A BITTER FEAST

ALSO BY DEBORAH CROMBIE

A Bitter Feast

A NOVEL

DEBORAH CROMBIE

WILLIAM MORROW
An Imprint of HarperCollins*Publishers*

A BITTER FEAST. Copyright © 2019 by Deborah Crombie. All rights reserved. Printed in the United States of America. No part of this book may be used or reproduced in any manner whatsoever without written permission except in the case of brief quotations embodied in critical articles and reviews. For information, address HarperCollins Publishers, 195 Broadway, New York, NY 10007.

HarperCollins books may be purchased for educational, business, or sales promotional use. For information, please email the Special Markets Department at SPsales@harpercollins.com.

FIRST EDITION

Photograph by Martyhoppe/Shutterstock, Inc.

Library of Congress Cataloging-in-Publication Data has been applied for.

ISBN 978-0-06-227166-2

19 20 21 22 23 LSC 10 9 8 7 6 5 4 3 2 1

For my brother Steve
1942–2018
Wherever he is sailing

ACKNOWLEDGMENTS

The village of Lower Slaughter in Gloucestershire is very much a real place. The Lamb, however, is entirely a product of my imagination, as are all the characters therein, and those characters' homes, farms, and cottages.

Many thanks to the staff at The Slaughters Manor House for their kindness and hospitality, and especially to Chef Nic Chappell for fabulous food, advice, and a tour of the manor house kitchen.

Thanks as well to my friend Chef Sean Currid in Phoenix, Arizona, for food advice, kitchen tours, and much of the original inspiration for this book.

To Chef Robert Lyford in McKinney, Texas, I owe the inspiration for Chef Viv Holland's charity luncheon menu.

I owe a huge debt, as always, to my first line readers, Diane Hale and Gigi Norwood. They correct me, inspire me, and keep me enthusiastic about writing—especially when I'm stuck in the book doldrums.

In the UK, Carol Chase, Steve Ullathorne, Karin Salvalaggio, Kerry Smith, Barb Jungr—you put the fun in book research! Thanks for invaluable hours, advice, and more than a few pub crawls.

My life and my writing are made much richer every day by my fellow Jungle Red Writers: Rhys Bowen, Lucy Burdette, Hallie Ephron, Jenn McKinlay, Hank Phillippi Ryan, and Julia Spencer-Fleming.

My book family at William Morrow is simply the best. Danielle Bartlett, Tavia Kowalchuk, Asanté Simons, Lynn Grady, Liate Stelik, you totally rock, and huge extra thanks to my incomparable editor, Carrie Feron.

Illustrator Laura Hartman Maestro has once again provided a magical map that brings the story to life, and she is as always a joy to work with.

My agent, Nancy Yost, deserves an array of medals for her patience and encouragement.

And last but not least, Rick, Kayti, Gage, and Wren, you inspire me every day. Love you to the moon and back.

St. Peter's Church

UPPER SLAUGHTER

River Eye

Polly

Joe's fishing hut

River

Eye

MacTavish

Beck House*

Becky Hill Road

Beck House *

Bella

Chelsea, London

Onslow Gdns

S. Parade

A3031

Viv's flat

Fulham Rd.

Chelsea Common

Britten St.

Old Church St.

Chelsea Old Town Hall

A3217

Beaufort

Mulberry Walk

Kings Road

B302

O'Reilly's

A3217

Street

Fergus's flat

Cheyne Walk

Chelsea Old Church

Albert Bridge

Mark's farm

River Thames

Battersea Park

map by Laura Hartman Maestro © 2019

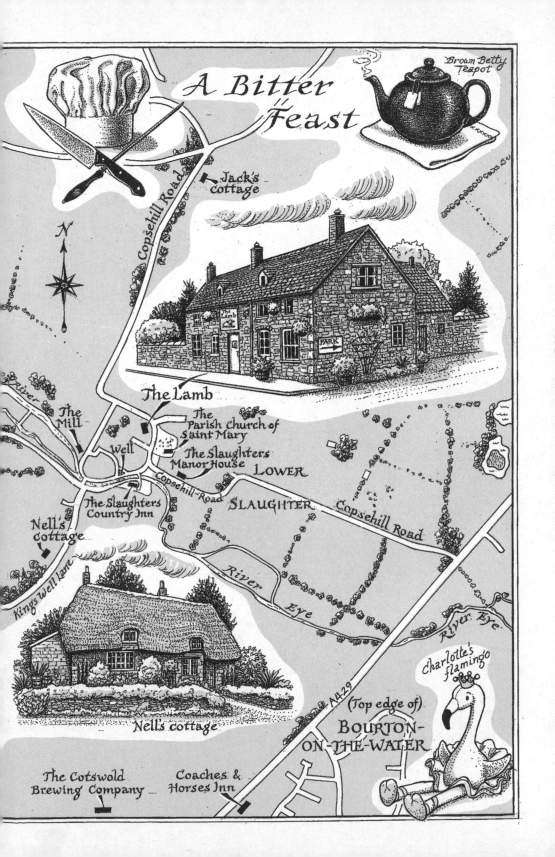

A Bitter Feast

Brown Betty Teapot

Jack's cottage

Copsehill Road

N

The Lamb

The Mill

River

Well

The Parish Church of Saint Mary

The Slaughters Manor House

LOWER

Copsehill Road

SLAUGHTER

Copsehill Road

The Slaughters Country Inn

Nell's cottage

Kings Well Lane

River Eye

River Eye

Charlotte's flamingo

Nell's cottage

A429

(Top edge of)
BOURTON-ON-THE-WATER

The Cotswold Brewing Company

Coaches & Horses Inn

CHAPTER ONE

She'd never been much of a sleeper. A good thing, she supposed, since getting by with little rest was a major requirement for a cook. That morning, she'd been up well before the September dawn. She'd made the farm runs, picking up the day's fresh veg for the pub. Then, home again, she'd made breakfast for her eleven-year-old daughter, Grace, before taking her to school. She treasured those quiet mornings with her daughter. Often it was the only time they managed to spend together outside of the restaurant kitchen.

Her brief hour on her own in the pub kitchen before the staff arrived for lunch service was priceless as well, and today doubly so. She'd scrubbed the walk-in fridge, organized the supplies, handwritten the day's menu for Bea, her manager, to copy. Now, apron-clad, she sat on the kitchen's back step, looking out over the little service area between the pub and the cottage that was the chef's attached accommodation. Sipping her first espresso of the day from the pub's machine, she ran over her to-do list for tomorrow's charity luncheon at Beck House, the Talbots' place.

Sudden doubt assailed her. What had she been thinking to commit to such a thing, catering an outdoor lunch for four dozen of the local well-to-do, as well as national food bloggers and restaurant critics?

When she'd come here with Grace, three years ago, glad of a regular job that put a roof over their heads and food in her daughter's mouth, she'd sworn to keep it simple. Good pub food. Pies, fish and chips, seasonal soups, a Sunday-roast lunch. She had done that, and done it well, judging by the daily packed house. Why, then, had she let herself be seduced into stretching past those self-imposed boundaries? "Something memorable, Viv. Something only you can do," Addie had said, with utter, breezy confidence. She'd taken the bait.

Well, she was in for it now, regardless, and she couldn't stop the little fizz of excitement in her veins. Everything, from starter to pudding, was made with local produce, and she'd spent weeks refining the menu.

That morning she'd already prepped the pub's smoker—a poor man's Kamado Joe—and put in one last lamb shoulder. Over the past few weeks she'd cooked and frozen more than half a dozen joints, but last night, in an attack of panic, she'd decided to do one more. The white beans with fennel that would accompany the meat had also been cooked and frozen, and were now defrosting in the cottage kitchen. She had a few things to finish up that afternoon, and a few that could only be done tomorrow morning, but overall she thought she was in good shape.

Taking a last sip of her coffee, she gazed absently beyond the mellow Cotswold stone of the storage shed and adjoining cottage to the hills rising away from the gentle valley of the River Eye. This was her favorite time of year, early autumn, had been since she was a child, growing up in these same Gloucestershire valleys. She'd never thought, after fifteen years in London, that she'd end up back here. But maybe it was a good thing. And maybe the charity lunch would be a good thing, too. She'd certainly paid her dues the last few years between catering jobs and the pub, and if she was totally honest, she missed the buzz of the bigger food world. Maybe it was time she stuck a toe back in those waters. What harm could it do, after all this time?

She tipped the dregs of her cup into the potted geranium by the back door. On with it, then, and let tomorrow bring what it would.

She was pushing herself up from the step when a tall shadow fell across the yard, blocking the morning sun, and when she looked up, her heart nearly stopped.

Nell Greene pushed a few bites of chicken-and-tarragon pie about on her plate. You could always count on the pub's made-from-scratch pies. Chef Viv's short-crust pastry was divine and a cold snap in the late-September weather had made Nell crave that sort of comfort. The pub's open fire beckoned as well, so she'd taken a seat in the bar near the hearth, rather than in the more formal dining areas on either side of the cozy center room.

But she'd felt odd, alone, in the midst of the Friday-night bustle, and had toyed with her food as she watched the evening sun slant through the pub's mullioned windows. Since her divorce, she'd found that she quite liked living on her own, but she had not got used to dining alone in public places. Watching couples always made her feel more awkward, and the sight of the two middle-aged and obviously married couples chatting over gins and newspapers brought a familiar twinge of jealousy. But tonight the young man and woman at the next table took the prize. They sat with their legs intertwined, kissing and nuzzling. When the blond woman ran her hand up inside the leg of the man's football shorts, Nell looked away, cringing with embarrassment. She suspected they were both married—but to other people. Nothing else would explain such a brazen display of—well, she supposed you could call it affection. At least she wasn't the only one alone tonight, she thought, glancing at the tall man in the fedora who had claimed the comfortably worn leather sofa in the corner.

He was, she guessed, a good ten years younger than she, perhaps in his midforties. Beneath the brown hat, his unruly dark blond hair curled to his shoulders. His beard, full but neatly trimmed, was a shade darker than his hair, but it failed to hide his strikingly deep dimples, visible when he'd smiled at the waitress. At first, she'd thought he must be meeting someone, but a half hour had passed and he was still alone.

Now, as though sensing her notice, he glanced up. Raising his eyebrows in the direction of the snogging couple, he gave her a small conspiratorial smile. Blushing, Nell managed to nod back. Then, slowly and deliberately, the man winked at her before turning his attention back to his food.

Nell felt mortified. Had he been mocking her? But there hadn't seemed any malice in his gesture, and after another moment spent nibbling at the remains of her pie, curiosity got the better of her and she glanced his way again. What was such a good-looking man doing on his own in the village pub on a Friday evening? Strangers weren't unusual, as the village was a draw for tourists and holidaymakers, but you seldom saw someone unfamiliar on their own.

He caught the barman's eye and touched his coffee cup. There was something in his manner that made her think he was used to getting what he wanted, and quickly. Well, why not? In spite of the slight eccentricity of the hat and the shoulder-length hair, his clothes were obviously expensive. Perhaps he was a guest at the posh manor house hotel in the village.

Nell watched as Jack, the bar manager, brought a fresh coffee from the kitchen and whisked away the man's empty cup. Why only coffee? Nell wondered.

Having found alcohol too easy a crutch in the early days of her divorce, she'd given it up except for the occasional social glass of wine. Now she no longer drank alone, and she felt a little more warmly disposed towards a fellow abstainer. She'd readied another smile when she saw that he was looking, not at her, but towards the kitchen.

Bea Abbott, the pub's manager, came through the kitchen door at the back of the bar. With a murmured word to Jack, she came round the bar and crossed the room towards the exit leading to the pub's small garden. It was odd, thought Nell, that she didn't stop to speak to any of the customers. Bea, with her dark curly hair and rimless glasses, was usually efficiently chatty. Nell had been glad to see her so well situated here.

In the corner, the man with the fedora watched the door close after Bea, then uncrossed his long legs and drummed his fingers on the table. His face was intent now, abstracted, and when his gaze passed over her, she knew she'd become invisible. Suddenly, he set his coffee cup down with a click and stood. He strode across the room, going round the bar and through the kitchen door without so much as a by-your-leave to Jack.

Nell sat openmouthed in surprise, but Jack merely frowned and went on wiping glasses with more force than necessary.

The snogging couple got up and went out the car park door, still entwined. The dining rooms on either side of the bar had begun to fill as Sarah, one of the servers, showed arriving customers to their tables. But over the increasing hum of conversation, Nell heard rising voices from the kitchen.

At first the voices were indistinct. Then Viv Holland said quite clearly, "You can't just waltz in here like this, demanding things. Who the hell do you think you are?" Nell was surprised. She'd never heard Viv, the spikily blond creator of the perfect pastry, raise her voice.

There was an answering rumble, indecipherable. The man in the hat, Nell guessed.

"No, you can't," said Viv, her voice now high and furious. "I won't do it. I told you—"

"Viv, come on, be reasonable." The man again, more clearly now, with a hint of cajoling. His accent, Nell decided, was Irish.

Viv muttered something.

"Well, if you're going to be a stubborn cow," the man said, sounding less patient now, "at least consider—"

"No." There was a crash, as if Viv had dropped something. Or thrown something. "You have no bloody right to ask it," she said, close to shouting. "Now get out. I mean it."

Conversation had died in the bar as the other patrons turned, wide-eyed, towards the kitchen. Jack stood, his hand frozen on the beer pull.

What on earth? wondered Nell, feeling terribly uncomfortable. She'd been intending to speak to Viv about Lady Adelaide's harvest lunch tomorrow, but now she didn't want to intrude.

The man came through the door into the bar, his expression grim. He pushed past Nell's table without a glance of acknowledgment and slammed his way out the garden door with a force that left it banging behind him. His camel hair coat remained behind, crumpled on the sofa.

"Are you certain your parents have room for us all?" From the passenger seat, Gemma James gave an anxious glance at her companion.

Melody Talbot laughed and shook her head. "Gemma, I told you not to worry. The house has eight bedrooms."

This brought Gemma little comfort. Eight bedrooms. What the bloody hell did someone do with eight bedrooms? Gemma had grown up in a two-bedroom flat over her parents' bakery in north London, sharing a room—not always amicably—with her sister. Although she now lived in a very nice house in Notting Hill, the accommodation was due more to circumstance than means, and she was still intimidated by real wealth. She was a working cop, a detective inspector, and such trappings didn't come with an ordinary copper's salary. Unless, of course, you were Melody Talbot.

She studied her friend. Small-framed, pretty, her dark hair growing out a bit from last spring's boy-short cut, Melody drove with confidence, her hands relaxed on the wheel of her little

Renault Clio. Melody was Gemma's detective sergeant, but it was only after they'd worked together for some time that Gemma had learned anything about Melody's background. There was good reason for Melody's reticence, Gemma now knew. Melody's father was the publisher of a major London newspaper, one known for investigative journalism that did not always favor the police. Melody had kept herself to herself, afraid of being ostracized if her colleagues learned of her connection, until the events of the last few months had forced her to open up a bit. Still, Gemma had only recently been invited to Melody's flat, and had never met her parents.

The invitation for Gemma and her family, and their friend Doug Cullen, to spend the weekend at Melody's parents' country house had come as a surprise. "Mum's putting on this big harvest festival do," Melody had said. "She wants to meet you and Duncan. And Doug, too, God knows why. Do come. Seriously." Moved by an unexpected vulnerability in Melody's expression, Gemma had impulsively agreed.

Now she wondered what on earth she'd been thinking.

They'd had to split up; Gemma and their almost four-year-old, Charlotte, traveling with Melody, while Duncan was coming on his own in the family car later that night. Their boys, Toby, seven, and Kit, fifteen, would come on the train tomorrow with Doug. Duncan and Doug, who worked on the same team at Holborn CID in central London, had been finishing up a case that afternoon, while Toby had not wanted to miss his Saturday-morning ballet class.

"Mummy," Charlotte said sleepily from the backseat, "are we there yet?"

"Almost, lovey," Gemma answered, although she had no idea. It had gone six, and they'd bypassed Oxford more than an hour ago and were now well into the Cotswold Hills. "Did you have a good sleep?" she asked, reaching back to give Charlotte a pat.

"I want my tea," Charlotte said plaintively.

"Soon, darling," Melody assured her. "And it will be a lovely tea, too. We really are almost there. You're going to love it."

Charlotte might, but Gemma was not at all certain about this country-house lark. She was a townie through and through. The city fit her like an old shoe, made her feel safe and comfortable. Outside of its confines she wasn't quite sure what to do with herself.

But she had to admit, as she watched the evening light fall across the rolling hills and sheep-strewn fields of Gloucestershire, that it was beautiful. They passed the turning for Bourton-on-the-Water, and a few minutes later Melody took a sharp left into a lane signposted THE SLAUGHTERS.

"Slaughters?" said Gemma, frowning. "You're taking the piss."

Melody grinned. "It doesn't mean what you think. It's a modernization of an Old English word for slough, or boggy place. At least that's one interpretation. There's Lower Slaughter and Upper Slaughter, and we are somewhere in between."

The lane was narrow, banked by hedges, and as the incline gently dropped it was increasingly covered by overarching trees. Gemma began to see long, low limestone cottages on either side of the lane, then a large manor house set back from the lane on the right. "Is that—"

Melody was already shaking her head. "Oh, no. That's the manor house. Seventeenth century. Much too grand for us. It's quite a posh hotel now."

They came into the village proper. Gemma saw a venerable church, and across from it, a long, low pub, its windows beginning to glow with lamplight. A glimpse of the hanging wooden sign showed a lamb on a green field. To their left, a pretty river ran under an arched bridge. "There's the other hotel, there, the inn," said Melody, pointing to a building covered with bright creeper on the far side of the bridge. "But the pub is definitely the place to eat for casual fare."

Their road crossed the bridge and followed alongside the river. All the buildings were the same honey-colored stone, except for a redbrick mill on the river's bend.

"What's that, Mummy?" asked Charlotte, pointing. "The round thing."

"It's a water wheel, sweetie. Is it still in use?" Gemma added to Melody.

"It's a museum. With a tea shop. Maybe we can go tomorrow." Melody glanced in her rearview mirror. "Would you like that, Char?"

"Yeah." Charlotte nodded, her halo of caramel ringlets bouncing.

They had left the village and were climbing now, the river lost to sight beyond green fields. The evening sun lay gold and flat across the hills rising away to either side.

As the road climbed, the hedges drew in until they were running through a tunnel of trees. At its end, Melody slowed and turned into a narrow drive. Before them, open parkland sloped down towards the river, but an avenue of trees lined the winding drive and shielded the distant view.

Gemma noticed Melody's hands tighten on the wheel as they entered a deeper wood. "The Woodland," said Melody. "Then the Wild Garden and the house. All very Arts and Crafts."

"Are we there? Are we there?" Charlotte jiggled in her car seat with excitement. Gemma found she was holding her breath.

The trees thinned, the drive dipped, and as they came out into the sunlight, Gemma gasped at the riot of color before her. Oranges, yellows, and purples filled the garden that rose in gentle terraces towards the house.

And the house! Built of the same pale Cotswold stone she'd seen in the village, it glowed in the late-evening light. There was a central gabled porch that rose to the height of the second-story slate-tiled roof, with wings either side. Leaded glass winked from the windows and a lazy spiral of wood smoke drifted from the central chimney. Blowsy pink roses climbed up either side of the porch.

"Oh, it's gorgeous," whispered Gemma. "Not at all the grand mansion I was picturing."

"Thank you. I think," Melody added, a wry twist to her lips. The drive swooped left round the garden, then the tires crunched as Melody pulled up the Renault on the graveled forecourt.

"Welcome to Beck House."

Duncan Kincaid watched the sun set from the A40. He had plenty of time to admire the spectacle, as the traffic was creeping along in annoying stops and starts. He'd rung Gemma to let her know he was held up. According to the radio, there was a major traffic incident just short of his exit. He supposed it was a good thing after all that the family hadn't traveled together, although he hadn't been thrilled about leaving the boys in London.

Of course, they would be all right tonight. Their family friend Wesley Howard had offered to stay with them. Then Kit would walk Toby to his ballet class in the morning, after which they'd meet

Doug Cullen at Paddington for the train. Not that Kit and Toby couldn't have traveled down alone, but Kincaid felt better knowing they'd have adult supervision.

The thought of Doug as "adult supervision" made him smile. Not that Doug wasn't past thirty now, but somehow he couldn't see his sergeant in a parental role. Doug had said he had a sculling event in the morning, but Kincaid suspected he was more reluctant to lose a Saturday morning in his garden. Since the spring, the garden had become Doug's new passion and he talked about it with the tediousness of the convert.

Kincaid also wondered how comfortable Doug felt about the visit to the Talbots' country home. They had both worked with Sir Ivan after the events of the spring, but neither had met his wife, and from Melody's description Lady Adelaide sounded quite formidable.

The sun sank below the horizon and he shifted restlessly, wishing he'd at least had the forethought to grab a sandwich and a bottle of water. But, hungry as he was, he was more concerned about his old car than his stomach. The Astra's engine had seemed a bit rough lately. He hoped the car didn't overheat with all the idling.

When the traffic finally began to move, he breathed a sigh of relief. It looked like the old beast would make it, after all. And perhaps he would even reach the Talbots' in time for dinner.

Dawdling, Nell sipped at her cold coffee. Outside, the dusk faded and lights winked on in the village. But neither Viv nor Bea emerged from the kitchen, nor did the man in the fedora return for his coat. Diners came and went, and Jack was too busy at the bar to chat. Reluctantly, Nell settled her check with Jack and let herself out into the crisp night.

The car park was now dark as pitch and the sharp air smelled of wood smoke and apples. Nell wondered if there might be a light frost by morning, and if the weather would hold for tomorrow's luncheon. She supposed that she would just show up at Beck House and do whatever was needed. Perhaps Lady Addie would know something about the mystery man, although Nell didn't think she was much of a one for gossip.

In the meantime, Bella, her border collie, was waiting for her evening walk, and the stars were hard and bright in the night sky. Nell took a breath of contentment as she unlocked her little Peugeot. This was a good life she had chosen, all in all.

Easing her way out of the car park, she took the old quarry road out of the village. Her cottage was close enough that she could have walked, but the lane was narrow and could be treacherous in the dark. Her headlamps glared against the hedges as the lane dipped and turned.

Suddenly, a figure appeared in the center of the road. Nell jammed on the brakes, skidding to a halt. The man in the fedora was walking away from her, in the center of the lane. He didn't turn or even seem aware of the car, and as she watched he staggered slightly. Was he drunk after all? Why was he walking away from the village, and without his coat?

Lowering her window, Nell called out, "Hello, there." When he didn't respond, she got out, leaving the engine idling, and walked towards him. "Excuse me! Do you need a lift? It's not safe walking these lanes in the dark."

He kept going, and it wasn't until she reached him and put a hand on his arm that he turned, as if startled. Immediately, she saw that he was not drunk, but ill. His face was pale, beaded with sweat in spite of the cold, and his eyes were unfocused. He swayed under her touch.

"Oh, dear," she said. "Do you not feel well? I think you need some help." He didn't resist as she grasped his elbow and guided him gently towards the car. She could feel him trembling. Should she take him back to the village? But then what? Not only did she not know where he was staying, there was no doctor.

The man swayed against her, mumbling something she couldn't understand. Nell made a decision. It would have to be Cheltenham. There was nothing nearer. "Right," she said briskly. "I can see you're ill. Let's get you in the car." She put an arm round him to support him. "We're taking you straight to hospital."

Kincaid's predictions turned out to have been overly optimistic. The traffic had slowed again, and it was fully dark by the time he finally left the Oxford ring road. The car was too old to have built-in sat-nav, and not wanting to stop to check his mobile, he trusted to his memory of the map he'd looked at earlier.

As he passed Burford, the land began to rise into the Cotswold Hills, as well as he could tell in the dark. Not far to go, then, but he had to laugh at the idea of the Talbots referring to their place as a "weekend" home. Perhaps they knew a way to circumvent the motorway traffic—or simply took the train to the nearest station, where they had a retainer waiting to fetch them. Or maybe they just took a helicopter, he thought, grinning.

A signpost loomed in the headlamps. It was the turnoff for

Bourton-on-the-Water, the nearest small town to the Talbots' village. Almost there, then. He was wondering if he should find a place to pull over and check the map on his mobile when headlamps blazed suddenly from his left, blinding him.

Before he could throw up a hand or hit the brake, there came a tearing impact, and all went dark.

CHAPTER TWO

Sound returned first. Gradually, Kincaid became aware of creaks and groans, like metal protesting, and then a sort of rhythmic ticking.

Smell came next. Burning rubber. Hot metal. Petrol.

His eyes flew open. At first the darkness seemed absolute. Then, as he began to make out shapes, nothing he saw made sense. When he tried to move, his head spun and a wave of nausea hit him.

Something warm trickled into his eye. Blinking, he reached down to touch his face—down, not up.

His orientation came back with a jarring click. He was upside down. What the hell had happened?

This time he moved more gingerly. Pain in his shoulder, a twinge of pain across his ribs. Seat belt. He was hanging upside down from his shoulder harness.

A flash of memory came. Lights. Bright lights on his left.

Shit. He must have been hit.

Take it easy, he told himself, stifling panic. Assess the situation.

Cautiously, he turned his head to the left, trying to focus. In the dimness he could make out a mass of metal and glass where the seat should have been. The passenger door.

"Shit." This time he managed to whisper it. He touched the collapsed remains of his airbag, thinking it had probably saved his life. From somewhere behind him came a strobe of light, then he heard a car door slam. A voice called out.

The smell of petrol grew stronger. His heart thudded. Bloody hell, the engine. Reaching up, he felt for the ignition and turned the key. He had to get out of the car.

Inching his right hand upwards, he felt for the door latch. There. When he pulled it, there was a satisfying thunk. Good. Not jammed. He pushed the door outwards a few inches, exhaling with relief when it seemed to move freely. Another foot and it stopped, caught, he thought, on a slight rise in the ground. Still, it was enough.

He took a breath, wincing at the pain in his ribs, then, bracing his right hand against the roof, he unbuckled the seat belt with his left. He eased his shoulders through the open door, then slithered out and back until he was free of the car.

Panting from the effort, he used the door to lever himself up until he stood, facing the bonnet. The glare from his own headlamps shone into impenetrable blackness, disorienting him. Slowly, using the door as a support against the dizziness, he turned, blinking against more lights. It took him a moment to understand that he was seeing the headlamps from two cars. The first was nose in to the hedge that bordered the verge. When he blinked against the glare, he could see that the vehicle's front end was crumpled like a child's smashed toy.

Behind that car, another stood at a slight angle to the road, its headlamps illuminating the wrecked vehicle—the car that had hit him, he realized, with a shock that made him grip the door a little harder. A figure moved, blocking the light momentarily.

"Sir, are you okay?" It was the woman's voice he'd heard before he climbed out of the car.

"I think so," he managed, his voice cracking. Clearing his throat, he tried again. "Yeah, I'm fine."

"Anyone else in the car?"

"No." Thank God, he thought .

"Okay, good. Hang on. I'm ringing for help." Her voice was calm, assured, but still he heard the tension beneath the words.

No one had emerged from the other car.

Fingers touching the underside of the Astra, he made his way to the end of the boot, then he stepped out towards the wrecked car, feeling his way across the uneven ground. The woman, who had knelt by the driver's-side door of the wreck, stood.

"Hey," she called. "You need to stay put."

"I can help."

As he drew nearer, he saw that she was dressed in a cardigan over what looked like hospital scrubs.

"I'm a police officer," he said. "Is anyone hurt? I think that car hit me."

He blinked as she shone a torch in his face.

"You're bleeding."

"It's a surface cut. I'm fine." He tried not to wince as pain shot through his ribs.

She looked back at the car against the hedge, seemed to hesitate. "Okay, look. I need to walk up the road to get a good signal. Can you just talk to this lady here while I do that?"

Kincaid nodded, then, realizing she probably couldn't see the gesture, said, "Don't worry. I've got it."

After an instant's pause, the woman started towards the road. "Right," she threw over her shoulder. "You know what to do."

Crossing the last few feet to the driver's door, he realized there was no sound from the car's engine. Had the Samaritan reached in and turned it off? Carefully, Kincaid lowered himself into a squat, wincing as pain shot through his knee. Touching the car for support, he peered into the driver's window.

A glance told him that the airbag had deployed and collapsed. And that the impact with his car had crumpled the front end of the small saloon into the car's interior. The driver was trapped. And she was conscious.

She turned her head towards him and whispered something he didn't understand.

"Help's coming," he said. "You're going to be fine."

Now he saw that there was a passenger beside her. A man. And he wasn't moving.

"I—" Her voice was a thread of sound now. She lifted her hand, reaching towards him, and he took it gently. Her fingers felt small in his, and warm. He thought her short hair was light in color, but he couldn't tell more in the dim light. She moved, as if to struggle.

"Shh." He gave her hand a squeeze. "Stay still. Are you in pain?"

She blinked, looking puzzled. "No. I—I don't know. Will you stay . . . with me?"

"Of course I will. We'll have you out of there in a tick, don't you worry." It was going to take the fire brigade, he thought, and probably the Jaws of Life. How long before they arrived? He caught the coppery scent of blood. "Just hang on," he said, as reassuringly as he could.

"I—" Her fingers moved in his. "I didn't mean . . ." Her voice faded and he thought, even in the dim light, that her skin had lost color.

"It's all right," he told her. "It was an accident." He thought he heard sirens in the distance.

"No." The woman turned her head until she could meet his gaze. "I didn't . . . He was . . ." Her fingers tightened in his. "Please," she whispered. "Tell them he—" And then the light went out in her eyes.

Viv knelt on the kitchen floor, chasing down slippery fingers of peeled potato with shaking hands. She'd dropped the pan of hand-cut chips destined for the deep fryer.

"Here, let me help," said Angelica, squatting beside her and reaching for the pan.

"No." Viv shook her head. "Can you do more chips? We've got to get them on or we'll fall behind." The hand-cut chips were one of the pub's signature dishes and the orders for fish and chips and steak frites would be piling up. It was Angelica, the line cook, who ordinarily prepped them before service.

"Okay. But how about you take a smoke break." It was a joke; a weak one. Viv didn't allow anyone who smoked to work in back or front of house, much less smoke out in the yard.

Viv chased down the last potato and stood, dumping the lot in the bin.

Ibby, her sous-chef, gave her a cold look as he squeezed past her with two starters of gravlax and horseradish cream. "We're *already* in the weeds. What were you thinking, letting that wanker in the kitchen?"

"I didn't let—" Viv stopped, pressing her lips together. There was no point in arguing with Ibby—Ibby, whose ever-present sense of grievance kept him from being the chef his cooking skills justified. "Just get on with it," she said.

His muttered, "Yes, Chef," as he set the plates on the pass was sullen, and she thought that she might actually, finally, fire him. But he was right. What had she been thinking?

She'd taken a breath and turned back to the pies puffing up in the oven, when Bea came in from the bar, her face flushed.

"What the hell happened in here?" Bea hissed. "Sarah says you had a row and half the restaurant heard it. And the tickets are piling up."

Viv met Bea's gaze. "Where is he? Is he still out there?"

"No. But he's left his coat."

Panic seized Viv. "Grace. Where's Grace?"

"She's watching telly in the cottage. I just checked on her."

Viv's hands shook with relief. "Good. I just didn't want—" She broke off as Jack came through from the bar.

The tiny kitchen was suddenly much too hot and filled with far too many bodies. "What the hell are you playing at, Viv?" Jack snapped his bar towel like a bullfighter throwing down a challenge. "Who the hell was that, swanning about the place all day in his poncey hat?"

They all stared at her. Waiting, for different reasons, to hear what she would say.

Finally, Viv spoke to Jack. "Fergus. Fergus O'Reilly. The chef. He was my chef, a long time ago."

Kincaid had shaken the driver, gently at first, then more forcefully. When there was no response, he'd shouted for the woman with the mobile phone.

"I think she's stopped breathing," he said when she reached him.

She deftly moved him aside. Feeling for the pulse in the driver's neck, she shook her head. "Bloody hell. I can't get to her, and I don't have any equipment."

The sirens grew louder. "We'll have to wait for the ambulance."

"But she—she was just talking to me. And what about him?" He gestured towards the passenger.

The woman shook her head. "He wasn't belted in. I'd guess his head hit the windscreen."

Kincaid looked at the driver again, and he knew that she was too still, much too still. A wave of dizziness hit him.

He must have swayed, because the next thing he knew he was sitting on the ground and the woman was steadying him with one hand while shining a torch in his eyes with the other. "You may be concussed," she said. "You've got a lump the size of a goose egg. Don't move."

The siren had grown deafening. Headlamps threw the woman's face into profile. She was about Gemma's age, with dark hair pulled back in a ponytail. Then the siren's wail stopped. Doors slammed, voices shouted. The woman left him. He stayed where he was, frozen, as the action flowed round him.

A boulder, he thought woozily. He might as well be a boulder in a stream. The water was so cold. Not water, he realized, but ground. The cold was seeping through his trousers. The night had turned chill. Why, he wondered, had the woman in the car had her window down? He was shivering now, his teeth beginning to chatter.

The woman came back to him, throwing a rough blanket over his shoulders. "Can you stand if I help you?"

Kincaid started to nod, then quickly thought better of it. She steadied him as he pushed himself up, then she supported him across the rough ground of the verge to her car. Opening the door, she eased him down onto the seat, examining his head in the light of the dome lamp. "You've got a good cut there, and one on your cheek, but the bleeding's let up. What else hurts?"

"Ribs," he managed with a grimace. "And my hand," he added with surprise, glancing down at his right hand. He could see bruising, and the beginning of swelling. "Why didn't I feel it?"

"Shock." She reached into the footwell and drew something out of a bag. "I keep a thermos in the car for the drive home." She unscrewed the cap and filled it. "Here. Drink up."

Kincaid took it left-handed, with shaking fingers. It was coffee, hot and milky. A few sips stopped his teeth chattering. He could see the ambulance crew moving round the wrecked car, their yellow safety jackets gleaming in the light of the flares they'd laid.

"The woman," he said. "The driver—"

His helper was shaking her head. "Nothing they could do. It's going to be a job to get both of them out. I can't imagine what happened. She always seemed such a careful person."

"You knew her?"

"Oh, not well. But I recognized her. Nell Greene. She was an administrator at my base hospital. In Cheltenham. A nice woman, but she left under some sort of cloud."

Nell, Kincaid thought. He wished he'd known. He kept hearing her voice, entreating him.

One of the yellow jackets loomed nearer. The woman, who'd been squatting beside the open car door, rose and spoke to him, their voices drifting down to Kincaid.

"Dead," the man said.

His companion gave him a puzzled look. "What are you talking about? We know they're dead."

"No. I mean the bloke in the passenger seat. There was barely a trickle from that head wound. I'd swear he was already bloody dead when the car crashed."

The woman in scrubs, he learned, was called Tracey, Tracey Woodman, and she'd been on her way home from an ambulance shift out of Cheltenham.

"I was only a half mile behind you," she told him. "I heard the crash." Her shoulders twitched in an involuntary shudder. "There's nothing else sounds like that. I feared the worst." She glanced down at him. "You were lucky."

One of the ambulance crew called to her and, after telling Kincaid firmly to stay put, she walked away. The police arrived shortly after, first one panda car, then a second. The fire brigade was not far behind. Kincaid watched as the police and the firefighters conferred with the medics, set flares across the road to redirect traffic, then began setting up a cordon round the accident scene. Used to being in charge, he felt oddly helpless. It was only when an officer came over to speak to him that he realized he not only had no transportation, he had no means of communication. His mobile had been on the car seat.

"My mobile phone," he said. "Did anyone find it?"

The officer, whose name badge read HAWKINS, shook his head.

"No joy, I'm afraid. You'll have to wait for the scene investigators to finish, and while I'm sure they'll do their best, that won't be any-time soon." Hawkins took Kincaid's details, raising his eyebrows at Kincaid's rank. Kincaid at least had identification. His driving license and warrant card were still in his jacket pocket. He winced as he drew them out. His hand was throbbing and every breath brought a stabbing pain in his ribs.

"And what were you doing here? Sir," Hawkins added hastily.

"Meeting my wife. We're visiting friends for the weekend. At Beck House."

This garnered another raised eyebrow. "Just so we can contact you, sir. And we'll need a blood draw before you leave the scene. You'll need to come into the station at Cheltenham to make a full statement tomorrow."

He'd thought about asking if he could borrow the officer's phone to ring Gemma when Tracey Woodman returned. "When they're finished with you, I'd be happy to give you a lift."

Kincaid accepted gratefully.

Woodman examined him, frowning. "You'll need that cut on your forehead stitched."

He shook his head, suddenly feeling exhausted. "Not to-night."

"Then let me at least clean you up a bit, after they stick you." Leading him over to the ambulance, she sat him on the tailgate, where one of the ambulance medics took a blood sample and labeled it. Then Woodman swabbed gently at the cut in his hair-line, finishing with some strips of tape. "There. You're going to look quite rakish, even once it's stitched. Downright piratical."

"My kids will be impressed." He managed a smile. "Not to

mention my wife. Once she gets over killing me for worrying her. I'm hours late, and I lost my mobile in the crash."

"Do you want to use mine to ring her?"

Kincaid thought, then shook his head, gingerly. "It's not far, I don't think. Better I tell her in person. It's Beck House, near Upper Slaughter."

Woodman whistled. "The Talbot place? You do move in fine company. You know," she added as they walked back to her car, "I think I heard at the hospital that Nell Greene had retired to one of the Slaughters. Inherited a cottage or something. We should all be so lucky." She glanced at the mangled remains of Nell Greene's little car and shrugged. "Or maybe not."

CHAPTER THREE

The Talbots had come out to greet Gemma and Melody as soon as Melody's car came to a full stop on the gravel drive. "My mum has radar. She'll have sensed us coming up the lane," Melody whispered as Gemma got out and lifted Charlotte from her car seat. Charlotte clung to her, taking in the house and the strangers with wide eyes.

Lady Adelaide Talbot had given her daughter a peck on the cheek, then held out her hands to Gemma. "I'm so pleased to meet you at last. And you must be Charlotte," she said, bending down so that she could look the child in the eye as Gemma let Charlotte slide to the ground. "Welcome to Beck House, darling. We're going to have lots of fun. Would you like to see the house?"

Charlotte nodded, still shy.

"Thank you for having us, Lady Adelaide," Gemma began, but Melody's mother was already shaking her head.

"Call me Addie. Everyone does. Can you imagine being saddled with Adelaide? And I'm only a lady when I'm not at home." Her smile was infectious and Gemma relaxed. Melody had always given her the impression that her mother was quite starchy. She'd been expecting prim, proper, and possibly matronly. Glancing at Melody, she thought she should have known better. Addie Talbot was small, dark-haired, and even more delicate than her daughter. She was also effortlessly elegant in a way that made Gemma doubt her own choice of work trousers and nubby jumper, and wonder just how badly her hair needed a brush.

To cover her discomfort, she exclaimed over the cascades of pink roses surrounding the front door. "Oh, these are gorgeous. What are they?"

"St. Swithun's. A David Austin climber. Ivan chose them because he misses his dreadful Newcastle weather," Addie added as she linked her arm through her husband's.

"St. Swithun's Day, if it does rain, full forty days it will remain," said Ivan with a twinkle. "Famously inaccurate."

"Do come in," Addie urged. "Ivan can bring your things." She took Charlotte's hand and whispered something in her ear that made her giggle.

From inside the house came the sound of excited barking, one dog a high, shrill yap, the other a deeper rumble. "Puppies," said Charlotte, jiggling with excitement now.

"We put the dogs in the study," explained Addie, nodding towards the room on the front of the house. "Until we knew if you were comfortable with them."

"Oh, we have tw—" Gemma began, just as an enormous furry head appeared in the window and a loud "Woof" rattled the glass.

Gemma and Charlotte both jumped, and all of the Talbots grinned. "That's MacTavish, Mum's dog," said Melody. "He's the size of a horse. But don't worry, he's a sweetheart."

"MacTavish?"

"He's a Scottish deerhound," Addie explained. "We thought he deserved something appropriately north of the border."

Ivan held the door for them, and Gemma caught her breath as she stepped inside. The covered entry opened into a large dark-beamed hall that ran the depth of the house. Sun falling through the west windows painted the pale cream walls with blocks of gold, and through windows on either side of a staircase at the back, Gemma saw a garden and the green of rising hills. A fire already crackled in a large fireplace set at a right angle to the front door.

"It's beautiful," Gemma murmured. "And so unusual."

"My great-grandfather built it in 1905," said Addie. "The architect was a disciple of Luytens and a devoted follower of the Arts and Crafts movement. They believed in function as well as comfort."

"I'll take you for a tour," put in Melody, nodding towards the study, where the barking was now interspersed with frantic whining, "but first things first. You might want to pick up Charlotte so that Mac doesn't knock her down."

Ivan opened the study door and the dogs came bounding out. The small bark, Gemma saw, belonged to a Jack Russell that leapt excitedly at Melody's legs. "That's Polly," said Melody, "Dad's favorite girl."

Ivan shook his head, laughing. "Jealousy will get you nowhere, sweetheart."

The deerhound, an enormous gray beast with a head so large he seemed almost prehistoric, trotted towards them. Charlotte buried her head in Gemma's shoulder and even Gemma tensed a bit. But the dog was as gentle as Melody had promised, and when he came to sniff and lick at Gemma's fingers, Charlotte reached out, too, and giggled at the dog's wet tongue.

Catching the heady scent of roses beneath the resinous smell of the fire, Gemma turned and saw a bowl filled with roses on a side table. Some were the pale pink of the climber by the front door, others deeper pinks and reds. "Are these all from your garden?" she asked.

Smiling, Addie said, "The last flush. It's a bit of a hobby."

Melody rolled her eyes. "A bit, yeah. You wouldn't think Mum is happiest with a trowel in her hand, would you? Come on, I'll show you round."

The house was smaller than Gemma had expected, and much more homey. From the deep Mediterranean blue of the sitting room that overlooked the gardens, to the pale blush pink of the kitchen/dining area that opened out from the kitchen side of the central fireplace, the place looked well lived in. Sir Ivan's deep red study faced the drive, as did a formal dining room. There were just enough touches of chintz to add country charm, enough leather to add masculinity, and the oil paintings of Cotswold landscapes glowed like jewels on the walls. The reds, pinks, and blues flowed from room to room in harmony, and Gemma couldn't help but notice that all the colors set off Addie Talbot's flawlessly pale complexion. She also realized that the casualness of the house was quite deliberately—and very expensively—achieved, with the sort of expertise that came only with generations of money and taste.

She felt suddenly much less at ease.

There were four bedrooms on the first floor, and four smaller bedrooms in what had once been the nursery and servants' quarters on the second floor. She and Duncan had been given a room on the first floor, adjoining a dressing room fitted with a small bed for Charlotte. The windows overlooked the gardens and the hills that were now only deep shadows in the dusk.

"This is perfect," she said to Melody. A shelf of worn books ran the length of the wall above the bed. The wallpaper was rose-sprigged, the bed linens white and puffy, but one corner of the room held a small desk and a slightly tattered slipper chair with an ottoman and reading lamp. "Was this room yours?" she asked, as it struck her.

Melody nodded. "And it usually still is, when I come to stay, but it's the only room other than Mum and Dad's with an en suite bath and a bed for Charlotte. I'm happy to take one of the guest rooms," she added before Gemma could protest. "And I certainly wasn't giving this one to Doug."

From the dressing room, Charlotte said, "Mummy, is this for me?"

Turning, Gemma saw that she meant not the little bed, but a picture book that had been placed on the pillow. When Gemma joined her, she saw that a note had been clipped to the front. "Charlotte, welcome to Beck House," she read. The heavy paper was signed with a large stylized *A*. "Yes, darling, it is," Gemma told her. "A present from Lady Addie. You'll have to thank her."

"It's an *Alfie*! A new one!" Charlotte clutched the book to her chest. The books by Shirley Hughes about a little boy named Alfie were Charlotte's favorites, as they had been Toby's.

"How thoughtful of your mother," Gemma told Melody.

"One of her many talents. She wanted everyone to feel welcome."

But Addie wouldn't have known that the books were Charlotte's favorites unless Melody had told her. Like mother, like daughter, Gemma thought, remembering all the seemingly casual little things that Melody did for her and for others on the team, things that meant she'd been paying attention to what pleased them.

"Your mum seems awfully calm for having such a big event tomorrow."

Melody laughed. "I wouldn't count on that. I would guarantee you that she's making last-minute calls right now, just making sure she has all her ducks in a row."

"What's the luncheon in aid of, exactly? You never said." Gemma had been in court that week, so she and Melody had spent most of the drive catching up on work news.

"The two local churches. Upper and Lower Slaughter are in different parishes, so supporting one without the other would be a political minefield." Melody frowned. "But I think the real reason is that Mum wants our local chef—remember the pub I pointed out?—to up her game. She's invited food critics and bloggers and the event will get lots of media attention. I hope Viv is up for it."

"Why wouldn't she be?"

"Rumor is that Viv was a rising star on the London food scene ten or twelve years ago. Then she just disappeared. Turned up here a couple of years ago and bought into the Lamb. Wanted a quiet life, apparently. I'd say she got that."

"Mummy." Book in one hand, Charlotte tugged at Gemma's jumper with the other. "Read it to me."

"Let's take it downstairs, shall we?" Melody told her. "Dad will have poured drinks and we don't want to keep them waiting."

"I can't think what's keeping him," said Gemma a few hours later. She felt it was rude to sit clutching her mobile in the Talbots' sitting room, but she'd tried Kincaid half a dozen times without a response. It was nearing nine o'clock and he should have arrived shortly after them. She'd even contemplated ringing Kit or Doug, to see if they'd heard from him, but didn't want to worry them unnecessarily.

"Do you want us to mount a search party?" asked Addie. Gemma thought she was joking until Addie continued, "Ivan can take the Land Rover while Melody and I take our cars. You need to stay with your daughter, of course."

"Oh, no, I'm sure he'll turn up," protested Gemma, shaking her head. Kincaid would be mortified if she called out the cavalry.

But Melody was frowning. "It's not like him."

"Maybe his mobile battery died," Gemma suggested, trying to convince herself. "It wouldn't be the first time he forgot his car charger. Or he could have had car trouble. I keep telling him he's got to replace the old boat, even if it hurts his dad's feelings." The Astra estate had been a gift from Hugh, Kincaid's father, when the demands of family life had finally forced Kincaid to give up driving his classic MG. A wife, three kids, and two dogs simply had not fit.

She put her phone on the side table and sipped at the brandy Sir Ivan had insisted on pouring her after dinner. Waiting for Kincaid, they'd put off the light supper the Talbots had prepared until Charlotte had been almost too sleepy to eat. Cold salads, pâté, cheeses, and bread had been laid out in the comfortable eating area in the kitchen.

"We didn't want to worry about getting a hot meal on the table with everyone in transit and the little one up past her bedtime," Addie had said. "I raided Daylesford Organic," she added with a conspiratorial smile. Gemma had no idea what she was talking about.

"The Fortnum and Mason of the countryside," Melody explained. "The poshest farm shop you can imagine. Run by the family who owns JCB." When Gemma still looked blank, she elaborated. "You know. Tractors. Earth movers. Pots of money. And the shop is so upmarket it even has a spa." When Gemma raised her eyebrows, Melody said, "Seriously. That's where you'll find all the Chipping Norton set. Even the Camerons, if the stars are in your favor."

Ivan's mouth twitched in amusement. "Or not, more like."

In spite of what she'd heard from Kincaid, Sir Ivan Talbot had been a surprise to Gemma. She'd seen photos, of course, so she'd known he was impressively tall and blond, but nothing had prepared her for his sheer presence. Or for the remnants of his Geordie accent. Melody had told her his story; a Newcastle grammar school boy, he'd come to London and taken a job as a fledgling reporter for the *Chronicle*, the newspaper owned by Addie's family. Smart and fiercely ambitious, his wooing of the boss's daughter had made London tongues wag. But anyone who wondered whether plain Ivan Talbot had courted Lady Adelaide Mann out of a desire to move up in the world had only to see the two of them together to know otherwise.

More and more of the running of the paper had fallen to Ivan, and when Addie's parents died, Ivan had taken over, shaping the paper to his vision. They had all, in the last few months, had reason to be thankful for it.

Gemma was wondering if there was any way she could tell him how much she appreciated what he'd done for Kincaid when both dogs lifted their heads, ears pricked. She heard it then, the crunch of tires on gravel, and then the dogs began to bark.

Later, Kincaid would only remember the swoop of the drive in the dark, then the shape of the house, blotting out the sky. It seemed formidable, but light shone from the lower windows, a good sign, surely.

Tracey Woodman brought the car to a halt in front of the door. Then, reaching up, she switched on the dome light and examined his face one more time. "Are you sure you're okay?" she asked. "I'd be happier if you'd go to A and E."

"I'm fine," Kincaid assured her. In fact, he didn't feel fine at all, but the last thing he wanted to do was go to hospital. "Nothing that a good night's sleep won't mend."

"Promise me you'll at least have someone look at that cut tomorrow. And at your hand."

Ouch. Obviously he hadn't managed to hide the fact that his hand was swelling and hurt like blazes. "Right. I will." He could hear dogs barking now, from inside the house.

Tracey seemed to hesitate a moment, then pulled her handbag from the footwell and dug round in it. She fished out a pen and a scrap of paper with a look of triumph. "Just in case you need anything," she said, scribbling, "like some more medical advice to ignore"—she looked up with a grin—"here's my number. I only live in Bourton."

"Thank you," Kincaid said, offering her his left hand. "Really." Light spilled from the door of the house. "I'd better go." As he climbed out and shut the car door, Tracey switched off the dome light, then gave him a friendly wave as she drove away.

Kincaid turned to see Gemma coming towards him, followed by Ivan Talbot, Melody, and a small, dark-haired woman he assumed must be Melody's mother. The barking continued from inside the house.

"Duncan! Where's your car? What happened? Are you all right?" Peering at him, Gemma touched his arm, her face creased with concern. "What have you done to your face? I was so worried."

"Long story." Managing a smile, he greeted Ivan. "Good to see you, sir."

"No 'sirs' here. Just Ivan. And this is my wife, Addie."

When Kincaid reached out to her, she waved his hand away. "Never mind that. Let's get you inside."

They led him into the house and introduced him to the dogs, who sniffed at him with more than usual doggy interest. He realized he must smell like blood—and God knew what else he had sat or crawled in on the side of the road.

"Let's get you a drink," said Ivan. "You look like you could use one. Whisky?"

"Yes, please. But, first, could I have a wash?" Kincaid turned to Gemma. "Where's Char?"

"Asleep, upstairs. But I'll just go make sure the dogs didn't wake her. Then, I want to know exactly what happened to you."

Kincaid scrubbed as well as his sore hand would allow, then dried his hands gingerly on the Talbots' fine linen bathroom towel. Then, he examined his forehead and cheek in the mirror, dabbing at the remaining dried blood with a wad of tissue from the toilet roll. Still, even tidied, he was not a pretty sight. No wonder Gemma had looked horrified. His jacket had a rip in the right shoulder but he had nothing to change into—his overnight bag, he realized, was still in his car. His knee was stinging, too, but he didn't feel like rolling up his trouser leg to check the damage.

The small downstairs loo was warm, and for a moment he was tempted to sink down on the toilet lid and close his eyes, just for a bit . . .

He shook himself and splashed a little water on the undamaged parts of his face. His hand throbbed—he would have to get some ice on it. By the time Gemma rapped on the door and said, "Are you okay, love?" he was as presentable as he was going to get. Coming out into the kitchen, he gave her a one-sided hug and rested his cheek against her hair for just an instant, but she pulled away so that she could look at him. She touched her fingers lightly to his cheek, then asked, "Where else are you hurt? And how badly?"

"I'm fine, really. Just banged up a bit."

Lady Addie had made him a plate of sandwiches. As she urged him into the sitting room, she said, "Whatever happened to you, I think you won't have eaten." He took the plate willingly, and he didn't object when Ivan waved him into the chair nearest the fire and handed him a crystal tumbler with a finger's worth of whisky. He wondered if he should drink it, as odd as he felt, but the first sip warmed him to his toes and he felt his muscles ease.

"The car," said Gemma. "What happened to the car? Did you—"

Ivan held up a hand. "Let the man eat, lass. Whatever it is, I imagine it will keep a few more minutes."

Kincaid bit into a ham and tomato sandwich. Suddenly, he was ravenous. As murmured conversation went on round him, he finished the ham, and then the cheese and pickle. Down-to-earth food, and delicious, the sort of thing he'd grown up on in Cheshire. When he'd finished, he set the plate aside and cradled the whisky in his left hand. The big dog, the deerhound, came over to him and settled against his feet with a sigh.

Melody smiled at him. "You're well and truly accepted now, if Mac likes you. He doesn't take to everyone like that."

"It's probably the sandwiches," Kincaid said, trying for humor. Ivan was watching him now, ready to hear his story, his big-boned face intent. The journalist was never far from the surface.

Kincaid took another sip of the whisky, then looked at Gemma as he said, "The car. It's . . . it's totaled, I think. There was a crash."

As he told them what had happened, Gemma came and sat beside him, her hand on his uninjured knee. She'd gone pale, the light dusting of freckles across her nose visible even in the lamplight. "Oh, my God," she whispered. "You could have been killed."

Ivan was frowning. "That's a well-marked junction. Anyone local would know it. You say they identified the woman who was driving?"

"The ambulance medic who stopped to help—the one who gave me a lift here—recognized her. She said her name was Nell Greene."

Addie Talbot looked shocked. "Nell? But that's—" She shook her head. "I can't believe it. Was she certain?"

"She said she knew her from work, that Nell Greene had been an administrator at the hospital."

"Yes, she was. She took early retirement and moved to Lower Slaughter from Cheltenham. She'd inherited a cottage from her aunt. It's just on the west side of the village." Still frowning, Addie continued, "It seems so unlikely that Nell would do something like that. I'd have said she was a careful person. Very responsible. In fact, she was one of my volunteer helpers for tomorrow."

"You say there was a passenger, a man?" asked Ivan.

Kincaid nodded. He hadn't mentioned the ambulance crew's speculation that the man had been dead before the crash. Nor had he told them that he'd been with Nell Greene in her last few minutes.

"Any identification?"

"Not that I heard. Tracey—the medic who stopped—didn't recognize him."

"Did Nell Greene have any family that need to be notified?" Melody asked.

"I suppose there's an ex somewhere—a doctor, I think," said Addie. "No children that I know of." Then her eyes widened. "The dog. Oh, dear. Someone will have to see to the dog. She'll be alone in the house."

"She?" asked Gemma.

"Yes, she's called Bella. A young border collie bitch. Training her was Nell's retirement project." For the first time, Addie's voice wobbled a little. "I think she was lonely, poor woman."

"Is there anyone who has access to the cottage?" asked Melody, as if her mother's show of emotion had in turn made her brisk.

Addie thought for a moment. "Mark Cain might. He's her nearest neighbor. And Bella was one of his puppies—he breeds working collies. I think he was helping Nell with the dog's training.

I'm sure he'll take Bella until something is sorted. I'll ring him straightaway."

Mark Cain stood with his mobile phone in his hand, staring at the ended call in shock. Nell, dead? How was that possible? He'd just seen her that afternoon. She and Bella had gone up the field with him and the dogs, Bella watching Sprig and Wally work the sheep. Nell had told him she meant to go to the pub for dinner, and she'd been excited about helping with tomorrow's lunch at the Talbots'.

He'd told Nell he might stop in the Lamb for a drink himself, but then at teatime he'd had a text from Viv telling him not to come to the pub. What the hell had that been about? He'd meant to text her now that the dinner service would be winding down—that was a lesson he'd learned quickly, not to interrupt the chef during the meal rush. But now, with this . . . He rubbed his face, feeling the end-of-day stubble. Good thing he hadn't poured his usual evening nightcap—he needed a clear head.

Nell . . . All Addie had said was that she'd been killed in an accident near the Bourton junction. But what the hell was Nell doing driving that way?

"Yes," he'd told Addie, Nell had given him a key, and he was happy to help out in any way possible.

The dogs were prancing round him now, thinking it was time to go out for the last constitutional of the evening, but he whistled them to their beds by the kitchen range. "Just wait, you two monkeys. You're going to have some company in a bit."

Poor Bella. She was quite bonded to Nell, who adored her. Had adored her, he corrected himself. She'd a talent for the sheep,

Bella, and there'd been times he'd wished he'd kept her for himself. But no one could have given a dog more love and care than Nell had done.

Well, for now, at least, Bella would come home with him. But first, he was going to stop by the pub and find out what the hell was up with Viv Holland.

From the far side of the pub car park, Ibby Azoulay saw Mark Cain pass the pub's main door and head round through the garden towards the kitchen. A regular ninja, the gentleman farmer, thought Ibby. Plonker. If Viv thought that nobody knew what was going on with her and Cain, she was just plain stupid. "Stupid," he muttered, liking the sound of it. "Stupid and bloody blind."

Ibby huddled into his jacket. The body heat he'd built up in the kitchen was dissipating in the sharp night air and he was glad he hadn't far to walk. But he stood in the shadows a moment longer, curious to see if Viv tossed Cain out on his ear. That was a discussion he'd like to have heard, if it had to do with Fergus O'Reilly.

Of course, if that bastard O'Reilly really was back in the picture, then he, Ibby, was well out of it. Bugger. He spat, then reached in his jacket pocket for his hidden packet of cigarettes. Stepping farther back into the passage that led from the car park to the lane behind the pub yard, he lit his first smoke of the day. He didn't dare smoke in the room he let from Bea Abbott—he didn't dare smoke anywhere that would leave a lingering odor on his clothes. Damn Viv and her rules. His palate was just fine, thank you very much, ciggies or no. He'd always been as good a cook as Viv. Better than Fergus, maybe . . . although there had been times in the glory days when Fergus had been pure magic in the kitchen. They'd all been a little in love with him.

And Fergus had used them for it, the son of a bitch.

Ibby took a last hard drag and threw the fag end into the hedge.

What the hell was Fergus O'Reilly doing, turning up here out of the blue? Offering Viv fame and fortune? That was rich, coming from him. He only hoped Viv had enough sense to turn it down. Because as much as Ibby groused about Viv's rules, and this dead-end, poky village, it was a good gig and he knew it. Their food was simple but top quality, and they'd begun to earn a reputation that was well deserved. The lunch tomorrow would definitely kick things up a notch, assuming they could pull it off.

And they would. Ibby would make sure of it. He'd worked in too many shithole kitchens since their London days, and been kicked out of more than a few of them. He didn't intend to let anything put him back there—especially bloody Fergus O'Reilly.

CHAPTER FOUR

Viv lay in the dark, watching the digital display on the clock. Four fifty-eight . . . four fifty-nine . . . When the numbers ticked over to five, she reached out from under the duvet and punched the alarm off. There was no point in staying in bed worrying when she could be up and making a start on the morning.

Had she slept at all? She'd drifted in and out of anxious dreams, dogged by a fear of being unprepared and by a vague sense of menace. Twice she'd got up to check on Grace, only to find her sleeping peacefully, her old stuffed rabbit clutched to her chest as if she were a toddler.

They'd argued when Viv had come in from the pub last night. Grace had been sullen, watching telly past her bedtime—and without her glasses, which Viv knew would give her a headache—and had refused to acknowledge her mother until Viv had snapped at her and switched off the television.

"Why did you say I couldn't talk to Fergus?" Grace had shouted at her then, tears starting. "He was nice. He asked about school, and about my bike."

"I've told you not to talk to—"

"Yeah, you're always telling me. But he wasn't a stranger. He knew you—"

"Just because I know him doesn't mean he's nice." Viv sat beside her on the sofa, ignoring Grace's flinch away from her. "Look, love, it's a long story and I'll tell you sometime, but not tonight. I just want you to be careful, okay? Not everybody is what they seem."

In Grace she saw her own reckless streak, the same one that had sent her off to work in a London kitchen at seventeen, as green as any country girl straight off the hay wagon. A little distrust would have seen her in good stead.

And Fergus, dear God. Why had she even introduced him to Grace? After disappearing mysteriously for a few hours after he'd scared her out of her wits that morning, he'd come back in the afternoon, all Irish blarney, trying to coax Viv into some hare-brained new scheme. She'd been standing in the yard arguing with him when Grace got home from school. Viv hadn't wanted to make a scene in front of Grace, and she'd had to get back to prepping for the dinner service, so she'd left them together. What had she been thinking?

That Fergus O'Reilly would have undergone some magical transformation in the years since she'd walked out on him and his bloody restaurant? That he suddenly had her best interests at heart?

Bollocks.

When she'd come to her senses, Fergus had been gone and

Grace had wandered into the kitchen looking suspiciously smitten. Viv had told her not to speak to him again and hoped that would be the end of it.

But Viv should have known she hadn't seen the last of Fergus. At the start of dinner service, he'd walked into the pub—her pub!—and picked his way through her menu as if he were a Michelin judge, then left the food barely tasted on the plates he'd sent back to the kitchen. By the time he'd strolled into the back without so much as a by-your-leave, she'd been ready to take his head off. And then he'd caused a scene that she was going to have a hard time explaining to anyone.

Bastard.

Well, she wasn't going to let him ruin this day. Fergus O'Reilly had caused enough damage in her life. She threw off the duvet, pulled on her whites, and headed for the pub.

Kincaid woke to the sound of running water. Gemma in the shower, he thought, fuzzily, then opened his eyes and squinted against light that seemed much too bright for their bedroom. Moving, he gasped as pain shot through his ribs, bringing recollection with it.

Not at home. He was in the guest room at the Talbots'. He'd wrecked his car. His head ached and his right hand throbbed. Gingerly, he lifted his swollen fingers and touched the knot on his forehead.

Gemma came out of the bathroom, wrapped in a towel. She'd pulled up her coppery hair in a clip but escaping tendrils curled from the steam. "You're awake," she said, perching on the edge of the bed. "I was going to let you sleep. How are you feeling?"

Wincing, Kincaid pulled himself into a sitting position. "Sore."

"And here I was thinking you looked a bit rakish." Gemma raised an eyebrow and patted his arm, letting her towel slip a few inches.

"I'll show you rakish," he said, reaching out to touch the exposed curve of her breast. Both his ribs and his hand protested. "Ow." He grimaced and sat back. "I'm bloody useless today."

Gemma eyed him critically. "You should take it easy."

He started to shake his head, then thought better of it. "I've got to make a statement. And I've got to see about the Astra."

"I'll drive you. I'm sure I can borrow Melody's car. And you need to have that cut looked at."

"I'll be fine," Kincaid said, without much conviction. "And what about Doug and the boys?" He'd meant to collect them in his car.

"I'm sure we can work out something. I suspect they have taxis even in the country." Gemma leaned over and kissed him very gently on the unbruised side of his forehead. "I'm just glad you're okay. You moaned and mumbled a good bit in your sleep last night."

"Did I?" Some of the dreams came back to him now, a confusion of flashing lights and the smell of blood. He'd told Gemma, when they were alone in their room last night, about the medics saying the passenger in the other car was dead before the impact. But he had not told her about Nell Greene's last few moments, and he found he still couldn't quite bring himself to talk about it. "Where's Char, then?" he asked, eager to change the subject.

"Downstairs. Helping." Gemma rolled her eyes and stood up. "And I had better get down there and rescue Melody."

"Nonsense," said Ivan, when Gemma proposed at breakfast that she should borrow Melody's little Renault to take Kincaid to the recovery yard and then to give his statement at the Cheltenham police station.

Startled, Kincaid looked at him as Melody said, "Dad—"

"I'll take the lad myself," Ivan went on before Melody could finish her protest. "Your mother needs all the help she can get this morning, and I am about as useful as the proverbial bull in the china shop."

Given that Ivan had made them a proper fried breakfast with all the aplomb of an accomplished cook, Kincaid suspected Ivan could turn a deft hand to just about anything. He didn't doubt, however, that Addie needed help. She'd greeted them when they came down, then gone out to oversee the setting up of the hired tables in the garden, taking a wide-eyed Charlotte with her. When he'd asked if she wasn't joining them for breakfast, Ivan had growled, "Yogurt and berries, that's all she'll eat," with a look of disgust. Addie's answering smile told him that this was a familiar argument.

"Sir," he said, then, at Ivan's glare, corrected himself. "Ivan. If Gemma's needed here, I'm sure I can get a taxi." Managing to shower, shave, and dress had convinced him he shouldn't attempt to drive, especially not a borrowed car. Not only was his right hand swollen and too tender to use, he felt surprisingly shaky and fuzzy-headed.

"Nonsense," Ivan repeated firmly. "It would cost you a fortune. Besides, I know a chap or two."

"But what about the boys?" Kincaid asked.

"I'll run into Moreton for Doug and the boys," said Melody. "Piece of cake."

Kincaid sat back, lifting his coffee cup in a left-handed salute. "You're a bossy lot, you Talbots."

Gemma shot Melody a grin. "I could have told you that."

The heady scent of caramel filled the quiet pub kitchen. Viv stood back, surveying her work with satisfaction.

The small glass jars filled with a spread made from local smoked trout were packed into a cool box. Earlier in the week, Grace had helped her make the labels for the jars, as well as for the two puddings which she would serve the same way. The guests would be encouraged to take home any that were left, as well as the larger jars of pickled vegetables. She'd fermented cabbage with radishes, and cauliflower with haricots verts and carrots. The spice mixtures were not as hot as traditional kimchee—a concession to the bland English palate—but still had a good bit of pop. The spicy, crunchy veg made a perfect counterpoint to the soft creaminess of the smoked lamb and beans.

Those she was serving together, in individual camping tins, to be warmed just before lunch in the Beck House warming ovens. It was all a bit precious, the jars and the tins, but she wanted the meal to be something people would remember.

She'd made a seeded crispbread for the potted trout course, and flatbreads to serve warm with the lamb and pickles. In between the trout and the lamb she planned a salad course—fresh greens, topped with roasted pear halves she'd done the previous day, a local soft blue cheese, and a drizzle of caramel. This was the course that had given her the most worry. It checked every foodie box, but would require last-minute assembly in the Beck House kitchen, and a good bit of willing volunteer help. She couldn't pull Ibby or Angelica from the pub kitchen on a busy autumn Saturday.

When the back door creaked open, she thought it might be Ibby, there to start lunch prep, but it was Bea, looking considerably the worse for wear. Her dark hair was tousled, her eyes shadowed, and instead of her usual work uniform of dark skirt and white blouse she wore sweatpants and an old T-shirt.

Bea headed straight for the coffee machine. When she'd started a cup, she turned to Viv. "Now, are you going to tell me what that was all about last night? Why the hell would you let him come here?"

"I didn't *let* him," Viv protested, all her calm from a moment before vanishing. "I have no idea how he tracked me down."

"I'll tell you how. It was this damned lunch." Bea waved a hand at Viv's carefully prepared courses. "You bloody well know it was. One of the food critics Addie Talbot invited had to have mentioned it. I told you this whole thing was a bad idea."

"Look." Viv wiped her hands on her apron and fetched the cream for Bea's coffee from the fridge. She hated seeing Bea so upset. Bea was the rock in their partnership, the dependable and steady half, and when she'd agreed to Addie Talbot's plan, she'd had no idea that Bea would be so set against it. But, then, she hadn't foreseen Fergus popping up, either. "It will be fine," she said, handing Bea the bottle. "He'll not come back after last night." She knew she was reassuring herself.

"No?" Bea was still scowling. "Not even for the camel hair coat he left in the bar?"

As Duncan and Ivan left the breakfast table to get ready for their run to Cheltenham, Gemma heard Melody's phone ding with a text. Frowning, Melody tapped an answer, then glanced up at Gemma, who'd stood to clear the table. "Um, slight change of plans," she said. "That was Doug. He and the boys are coming early. So I'll run pick them up now, if you don't mind giving Mummy a hand in the garden."

"Wait." Gemma gave Melody a sharp look. "Why didn't they tell us they were coming early? What about Toby's class?" Realization dawned. "You told Doug about the accident, didn't you?"

"I might have just texted him last night." Melody smiled a little apologetically. "Can you imagine what he'd have said if he'd shown up at noon and no one had told him what happened to Duncan?"

Gemma had to admit she had a point. And she would be glad to have the boys with them sooner rather than later—although she wasn't sure that Toby's presence would help with the luncheon prep. Still, she didn't like being left out of the loop. "I can pick them up, if you don't mind me borrowing your car," she said, realizing how much she really hated being dependent on someone else for transport.

"No, I'll go." Melody was already grabbing her bag from the sideboard. "I know the way, and the train's due in twenty minutes. Don't worry about the washing up. I'll do it when I get back." Then she was gone.

Gemma gazed after her. Duncan had been right about the Talbot bossiness. She'd been managed, and she wondered if there was more to Melody's tactic than convenience.

From the garden came the Jack Russell's high-pitched yips, and Charlotte's even more shrill squeal of excitement. Gemma realized she'd left the child in Addie's care too long. She stacked the breakfast plates in the sink and headed for the French doors that led to the terrace.

She stepped out into the crisp morning and stopped, her breath catching at the sight that greeted her. Last night, she'd only glimpsed the garden through the windows in the fading dusk, and then her gaze had been caught by the distant hills.

Now, she marveled at the riot of color and symmetry spread before her. The flagged terrace merged into a smooth expanse of emerald lawn anchored by a rose-draped pergola. Two long tables had been set up in the grass on either side.

At the lawn's edge she could see drifts of flowers bisected by a shallow flight of steps, and beyond that, more green lawns and steps, leading her eyes down to the curve of the little river.

On either side of the top lawn, double herbaceous borders blazed in a profusion of late-summer reds and golds. She'd no idea so many different flowers even existed.

"Mummy!" Charlotte came running to her from the pergola, the terrier at her heels. "I've been throwing the ball for Polly. She likes it."

"I'll bet she does." Gemma gave her a squeeze. Mac the deer-hound lay in a patch of shade cast by the pergola, massive head on his paws, watching Charlotte as if he'd been given the charge.

"There's a bowling lawn, and a tennis lawn. Miss Addie says we can play after the lunch."

"Where is Miss Addie?" Gemma asked, a little concerned that Charlotte had been left on her own. But just then, the big dog raised his head, and she saw Addie coming from the left, her arms filled with a bundle of fabric.

"Just getting the tablecloths," Addie explained. "I had them in the glasshouse."

Gemma thought she must have meant greenhouse, but when she looked in that direction she saw that it was, quite literally, a glass house, glass and white wrought iron with a peaked roof.

"My grandfather's folly," said Addie, following her gaze. "Or at least so everyone thought at the time. It's Victorian. He found it on an estate that was being razed in the thirties, had it taken down and reassembled. A good thing, too, as otherwise the iron might have gone for scrap in the war. Now, of course, the glasshouse is priceless."

"It's beautiful," said Gemma. "And the garden, it's—" She shook her head and waved a hand at the surroundings. "I've never seen anything like this. It's spectacular."

Addie smiled. "We've made an effort to return it to something like its Edwardian glory. Jekyll-esque, if not pure Gertrude Jekyll." Gemma's incomprehension must have shown, because she added, "Gertrude Jekyll was the most brilliant of the Arts and Crafts garden designers. Family letters say she consulted with the architect who designed the house, but we've never found any actual plans. I'll give you a proper tour after lunch. But in the meantime," she went on, dumping the red-and-white-checked bundle on one of the hire tables, "we'd better get a move on. Where's Melody?"

"Oh. I came to tell you." Gemma explained about the early arrival and the train. "So I'm afraid you're stuck with me for a bit."

Addie glanced at her watch. "My assistant, Roz, should be here soon, and she's rounded up some of the village ladies to help with the serving. So if you could just help me get the tables laid—" Her phone dinged. Checking the text, she said, "That's Viv, our chef. She's in the drive and the house is locked. Would you mind letting her in? She's got things for the kitchen."

Gemma checked to make sure Charlotte wasn't being a nuisance, but she was sitting quietly on the top step, the terrier beside her. "Of course."

Hurrying back through the house, she opened the front door. A woman in a chef's jacket and checked trousers was pulling plastic tubs from the back of a small van. She was slender—perhaps a little too thin—with short, blond, carelessly spiked hair. Beside her stood a girl, hands in hoodie pockets, a scowl on her small be-spectacled face. Her mop of light brown hair was almost as curly as Charlotte's.

"Hi, I'm Gemma. Addie sent me to help."

The woman set the tub down and held out a hand to Gemma. "I'm Viv. Viv Holland. And this is my daughter, Grace."

The girl managed a nod and a mumbled "Nice to meet you," but kept her gaze firmly on Gemma's feet.

"Tell me what goes where," Gemma said, gesturing at the van's contents.

"Everything in the scullery to start with. Then we can sort it out." Viv handed Gemma the tub she'd set down, then picked out a smaller one for Grace. "Here, love, take the pears. They're not so heavy. You know where to go."

As Viv pulled out a cool box, Grace trudged towards the open front door as if the tub were filled with lead.

"She's eleven," Viv said with a sigh.

"Oh. That explains it, then," Gemma replied with a grin. Now, she saw that Viv Holland was not as young as she'd first thought, and that she looked hollow-eyed with exhaustion.

"You have kids?" Viv asked as they entered the house.

"Three. My daughter's in the garden with Addie, and the boys should be here any moment with Melody." She followed Viv through the kitchen into a room she hadn't noticed, a right angle in the far corner of the house. There was a utility sink, a dishwasher, a large fridge, and two built-in warming ovens. A door opened onto the terrace. The far end of the room held racks of Wellies and pegs for anoraks.

Grace went out onto the terrace and ran to greet the dogs, suddenly looking more like a child than a sulky preteen.

"Is it just you and Addie, then?" she added with a frown, glancing out. "I thought Nell was helping out this morning."

"Nell?" Gemma echoed, realizing with dismay that Viv hadn't heard the news.

"Yeah. Nell Greene, from the village. Nice woman. She's supposed to be doing the setup."

"Viv." Gemma touched her arm. "I'm sorry, but there's something you should know."

CHAPTER FIVE

"Why is it," asked Ivan, "that senior police officers are always total idiots in films and on the telly? I haven't found that to be the case." He gave Kincaid a sideways glance. "And you're a superintendent, after all."

"But not a chief superintendent," Kincaid replied with a grin. "Therein lies the difference."

"Well, your own super—former super, I should say—is not bad at all, and I think you'll pass ACC Shelton. Why haven't you gone for promotion?" added Ivan, this time keeping his eyes on the road.

"Because I don't play golf," Kincaid quipped, refusing to be drawn, even by Ivan.

"Neither do I," said Ivan. "Bloody waste of time, if you ask me." Kincaid surveyed the workaday interior of Ivan's country car.

It was a classic Land Rover Defender from the 1980s, dark blue and lovingly restored. His father would love it, but it was certainly unexpected for a man of Ivan's position.

He wondered how Ivan Talbot managed to navigate the spaces between his working-class background and his roles as a newspaper baron and a country gent with such apparent ease. "Isn't it expected of you, the golfing?" he asked.

"The nice thing about money," Ivan said, "I learned early on. You don't have to do what people expect. Not that folks expected much of me in the beginning," he added with a shrug of his big shoulders.

"That didn't bother you?"

"I came from a two-up, two-down with the necessary in the back garden. My nan struggled to put tea on the table. How could they damage me? Not to mention I had Addie and the paper. Folks could think what they liked."

Kincaid thought that one of the secrets to Ivan's success—and his integrity—was just that: he met no one's expectations but his own.

The green rolling countryside had flashed by them as they left the village, and it wasn't until Ivan pulled to a stop at a T-junction that he realized where he was. The depressions left by the wrecked cars were still visible in the turf on the opposite verge. "Wait," he said. "This is where she—Nell Greene— She must have come this way."

Checking the rear mirror, Ivan idled the Land Rover at the stop. "This road's the fastest way from the village to Cheltenham or Gloucester. All the surrounding villages use it."

"But—" Kincaid surveyed the junction with dismay. "If she used this road regularly, how could she miss the stop?"

"Nell Greene, you mean?"

Kincaid nodded. His head hurt and he felt suddenly queasy. Why did he keep smelling blood?

"Maybe she felt ill," Ivan suggested.

"Yes, but—" Kincaid stopped. That didn't explain the dead passenger. Damn. He hated not having access to information. Maybe the local force had an identity on the man. Ivan turned into the main road and they left the junction behind, but that didn't stop the scene from replaying in Kincaid's head.

"Sorry, mate." The man at the recovery yard in Cheltenham shook his head as Kincaid surveyed what remained of the Astra. "We've sent photos to your insurer. I'm sure they'll be in touch. On the plus side, we recovered your mobile phone and an overnight bag. They're in the office."

But the phone, when removed from its plastic bag, was a total loss, its screen and casing shattered.

Ivan, who had come into the office with him, touched him on the shoulder. "Phone shop first, police station second."

While Ivan drove to a nearby shopping district, Kincaid tried to come to grips with the loss of the car. Not that he hadn't expected it, but seeing it had still been a shock. It was stupid, he knew. The Astra had little monetary value, and they had all hated it. But it had been a gift from his dad, and somehow the destruction of the car brought home his dad's fragile health. He would have to tell his parents the car was gone. And then what? He had no idea what he would do to replace it.

While Kincaid dealt with the purchase of a new mobile phone and the data transfer, Ivan brought them coffee from a nearby Caffè Nero.

"I remembered how you liked it from breakfast," Ivan said as they walked back to the Land Rover. "All set?"

Kincaid scrolled through text messages. There was one from Gemma: "Doug and boys coming early. All under control. Love you."

"Yes." Kincaid looked up, trying to place where they were on the map of Cheltenham he'd looked at that morning. "Are we close enough to walk to the station?"

"Not unless you're very fit," said Ivan. "We're going to county HQ outside Gloucester."

"Wally! Sprig!" Mark Cain whistled his dogs to him in the farmyard, then added, "Bella, good girl," as the black-and-white bitch trotted behind them. He rubbed her head as she came to him, then finished locking the four-wheeler in the barn. He'd done his morning check on the flocks, Bella following the other dogs without much prompting, but he wondered how she'd do left on her own in the house when she'd been used to Nell being home most of the day.

Well, needs must. She'd have to get used to it, at least for the time being. He hadn't heard from anyone about the dog and had no idea who to contact. He'd ask Addie at the luncheon.

He checked his phone for at least the tenth time that morning, but there was nothing from Addie, and still no call or text from Viv. Damn it, he was starting to feel like some kind of stalker. When he'd gone to the pub last night, he'd found only the waitstaff, closing up. Jack, Sarah said, had left early, and Viv had gone to bed, big day tomorrow and all that. When he'd rung Viv again from the courtyard, his call had gone straight to voice mail.

His irritation had turned to unease. They might not have an official relationship, but Viv had certainly never avoided him. Something was wrong, really wrong, and he'd sworn in frustration because he'd no idea what it was. The news about Nell had been bad enough without this added worry.

Leaving the pub, he'd gone back up the lane to Nell's cottage and let himself in with the key neatly labeled NELL with sticky tape.

Of course she'd labeled her key, he'd thought. Organized to a T, that was Nell. It had been her one fault in training Bella, always wanting to follow the rules. Sometimes, with dogs and sheep, you had to follow your instincts.

Was it instinct that had failed her on the road?

He'd entered the dark house with reluctance. It felt intrusive, and he hadn't been able to shake the idea that Nell might just be asleep, that there had been some terrible mistake. But the cottage had been silent, and Bella had been frantically happy to see him, and to go out. When she'd finished her business, she jumped willingly into the Land Rover. Going back into the house for the dog's bed, he'd stood for a moment in Nell's kitchen. The place was as neat as Nell herself. The only thing out of place was a copy of the *Times* folded to the day's crossword, half finished, pencil beside it. He'd closed the door and locked it firmly behind him.

Now, he shut the dogs in the kitchen and drove the Land Rover down to the pub. The village was starting to fill up with walkers, cars lining every available space on the verges, but the pub's "customers only" car park was still empty. There was a half hour yet to morning coffee. But Viv's van, he saw immediately, was already gone.

Going in through the main door, he found Jack already behind the bar, his usually cheerful face set in a scowl. The pub smelled welcoming, like coffee and baking bread. Viv had told him that morning coffee was a growing moneymaker for pubs, and that it was well worth it to stock top-tier coffee and serve fresh-baked pastries. The scents, however, were obviously not working their magic on Jack this morning. "Did you see them?" he asked, before Mark could even greet him.

"What? Who?" asked Mark, stopping at the bar.

"Bloody police." Jack shook his head. "Asking about Nell Greene. Have you heard what happened to her?"

Mark nodded. "I've got her dog. Addie Talbot rang me last night."

"Addie? How did the Talbots find out before anyone else in the village?" Jack sounded incensed.

"No idea. But it's a dreadful thing. I still can't believe it."

Jack picked up a wineglass by the neck as if he might strangle it. "Did Addie tell you there was a bloke in the car with Nell?"

"No. I only heard the crash was at the Bourton T-junction—"

"He was killed, too, this bloke, but apparently the cops don't know who he was. No ID. The thing is, Nell was here last night, on her own."

"She said she might come. I meant to, but—"

"They gave me a description of the guy in her car. He was here, too."

"What?" Mark stared at him. "You're not suggesting that Nell picked up some stranger?" He couldn't imagine anything less likely, but if his own ex-wife had taught him one thing, it was that you could never be certain what people might do.

"Stranger to her, maybe. But not to some." Jack polished the wineglass with renewed force.

Baffled, Mark said, "What are you talking about?"

"I told them," said Jack, "to ask Chef."

Viv stared at Gemma, her expression blank. Then she let out a puff of breath and slumped against the work top. "That's terrible. Poor Nell."

"Did you know her well?" asked Gemma.

"No, not really. But she was . . . nice." Viv grimaced. "That sounds a bit 'faintest of praise,' but she did seem to be a genuinely nice person. Done wrong by her ex, if rumors are anything to go by, although she never said so herself. I'd chat with her when she came in for a meal, if I wasn't too busy. She was interested in food. And she seemed a bit lonely. She'd been so excited about this luncheon," Viv added, her eyes glazing with tears. "Sorry." She sniffed and wiped a hand across her eyes. "It's just the shock." Straightening up, she said, "We should be getting on with things," and led the way out the door onto the terrace.

"Oh, it looks lovely," she breathed, gazing at the tables, now covered in red-and-white-checked cloths. Addie was laying each place with an assortment of vintage china and glassware. "Addie must have raided every Oxfam shop in five counties for this much stuff."

Looking up, Addie called out, "The plates for the salad course are in the scullery." Then, she came to them, saying, "Oh, dear. Gemma's told you about Nell."

Grace had apparently got over her sulks enough to play with Charlotte, and the two girls were marching up and down the garden steps, followed by the now-panting terrier.

"Oh," said Viv, as if the sight of Polly had reminded her. "The dog. What about her lovely dog?"

"Mark Cain has her," answered Addie, and Viv nodded as if that made sense, but the nod was followed by a little frown. "But he didn't—" She shook her head. "Never mind. We need to get the cold jars in the fridge and the tins in the warming ovens. And where the hell is Joe with my salad greens?"

"He's in the kitchen garden, cutting the flowers for the table. He picked the greens first thing—they're in buckets in the glass-house."

"Who's Joe?" asked Gemma.

"My business partner," said Addie. "He manages the gardens here, and sells the extra produce he grows in the kitchen garden to the local restaurant trade. I take a percentage." She smiled. "Melody will tell you it's quite feudal."

"It's brilliant stuff, is what it is," Viv put in. "Seasonal, all or-ganic, heritage varieties. He started out just growing for the pub and now every restaurant in the area is fighting over his veg, in-cluding the Michelin-rated kitchen up the hill." She nodded in the direction of Upper Slaughter. "Addie better watch out or he'll be digging up the rose garden for more growing room."

Addie smiled. "Over my dead body. But I'll send him up to the house with the salad stuff. He should—"

Whatever she'd been about to say was drowned out by a sudden cacophony of barking. Both Polly and Mac stood, facing the house, hackles up.

A tawny-haired woman in black trousers and a white top came out of the kitchen French doors.

"Oh, hush, Polly, Mac," said Addie. "It's just Roz—"

But behind the woman came two uniformed constables, a man and a woman. Unexpected visits from uniform were seldom good news.

"Grace," called Addie. "Will you take the dogs up to the glasshouse and ask Joe to put them inside for a few minutes?"

Grace obeyed with only a curious glance for the officers, and the dogs went willingly. Charlotte, sensing something, came to Gemma and wrapped her arms round Gemma's leg.

"Here, you go with Grace, lovey." Gemma gave her a pat and watched with relief as she ran to catch up to the older girl. Whatever the officers wanted, she doubted a four-year-old needed to hear it.

Addie's assistant, Roz, murmured something to the female constable as they crossed the terrace. As they reached the lawn, she called out, "Addie, these officers would like to speak to Viv."

Viv, who'd been looking impatient at the delay, frowned. "How can I help you?"

"Miss Holland?" asked the female officer. Her name badge read PC MURRAY, and her companion was PC MCCABE. Murray and McCabe made Gemma think of an old-fashioned comedy duo, but these two were not smiling.

"Yes, I'm Viv Holland. Is there a problem?" Suddenly looking anxious, Viv added, "Is everything all right at the pub?"

"Yes, ma'am," said PC Murray. "But your barman"—she pulled a small notepad from her uniform pocket and consulted it—"Mr. Jack Doyle, told us we might find you here. We were hoping you might be able to help us identify a man who was involved in a traffic incident last night."

Gemma realized immediately who they meant, but it was

obvious from Viv's bemused expression that she had no idea where this was going.

McCabe spoke for the first time. "Ma'am, a Mrs. Greene from Lower Slaughter was also involved in the incident."

"Nell? Yes, I just heard," said Viv, sounding thoroughly puzzled. "Terrible. But what has that to do with—"

"It seems that Mrs. Greene was in your establishment, the Lamb—"

"Yes, I know the name of my pub—"

"The Lamb," McCabe went on, unperturbed, and Gemma was beginning to find him as annoying as Viv apparently did, "until approximately 8 p.m. last night. As was a gentleman your barman described as being mid to late forties, a bit over six feet tall, brown eyes, with shoulder-length blondish hair. Your barkeep intimated that you could identify this gentleman."

Viv stared at him. "Fergus? Are you talking about Fergus?"

"And that would be Fergus who, ma'am?"

"Fergus O'Reilly, of course," Viv snapped. "But why the hell didn't you ask him yourself?"

Murray stepped in, her voice gentle. "Ma'am, the gentleman had no ID. And I'm afraid he was deceased."

"What?" The color drained from Viv's face. "Are you telling me that Fergus is dead?"

Addie had a hand on Viv's shoulder as Gemma pulled a chair from the luncheon table. Together, they eased Viv into it.

"Roz," said Addie, "would you fetch Viv a glass of water?" Nodding, Roz turned away, but Gemma thought she looked almost as shocked as Viv.

"Viv, darling." Addie gave Viv's shoulder a squeeze. "Take your time."

"His wallet," Viv whispered. "He couldn't stand having it in his trouser pocket, especially when he was cooking. He always kept it in his coat. And last night . . . after . . ." She swallowed. "Last night, when he left the pub, he left his coat."

With its curved glass front and flat roof, the Gloucester Constabulary Headquarters at Quedgeley looked more like an aquatic center to Kincaid. At night, he suspected it might look like an alien spaceship.

"It's green," said Ivan, with proprietary pride as he pulled up the Land Rover in Visitors' Parking. "The architectural firm came highly recommended."

So he'd had a hand in the planning, Kincaid thought, and wondered what Ivan *didn't* have a hand in. Although he had to admit the headquarters building was a damned sight more appealing than the Brutalist concrete facade of his own Holborn Police Station. Maybe he should petition Ivan to improve the Met's architecture.

"I thought we'd have a chat with Mike Shelton." Ivan gave Kincaid a sideways grin. "Who doesn't golf."

Mike Shelton, Kincaid soon learned, was Michael Shelton, Assistant Chief Constable, Operations, a slender, dark-haired man in his forties. Young for an ACC, Kincaid thought, as Shelton greeted them and shook hands warmly. He was in casual clothes rather than in uniform, and it wasn't until Ivan said, "Thanks for taking the time to see us on a Saturday, Mike," that Kincaid realized Ivan must have rung him and requested the meeting, probably while Kincaid was dealing with his phone.

"Not a problem," Shelton said easily. "I had some things to finish up this morning as it was. How's the Defender?" he asked when they were settled in the conference chairs in his glass-walled office.

It took Kincaid a moment to realize he was talking about Ivan's car. So Shelton was a Land Rover enthusiast as well. "Tip-top," Ivan answered. "Did you find the '90 station wagon you've been looking for?"

"Not yet, but I'm not giving up. It's the perfect thing for holding the kids, the dogs, and the camping gear, and it's dependable enough to get us round Scotland next summer."

"Mike's quite a walker," Ivan explained to Kincaid.

"I'll be in your neck of the woods tomorrow," said Shelton. "We're doing Slaughters Vale."

Kincaid recognized the name. He'd looked up some of the local walks, hoping to get out with the kids over the weekend. Now he wasn't even sure he could manage the trek from Beck House to Lower Slaughter. His breakfast dose of pain relievers was beginning to wear off, his arm was throbbing, and his head felt like someone had taken an ax to it.

A uniformed constable brought in a tray with a freshly brewed pot of tea and three china cups. There were definite perks to being an ACC, Kincaid thought. The strong malty tea was welcome.

When they all had their cups filled, Shelton examined Kincaid. "Ivan tells me you were in an odd accident last night. You look a bit the worse for wear."

"Considerably better than the other people," Kincaid said with a grimace.

Retrieving a folder from his desk, Shelton slipped on a pair of reading glasses, making him look more like a college professor than a policeman, and scanned a report. "Mrs. Nell Greene, of Lower Slaughter, the driver of the vehicle, died at the scene of the accident. No trace of alcohol or drugs, according to the prelimi-

nary report. Unidentified male passenger, also dead at the scene."
He peered at Kincaid over the glasses. "Except the ambulance
crew stated that they thought life was extinct before the collision.
There was minimal bleeding from severe trauma injuries. That is
odd." Glancing at Ivan, he added, "I understand you knew Mrs.
Greene personally?"

"Not well. My wife knew her better. Mrs. Greene was fairly
new to the area but had made an effort to become involved in local
activities."

"And yet your wife didn't recognize the passenger from Mr.
Kincaid's description?"

"No. And he didn't sound like anyone that we know from the
village."

Shelton looked at the report again. "We've sent uniform to try
to track down an ID, and routine postmortems are scheduled for
both victims. Family liaison has tried to contact Mrs. Greene's
ex-husband. Any other next of kin that you know of?"

Ivan shook his head. "My wife has asked Nell's neighbor to look
after her dog."

"Well, I'd put her failure to yield down to driver distraction—
usually these days it's a mobile phone if alcohol isn't involved. But
I don't like the dead passenger. Nor do I like odd things on my
watch." Returning the folder to his desk, Shelton picked up the
phone and said, "Tammy, send Booth in, will you?" Hanging up,
he continued to Ivan and Kincaid, "One of my DIs is in today. I'll
have him take your statement, Mr. Kincaid, and then we'll take it
from there."

There was a sharp knock on Shelton's door. The man who entered wore an expression about as welcoming as a granite rock

face. Unlike Shelton, he wore a suit. It was charcoal, and well cut enough to show off the muscles beneath the shoulders of his jacket. With a curly earpiece, he could have doubled as a Royal Protection Officer.

"DI Booth, I don't think you've met Mr. Talbot. And this is Detective Superintendent Kincaid, from the Met." They stood to shake Booth's hand. Kincaid offered his left, and was glad he had. The man had a grip that could crush uninjured fingers. "Mr. Kincaid was a victim in an accident last night. I've sent you the report, Colin, if you could have a look." While phrased as a request, it was obviously an order.

"Sir," said Booth, with ill-concealed irritation. "I was just—"

"And if you could have Mr. Kincaid go over the statement he gave to uniform last night and sign it. I believe Mr. Kincaid and Mr. Talbot have places to be."

"Sir." The look Booth gave Kincaid said that he had places to be as well, and that he was not the least bit amused by his ACC's request. But he said, "Why don't you step into my office, Superintendent?" and turned on his heel.

Kincaid followed Booth into a much smaller office. Booth waved him into a visitor's chair, then sat behind his desk with an exasperated thump. "What's all this bollocks, then?" he said without preamble. "That's Ivan Talbot, the newspaper baron. Must be nice to have him throwing his weight round on your behalf."

"Not on my behalf, no. Read the report and you can decide if it's bollocks or not. And I'm sorry to muck up your Saturday."

Booth shrugged, his expression softening a little. "Kid has a football match at one. I'm in trouble if I miss it."

"I know what you mean." Kincaid cocked his head, replaying what he'd heard. "You're from Manchester."

"My northern vowels give me away?"

"I grew up in Cheshire, in Nantwich."

"Ah. Close enough." Booth looked at him with more interest. "Man U or City?"

"Liverpool."

"Bugger." Booth shook his head. "That's too bad. I thought we might be long-lost brothers." There was a hint of a smile on his dark face. "Except you're all citified now. How long have you been in the Met?"

"More than twenty years. But I have a good friend in Cheshire, Ronnie Babcock."

Booth's eyebrows went up. "DCI Babcock? Bloke looks like he's had his face smashed in once too often?"

Kincaid grinned. "That's the one." He thought mentioning that Ronnie Babcock was his sister's boyfriend might be gilding the lily.

"He's one of the good ones, Babcock." Booth considered Kincaid a moment, then said, "In which case maybe you should just bugger the report and tell me what happened."

"A nice, middle-aged divorcée, who was not drinking, plowed straight through a T-junction and hit me broadside," Kincaid said. "My car rolled. The front end of hers was crushed. She was trapped. I held her hand as she died." Why he was prompted to tell Booth this, when he hadn't even told Gemma, Kincaid didn't know. He cleared his throat and went on. "The thing is, there was an unidentified passenger, a man, also dead. But the medics think he died before the crash."

"Got your copper's instincts going, I take it?" Booth said, frowning.

"I'd just like to know what happened."

Booth sighed. "I get that, mate. I really do. But—"

There was a rap on the door and ACC Shelton came in. "Sorry to interrupt. Sir Ivan just got a call from his wife. Someone has identified the man in the car. His name is Fergus O'Reilly."

"Fergus O'Reilly? Not Fergus O'Reilly the chef?" said Booth. "Oh, bloody hell."

CHAPTER SIX

Addie had excused herself for a moment, whispering to Gemma that she was ringing Ivan. When she returned, seeing that PC Murray had her pencil poised over her little notebook, she said, "Let's move to the terrace, shall we? And give Chef Holland a moment." Gemma helped her encourage Viv from the folding chair on the lawn to a proper chair on the terrace.

"I'm fine, really," Viv protested. "It's just—it's just a shock, that's all." But Gemma thought she still looked shaky, and her voice was high and breathless.

The kitchen door opened and Roz came out bearing not a glass of water, but a tray with a teapot and a half a dozen mismatched mugs. "I thought we could all use some fortifying," Roz said, setting out the mugs on a table. When Gemma stood to help, Roz added to her quietly, "Sorry we weren't properly introduced. I'm Rosalind Dunning. You must be Melody's friend."

"Gemma James. I work with Melody."

As Roz poured the tea, Gemma caught the strong, malty scent on the warm air. She gave the first two mugs to Viv and Addie, the second two to the uniformed officers, while taking the opportunity to examine her companion. Roz Dunning was an attractive woman, perhaps a bit older than Gemma had first thought—up close, the tiny lines at the corners of her eyes and mouth were visible.

By the time Roz had offered milk and sugar, Gemma was glad to see that Viv had regained a little color. A good thing, too, as PC Murray had opened her notebook again.

"Ms. Holland," said Murray, "can you tell us how you knew Mr. O'Reilly?"

Viv swallowed. "I used to work for him in London, a long time ago. In his restaurant. But I hadn't seen him since then, until yesterday."

"Do you know what he was doing in Lower Slaughter?"

"No. He just showed up at my pub. Said he wanted to catch up, for old time's sake." Viv shot Addie a glance that might have been accusing. "He'd heard something about the luncheon today. He—he stayed for dinner at the pub," she added, looking at her hands.

PC Murray made a note, then asked, "Do you know where Mr. O'Reilly was staying?"

"Not a clue," Viv said more firmly. "But it can't have been far if he left his coat."

"Did he know Mrs. Nell Greene?"

Viv frowned. "I can't imagine that he did."

"Did you see them leave the pub together?"

"No. I was in the kitchen. It was Friday-night service," she added, as if it should have been obvious.

Murray made another note, then asked, "Do you have a London address for Mr. O'Reilly?"

"No idea. He used to rent a flat in Chelsea, but I don't remember the street. As I said, it was a long time ago. Look, I have to—"

"Just a couple more things, Ms. Holland. Is there anyone who should be notified as Mr. O'Reilly's next of kin?"

Viv paled again. "Oh, God, no. He didn't have any family that I know of. That was part of Fergus's myth—you know, the Irish orphan. They were all killed in Belfast in the eighties."

A young man in jeans came from the direction of the glasshouse, carrying two pails brimming over with salad leaves. "Look, sorry to interrupt," he said when he reached the terrace, "but what do you want me to do with these greens, Viv? They're going to wilt." He turned to Addie. "And what about the kids? I've given them some veg to sort but I can't keep them occupied all day." He had a shock of unruly brown hair and a neatly trimmed beard, and a heavier local accent than Gemma had heard so far. Joe the gardener, she assumed.

"I'm so sorry," she said, standing. "I'll just fetch Char—"

But PC Murray stood as well, and the silent McCabe followed suit. "Thank you all for your time," Murray said, with a nod to Addie. "We'll let you get on with things. Just one more question for Ms. Holland." She'd put her notebook away, but Gemma guessed what was coming. "A formal identification of the body will be necessary. Can you come to the mortuary at headquarters? At your convenience, of course."

MAY 2006

The first thing Viv did every morning when she arrived at O'Reilly's was clean the vent hoods, which had been left in the sink to soak.

Ibby had mocked her, saying, "Women's work," but she was used to that and she didn't care. Any kitchen she worked in was going to be clean.

"You think any Michelin-starred restaurant has greasy vents?" she asked.

She'd been in enough London kitchens. At eighteen, she'd left her home in Evesham, having saved up the money she'd made working at the café next to her mum's antiques shop, and set off for the city she knew mostly from television shows.

For her mum, the good life had meant her shop. For her dad, a former London banker, it was a smallholding, raising chickens and pigs and his own veg. Viv had helped him in the farmhouse kitchen for as long as she could remember, and the older she grew, the more she loved it. When her friends were listening to the Spice Girls, Viv was glued to MasterChef *on the telly and daydreaming about what she could make for dinner.*

For her sixteenth birthday, her parents took her to the Michelin-starred Le Champignon Sauvage in Cheltenham. The food had been sublime, beyond anything she had even imagined, as if every component tasted somehow more itself. She'd spent weeks afterwards trying to re-create the things she'd tasted, crying in frustration when she couldn't duplicate what she'd eaten.

Now, she saw that meal as the moment her future crystallized. She knew then that she was going to cook.

In the five years she'd been in London, she'd worked her way up from restaurant to restaurant, dishwasher to line cook, in some of the best places in west London. A year ago, she'd set her sights on O'Reilly's in Chelsea. It had the up-and-coming buzz, and Fergus O'Reilly was the chef everyone was talking about as the next Marco Pierre White or Gordon Ramsay. When a job came up on day prep, she'd jumped at it, even though she knew she was good enough to be on the line.

When she sat down for an interview across from O'Reilly in the tiny basement room that served as the restaurant's office, she'd found herself unexpectedly tongue-tied. She'd seen him in photos, and in cookery and interview segments, but none of that had prepared her for his height, or for how stunningly good-looking the man was in person. With his curly dark blond hair and deep dimples, he was reputed to have women swooning over him, but none of that charm was wasted on her that morning.

"I don't like women in my kitchen," he'd said bluntly, with his Belfast accent. He must have seen her start to bridle because he added, "I don't mean women can't cook, so don't go getting all flustered. But women cause problems in the crew and I won't have any of that emotional shite on my patch, understood?"

"Yes, Chef," Viv had managed to mumble. She was glad she'd worn a T-shirt and kitchen overalls and not a stitch of makeup.

"Good. My day prep cook quit because he said it was too hard. Can you fucking believe that?" He glared at her as if it were her fault. "You'd better tell me now if it's going to be too much for you."

"No, Chef. I can do it," she'd said, looking him straight in the eye. She'd started the next day.

It was hard, she found out soon enough, ten hours a day of working her bum off. The job was as much about organization as physical labor, but she liked that, liked the routine and the sense of accomplishment, liked that everything that came off the line at dinner service depended on how good a job she'd done.

Fergus O'Reilly, however, she thought as she dumped twenty pounds of veal bones into a stockpot, was another kettle of fish.

He was mercurial, prone to shouting at the staff over the least little detail, while ignoring things that drove her bonkers, like the dirty vent hoods. But when he cooked, he was absolutely bloody brilliant, making the kind of food she'd dreamed about since that sixteenth birthday dinner. And lately he'd been listening to her suggestions and a couple of her ideas had turned up on the menu.

But she wanted to be back on the hot line—she missed the adrenaline rush of service and the challenge of getting the plates up. When a spot opened up on the line, she was going for it, no matter what it took.

"What about this one?" Kit shoved his phone across the train carriage table towards Doug Cullen. With an exaggerated sigh, Doug lowered the tabloid he'd picked up at Paddington Station. This must be the tenth car Kit had shown him in the last hour and a half.

"A Volvo?" It was a sleek and powerful S90 saloon. "That's pretty hot." Doug slid the phone back. "But your dad doesn't need hot. He needs boring. How do you think you lot and the dogs would fit in that?"

Kit rolled his eyes and elbowed his younger brother. "We could leave him home."

Toby, earbuds in and eyes glued to the iPad Kit had let him use, was oblivious.

"You sure what he's watching is okay?" Doug asked, a little nervous with his temporary parental role and Toby's access to the Internet.

Glancing at the screen, Kit said, "Ballet. And more ballet.

Justin Peck again." Toby had discovered the New York City Ballet's resident choreographer and was in the grip of adulation. Kit
scrolled through his phone, then handed it back to Doug. "What
about this one?"

A Mercedes SUV this time. Doug snorted. "Not bloody likely.
That's not a cop's car. And you don't even know for certain that the
Astra can't be fixed. Not to mention that your dad could have been
killed." He regretted the words as soon as they left his mouth. It
was a horrible thing to say to a boy who had lost his mum.

Kit glanced away and shrugged, his mouth set in a scowl. "But
he wasn't. He's fine."

But it had been Kit, when Doug had rung him about the accident last night, who'd insisted on coming early, as if he had to see
for himself that Duncan wasn't seriously hurt.

"Of course he is," Doug said, then breathed a sigh of relief as the
announcement for Kingham came over the train's address system.
"Come on, you two, get your things together. Moreton-on-Marsh
is the next stop. Melody's picking us up."

As the train pulled into Moreton a few minutes later, he saw
Melody waiting on the platform. In faded jeans and T-shirt, she
looked more like a teenager than a seasoned detective sergeant.
Her face, too, looked more relaxed than he'd seen in ages, which
surprised him. Usually, encounters with her parents left her tense
and edgy. Maybe it was the country air that agreed with her. Then,
she saw them, and waved.

When they'd disembarked, she gave Toby's straw-fair hair a
friendly tousle. "Good journey?" she asked.

"Boring," Kit and Toby said in unison. "Is there anything to
eat?" Toby added. "I'm starving."

Doug rolled his eyes. "You had tea and biscuits on the train."

"But that was hours ago," Toby protested.

"I think there's a packet of crisps in the car," Melody said. "Whoever gets there first has dibs."

Toby whooped and took off towards the car park. "No, you don't," shouted Kit, sprinting after him, his rucksack swinging wildly from his hand.

"You survived," Melody said to Doug as they followed the boys at a more sedate pace.

"Barely. Kit is already car shopping for his dad. I'm surprised he hasn't picked out a Lamborghini."

"Dad's taken Duncan to the recovery yard this morning, but it doesn't sound like the prospects are good. Listen." She touched Doug's arm, slowing him down as the boys reached the little Renault. "I thought you should know. Both passengers in the other car were killed. Dad's taking Duncan to make a statement this morning as well."

"But there's no question of him being at fault?" Doug asked, frowning.

"No, I don't think so. But he's pretty battered. And my mum and dad knew the driver. She was from the village. They say they can't imagine how it could have happened." Opening the Clio's tailgate with her fob, Melody called out, "Bags in the back." As she and Doug reached the car, she pulled a shopping bag from the cargo space, adding, "And look. Two bags of cheese and onion crisps. Emergency rations. Just don't get crumbs all over."

The boys squeezed in on either side of Charlotte's car seat, opening the crisps, as Doug got in the passenger front seat. Just how lucky had Duncan been, he wondered, to walk away from that sort of crash? He'd seen enough when he was in uniform to know how bad it might have been.

As Melody pulled out into the high street, he had a glimpse of low buildings in golden Cotswold stone, colorful awnings, and a bustle of people. "You should see it on market day," said Melody, following his gaze. "It's bonkers."

For the first time, he really grasped that Melody had spent a good part of her childhood here. She'd always seemed such a quintessential city dweller. "Is it far, your parents' house?" he asked.

"No. We'll be there in a quarter hour. A good thing, too. Gemma's helping, but Mum will need us as well, even with the local volunteers."

"You invited me so you could make me work?"

Melody gave him a sideways grin. "Of course. Why else?"

"What about Andy? You do know he's back?"

This earned him a glare. "Of course I do."

"You didn't invite him?"

"No," Melody snapped.

Doug studied her. "You still haven't told your parents about him, have you?" Melody and rock guitarist Andy Monahan had been seeing each other since the previous winter, but Melody had made every effort to keep it low profile, especially after what had happened at St. Pancras.

"None of your business," she said now.

As Melody pulled up to a junction, Doug unfolded the newspaper he'd been reading on the train. "Look. I thought you should see this." He wasn't sure if he was being kind or cruel.

Doug watched as Melody glanced down at the photo. In it was Andy, coming out of arrivals at Heathrow. He had his arm round his girl-singer bandmate, Poppy Jones, who was standing on tiptoe to kiss him on the cheek. They were laughing.

"That's photo-op bollocks," said Melody, putting the car into gear, but her lips were set in a tight line for the rest of the journey.

"Did you know him?" Kincaid asked Booth, surprised by his reaction to the news of the passenger's identity.

"Well, no, not personally," said Booth. "But I met him. My wife is a bit of a foodie. More than a bit, actually. When O'Reilly's—his London restaurant—was the big buzz on the food scene, I took her to London for the day and I surprised her with dinner reservations at O'Reilly's." Booth fidgeted with a pen on his desk. "I proposed to her there. Fergus O'Reilly himself came out from the kitchen to congratulate us." Shaking his head, he added, "My wife will be gutted. She was that upset when we heard the restaurant had gone under."

"I'd heard of the place," said Shelton, who still stood in the office doorway. "What happened to it?"

Booth shrugged. "I don't know."

"Can you take a look at the body and confirm the ID?" Shelton asked.

"It's been more than ten years, but, yeah, I can probably do that. He was a pretty distinctive-looking bloke. My wife went on and on about his damned dimples." Booth grimaced. "I'm not looking forward to telling Jess. We're coming up on our anniversary, so she'll really take it hard."

Ivan came into the office behind Shelton and the cramped space suddenly felt much smaller.

"It seems DI Booth knew the deceased," Shelton told him. "What the hell was a well-known London chef doing in a car in Lower Slaughter?"

"According to my wife, our local chef, Vivian Holland, had some connection with him. And he was in her pub last night, so that explains at least part of it."

"But not what he was doing in Nell Greene's car," put in Kincaid. "Or why he was dead when they crashed."

"Well, I can see I'm not going to make my son's football match." Booth's sigh was belied by the gleam of interest in his eyes. "I'll have a look at Mr. O'Reilly, and have a word with the pathologist, see if she has any idea yet what killed him. Then, I'd better have a chat with your lady chef."

Ivan looked horrified. "DI Booth, I hope that can wait until this afternoon. Viv Holland is catering a charity luncheon for fifty people at our house today. If anything disrupts that, my wife is likely to kill *me*."

CHAPTER SEVEN

A shower and a change into her work clothes had given Bea Abbott
a chance to cool down after her row with Viv. She pulled her curly
hair into a tight twist—she'd no patience to fool with it today—
and swiped at her mouth with a lipstick.

On her way out the door, she gave her usual grimace at the state
of the garden. She'd had visions, when she'd bought the semide-
tached house behind the mill in Lower Slaughter, of turning the
overgrown small front garden into a colorful riot of cottage borders. But somehow, between work at the pub and helping to look
after Grace, the dream never seemed to materialize.

Nor had her vision included a lodger in the person of Ibby, the
sous-chef. But there were no rental accommodations in the village,
so Bea had agreed to house him. Frowning, she nudged a cigarette
end on the gravel drive with the toe of her court shoe. Ibby had

promised not to smoke round the cottage, just as he'd promised not to park his old RAV4 in the drive, where it now sat.

But she had bigger problems to solve today than her errant lodger. Leaving her own car garaged, she walked down Malthouse Lane and then along the river towards the pub. It was a sunny autumn Saturday, crisp as an apple, perfect as a watercolor. The village was already filling with walkers and Lycra-clad bicyclists—they would need all hands on deck in the Lamb today and she hoped Ibby was up to the job.

When she reached the pub, the car park had begun to fill. It was eleven o'clock and morning coffee would just be ticking over into lunch service. Entering through the car park entrance, she popped her bag into her tiny cubbyhole of an office. Her heart sank when she saw that Fergus O'Reilly's coat was still there. Damn the man. Just how much more trouble was he going to cause?

She'd been dead set against Viv doing this charity luncheon for Addie Talbot, but now that they were committed, she didn't want anything going wrong that would reflect badly on the pub. Viv's van was gone from the yard, so at least she'd got off for Beck House. She'd just check with Jack to make sure Fergus hadn't been in.

But when she walked into the dining area, there was no one at the bar, and she could hear raised voices in the kitchen. The few patrons at the bar tables were looking up curiously.

Bea gave them a nod and a tight smile before charging through the swinging door.

The kitchen smelled of scorched coffee and burning garlic. Ibby and Jack stood facing each other, both bristling and up on the balls of their feet.

"You stupid git," Ibby shouted. "How the hell could you let the police tell her?"

"Keep it down in here," Bea snapped at them. "And tell who what?"

"Chef," said Ibby, turning to her. "Some cops came in, talking some rubbish about a car crash with—"

"Nell Greene," broke in Jack. "They said Nell was in an accident last night. She's dead."

"What?" Bea felt her stomach tighten. "But she can't have been. She was here for dinner—"

"It must have happened right after she left," Jack went on. "And that bloke, the poncey one that came in the kitchen, was with her."

"What? Do you mean Fergus O'Reilly? With Nell?" Bea shook her head against the fog that seemed to be invading her brain. "That's insane. Why would O'Reilly be in Nell's car?"

"Well, you can't ask him, can you?" Ibby picked up his knife and turned back to his cutting board, slamming the flat of the blade down on a head of garlic so hard that cloves shot out and skittered off onto the floor. "The fucker's dead, too."

"What?" Bea whispered. "But—but he can't be—"

"And Jack here took it on himself to send the cops to ask Viv to identify him. Chef can be a right bitch sometimes, but she didn't deserve that."

"I didn't know," Jack protested. "I thought—"

"You didn't think. You're a freaking idiot." Ibby whacked the garlic again. He looked dangerously piratical with the red bandanna he wore over his hair in the kitchen, his dark olive skin glistening against his whites. But there was something more than fury in the tight set of his mouth and the forceful wielding of his knife. It was a moment before Bea recognized it as grief.

It was Roz who seemed to recover from the shock first. "Viv, darling, I am so sorry. This must be dreadful for you."

Viv shook herself as if coming up from deep water. "I can't believe it. Surely there's been some mistake?"

"What are you talking about?" asked the young man with the salad greens. "You okay, Viv?"

When no one else spoke, Gemma took it on herself to explain. "A chef Viv used to work for. In London. He was killed last night."

"Along with Nell Greene," said Addie. "You remember Nell, Joe?"

Joe looked blank.

"I'll just go fetch the children," Gemma began again, jumping up, when there was a chorus of barks and the two girls, followed by the dogs, came running from the direction of the glasshouse.

"Mummy," said Grace, tugging at Viv's apron. "Joe left us. You said he should stay with us."

"I was coming right back." Joe shot her a frown.

Always quick to pick up on tension in the air, Charlotte attached herself to Gemma, burying her face in Gemma's shirt.

"Well, you're all here now," Addie said briskly. "And we've some decisions to make. Viv, I know this must be terribly upsetting. If you feel you can't go on—"

"No." Viv stood, too. "No. Of course I'm not going to let you down. But we've got to get moving. I'll—I'll deal with all this later."

"Right." Addie nodded her approval. "It's eleven o'clock. The guests are due to arrive at twelve thirty. Roz, can you get your village ladies here to help with the serving? And, Viv, what do you need us to do?"

Viv's back grew visibly straighter. "Joe, we'll need more greens. And someone to wash and dry them, then arrange them on the plates. We need the tables completely set, and the jugs and ice ready for the prelunch Aperol cocktails. Addie, if you could—"

"Mummy." Grace tugged at Viv's apron with more force. "What happened? Why were the police here?"

"Oh, darling, I'm so sorry." Viv wrapped an arm round her daughter. "There was an accident. Last night. You know Mrs. Greene, the nice lady with the collie—?"

"Of course I do," interrupted Grace. "I've helped Mark with Bella's training."

"Of course you have." Viv turned Grace to face her. "I'm afraid Mrs. Greene died in the accident."

Grace digested this, her small face creased in a frown. "Who's going to look after Bella?" she asked.

"She's with Mark," Addie told her. The penny dropped for Gemma. Mark was the man that Addie had called last night. "I'm sure he'll take good care of her until someone can be found to take her—"

"No," Grace wailed, starting to cry. "I don't want Bella to go away—"

"Hush, hush now, love. We can talk about that later." Viv pulled her daughter into a hug while sending an imploring glance at Addie. "Mummy has to get to work now."

"You always have to work." Grace, still sniffing, pulled away from her mother.

"Charlotte," said Gemma, giving her own daughter a squeeze, "why don't you take Grace to watch for your brothers. They should be here any—speak of the devil," she added as the terrace doors opened and Melody came out, followed by Doug and the boys.

Gemma found herself extraordinarily glad to see them all, but even in the midst of the greetings and introductions, she couldn't help wondering why Viv had failed to tell Grace that there had been another victim in last night's accident.

Melody hadn't expected to come back to a crisis. After quick introductions, her mother took her aside and explained the situation.

"Fergus O'Reilly," Melody whispered, glancing at Viv. "I can't believe it. What the hell was he doing here, of all places?" He'd been big in the London restaurant scene for a few years, but she realized she hadn't heard much about him recently.

"Well, whatever it was, we've got to get this lunch organized," Addie said, and Melody could feel the fizz of her energy. Addie nodded towards Doug, standing on the edge of the terrace, looking out over the gardens. "But first you should see to your friend. He looks a bit lost."

When Melody reached Doug, he glanced at her, then went back to his gazing. The lawns and the borders were beginning to shimmer as the sun inched towards midday, and the air was heavy with the scent from the roses on the pergola. "You're full of bollocks, you know that?" Doug said.

"What? What are you talking about?" That was the last thing Melody expected.

"This. You said you didn't know anything about gardening."

"I don't. Not really," Melody protested.

"This"—Doug waved a hand at the vista—"this is a Gertrude Jekyll garden. I've been reading, you know."

"Well"—Melody hesitated—"you can say it's an approximation

of a Jekyll garden. The house was built in 1905, so it's appropriate. But it's not an exact copy."

Doug shook his head. "You are such a liar. You said you didn't know anything, and you live with *this*."

"*Lived* with this. Summers and holidays." Melody was irritated now. "And it's Mum's thing, not mine. As it was my grandmother's before that. I was riding ponies when I wasn't at school."

"Still—"

She put her hands on her hips. "Okay, so maybe I absorbed a little bit. I was friends with the old bloke who used to help out. How do you think I knew where to put your herbaceous borders, and what should go in them? Maybe I just didn't want to sound like a conceited git."

Doug's lips relaxed at the corners and she knew she'd got him. "God forbid you should sound conceited." He shrugged his shoulders. "I mean, I knew you were posh, but this—"

"What? You thought my parents lived in a hut? Get over yourself, Dougie. Who's the Eton Old Boy? You must have gone home with mates who lived in freaking Downton Abbey."

When she saw his expression, she knew she'd touched a nerve. Doug had indeed gone to Eton, but he'd been a scholarship boy, his father a solicitor in St. Albans. Doug's inferiority complex had followed him ever since.

Melody gave his arm a little shake. "Never mind. I did go home with friends like that, and I guarantee you didn't miss much. Now, as posh as we may be, we have work to do. And there's something else." She told him about O'Reilly.

The light glinted off Doug's glasses as he turned to look at her. "Bloody hell. That's a turnup. Does Duncan know?"

"Mum rang Dad, so I'd assume so." Melody glanced back at the terrace. The children were playing with the dogs. Her mother and Gemma were finishing the tables. Viv had disappeared, presumably to oversee the kitchen, and Roz must be rounding up the village helpers. "What I don't understand," Melody said thoughtfully, "is why Viv never said she'd worked with Fergus O'Reilly. Surely, as a chef, a name like that would have made her reputation."

Kit stood at the scullery sink, washing salad leaves. He'd offered to help the gardener, Joe, carry the pails from the greenhouse. Then, once inside, he'd seen what looked like dismay on the chef's face as she contemplated the job ahead. Shyly, he'd volunteered.

"Good lad," she'd said, seeming to really see him for the first time, and he'd flushed uncomfortably. "You know how to do it, right? Make certain to get all the grit out, but be gentle. The leaves will tear easily."

Kit nodded. "I do it all the time at home."

"You know how to dry them, then, too?" Chef Viv dug in one of the plastic crates stacked by the sink. "Here's a stack of clean tea towels. You can lay the leaves out on those and pat them dry, then fold them in the damp towels so that they'll stay fresh until we can plate them. Oh, and pick out any damaged leaves, okay?"

"Got it," Kit had told her, with more confidence than he felt. But it was an easy enough task, as long as he was careful. When the chef had gone into the main kitchen, he'd nibbled a damaged leaf before tossing it in the bin. It tasted slightly bitter, but really fresh, and somehow even more like salad than the produce from the veg stalls at Portobello Market. He wondered what she meant to do with it.

He was almost finished with the second pail when he heard talking from the kitchen. A woman's voice he didn't recognize said, "Viv! I came as soon as I heard. Oh, my God. I'm so sorry."

"Christ, Bea," said Chef Viv. "I can't believe it. How could he? How could he do this?" She sounded near tears.

"I don't think he meant to get himself killed, darling," the person called Bea soothed. "For all his faults, that's the last thing I can imagine."

"But why here? And what was he doing with *her*, of all people?" Viv groaned. "Oh, that sounds terrible, as if I didn't care about poor Nell. But, Bea, they want me to . . . to identify— I don't know if I can—"

"I know, darling. I'll come with you, don't worry."

"But what am I going to tell—"

The scullery door slammed open and Grace, the gangly kid with the glasses, came bursting in. "Mum? Mum?"

"In here, love."

"Lady Addie says, do we need a spoon for each pudding?" Grace called without going into the kitchen, giving Kit a shy glance.

"No, just one is fine. They get to choose one pudding, not both. They can pass them round if they want."

"Okay." Grace grinned at Kit and banged out again.

"Do you need a hand in here?" came Bea's voice again. "I'd better pay my respects to Addie and see what needs doing out there."

"No, you go on. I've got things in hand for the moment. And I've a helper in the scullery."

A moment later, a small, dark-haired woman popped her head round the kitchen door. "Oh, hello," she said. "And who are you?"

"I'm Kit. Kit McClellan." Kit wiped his hand on a tea towel and held it out to her.

With a raised eyebrow, the woman took it and said, "Ooh, manners. How nice. Viv certainly knows how to pick her labor." With that, she went out onto the terrace. There had been something condescending in her manner that rubbed Kit the wrong way. Why did everyone think teenagers were boors?

Chef Viv came back into the scullery carrying a tray filled with foil-wrapped packets and began placing the packages in the scullery warming oven.

"What are those?" Kit asked.

"Flatbreads to go with the lamb and white beans. I made them this morning. We'll keep them on low until time to serve them." Coming over to Kit, she lifted the tea towels and examined his lettuces. "Great job." When she smiled at him, he saw that her eyes were red-rimmed.

Kit didn't know what she and Bea had been talking about, but obviously it was bad—someone had died. He didn't feel he could ask, though, so instead, he said, "Who was that lady who just came through?"

"Oh. That was Bea. She's my business partner. She's in charge of front of house at my pub."

"Oh, right," Kit said, nodding. "And you're back of house."

Viv looked at him curiously. "You know a bit about restaurants?"

"I have a friend who's a chef." Wesley might say he was stretching it a bit, but then Wesley never gave himself credit. "And I like doing things in the kitchen."

"Hmm." Viv eyed him speculatively. "Do you think you could plate these greens for me? It will be a bit fiddly."

"I can do fiddly."

"Right, then. I'll show you." She went into the kitchen and came back with a tall stack of mismatched china salad plates. Taking one, she arranged a handful of salad leaves, placing them carefully. "See, some of them are darker or redder, so see if you can use those for accents, a bit like a painting. Why don't you give it a try?"

Taking a plate, Kit did his best to copy her, hoping she wouldn't notice his nerves.

"Very nice." Viv tweaked a leaf. "You have a good eye. Just keep that up and we'll have you working the cold line in a real restaurant."

"What goes on this?" he asked, to cover his embarrassment at the compliment.

"You'll see." This time her smile reached her eyes.

Grace came in again from the terrace as Kit was beginning to run out of room on the scullery work top for the salad plates. "Wow," she said. "My mum let you do that?"

Kit shrugged. "She said it was okay."

"She never lets me do anything. She says I'm too young." Grace sounded aggrieved.

"Would you like to help her?" Kit asked.

Frowning, Grace chewed her lip. "Well, yeah. 'Course I would. I get really tired of being told I can't do things."

"Part of being a kid, I guess." Kit finished another plate and stepped back to check his handiwork. "How old are you?" he asked, glancing at her. Her glasses looked too big for her small face, and her hair was a tangle that could have held birds' nests.

"Eleven. People think I'm older because I'm tall for my age."

Kit hid a grin. He'd put her at ten.

"How old are you?" Grace asked.

"Fifteen."

"Wow," she breathed.

Kit felt embarrassed by her awe. "Look, can you help me make room for some more of these plates?"

"Sure." Together they moved some canisters to the back of the work top and shifted plates, Kit keeping an eye on Grace to make sure she was careful.

"Do you live in the pub?" he asked. Melody had pointed it out to him as they'd passed through the place with the funny name—Lower Slaughter. The sight of the village had given him a pang. It reminded him of where he'd lived in Cambridgeshire until he was eleven, before his mum died.

"Behind it," Grace said. "There's a separate cottage."

"That must be cool."

Grace rolled her eyes. "Not really. I want to live in a real house. With a dog. And you know, like a normal life."

"Nobody's life is normal."

That earned him another eye roll. "You sound like my mum."

"Well, it's true." Kit went back to plating greens. Maybe he could ask Grace about the conversation in the kitchen. "I heard your mum say somebody died."

"Yeah. A lady. Nell. She was nice. I helped train her dog." The girl looked down and brushed her hands on her jeans. "I never knew anybody who died before. It's weird." She seemed younger than eleven then, and Kit felt suddenly ancient.

"Yeah," he said. "It is."

CHAPTER EIGHT

They were late.

After leaving police headquarters, Ivan had driven back through Cheltenham, insisting that Kincaid see his GP. "No point in taking you to A and E," Ivan said. "The wait would be hours."

"But I'm fine," Kincaid had protested.

Ivan shot him a glance. "Obviously, you're not. You wince every time you move and I can see that your hand is useless. I've already rung my doctor. She's meeting us at her surgery. At the very least she can give you some tablets for the pain."

Having realized by now that trying to stop Ivan Talbot in action was akin to trying to halt a juggernaut, Kincaid had said merely, "I'll not be responsible to Addie if we miss the lunch." The truth was that his ribs and his hand hurt like hell, and his head felt like someone was pounding it with an anvil.

He'd expected some snazzy upmarket practice, but the surgery occupied the ground floor of a Georgian town house and the rooms were just worn enough to feel comfortable.

"Saunders," the doctor said, when Ivan introduced him. "Ivan said you had a bit of a banging. Let's have a look at you."

Leaving Ivan in the waiting room, she sat Kincaid on a scuffed leather exam table and had him take off his shirt. "Bit difficult for you, doing things left-handed, I see," she commented, examining his right hand with strong but gentle fingers. "Well, I don't think you've broken anything here." Moving on to his ribs, she pressed until he let out a grunt of pain. Then she held a cold stethoscope to his bare back and had him take deep breaths.

"Well, I don't think you've punctured anything," said Dr. Saunders. "I'm going to give you some painkillers. But if you feel any difficulty breathing, it's straight to the A and E. Got that?"

Kincaid nodded carefully.

"Right, then," she said. "Let's have a look at your head." She'd shined a light in his eyes, then manipulated his head and face with the same gentle fingers. "I'm going to give this cut on your forehead a couple of stitches," she told him. "Unless you'd really like to have a battle scar."

"Don't want to give my kids any copycat ideas," Kincaid managed, closing his eyes and trying not to flinch as she applied a local anesthetic. As she worked, he said, "How is it that you know the Talbots?"

"Oh, everyone round here knows the Talbots." Kincaid could hear the amusement in her voice. "But my dad was doctor to the Manns—that's Addie's parents—and my grandfather was doctor to her grandparents. Addie and I were at the same boarding school."

Cheltenham, it seemed, was the sort of town where everyone knew everyone else's business. "Did you know the woman who died in the accident last night?" he asked. "Nell Greene? I was told she was an administrator at the hospital here."

"Yes, I knew Nell. Ivan told me what happened." Dr. Saunders snipped a piece of tape and applied it to his forehead. "I was sorry to hear it. And just when she was beginning to put herself back together." She snipped again and applied more tape with firm pressure. "Now, that should do you, but if you have any dizziness or headaches that last for more than a day, you should get a scan."

With that cheerful rejoinder, she left him to put on his shirt and join Ivan.

When they emerged from the leafy tunnel of upper Becky Hill Road, the verge outside the entrance to Beck House was already lined with cars. A young bearded man was turning cars away from the Beck House drive. Ivan raised a hand to him, and as they reached the house, Kincaid saw that the graveled forecourt was filled as well.

Ivan garaged the car, and as they walked back across the drive he stopped for a moment, scanning the sky and raising his nose to the wind. "So far, so good," he told Kincaid. The day was still fine, and warm enough to encourage shirtsleeves. "Fingers crossed."

A handsome woman dressed in elegant but efficient-looking dark trousers and blouse met them at the open door. "Sir Ivan. We were getting quite worried about you." She gave Kincaid an interested look as she stepped aside.

"We had some things to attend to," said Ivan easily. "Duncan, this is Rosalind Dunning, my wife's personal secretary. Where is Lady Addie, Roz?"

"In the garden. Almost everyone has arrived."

"And Viv?"

"In the kitchen."

"Well, hold the fort. There are some stragglers coming in now." Ivan headed for the kitchen and Kincaid followed, curious.

There was no mistaking the woman who stood at the stove, her back to them. Tall and slender, she wore a white chef's jacket and houndstooth trousers. Her short blond hair was platinum pale and stood up on top as if she'd been raking her hands through it. Kincaid thought he heard her mutter, "Bloody caramel," before she turned, whisk in hand, and gave a little gasp. "Sir Ivan. I didn't hear you."

"Not to worry, Viv. I know you're rushed off your feet. I just wanted to say I was sorry about your friend."

"I— He wasn't— But thank you."

Kincaid thought that under other circumstances, Viv Holland would be more than attractive. She had the good bones necessary to carry off the boy-short hair, and her very fair skin and light blue eyes suggested that the platinum hair might be natural.

At the moment, however, her eyes were red-rimmed and she rubbed the back of her whisk-free hand across her cheeks. "Sorry," she added, with a glance at Kincaid. "I didn't mean to be rude. You look as if you've been in the wars."

"This is Duncan Kincaid," said Ivan. "I think you'll have met his wife, Gemma."

"Yes, Gemma's been a brick. Nice to meet you."

Kincaid realized Viv Holland must have no idea he'd been in the accident that had killed Nell Greene and Fergus O'Reilly, and now was certainly not the time to tell her.

"We'll get out of your—" he began, when he heard a door bang and his son came barreling into the kitchen.

"Chef Viv—" said Kit, then stopped when he saw them. "Dad!" He reached Kincaid in two long strides and threw his arms round him as if he were Charlotte's age.

"Ow," Kincaid managed, on an indrawn breath. "I'm glad to see you, too. But take it easy, sport."

Kit stepped back. "Oh, sorry. I didn't mean— I just—" He took in Kincaid's bandaged hand and head. "You're really hurt."

"I'm fine. Just a bit sore. I—"

"Oh, of course, you're Kit's dad," said Viv. "How stupid of me." She beamed at him then, her obvious pleasure erasing the stress lines from her face. "Kit's the best. He's been my sous-chef today. I'd never have managed without him."

Kit colored with what Kincaid guessed was embarrassment and pride. "Anyone could have done it," Kit mumbled, retreating towards the scullery. To Viv, he said, "Lady Addie sent me to tell you that all the trout pots are on the tables. She's going to seat people in just a few minutes."

"That's our cue, I think," Kincaid was saying, once again trying to make an exit, when the sound of raised voices came from the front hall.

A moment later, a large man entered the kitchen. Kincaid registered broad shoulders constrained in a navy sports jacket, and as the man's glance raked him, vivid blue eyes in an outdoorsy tanned face.

"Viv." The man almost knocked into Ivan as he came to a halt, but he seemed oblivious. "Viv, I've been trying to reach you. What the hell is going on? What's this about some bloke who was in the pub being in the car with Nell?"

"Mark!" The smile on Viv's face vanished. "What are you doing in here? I can't—I can't talk about this right now."

Roz Dunning appeared, from the hall. "Sir Ivan, I told Mark that Viv was busy—"

"It's all right, Roz. Just mind the door and make certain everyone gets headed to the garden." Then Ivan turned to the interloper, putting a firm hand on the man's shoulder. "Mark." Kincaid's fuzzy brain made the connection. This was the man with the collies. But what did he have to do with Viv Holland? "I'm sure you and Viv can get this all sorted," Ivan continued, "but Viv has had a bit of a shock, and she needs to concentrate on the lunch now."

"But I don't understand—"

"The one thing I completely understand is that Addie will have us strung up if we don't get out of Viv's way and join the party. Let's get a drink, shall we?"

Adroitly, he used his grip on the man's shoulder to turn him round and head him out of the kitchen. Following, Kincaid saw Mark send a last troubled glance towards Viv Holland.

Standing at the far edge of the terrace, Melody surveyed the party in progress. She had to admit that her mum had managed to pull it off. In spite of the tragedies, an injured guest, a traumatized chef, and a visit from the police, the luncheon was going swimmingly.

Craft cocktails in hand, the luncheon guests chatted on the terrace or drifted about the garden admiring the herbaceous borders, waiting for the signal to take their seats. The long pine tables on the pergola lawn, red-and-white-checked cloths tossed casually across them, looked just rustic enough to offset the delicacy of the mismatched vintage china and glassware. Multihued dahlias mixed with bronze rose hips spilled carelessly from the large jam jars scattered along the tables, but Melody, recognizing her mother's fine hand in the arranging, knew that the artlessness was carefully achieved.

A little sigh escaped her. She felt awkward, as always, held up to her mother's talents. Doug, she saw, was still admiring the garden—and her mum—with wide-eyed rapture. Before she could go too far down that resentful road, Gemma appeared beside her, having fetched two drinks. She handed one to Melody and raised her own glass. "Cheers. We deserve this. Wow," she added, eyes wide, when she'd taken a sip. "That's fabulous. What's in it?"

Melody took a meditative swallow. "Local gin, I'm sure. See, that's the distiller over there." She nodded discreetly towards a young man with shaggy brown hair who was deep in animated conversation with a small round woman in an unfortunate russet tunic that made her look like an apple. "Mixed with local craft-distilled ginger beer. And fresh lime, I think. And"—she studied her glass—"something to make it pink and slightly bitter. Aperol, maybe. I think it's Viv's recipe from the pub."

"Whatever it is, I like it." Gemma sipped some more. "Who are all these people?" she asked, surveying the crowd.

"Local VIPs from the parish and the villages. The vicar. Farmers and food producers. The woman by the dishy distiller makes the most amazing cheeses. And see that tall, dark, brooding bloke over by the pergola, the one that looks straight out of a romance novel? He owns the cider orchard. Unfortunately for his single admirers, he's happily married and has four kids. Mum is serving some of his cider at lunch, so be warned—that stuff is straight out of the cask and will hit you like a sledgehammer."

Gemma grinned. "Point taken. But some of these people look like city types to me."

"There are some food bloggers and restaurant critics. I don't know them, but I saw the guest list. And that man"—Melody gave another nod, this time in the direction of a middle-aged, balding man in a seersucker jacket who was waving his glass as he held forth to Addie—"is the food critic for the paper. Dreadful taste in clothes, but he's a big gun."

"So lots of pressure—and big opportunities—for Viv," Gemma said thoughtfully. Melody, familiar with Gemma's thought processes, sipped her pink drink and watched her, waiting to see what would come next. "Your dad," Gemma continued. "How's he going to handle the death of a celebrity chef practically on his doorstep?"

"I've been wondering the same thing." Melody had seen her dad arrive with Kincaid. "I don't think he can afford to have another source scoop the paper. And if he leads with the story, it's bound to come out that Mum and Dad live in the village, but it would at least give him damage control."

"Surely they don't try to keep that secret?"

"No. But they don't advertise it, either, and it's not usually newsworthy . . ."

"Awkward for Viv, though," said Gemma. "Won't it cast a pall on this lunch?"

Melody shrugged. "Maybe not. You know what they say—"

"Any publicity is good publicity," Gemma finished for her.

Thinking of Viv's stricken face, Melody wasn't so sure. What exactly had Viv's relationship been with Fergus O'Reilly, and why had she never mentioned it?

Well, people had their reasons for keeping things to themselves, as she very well knew. But the thought of relationships had struck a nerve. She'd managed to keep the photo Doug had shown her that morning pushed to the back of her mind as long as she was busy. She knew that she and Andy had agreed from the beginning not to make their relationship public. She, because she didn't want the attention at work or from her parents. Andy, because both his and Poppy's managers had stressed that fans liked to imagine there was a hint of romance between the two. But that photo? Really? What was he thinking?

Damn Doug for showing it to her. And damn Andy for prostituting himself for the tabloids. Assuming that was what he was doing. But what if what the camera had captured had been real?

Her mobile, tucked in the little bag she'd thrown over the shoulder of her sundress, rang. When she fished it out, Andy's face popped up on the lock screen as if summoned. Melody stared at it for a long moment, aware of Gemma's gaze.

Then she swiped Decline and dropped the mobile back into her bag.

Kincaid had spotted Gemma as soon as he stepped out on the terrace. She'd been adjusting the chairs at one of the long, decorated tables, but as soon as she saw him she hurried to him, her brow creased in a frown of concern.

"Darling, did Ivan take you to hospital after all?"

"No. Just his doctor in Cheltenham. She says I'm fine."

"You don't look fine."

"Don't worry." He pulled her in for a hug with his good arm and kissed her forehead. "I've seen Kit, but where are the rest of the hooligans?"

"They're with Viv Holland's daughter, Grace, and the dogs in the sitting room. Addie's organized some games and snacks for them in there. I did make Toby and Charlotte change, and it was a struggle, I can tell you. But Kit's been—"

She was interrupted by Addie, who took her by the arm, saying, "Gemma, darling, do you mind? I've some guests who are dying to meet you."

Then Ivan brought someone to meet Kincaid, and when he turned to find Gemma again, she'd been seated at Addie's table between two rather florid-looking gentlemen in country tweeds.

Feeling suddenly woozy, he took a chair at the nearest table and found he'd sat beside the man who'd accosted Viv Holland in the kitchen. From the frown on the chap's face, he was still angry, and he knocked back a glass of the pink gin drink as if it were water. Kincaid had taken one sip from the glass a server had offered him and decided his head felt fuzzy enough without alcoholic help.

"I'm Duncan Kincaid," he said, holding out his uninjured hand. "I think you must be the fellow who's looking after Nell Greene's dog."

This earned him a stare, but lessened the scowl a bit. "Mark Cain." Cain gave his hand a perfunctory shake, but his grip was firm and dry. "How'd you know about Bella?"

"My wife works with Melody Talbot. That's Gemma, over there." He gestured at the next table. Ensconced between the two men, who both seemed to be talking to her, Gemma, in her red poppy-print sundress, looked as if she'd been dropped into the setting by a painter. "She and I and our kids are guests of the Talbots for the weekend. I'm very sorry about your friend Nell."

Shaking his head, Cain took another sip of his drink. "I still can't believe it. She was fine yesterday. I suppose you never think you can lose someone in the blink of an eye." He gave Kincaid a closer inspection. "What happened to you, then?"

"The same accident," Kincaid said, a little reluctantly, but it would have to come out, and he had questions of his own.

Cain frowned at him. "What? What do you mean?"

"I was in the other car."

"Oh. My God." Cain seemed to deflate, his skin blanching under the tan. "I heard the accident was at the T-junction, but somehow I didn't think about anyone else being involved . . . You must have— Did you see her? Nell?"

"Only for a moment." Kincaid was unwilling to share more. Everyone was seated now, and cheerful women in aprons had brought round baskets, some filled with crisp, seed-coated crackers, others with small labeled jars. "I take it we're to help ourselves, picnic style," he said in an effort to defuse the tension. He picked up the little pot.

Ignoring the food, Cain clutched his drink and said, "Did you see him, too? The man with Nell?"

"Not really," Kincaid hedged. "It was pretty chaotic."

"Oh, Christ," Cain said, as realization seemed to strike him. "That was thoughtless of me. I can see you were hurt. Very lucky to be in one piece, I imagine. And your car?"

"Totaled. But as you said, I was very lucky."

"I just wondered . . ." Cain fiddled with his glass. "Well, if you had any idea who the bloke was. Jack, the barman at the Lamb, said he was in the pub last night. But he wasn't with Nell, at least not then."

Kincaid had no intention of giving him Fergus O'Reilly's name—information that was, as far as he knew, known only to the police, the Talbots, and Viv Holland, and was still speculative. "Not being local, I'm not really in the loop," he said with a shrug. Taking a bite of what turned out to be trout spread, he realized that he was starving. "This is amazing."

"The trout is from a trout farm near Stow. They smoke it themselves. And of course the recipe for the spread is Viv's."

"I take it you're friends with Chef Viv."

Cain frowned and took another slug of his drink. Had he even registered that Kincaid had been in the kitchen when he'd shouted at her? But then he gave Kincaid a sharp look and said, "Heard that, did you? Well, obviously, I thought we were . . . I suppose you could say 'friends.' Very low key, you understand, because this is a small place and Viv didn't want tongues wagging. But as of yesterday evening, Viv has cut me off like I was the plague. And Jack, the barman at the pub, said Viv knew the bloke in the car with Nell, and Jack sent the cops up here to talk to her about him."

"Ah." Kincaid ate some more trout spread while he thought about this. "I can see you'd want to know what was going on," he offered encouragingly, while wondering why Viv Holland's avoidance of Cain had coincided with the arrival of the London celebrity chef in Lower Slaughter. "Well, I'm sure it will all make sense," he added with more assurance than he felt. His brain seemed thick as treacle. At the next table, Gemma was laughing at something one of the men had said, and Kincaid was beginning to wish he'd sat somewhere other than next to Mark Cain.

The aproned ladies were now serving plates of salad. Looking for a safer subject, Kincaid asked, "How is Nell's dog?"

"Bella? She was a pup out of one of my litters, so she's used to me and the other dogs. But I can tell she misses Nell. I don't dare leave her out for fear she'll try to go back to Nell's cottage."

Cain looked so distressed that Kincaid tried once more. "Lady Addie and Chef Viv have done a great job of putting this lunch together. I understand everything was supplied by local producers."

"I am a local producer," said Mark Cain, sounding offended. "It's my lamb Viv is serving as the main course."

The aproned servers and the flowers blazing in the borders and the edges of the bright checked tablecloths fluttering in a rising breeze all seemed to run together in a blur of motion and color. Gemma blinked, gave her head a little shake to clear it, then wished she hadn't. She frowned at her empty glass. Apparently, Melody hadn't been joking about the strength of the cider, especially added to the potent prelunch gin cocktail. Still, all's well that ends well, she thought, leaning back in her chair with a little sigh of contentment. The two men, both local landowners, who'd monopolized her over lunch—making her feel as though coming from London was exotic—had turned to other guests, and she was free to get her bearings.

At least she could see Duncan where he sat at the next table, next to a man who looked hard going. Maybe she'd been lucky with her gentlemen farmer companions. Kincaid looked up and caught her eye. She rolled her eyes a tiny bit and he grinned. Perhaps, she thought, they could salvage this weekend that had started out so badly.

She might even decide she liked the country.

The only blot on the cider-induced rosiness of her mood was Viv Holland's distress. But when Addie had brought Viv out during the pudding course to thank her for her catering, Viv had looked flushed with pleasure.

Even with the quirky presentation, the food, Gemma had to admit, had been divine. From the creamy, smoky trout spread, to the delicate salad with roasted pears, caramel, and a local blue cheese, to the meltingly tender lamb and white beans served in camping tins, it had been of absolute star quality. What, Gemma had to wonder, was a chef so talented doing in this tiny village?

She nibbled at the last bit of her pudding. The little jam jar she'd chosen had held a mixed berry crumble with a tangy layer of crème fraîche—a dessert she suspected she'd find herself dreaming about. All round her, spoons were being laid down and empty jars examined in hopes of finding a smidgen more.

Soon the party would be breaking up. Gemma sighed again and stretched, wondering if she'd be able to cadge a cup of tea while helping with the clearing up, and if she could get Kincaid to go upstairs for a rest.

The colors in the garden suddenly dimmed. Looking up, she saw that the recent flutter of breeze had heralded a smattering of fast-moving clouds. Within moments, they had spread over the brilliant blue sky like a sugar glaze on a cake. She shivered, suddenly chilled, and wondered if she might fetch a cardigan. Glancing towards Addie at the head of the table, she waited for the signal to rise.

Addie stood, tapping her spoon on a glass. "Thank you, everyone, for joining us today, for the best the Cotswolds have to offer.

We hope you will—" She stopped, giving a startled glance at the house. Turning to follow her gaze, Gemma saw that Roz Dunning had come out onto the terrace, followed by a big, dark-skinned man in a very dark suit. The man stood for a moment, surveying the group. Between the suit, the posture, and the expression on his face, he might as well have had "cop" emblazoned on his forehead. And not just "cop," but "detective."

Gemma's heart sank. So much for the salvaged weekend. Whatever had brought him, it was official, and it was not good news.

CHAPTER NINE

Kincaid stood up so quickly that he tipped over his folding chair, wrenching his arm in the process of righting it. What the hell was Colin Booth doing here? In his dark suit, he looked like a crow among the summer pigeons. Ivan had already risen and was heading towards the terrace. Addie, Kincaid realized, had quickly recovered her poise and was thanking the guests.

When Kincaid reached the terrace a moment behind Ivan, Booth was saying quietly, "So sorry for the interruption, Sir Ivan. But I've had a word with the pathologist, and she's found an excess of digitalis in our male accident victim's system."

"Digitalis?" said Ivan, frowning. "Isn't that foxglove?"

"Yes. At least as a precursor. Apparently, once it's broken down in the body, it's hard to differentiate between digitalis and its derivative digoxin."

"That's heart medication."

"Used for a number of conditions," agreed Booth, "or at least that's what the good doctor tells me. So it's essential that we learn—"

"Have you confirmed his identity?" Kincaid broke in.

Instead of meeting Kincaid's eyes, Booth shoved his hands in his trouser pockets and surveyed the garden. "I had a look at him. As far as I can determine, yes. But we'll need an identification from someone who knew him better personally."

Kincaid guessed at Booth's discomfort. It was one thing to deal with the death of a stranger, but quite another to be faced with someone you knew, however casually or briefly.

"What about Nell Greene?" he asked.

"The pathologist is running the tests now."

"Wait." Ivan looked from Booth to Kincaid. "Surely you're not suggesting that they were poisoned?"

Booth shifted on his feet. "I can't say, sir. But we will have to ask some questions about Mr. O'Reilly, ascertain what he might have been taking, or have, um, encountered. And I need that formal ID as soon as possible."

Addie appeared at Ivan's side. "What seems to be the problem, darling?"

Ivan put a casual arm across her shoulders. "Addie, this is Detective Inspector Booth, from Gloucester CID. Inspector Booth, my wife, Lady Adelaide. Inspector Booth needs a word—in private—with Viv. It's about last night's accident."

"Of course." Addie gave Booth her most gracious public smile. "Let me see what I can arrange. Ivan and I have to attend to our guests, but perhaps we can deputize our daughter to help you." She gave Ivan's arm a squeeze and left them, her stride purposeful.

Kincaid looked round for Gemma, saw that she had risen, but was still hemmed in by her gentlemen admirers. He caught her questioning glance and shrugged. It seemed to him that Booth was studying the garden with undue attention. Was there foxglove in the borders? He couldn't recall seeing it, but then his memory of his quick tour of the garden before breakfast that morning seemed a century ago. "Surely someone would know if Nell had a heart condition," he said. Was he hoping to excuse her, find a logical reason why she had plowed into his car? But if Nell had been poisoned, she had still been alive when they crashed. Nothing made sense. He didn't seem to be able to focus on anything more than a few seconds.

Kincaid saw Addie speak to Melody, then Melody started across the lawn towards them, but as he watched, his vision seemed to darken round the edges.

"Are you quite all right, Duncan?" asked Ivan, his voice sounding very far away.

"I think," Kincaid managed, "I might need a bit of a lie-down."

With her mother's whispered instructions in her ear, Melody pasted on a smile and went to meet the newcomer.

"So sorry to disturb the party," Booth said as he shook her hand. He was quite good-looking, Melody decided, and his clasp was warm and dry.

"If you could take DI Booth into the sitting room," her father said, "and then fetch Vivian?" He turned to Booth. "Let us at least get you a coffee."

This was framed as a statement rather than a question, and Melody saw Booth hesitate before he said, "Thanks. That's kind of you, sir." She could tell that he felt awkward, but she also saw that he was taking everything in with alert curiosity. She wouldn't want to have secrets from this man.

"Good. Let us know if you need anything else." Ivan gave Booth's hand a hearty shake, and a moment later was chatting with guests who were all now rising from their tables. Kincaid excused himself as well, making a rather unsteady beeline for Gemma. Melody thought he'd looked a bit green about the gills.

Left alone with Booth, she led the way through the house to the blue sitting room. "You're from Gloucester HQ, then?" she asked.

"Yes. Your father paid us a visit this morning."

"Ah. I see." Melody did, indeed.

"Lovely house," commented Booth. "Very comfortable. Not what I expected."

"My parents seldom do the expected," Melody said.

Rather than taking the offered seat, Booth stood gazing out the sitting room window at the milling crowd in the garden.

"How do you take your coffee, Mr. Booth?" Melody asked from the door.

Booth turned, and she thought she saw the corner of his mouth quirk in a smile. "Black, thank you."

She left him and bumped straight into Doug Cullen in the hall. "Who's the cop?" whispered Doug, catching her by the shoulders. "What's going on?"

"Gloucester CID. He wants to talk to Viv."

"About O'Reilly? I want in on that."

"Shh," Melody admonished, finger to her lips. "Then go keep him company while I fetch Viv. Otherwise, I think he'll have unearthed all of our family secrets."

When she returned with Viv, and carrying Booth's cup of

coffee, she found Doug and Booth comfortably ensconced on the sofas, chatting about, of all things, rowing.

Booth stood to greet Viv, who looked as if her legs might give way at any moment.

"Well, we'll leave you to it, then," said Melody, giving Doug the eye when Viv had taken a seat.

"No, please. I'd like you to stay, Melody. You, too," Viv added with a glance at Doug. "If that's all right with Inspector Booth."

Melody was surprised. She didn't really know Viv Holland all that well. When she came to the country for weekends or holidays, her parents often took her to dinner at the pub. Viv would come out from the kitchen to speak to them, but their conversations had revolved round the food, and the usual village topic, the weather. She wasn't even sure if Viv knew what she did for a living.

"Certainly." Booth nodded at Melody and Doug, then turned to Viv. "Miss Holland— It is 'miss,' isn't it?"

"Yes," Viv answered, sounding hoarse. Melody sat beside her on the sofa.

"I'm sorry to bother you. I realize you've had a busy day."

Viv sat forward, fingers kneading at the hem of her white chef's jacket. "I have to clear up. And then get ready for service at the pub—Saturday is our busiest night."

"I do have to ask you some questions." Booth sounded almost gentle, which put Melody on alert. Booth was not just going through the motions, then. "I understand you knew Fergus O'Reilly."

"Yes. I worked for him. At his restaurant in Chelsea."

"O'Reilly's?"

"Yes. Did you know it?"

Booth gave her a disarming smile. "Oh, yes. I ate there, once.

I had the duck breast with farro risotto and duck confit. I think it was the best meal I've ever eaten."

Viv's look of surprise would have been comical under other circumstances.

"O'Reilly was ahead of his time with the farro, don't you think?" Booth added. When Viv nodded, he went on. "You were there, then? It would have been"—Booth closed his eyes for a moment, as if counting to himself—"twelve years ago."

"Yes, I—I think I was. I worked there for a couple of years. But it was a long time ago."

"But you'd had recent contact with Mr. O'Reilly?"

"Before yesterday, I hadn't seen or heard from him in years, not since I left the restaurant. I told the officers that this morning. He just showed up yesterday morning, in the yard of the pub."

"Did he say why he was there?"

"He said he'd heard about the luncheon. Lady Addie did a lot of promotion."

"But he wasn't a guest?" asked Booth.

"No. The tickets were sold out."

Booth raised an eyebrow. "He came all the way from London for a luncheon he couldn't attend?"

Viv shrugged. "I think he was hoping I could get him a ticket. But it was limited seating. There was no way I could add someone, even if I'd wanted to."

"I'm not following this," broke in Melody, forgetting for a moment that it wasn't her job to ask questions. "Why would Fergus O'Reilly want to come to my mother's luncheon? Unless . . ." Melody didn't like where the thought was taking her. "Unless he wanted something from my parents?"

"Oh, no." Viv sounded shocked. "It wasn't your parents he wanted something from. It was me." When they all looked at her expectantly, she sighed. "He had some crazy idea. Fergus always had mad ideas. He said there were some mysterious London backers who were offering him a great deal on a new restaurant. He wanted me to come back to London and run the kitchen." She must have read disbelief in their faces because she went on, "It's not unusual. Chefs are always recruiting other chefs for projects, especially someone they've cooked with before."

"What did you tell him?" Melody asked.

"No, of course," Viv said sharply. "My life and my business are here. But I wish I'd been . . . kinder about it. If I'd known . . ." She shook her head. "Look. I'm very sorry that Fergus is dead. But I don't understand why you're asking me these things."

Booth gave Melody a quelling glance. "Was Mr. O'Reilly on any heart medication?" he asked Viv.

"What? No. At least not as far as I know."

"Can you tell us where he was staying?"

"I have no idea. He didn't tell me."

"Do you know if he had a car in the village?"

"If he did, I didn't see it in the pub car park. But Fergus didn't like driving. He never kept a car in London."

"Do you have any idea where Mr. O'Reilly was living?"

"Absolutely none. I told your officers this morning. But . . . he always left his wallet in his coat—I told them that, too—and as far as I know his coat is still at the pub."

Booth took a moment to make a note on his phone. From his expression, Melody thought she would not want to be the officer who had failed to follow up on the coat.

Viv had half risen when Booth looked up and said, "What about Nell Greene? What was her connection to Mr. O'Reilly?"

"I have no idea. I told you, I hadn't seen him in years. And I honestly didn't know Nell well at all. Look, I really must—"

"I'm afraid whatever it is will have to wait a bit longer." Booth set his empty cup on the coffee table and stood. "Before we go any further, I need you to make a formal identification."

"But I don't want— And I've got to load food in my van—"

"In that case, it might be easiest if you come with me."

Sitting in the leather passenger seat of DI Booth's Volvo, Viv felt like she'd been hijacked. She'd protested, but Melody had whispered in her ear, "Best get it over with. It won't get easier." Then more loudly, Melody had added, "Don't worry, we'll load the van and drive it down to the pub. And we'll get Grace home."

Viv had insisted on talking to Grace first. She'd found her in the scullery with Kit, who hadn't even needed a word to realize that Viv wanted a moment alone with her daughter. When Kit had gone out, Viv had leaned down, eye level with Grace, and said, "Sweetie, the man who was here yesterday—"

"You mean Fergus." Grace glared at her.

"Yes, Fergus. I'm afraid the police think he was in the car crash last night as well as Miss Nell. I have to go to the . . . hospital, to—to be certain it's him."

"But he's going to be okay," Grace said, suddenly looking small and frightened and much younger than her eleven years.

"No, sweetie." Viv took a breath. "He's not going to be okay. He died, too."

Grace stared at her, then shook her head, her hair flying. "No.

He can't be. I don't believe you." When Viv reached for her, she backed up as if she'd been slapped. "I hate you," Grace spat at her. "You're just saying that to be mean." Then she ran out the terrace door after Kit.

Now, sitting huddled in her dirty chef's jacket in Booth's car, Viv felt ill with dread. What if what happened was somehow her fault? Two people who had been in her restaurant last night were dead. She didn't remember Nell ever drinking much, and she didn't think Fergus had been drinking when he came into the kitchen last night. In any case, Jack wouldn't have overserved them, although Nell had lived close enough to walk home. And Fergus, where the hell had Fergus come from?

Had there been anything different about him? She glanced at Booth. "Why did you ask if Fergus was taking heart medication?"

Booth seemed to hesitate, then shrugged. "The pathologist found digitalis in his system."

"Digitalis? You mean like foxglove?"

"Well, it could be. A form of digitalis is used in heart medication, as well as other things."

"But—" Viv frowned, thinking. Could Fergus have been ill? Was that what had prompted his sudden appearance?

"What are you thinking?" asked Booth.

"Well, it's just, chefs lead pretty hard lives. And Fergus— Fergus liked to party as hard as he worked."

"You mean he did coke?"

Viv wished she hadn't said anything, but in for a penny . . . "I just wondered if his lifestyle might have had long-term repercussions."

"You said he showed up yesterday morning and made you this proposition. Then what?"

"I told him I wasn't interested. He left."

"Did he tell you he was coming back for dinner?"

"No. He just appeared again late in the afternoon, in the yard, but I didn't really speak to him then. I was getting ready for service."

"But you knew he was in the restaurant later in the evening?"

"Only because Jack—my bartender—told me. And Jack had no idea who he was, just that he was making a nuisance of himself, ordering things and sending them back."

"But you didn't talk to him yourself?"

Viv hesitated again, but there was nothing for it. She wasn't going to tell an outright lie, no matter how bad the truth made her look. "He came into the kitchen. You can't just walk into another chef's kitchen and start throwing your weight around. But that was Fergus for you. Boundaries were never his strong suit."

Glancing at her, Booth said, "I take it you two didn't get on." He turned his attention back to the road, his hands relaxed on the wheel.

Viv blinked furiously against a sudden and unexpected wash of tears. "Oh, we did. Once."

DECEMBER 2006
They were in the weeds, had been since the start of service when they'd had two unexpectedly large parties order at the same time.

It had taken Viv six months to work her way on to the fryer station on the hot line at O'Reilly's. She'd almost quit half a dozen times, but the stubborn streak that had got her through her first few kitchens kept her going. It was the first time she'd ever worked in a kitchen where not even the pastry chef was female. Sometimes she thought she'd accidentally walked into the eighties—or maybe the sixties.

She learned never to go in the walk-in fridge alone, and especially not with John, the pastry chef. When he'd cornered her at the stove one day, she'd accidentally *tipped a pot of boiling water on the tips of his clogs. But John was a bit of a friendly puppy—he was out of line but there was no malice in it. Guy, the sous-chef, was another story. He gave her the creeps even when he looked at her. She avoided him as much as possible but it was hard when he was on sauté and she was next to him on the fryer. The kitchen was cramped, but even so they were understaffed for the amount of covers they were doing every night. The restaurant was getting good press, and the food was consistently improving, thanks in no small part to her, she thought. Even when Fergus had moved her on to the hot line when one of the cooks had quit, she'd kept on with the daytime prep. It allowed her to control the quality of the food, and Fergus had turned more and more of the ordering over to her.*

Popping a new batch of their signature Parmesan and courgette puffs into the deep fryer, she glanced over at Fergus, plating at the pass. His long hair was pulled back in a ponytail, revealing the deep dimple that showed even when he was frowning in concentration. He bent over a plate, adjusting a bit of garnish with the tweezers in one hand, adding a dot of bright green pea purée from a squeeze bottle in the other.

"Pay bloody attention, can't you?" Guy snapped at her.

"Sorry," she said automatically, pulling up the fryer basket and dumping the puffs on a kitchen-towel-lined baking pan to drain. They were perfect, and would go on the plates with the scallops and the pea purée.

Guy passed the hot puffs to Fergus, then turned back and patted her on the bum just as she was lowering another batch into the oil. His hand slid between her legs and squeezed. "And next time why don't you give me some of that while you're at it, darling?"

She spun round with the basket, still dripping hot oil, in her hand. "Keep your hands off me."

"Whoa, whoa, sorry." He backed away, holding up his hands. "Just a little joke."

"Not. A. Joke. You do that again and you really will be sorry."

Fergus had looked up from his plating. "Shut it, the both of you. I told you I didn't want any of that shite in my kitchen."

She was furious, the blood pounding in her ears. "Then tell this arsehole to keep his fucking hands off me. I'm just doing my job."

Fergus looked from one to the other. She couldn't tell what he was thinking—she'd learned she often couldn't read him. What the hell had she just done? "You." He pointed his tweezers at Guy. "She's right. You are an arsehole, and she's been doing half your work. You're fired."

"You can't do that." Guy sounded more incredulous than indignant.

"I can. Get your kit and get out of my kitchen."

For a moment, Viv thought Guy was going to punch Fergus. Then he shook his head. "You're off your nut, you know that, Fergus? Who's going to work sauté?"

"She is. Now bugger off. I'm not telling you again." Fergus turned back to his plating.

Guy took a step towards Viv. "You bitch." Spit sprayed her face. "You are so going to regret this." Then he turned on his heel and shoved his way out of the kitchen, knocking into Mikey, who was on garde-manger, and very nearly making him lose his grip on a tray of veg.

More orders were piling up at the pass.

Ibby said, "But, Chef. I'm on grill. I should be—"

Fergus lowered his voice. "You'll do fryer as well. Get those orders up now." Fergus wasn't a shouter, but that didn't mean he didn't have a ferocious temper. Viv had learned that when he dropped his voice, you had better watch out.

"Yes, Chef," she and Ibby said at the same time, but Ibby gave her a venomous look.

Shit. The bastards. Moving to the sauté station, Viv poured oil in the pan. Her hands were shaking. She'd been sure she'd be the one walking. Why hadn't Fergus fired her? She placed the waiting scallops in the pan, pressed them with the spatula. She must do this right.

By the time she'd passed the finished scallops to Fergus, concentration on the task had begun to slow her racing heart. Fergus pressed a scallop with his finger, nodded, and began adding them to the plates. A wave of relief made Viv feel light-headed, but she forced herself to focus on the orders. Within half an hour, even with a man down, service was running smoothly. Even Ibby seemed to have got over his sulks and together they made a good team.

By the end of the night, customers were coming to the pass to *thank Fergus—or if they were female, to look at Fergus, Viv thought with a roll of her eyes.*

When they'd closed the kitchen down, Viv went, as usual, to get her coat and bag from the little basement office. Their space was too cramped for a locker room. The blokes changed in the storage cupboard off the walk-in. Viv had taken to just changing her shoes and switching out her chef's jacket for a sweater in the tiny staff toilet. Tonight she was too tired even to do that. She was pulling her coat off the hook when Fergus stuck his head round the door.

"Oi, Viv. Come for a drink." Most nights after service, Fergus and the rest of the blokes would go to one of the clubs on the King's Road and drink until the wee hours, but Viv had never been invited. Nor had she wanted to try to be one of the boys—that way lay pathetic.

"Oh, thanks, Chef, but I'd better—"

Fergus stepped all the way into the room and said quietly, "Listen, I don't want you walking out of here on your own to-night, okay? Just a precaution."

Oh, hell. Guy. Viv had forgotten all about him. She frowned. "You don't think Guy would—"

"He'll get over himself, or at least he will when he gets another job. But meanwhile there's no sense in being stupid."

"Oh, right." Now that she thought about it, Viv did not want to walk out of the restaurant's dark back entrance by herself. "Okay."

"Get changed, then." Fergus went out, leaving Viv to con-template going to a club in the trainers she'd worn to work that morning, with a woolly jumper over her checked kitchen trousers.

Oh, well, what the hell. Why not? She was still so buzzed with the service adrenaline that she'd never be able to sleep, anyway.

They left the restaurant together, all except John, who'd begged off, rather to Viv's relief as she didn't fancy dodging another groper. The night had turned a deep, sharp, biting cold, and their breaths puffed out before them as they walked. Fergus fell into step beside her, matching his long stride to hers, and for the first time she felt comfortable in his presence outside the kitchen. Their foot-steps were barely audible on the pavement. Ahead of them, Ibby and Mikey were arguing over the latest football results, but even the sound of their voices seemed muffled by the cold.

When she could see the lights of the King's Road ahead, she said into the silence, "Why did you fire him, and not me?"

She sensed Fergus shrug beneath his heavy coat. "Simple. You're a better cook."

CHAPTER TEN

Having seen Grace run out of the scullery, Kit had returned to the kitchen and found Viv staring at the stacks of dirty dishes with her hands in her hair.

"I have to go," she said, looking up at him. "To the police headquarters, with Detective Booth. They—they need me to do something. And I don't know how I'm going to get all this mess sorted."

Kit had seen the man in the dark suit, on the terrace with his dad and Sir Ivan, and had wondered who he was. "Can I help?"

Some of the tension seemed to go out of the chef's shoulders. She gave him a smile that he could see took an effort. "You don't mind?"

He shook his head. "No, honestly."

"Okay, then. All the jars and the camping tins need to go back to the pub. If you can load them in the van, they'll go in the dish-washer there. But all of Lady Addie's things need to be rinsed and put in the dishwashers here. You know there's a second one in the scullery?"

"Got it."

Kit followed her out to the drive, where the detective was wait-ing, and watched them get into the black Volvo and drive away.

Puzzled about what had happened, he'd gone looking for Gemma and found her bringing in yet another tray from the garden.

"Why did Chef Viv have to go with the detective?" he asked. "She can't have done anything wrong."

"No, love, I'm sure she hasn't." Gemma deposited the tray on the scullery work top and turned to him, her expression serious. "But the people in the car that crashed into your dad last night both died, and it seems that Viv knew one of them, the man, from when she used to work in London. Detective Inspector Booth just wanted her to confirm the man's identification."

"She's not in trouble, then?" Hating the squeak in his voice, Kit started unloading plates from Gemma's tray.

"No, of course not." Gemma touched his shoulder so that he had to look at her. "You were a big help today. You two really hit it off, didn't you?"

He nodded. "She's cool. I like helping," he added, shrugging to indicate that it was no big deal. He did a good bit of the cooking at home, and sometimes he even helped their friend Wesley Howard in the kitchen of the café where Wesley worked part-time. But today with Viv had been different. He'd felt, not just important, but . . . essential. That was it. Like she really couldn't have man-aged without him—and her a real professional chef.

"I'm sorry this weekend isn't turning out the way we'd planned," Gemma said, shifting the last of the plates.

"It's okay." Kit thought of the walks he and his dad had planned, just the two of them. They'd downloaded maps and worked out routes, and even filled day packs with compasses and snacks and bottles of water.

When he asked why they needed compasses, his dad had teased him. "You can't do everything on your phone. It's the country. You might not even have a signal."

Obviously, those walks were not going to happen. But if Kit had been disappointed, just for a bit, it had scared him to see his dad with his head and hand bandaged. And that was before he knew that the other people in the crash had died. He felt stupid for having gone on to Doug about a new car. "Dad's going to be okay, isn't he?" he said to Gemma now, feeling the knife prick of worry.

"He's fine. Just a little banged up." Gemma put her arm round him and gave him a quick squeeze. "He's having a rest. I'll go and check on him as soon as we get things squared away here."

They had worked in companionable silence, rinsing and filling the dishwashers, the clink of china and glassware a counterpoint to the regular chatter of voices from the front hall as the Talbots said goodbye to their guests. The ladies from the village who'd helped with the serving left as well, and through the open scullery door, he heard faint bangs and thumps as Doug and Melody and the gardener, Joe, folded chairs and broke down tables.

Roz, the blond woman who seemed to work for Lady Addie, came in with an armload of tablecloths for the washing machine. She looked a little flustered, Kit thought. Behind her was Melody, with another bundle of linens.

"Has anyone seen Grace?" Melody asked. "I told Viv I'd drive the van down to the pub and take Grace home as well."

"I've no idea," snapped Roz. "I've enough to do without child minding."

Kit saw Gemma's eyebrows go up at her tone. "I've put Toby and Charlotte in the sitting room with a video," she said, mildly, "but Grace wasn't with them."

"I'll find her," Kit volunteered, feeling suddenly hemmed in by the air of tension in the room.

He went out the scullery door onto the terrace. The tables and chairs had vanished and the lawn looked as pristine as a bowling green. Doug stood at the edge, his back to the house, deep in discussion with Joe. The earlier spatter of rain had stopped and the sky had begun to clear; the rain had brought a little chill to the air.

"Has anyone seen Grace?" Kit called.

"Grace?" Doug turned, looking puzzled.

"The kid with the glasses." Too late, Kit wondered if Doug would think that was rude, but Doug had already turned back to the view.

"Not lately," said Joe.

"What about the dogs?"

"No idea."

"Okay, thanks." Kit wondered why everyone connected with Beck House seemed to be cross. The food had been super, and from what he'd seen, the luncheon had been a big success.

Leaving them, he'd wandered in the direction of the glasshouse and the storage shed—although *shed* seemed the wrong word for the sturdy, stone-walled building. He peeked inside, seeing nothing but stacked tables and chairs, mowers and gardening equipment.

Next, he poked his head into the muggy warmth of the glass-house. It smelled like the potting soil Gemma used for the gerani-ums on their patio. Long tables covered with pots and plants and plastic trays stretched down either side of the building. The floor held bags of soil and fertilizer and wooden crates filled with more gardening tools. He was about to move on when he heard a sound.

"Grace?" he called, then stood still to listen.

There it was again, a little snuffle. He walked down the center aisle, peering behind things, until he came to some crates that were double stacked a few feet from the end. There was a space between the crates and the back of the building, and in it was Grace, sitting on the dirt floor with her arms wrapped round her bony knees. "Grace? What are you doing in here? Everyone is looking for you."

"Go away." Her face was tear-streaked and her nose red as a Christmas bulb.

Kit brushed away a few cobwebs and sat down beside her. "Melody wants to take you back to the pub."

"I don't want to go home." Grace wiped her nose on the sleeve of her jumper. "I don't want to talk to you, either." She turned her face away.

"Why? I thought we were friends, earlier."

Grace gave a little hiccup and the tears started sliding down her face again. "That was . . . before."

"Did I do something?"

Shaking her head, she wailed, "Nooo." She swiped at her eyes, knocking off her glasses. Kit picked them up and polished them on the hem of his T-shirt, then handed them back without looking at her. "Thanks," Grace mumbled. "It's nothing to do with you."

Kit thought for a moment. Grace had seemed fine until her mum had spoken to her in the scullery. "Are you worried about your mum having to go to the police, then?"

"No." Grace gave him an offended scowl, as if it were ridiculous to think she'd be worried about her mother. Kit had to bite his tongue. This was clearly not the time to tell her that her mum was nice and that she was lucky to have her.

If it wasn't about her mum, then, was Grace upset about the car crash? He frowned. They had talked about the lady, Nell, and Grace had seemed to be okay with that. But she hadn't known about the man, then, had she? Was that what Chef Viv had told her in the scullery?

"Grace, is this about the bloke who died in the crash?"

This time she sobbed in earnest and hugged her knees tighter. "I can't believe he's dead. He was—he was nice to me."

"You knew him?"

She nodded, gulping. "He— He was— He said he—"

"Kit?" came Gemma's voice. "Are you in here?"

"Coming," he called. Standing, he brushed off the seat of his jeans and held out a hand to Grace. "We'd better go. But I'll try to come down the pub," he whispered. "If you want to talk."

Booth watched Viv Holland as she stood at the mortuary viewing window, her hands clenched into fists at her sides. On the other side of the glass, the attendant pulled back the sheet. Viv gave a little gasp, then stood motionless for a long moment.

"Is it Fergus O'Reilly?" Booth asked. The crush injury at the top of the man's forehead had not marred his profile, and there had been no blood to wash out of his long, curling hair. O'Reilly's other injuries had been minor, surprisingly.

Her shoulders slumping, Viv nodded, then reached out and

touched the glass, very gently. "I know it sounds trite, but he looks so . . . peaceful. Fergus was always moving. If he wasn't cooking, he was talking, or pacing, or fiddling with something. That . . . injury"—she nodded towards O'Reilly's head—"did it— I don't like to think of him being in pain."

Booth wasn't ready to tell her O'Reilly hadn't died in the crash. "I doubt he suffered," he said, which was neutral enough. "Did Mr. O'Reilly have any distinguishing marks?"

"A tattoo. On his left forearm. Fergus didn't approve of tattoos, but we talked him into it one night."

"We?"

"The cooks." Viv pushed up the left sleeve of her chef's tunic. "Like this." On her forearm, a small chef's knife and a honing rod were crossed beneath a stylized toque. Above the toque floated a tiny rosette.

Booth spoke to the mortuary attendant through the speaker, and the woman lifted the sheet to reveal O'Reilly's left forearm. The tattoo matched.

Viv turned away, her eyes swimming with tears, as if that small thing had hurt her more than the sight of O'Reilly's face. "Can we go now?" she said abruptly. "I've got to get back to the pub."

When they reached the car park, Booth saw that the earlier shower had stopped while they were inside. The sky still looked threatening to the west, however, so there might be more rain to come. "You had a lot of faith in the weather forecast, planning an outside luncheon today," Booth said as he unlocked the car, hoping to relax the atmosphere between them.

Viv didn't answer until she'd fastened her seat belt. "Addie had a marquee on hold until midmorning. But, yeah, we scraped by." She fell silent as he drove, her face half turned away from him.

She looked, Booth realized, exhausted. When, after a moment, he said, "I am sorry about your friend," she started as if she'd been miles away.

"I wouldn't exactly call Fergus a friend."

"Former employer, then. In any case, I know that what you've just done is very difficult."

Viv just nodded.

Booth tried another tack. "You're not in touch with anyone else who knew him?"

"Well, of course, there's Ibby——" she began, then, on a rising note of distress, "Oh, dear God, I'll have to tell Ibby. I didn't even think about him—— How could I be so——"

"Who's Ibby?" broke in Booth.

"My sous-chef." Viv took a breath. "We both used to work for Fergus."

"Did he still keep in contact with O'Reilly?"

"Christ, no," she said, then shot him an abashed glance. "I mean, no, I doubt it. I'm sure Ibby would have mentioned it," she added, but she sounded a little uncertain. She was silent again, her hands, which had been open in her lap, were now tightly clasped.

But when Booth glanced at her a few moments later, her eyes were closed and her face had relaxed. He thought she might have actually fallen asleep. He didn't disturb her, glad of the time to think about what he should do.

He was certain that there were things Viv Holland was not telling him. What he didn't know was whether or not those things had any bearing on the deaths of Fergus O'Reilly and Nell Greene. He sensed that Viv was an intensely private person, and that even the little she'd shared with him had been under duress.

As for now, he only had a suspicious death, not a crime. Was he justified in pulling in more manpower, from either uniform or CID, until he knew if O'Reilly had been taking prescribed medication that might have killed him?

He could, he thought, do a little digging himself. His curiosity was aroused, he had to admit. How often did he have a celebrity death on his doorstep—much less the death of a celebrity he had admired and had actually met?

And, having had a word with Doug Cullen—make that Metropolitan Police Detective Sergeant Doug Cullen—while Viv was speaking to her daughter, he now knew he had an entire contingent of coppers at hand.

Kincaid woke to the touch of a cool hand on his forehead. Opening his eyes, he found Gemma sitting on the edge of the bed, studying him, her brow creased in a frown. "What is it?" he managed to mumble, his mouth dry from the pain pill he'd swallowed when he came upstairs.

"You were dreaming again, muttering in your sleep."

"Was I?" He tried to hang on to a fragment from the jumbled images that teased at his consciousness, but it was gone. "I can't remember."

"I thought you might have a fever, but you're cool."

"I know I am," he replied, summoning a grin. Sitting up a bit, he was glad to find that his head didn't swim. He slipped his good arm round her waist. "Come to bed."

"I think you must have a concussion," said Gemma. "It's the middle of the afternoon in someone else's house, and the children will pop in any minute. Besides, I'd hurt you." She smiled and leaned down to kiss the corner of his mouth very gently.

"Ow."

"See? I told you so."

Pushing himself farther up in the bed, he flexed his right arm and hand gingerly, then moved his head. Nothing spun. "I feel better. Those pills must be magic." He released Gemma and reached for the glass of water he'd left on the bedside table. "What's going on?"

"DI Booth took Viv to make the identification. We have all of her things packed into her van. Melody's going to drive the van to the pub and I'm going to take the kids to the village in Melody's car. They want to get ice creams at the mill."

"Melody must have told them about the ice creams."

Laughing, Gemma said, "I'm not taking responsibility. But they could use an outing and I want to see the village—and the pub. I'll help Melody and Doug unload the van. I'm not sure who's on hand at the pub if Viv's not back."

Kincaid swung his legs off the bed. So far so good. "I'm coming, too."

"Are you sure you're up to it?"

"If I managed to keep up with Ivan this morning, I could probably run a marathon."

Gemma started to speak, then hesitated.

"What is it, love?"

"I wasn't sure if you were feeling up to it. But Melody got the key to Nell Greene's cottage from Mark Cain. I thought you might like to be the one to give it to DI Booth."

Joe had loaded all Viv's equipment into her van, helped by the tall, lanky kid who was visiting—Kit, he thought the boy was called—

and Melody, and Melody's friend from London, the one who was mad on gardening. He hadn't needed to be told that the friend was a cop. With his round glasses and neatly pressed chinos, the guy looked more like a programmer, but he had that quiet, watchful air all cops seemed to acquire, natural as breathing.

A half hour later, Melody and Grace and Melody's friend had squeezed into the van, while the pretty copper-haired woman and the other bloke, the one who'd been in the car crash, got into Melody's car with the three kids. When they'd all driven away, he raked the gravel forecourt until it formed perfect undulating ripples, like the sand in a Japanese meditation garden.

It wouldn't last. Of course it wouldn't. Nor did the trimming and tidying he did every day in the gardens, but that didn't mean that it wasn't worth the doing, in and of itself. He understood Viv, with her constant battle to master elements that were of necessity fleeting.

Going round the side of the house, he put the rake away in the shed, then made his way through the kitchen garden and down the walk that ran along the outside of the formal hedges. At the end of the last hedge, he crossed the bottom lawn and entered the thicket of trees that bordered the river. The arching branches hid him now from any casual observer. He didn't want to speak to anyone, not until he'd had time to think about what he'd heard.

His carefully tended path through the trees ended in a small clearing on the river's edge. The one-room fishing hut—built by Addie's great-grandfather shortly after the construction of the house—hugged the shoreline. Here, the river had been partially dammed so that it widened into a good-sized trout pool, and the hut's large covered porch extended a few feet over the water.

When he'd first come to work here, he'd found the hut neglected since Addie's father's death—Ivan Talbot was no fisherman. Joe, fascinated by the place, had offered to make the necessary repairs. He'd mended the fishing tackle as well, and would cast a line when he'd finished his day's work in the gardens. More and more often, he spent the night on a camp bed in the hut rather than driving back to his small, barren flat in Moreton.

When Addie caught on to his overnight stays, she'd offered to let him live there if he wanted to make the place more habitable. "But surely you'll miss the nightlife, and your friends," she'd said.

"I don't think you can say that Moreton-in-Marsh has night-life," he'd answered with a smile. He didn't add that he didn't have any friends he could be bothered to keep up with. The oldest of six in a cramped house, he'd never wanted anything as much as to be alone.

Once settled in the hut, he fished, he cooked simple meals on the camp stove, and read his books on landscape design and plants and philosophy. On warm evenings, he stretched out on the little dock and watched the stars. In the winter, he warmed himself by the wood-burning stove. The lack of company bothered him not at all.

But he had, unfortunately, missed sex, and that had been his undoing.

The shade from the riverside sycamores kept the hut cool on warm days, but it also meant the room grew dim in the after-noons. Lighting the lamp that hung from the beamed ceiling, he took a glass from one of the storage shelves and reached for the seldom-drunk bottle of single malt. He'd just poured a generous finger when he heard footsteps on the porch, then the hut door was yanked open.

Without turning, he said, "What do you want, Roz?"

"Pour me one of those." She sat, uninvited, on the edge of the camp bed.

Joe took down another glass and splashed some whisky into it. When he turned, he saw that she was far from her usual calm and collected self. Her hair had come loose from its customary twist. Her perfect lipstick had vanished, and her blouse was half untucked from the waistband of her dark trousers. A few weeks ago, he'd have been aroused at the sight of Roz disheveled. Now, he said, "Drink up and get out."

"Sit down, darling, for heaven's sake." Her lips formed a pout.

He knocked back enough single malt to set his throat on fire and stayed where he was. "What do you want, Roz?" he said again.

"Did you hear . . . about him?" When she lifted her glass, he saw that her hand was shaking.

"One of the church ladies told me. You know what gossip is like in the villages."

Roz flushed. "That was beneath you. So . . . Did you talk to Viv?"

"Really? And what should I have said when she was being taken to identify the body? You are a harpy, Roz."

She gave him a calculating look over the rim of her glass. "That never bothered you before."

"Yes, well." He shrugged. "We all make mistakes."

She looked hurt. "I never thought you'd be so petty, darling Joe."

To tell the truth, it had surprised him as well. Their relationship had seemed the perfect liaison of convenience. She was almost twenty years older, with her own home, a good job. There was none of the pressure to do the things required of a conventional relationship—to marry, to settle down, have kids, buy a little box on a housing estate.

It had been ideal. Until the day when he'd walked in on her in Beck House.

She raised an arched eyebrow. "You're not going to tell anyone, are you? About him?"

Unmoved by her appeal, he said, "Why shouldn't I?"

Roz took another swallow of the Glenlivet and licked her lips. "Because, if you do, I'll tell Addie you've been skimming."

He stared at her. "You bitch." Swallowing hard, he tried to tamp down the rage. "You know I wasn't— I'm a partner, for God's sake, and I'll pay the bloody money back."

"Then why not tell Addie? What did you need the money for, anyway, Joe? Some problem with your pack of relatives?"

"None of your damned business," he ground out through clenched teeth.

"Well, whatever it was, I doubt it will make a difference to Addie." Her smile was vicious.

"Damn you, Roz. Get out." He crossed the room in one long stride and yanked her up by her arm. The remains of her whisky splashed over them both, the fumes filling his nose like brimstone. He shoved her towards the door. "And don't come down here again. I swear I'll hurt you if you do."

CHAPTER ELEVEN

A glance to her left showed Gemma that there were still people on the small terrace of the Old Mill, on the other side of the river. Slowing, she said, "Looks like they're still open." A couple with a spaniel on a lead appeared round the corner of the building, licking ice cream cones. "And still serving ice cream," Gemma added. Checking that there was no traffic coming, she pulled onto the tiny bit of verge at the edge of the small roundabout and stopped. They could cross the stone footbridge to the mill. "Hop out, you lot."

Toby was first out, of course, whooping. Kit took the time to unbuckle Charlotte from her booster seat and help her from the car.

"Mummy." Charlotte stood at her window. "You need an ice cream, too." Her little face puckered with the gravity of this announcement.

Gemma laughed, thinking of the state of her waistband after

Viv's lunch. "Not today, love. How about you taste it for me and tell me which one is best. Maybe I'll have one tomorrow."

"Are you sure?" asked Kincaid, leaning back into the car.

For a moment she was tempted. Tempted to hold Charlotte on her lap while she dripped ice cream, tempted to listen to Kit explain the mechanics of the water mill. Tempted to scold Toby for trying to climb the terrace railing. Tempted, most of all, to take in the sight of Kincaid, bruised but whole. She sighed. "No. I promised I'd help. And you are not lifting boxes, so don't even think about it." Wagging a finger at him, she gave him her most severe frown.

Seeing Kit hesitate, gazing in the direction the van had taken, she wondered if he was worried about Viv. Toby was already on the bridge, tightrope-walking on the low stone parapet. "Go," she told Kincaid and Kit. "Before Toby falls in the river. I'll be at the pub." She pointed down the road. "You can't miss it, on the left after the big bridge and the main roundabout, across from the church. You can find me when you're finished." Waving at them, she drove on before she could change her mind.

The village glowed in the afternoon light, golden stone buildings festooned with the brilliant scarlet of creeper, the pathways busy with families, dogs, and cyclists. She passed the well and crossed the river, and there was the long, low pub as she remembered it from the previous evening, when lights had been aglow in the windows. Today she drove past, making a sharp left into the car park. She found an empty space easily—it was the lull between afternoon tea and happy-hour drinks. Looking round for the van, she saw that Melody had pulled it through an arch into an inner courtyard.

The van's rear doors were open. Melody and Doug and a wiry,

olive-skinned man in a cook's apron were sliding crates from the back. Grace stood to one side, hands in her anorak pockets, watching them. "Grace," called Gemma. "Are you sure you don't want an ice cream? The kids are all at the Old Mill with their dad and they'd love you to join them."

Grace shook her head and disappeared into the building across the courtyard from the pub.

"Viv not back yet?" Gemma asked as she reached the van. "Grace has a bee in her bonnet about something. And I thought all the kids were getting on well."

Melody balanced a crate of jam jars on her hip. "Gemma, this is Ibby, Viv's sous-chef." She nodded towards the man in the apron.

He put out a hand. "Hiya." Gemma had a glimpse of the colorful tattoos on his forearm, vegetables twining round a chef's knife, and the words *mise en place* in flowing script.

Bea Abbott, whom Gemma had met very briefly in the kitchen at Beck House, came out from the pub's service entrance. When she saw Gemma, her face fell. "Oh. I thought you were Viv. What on earth is keeping her?" Apparently, she hadn't expected an answer because she immediately turned to Ibby and added, "Hurry up, can't you? Evening rush is going to start any minute, and we've got full bookings. Of all the days for this to happen, it would have to be Saturday."

Gemma had to bite her tongue to keep from saying she doubted Nell Greene and Fergus O'Reilly had died just to inconvenience Bea. She was saved by the crunch of tires on gravel as a black Volvo pulled into the car park. Viv got out and came towards them, followed by Detective Inspector Booth.

Bea greeted them with her hands outstretched. "Viv, what's kept you? I was so worried—"

But Viv walked past her and stopped in front of Ibby. She looked at him and simply nodded.

"Oh, man." Ibby shook his head. "The bugger. God damn him."

Viv took his arm and turned him away. "Come on. Let's see what state the kitchen's in."

"It's a positive ID, then?" Melody asked Booth quietly.

"Yes, I'm afraid so." Booth turned to Bea. "Colin Booth, Gloucester CID. And you are?" Gemma noticed that he hadn't used his rank, and that in the few moments since he'd arrived he had very unobtrusively loosened the knot in his tie. She was beginning to like Colin Booth.

"Oh," Melody broke in before Bea could answer. "So sorry. This is Bea Abbott. She's—"

Bea spoke for herself. "I'm Vivian's business partner and the pub's manager. This is a terrible business, er, Mr. Booth." Not knowing Booth's rank had obviously put her wrong-footed, but she recovered quickly. "What can we do to assist you?"

"I understand Mr. O'Reilly left a coat?"

"Yes. It's in my office. I'll just fetch it." Bea turned away briskly, as if that was all there was to it.

Booth stopped her. "Miss Abbott, I'll need to have a word with your staff about Mr. O'Reilly's visit—or visits—to the pub yesterday. Is there someplace I can speak with them?"

"All of them? But it's—" She glanced at her watch. "It's almost time for dinner service, and as I said—"

"This won't take long, Miss Abbott." A clear command.

"Oh, all right," said Bea, sounding more exasperated than ungracious. "I suppose you can use the small dining room. It's not set up yet." She turned to lead him inside.

Melody and Doug were headed towards the kitchen with more crates.

Gemma hesitated for a moment, then glanced at Booth. He was watching her, and he gave her the slightest of nods before following Bea Abbott. Slipping her hands in her jacket pockets, Gemma trailed along a few feet behind him, as if she had nothing better to do.

As she entered the pub, Gemma looked round curiously. Booth and Bea had stepped into a small office just to the left of the door. Ahead was a small dining room, separated from a bar lounge area to the right by an inglenook fireplace. Looking through the lounge, she saw another dining area through a doorway on its far side. The burly, balding man behind the bar looked curiously back at her.

The pub was certainly an appealing place, with white-painted paneled walls offset by dark polished wood and leather furnishings, and red dhurrie carpets on the stone-flagged floors.

In the office, Bea handed Booth a long camel hair coat and said, "If you want to have a seat, I'll just fetch everyone."

Booth stopped her. "Before you do that, can you tell me where this coat was found?"

"Where he was sitting. There, in the corner." Bea pointed to a leather sofa in the L-shaped nook that formed the far corner of the lounge.

"Did anyone see him leave?"

"I don't know. Maybe Jack—he's the bartender—or Sarah, who's one of the waitstaff. All I know is that when I came in to close up, it was there."

"But you knew who the coat belonged to?"

Shifting impatiently, Bea said, "Well, yes, of course."

"You were acquainted with Mr. O'Reilly, then?"

"I—" Bea stopped and took a breath. "I'm not sure I'd say acquainted. I'd never met him before yesterday afternoon. But obviously I knew who he was."

"From Miss Holland?"

"Well, yes, but I'd have recognized him regardless. From his books and everything. But I was surprised to see him standing in the yard yesterday afternoon."

Surprised and not thrilled, thought Gemma, who seemed to have done a good job of fading into the woodwork. Booth, she was sure, was well aware that she was still standing in the hallway.

Feeling in one of the coat pockets, Booth pulled out a wallet and flipped it open. He nodded as he rifled through it. "National insurance. Credit cards. A photo ID but no driving license—in which case we'll have to find out how he got here—but there's nothing with a London address." Shifting the coat, he retrieved a mobile phone from the other pocket. It was a sleek new iPhone, but Gemma could see that when he pressed the power button, nothing happened. Even charged, it would be pass coded. Booth shrugged. "That won't be much help at the moment." Frowning, he felt the rest of the coat. "There's no room key here—"

A couple came in from the car park with their dogs, two handsome Belgian shepherds, and they all had to step back to let them pass. Bea gave them a friendly greeting, then turned back to Booth. "If you're going to speak to the staff, it will have to be soon. I can cover the bar for Jack for a few minutes, but everyone's going to be needed in the kitchen."

"I'll just step into the kitchen then," said Booth with a smile. "And then I'll have a word with Jack afterwards. No need to disrupt your routine more than necessary."

"But you can't go into the kitchen." Bea looked as if he'd just suggested sacrilege. "They're working and there's no room—"

"I've been in a kitchen or two. I'm sure Chef Viv can put up with me for a couple of minutes." Booth's tone was firm. Gemma moved out of his way as he stepped round the bar and pushed through a swinging door into the kitchen.

This left Gemma standing a little awkwardly in the hallway. She was wondering where Doug and Melody had got to when Bea said, close enough to make her jump, "Can I help you with something? It's Gemma, isn't it? You're staying with the Talbots?"

"Yes, that's right. I was just waiting for Melody and my hus—"

"Thanks for all your help this morning. I didn't have a chance to say earlier. I had to rush back to deal with the lunch service here." Taking off her rimless glasses, Bea pinched the bridge of her nose. "It was a beastly day." Her voice wavered at the end, and when she looked up at Gemma, her eyes were glistening.

"I'm so sorry," Gemma hastened to say. "I'm sure this has all been a dreadful shock. We were pretty shaken up, too."

Realization flooded Bea's face. "Oh, God. I'm an idiot. It was your husband in the other car, wasn't it? Viv told me. I'm so sorry. Is he all right?"

"He's fine. Just a bit banged up. We were very lucky." Just talking about it made Gemma feel a little weak-kneed, but Bea looked so distressed that she added, "You can see for yourself. He's meeting me here in just a bit."

Before Bea could respond, a plump woman in a server's apron appeared from the other dining area. "Bea," she called, "we've got an eight-top booked for six o'clock. Could you help me shift the tables and set up?"

"Don't mind me," Gemma said to Bea. "I'll just have a seat in the bar." She could have gone outside to look for the others—she had Melody's keys, after all—but the bartender was still giving her darting little glances.

"Have something on the house, do," Bea insisted, looking harried again as she hurried off to help.

Smiling at the couple with the dogs, who had been served their drinks and had settled at a table with their newspapers, the dogs under their feet, Gemma made her way to the bar.

"What will it be, then?" asked the bartender, who had obviously been listening to her conversation.

"What do you suggest?"

"Do you fancy gin?"

"Oh, yes. I do." Gemma glanced at her watch. It had gone five, and after the day she'd had, she certainly thought she could justify a little tipple. "A G and T?"

"If I could suggest . . ." He pulled a smart-looking black bottle from the shelf behind the bar. "Our local Cotswolds Dry Gin, on ice with a twist of grapefruit."

"Grapefruit? Really?"

"Trust me on this one." If not for the local accent, he might have been an East End bouncer, but a smile transformed his broad face.

"Okay, you've convinced me. I'll give it a try."

She watched as he put a few ice cubes in a heavy glass, then expertly curled a strip of grapefruit rind from one of the fruits in a bowl on the bar top. "This must be a favorite," she commented, nodding at the supply of grapefruit nestled in the bowl along with the usual lemons and limes.

He poured a generous measure from the black bottle and handed it to her with a cocktail napkin. "See for yourself."

Gemma wasn't in the habit of drinking gin neat, so she sniffed, then took a tentative sip. The flavors exploded in her mouth—coriander and juniper and lavender and lime and . . . grapefruit. "Oh, wow," she said, when her eyes stopped watering. "That is amazing. I'm converted." She held out a hand. "I'm Gemma, by the way."

"Jack." His grip was quick and firm and her hand felt delicate in his grasp. Studying him, Gemma wondered if he might be ex-military. "You're a cop," he said, as if he'd been reading her signals, too.

"Detective in the Met," she agreed. "My husband, too."

"Ah." Jack polished a glass. "That I didn't know."

"I work with Melody Talbot. She invited us for the weekend." Gemma took another appreciative sip of the gin.

"Good lass, Melody. But not the best weekend for your husband." Jack nodded towards Bea's office. "I couldn't help but overhear. I take it you weren't in the car with him last night, then."

"No. I came down with Melody and our little daughter earlier in the afternoon."

"Well, I'm glad for that. And glad your husband is all right. It's just"—the wineglass gleamed in Jack's hand but he gave the rim another rub—"it's just that I wondered—I liked Nell, you see. She was a nice woman. Wouldn't have hurt a hair on anyone's head. It's bad enough that she's dead, but I don't like thinking she was responsible for such a thing."

Gemma didn't want to steal a march on DI Booth, but her pulse quickened as she realized Jack might have been one of the last people to have seen the crash victims alive. "I understand she was here last night?"

Jack nodded. "She had dinner in the bar. She didn't like to eat in the dining room on her own, said she felt more comfortable in here," he added, with what sounded like proprietary pride.

"Did you notice anything unusual about her last night?"

His broad forehead creased. "I've been over and over it since we heard the news. She was quiet, maybe not as chatty as usual, and she didn't eat much. She stayed for a good long while, too, after she'd finished her chicken pie and her coffee. I wondered that she didn't bring Bella—that's her dog—but she might have come straight to the pub from somewhere other than home."

Gemma was now casting anxious glances towards the kitchen, where she could pick out the occasional rumble of Booth's voice among the others. Smells were beginning to percolate into the bar as well—roasting meat and frying potatoes, she thought. Her stomach rumbled, in spite of her earlier protestations about the ice cream.

Crossing her fingers for a few more uninterrupted minutes, she said, "And did you see her speaking with Mr. O'Reilly?"

"Him." Jack set the wineglass on the bar with such a smack that the couple with the shepherds looked up at him curiously and the dogs raised their heads. Lowering his voice, he said, "That one, showing up here, with his silly hat and coat. Ordering Viv's food and sending it back to the kitchen with his little comments. 'Tell Chef the pastry is quite soggy,' and that on her steak and Hook Norton Pie. Everyone knows Viv makes the best pastry in the county. Or, 'Tell Chef the pork is overdone,' on the Todenham Manor cutlet."

"Was he friendly with Nell—Mrs. Greene?"

"I never saw him speak to her."

"But they left together?"

"No." Jack pulled another wineglass from the overhead rack. Nodding at Gemma's drink, he said, "Get you another?"

"Oh, gosh, no thank you." Gemma hadn't realized she'd finished it. She felt a bit light-headed. She wondered why Jack was suddenly less forthcoming. There was no sign of Booth, and Bea still seemed to be busy in the other dining room. "I understand he left his coat."

"That he did. Walked out on his check, too." Jack flushed. "That sounds petty of me, considering, but at the time . . ."

"I understand," Gemma assured him. "Did he seem in a hurry?"

Jack glanced round, then seemed to come to a decision. Dropping his voice almost to a whisper, he said, "More like royally pissed off. There was . . . a bit of a row. In the kitchen."

"He was in the kitchen?"

"Got up from his table, came round the bar, and blew right past me."

Gemma was surprised. She thought Jack could have stopped a small tank.

As if he'd sensed her criticism, Jack shrugged, looking down. "He'd been hanging round all day. He was in the courtyard with Chef when I got to work, so last night I figured he had her permission. But next thing I know there's a crash and he comes storming out again and goes straight out the door."

"You didn't go after him?"

"He'd left his things. I thought he'd just gone out for a smoke or something. And I went in the kitchen to make sure everything was okay. Viv had dropped a pan of chips. A right mess, it was."

"What about Mrs. Greene?"

"She stayed for a while longer, just drinking coffee. Maybe ten or fifteen minutes. It crossed my mind to ask if she was all right, but with everything else . . ." He looked at Gemma, his hands finally still. "If only I'd spoken to her, asked her if she was okay . . . I had no idea I'd never see her again. I feel I'm somehow to blame."

CHAPTER TWELVE

The arrival of new customers took Jack's attention. Gemma gave him a wave of thanks and headed for the exit. It was getting on towards dinnertime and the place was filling up. Surely Melody and Doug had finished helping with the unloading of Viv's van. And where were Duncan and the kids?

When she stepped outside, she saw that dark clouds had begun to build up again, bringing an early twilight. The breeze had died and the perfume from the rambling roses that grew on the side of the kitchen extension hung heavy in the air. She was about to round the corner into the courtyard when she heard voices. Peering past the roses, she saw Viv, standing by the kitchen steps, and with her the man who'd sat glowering next to Kincaid all through the luncheon. Something in their body language made her stop, half shielded by the twining rose canes.

"You have to tell me what's wrong, Viv," the man said, sounding not angry but distressed. "Did I do something to upset you?"

"No, no, nothing like that. I promise it's nothing to do with you. I'm sorry if you thought that. It's been a horrible day." She stepped into his arms and rested her head against his shoulder for a moment. Then, with a glance towards the kitchen, she stepped back. "I thought I'd left it all behind, my old life. I should have known I couldn't—" She shook her head.

"Addie said you knew the fellow who was in the car with Nell."

"I worked for him, years ago. But—it was . . . complicated. I'll tell you, but not now. And not here." Viv turned away, but the man reached out and caught her arm.

"Viv, did you still have feelings for him?"

"Feelings?" Viv pulled away and crossed her arms tightly over her chest. "Yes. I hated his guts."

When Kincaid and the rather sticky children followed the ENTRANCE sign and rounded the end of the pub, he saw Gemma apparently sniffing the pink roses that adorned the side of the building. She jumped guiltily and came towards them with a bright smile. "I was wondering where you'd got to."

"You know you're allowed to smell the roses, love," he teased.

She gave him an arch look and bent down to Charlotte, who was holding out an enormous scarlet leaf.

"We found this for you, Mummy."

"We didn't pick it," Toby offered. "It was on the ground."

"That's even nicer than ice cream," Gemma told them.

"I had strawberry," said Charlotte. "I tried to bring you some but it melted." She held out the splotchy front of her T-shirt as evidence.

They had all had ice creams, and perused the gift shop at the Old Mill to the sounds of 1940s jazz. Kincaid had bought a book on local walks. Afterwards, they'd examined the mill wheel, then meandered along the Eye, looking for trout in the clear water and picking up leaves dropped by the creeper growing on the walls of the inn.

The children had spotted the play area in the garden behind the pub. "Can we go see, Mummy?" Charlotte tugged at Gemma's hand.

"Go on, then. We'll be right behind you," Gemma said, waving them off. Kit sauntered behind the younger two, looking round curiously.

"Is Viv back?" Kincaid asked when the children were out of earshot. "Was it a positive ID?"

Gemma nodded. "And Booth's still here."

As they entered the courtyard, Kincaid saw Melody and Doug sitting at a picnic table in the garden. Doug had a pint and Melody had what looked like a mug of tea. They were talking to Mark Cain, who had sat next to Kincaid at the luncheon. Cain looked considerably less aggravated than earlier in the day, and Kincaid wondered what had improved his mood.

"Hello, again," Cain said, shaking Kincaid's hand, then turning to Gemma.

"Hello. I'm Gemma James, Duncan's wife." Gemma gave Cain a smile, but Kincaid recognized the curiosity in her glance.

"Mark Cain. I've come to see if Grace would like to take Bella for a walk. Bella's Nell's dog," he added. "I'm looking after her."

"I think Lady Addie said she was one of your puppies?"

"Yes. And I was helping Nell with some obedience training."
He shook his head. "I still can't believe it, that Nell's gone."

"I understand you were her neighbor?"

"Yes. Nell's cottage is up King's Well Lane—the turning is opposite the mill. My farm is the next place beyond it." Cain frowned.
"Nell would have driven right past me last night."

Kincaid could visualize the lane—he'd gone that way with
Ivan that morning. And when he'd glanced at the walking guide
he'd bought in the mill shop, he'd seen that the lane was part of a
designated-walks loop. He thought he remembered seeing a farm
gate, but there had been nothing beyond that other than the junction that led to the main road. Where had Nell Greene been going?

Melody and Doug had finished their drinks and risen to join
them. "I've given Mark's key to the cottage to DI Booth," said
Melody. "And we'd better get organized to go back to the house.
Duncan, I thought you and Gemma and Charlotte could ride with
me, and Doug could walk up with the boys."

Kincaid started to say he didn't need a ride, then remembered
the grade of the hill and wondered if he felt quite up to the climb.

"She's coddling you," said Gemma with a smile. "And you'd
better not think of arguing."

They all looked up as DI Booth came out of the kitchen entrance, followed by Viv Holland. Booth carried a man's camel hair
overcoat.

"Is that O'Reilly's?" Melody asked.

"Yes, but not much help, I'm afraid. There's nothing with a
London address or anything to indicate where he was staying in
the area." Booth turned to Viv. "Do you have any suggestions,
Miss Holland?"

"There are only two places here in the village, the inn and the manor house. Knowing Fergus, I'd try the manor first. It's a bit more his style." Her smile was pinched. "You'll find it just the other side of the church." To Melody, Doug, and Gemma, she added, "Thank you all so much for your help. I don't know how I'd have managed otherwise. Now, if you don't mind, there's someone else I need to thank." She walked across the garden to the play area, where Kit was helping Charlotte on the slide.

Kincaid noticed that she had not acknowledged Mark Cain.

"You'll be checking on Nell Greene's cottage as well as the hotels?" he asked Booth. "I wondered if I might tag along."

"Of course," Booth said. "I'll run you up to Beck House afterwards."

Leaving the pub, Kincaid and Booth crossed the road at the main roundabout and took the paved path that meandered alongside the Eye, the river here wider and deeper than it had been beside the mill. Across the road, a wall of golden Cotswold brick with ironwork insets bordered the tarmac, partially concealing the manor house.

"You think there's something in these deaths, then?" Kincaid asked Booth.

"I certainly think the whole business is odd. But I don't have enough yet to justify authorizing overtime on a Saturday night." Booth shot Kincaid an amused glance. "Hence my appreciation of another set of eyes and ears."

"Happy to oblige."

Booth walked on another few yards before he added, "Did you have a particular reason for wanting to see the woman's cottage?"

"Nell." Kincaid spoke with more force than necessary, then

took a breath. "Mrs. Greene. Sorry. Didn't mean to snap. It's just that no one's accounts of her—or my impression—seem to match up with what happened last night."

"None of the staff I just interviewed at the pub saw any interaction between Mrs. Greene and Fergus O'Reilly. According to the bartender, O'Reilly left about twenty minutes before Mrs. Greene."

They'd reached the ornate pineapple-topped gates flanking the manor house drive. Kincaid looked back towards the pub, just visible in the fading light. "What time was this?"

"Fully dark, according to the bartender. Half seven, he guessed."

So only a short time before Nell had run into him on the A429. How long had the drive from the village to the intersection taken Ivan that morning? Ten minutes? So, however O'Reilly had ended up in Nell's car, it had to have happened very shortly after she left the pub. "Were they even sitting near each other?" he asked.

"Not according to the barman. If I had the resources, I'd track down the other customers in the bar."

As they crossed the road and entered the manor drive, Kincaid gazed across a broad sweep of green lawn to the house itself. Lights had begun to wink on in all three stories. Above the roofline, dark clouds were massing, and the golden facade of the house seemed to glow against the looming backdrop. This was the place Kincaid had glimpsed when Tracey Woodman had driven him to the Talbots', the place he had thought was Beck House.

This house, unlike the Talbots' comfortable Arts and Crafts home, he guessed to be at least seventeenth century. "If O'Reilly was staying here, he certainly went for posh," he said as they walked up the curving drive, their feet crunching on the manicured gravel.

A flight of steps on the left of the covered porch took them up to the elevated ground floor and a glassed-in entry. "Airlock," Kincaid murmured as they stepped through the second set of doors into reception, and Booth's lips twitched in a smile.

The house might be Tudor, but there was nothing fussy about the large central hall that greeted them. The cream walls and gleaming white woodwork were anchored by a chevron-patterned blond wood floor and a long, sleek reception desk. The young woman behind the desk was sleek as well, with bobbed dark hair and a crisp white blouse. "Can I help you?" she asked with professional courtesy, but her brow creased as she inspected them.

Kincaid realized they must look an odd couple, Booth with his expensive suit, he in his slightly rumpled sports jacket—not to mention his bruises and bandages and a few drips of pistachio ice cream on his shirtfront. Booth stepped up to the desk and flashed a blinding smile along with his warrant card.

Pulling up an online photo of Fergus O'Reilly on his mobile phone, Booth inquired if he was a guest of the hotel.

"Mr. O'Reilly?" The woman's frown deepened. "Is there some sort of problem?"

"I'm afraid Mr. O'Reilly has been in an accident. And this is an official inquiry. Can you confirm that he was a guest here?"

"Well, yes, but— What's happened to him?"

"Mr. O'Reilly was killed in an automobile crash yesterday evening," Booth said.

"Oh." Her eyes widened. "That's awful. I can't believe it." She paused for a moment, her brow puckering again. "Although I did wonder . . ."

"You wondered what? Miss"—Booth glanced at her name tag— "Jane."

"Mr. O'Reilly never picked up his key last night. He'd left it at the desk. He didn't come in the night before, either, but he used his room yesterday morning. Housekeeping said nothing had been touched today."

"O'Reilly didn't sleep in his room night before last?" Kincaid asked.

"Well, I can't be certain," said Jane. "But he didn't pick up his key before I went off duty at eleven, and housekeeping said his bed hadn't been slept in." She looked suddenly uncomfortable. "We pride ourselves on our attention to our guests."

"Of course," Booth said. "I take it Mr. O'Reilly had booked through tonight?"

Jane checked her computer. "Yes, the booking was for three nights." She hesitated for a moment, then said, "I don't want to sound insensitive, but what are we to do about his room? We have guests booked into it tomorrow. Will someone be coming for his things?"

"I'd suggest that you have your manager pack his things and hold them until further notice. In the meantime, my colleague and I need to have a look at his room."

"Oh." The young woman hesitated again. "I'm not sure— Maybe I should contact my manager—"

"I promise this won't take long and that we'll be very discreet. I certainly don't think you'd want uniformed officers here."

The idea of such disruption to the hotel did the trick. "Well, if you're certain . . ." Jane reached into a cabinet under the reception desk.

When she'd retrieved the keys, Kincaid took the opportunity to ask, "Did you talk with Mr. O'Reilly at all during his stay?"

"Not more than the usual chitchat. I think I asked about his journey, and if he would be needing to park a car. He said he'd come by train and had got a taxi from the Moreton station."

"Did he say why he was visiting Lower Slaughter?"

Jane shook her head. "No. He was nice enough—quite the charmer, I'd say—but it was a bit perfunctory. He seemed . . . distracted."

"Did he meet anyone here at the hotel?"

"I don't think so. He had a drink in the bar the first night." She nodded to the right of reception. Kincaid had noticed the bar when they'd come in, a stunning room with a free-standing horseshoe-shaped bar and blush velvet–covered bar stools. Gemma would love it.

"He was alone?" Booth put in.

"As far as I know. I was on duty that evening and I pretty much see anyone coming or going." She thought for a moment. "There was something, though. It was not long after he'd given me his keys. I went out to help some late arrivals with their luggage. Mr. O'Reilly was talking to someone in the garden, over near the churchyard entrance. A woman. Blond, I think."

"You didn't recognize her?"

"No, it was just an impression, really. A woman's shape, a flash of light on her hair. I'm sorry."

"You've been very helpful," Booth said. "Can you tell us what time this was?"

"It was after he'd been in the bar. Half eight, maybe? I came back inside and I didn't see him again." Coming round the desk, she said, "If you'll follow me," and led them up the wide central staircase to a room on the first floor. She unlocked the door and stood aside, then hesitated. "Are you certain this is all right? I feel I should stay, but I can't leave the desk unattended . . ."

"We won't be long," Booth assured her, and closed the door firmly. "I suspect she thinks you look disreputable," he said to Kincaid, grinning. "But I thought she'd have doubted me if I'd told her you were a detective superintendent."

Kincaid grimaced. "Ouch. That does nothing for my confidence." Looking round the room, he saw that the bed had been turned down by housekeeping, but not slept in. A partially open duffel bag sat on the bench at the foot of the bed, and one of the bedside tables held a dog-eared paperback thriller.

"Somehow I'd have expected better literary taste," Booth commented. "Something on food, or at least an Irish noir detective novel."

While Booth looked through the duffel, Kincaid opened the wardrobe. Hanging in it were a sports jacket, a couple of cotton button-down shirts, and a pair of wool trousers. The clothes were expensive brands, but he noticed that the shirts were beginning to wear at the collars and cuffs. The pair of lace-up dress shoes in the bottom of the wardrobe looked bespoke, but when he examined them more closely, he saw that the heels were wearing. "He liked his clothes, but they were getting a bit shabby. Anything in the duffel?" he asked as he checked the pockets of the jacket and the trousers.

"Socks and underwear. A pair of jeans and a T-shirt."

"No medication?"

Booth shook his head. "I'll check the bathroom."

Following him, Kincaid watched as he went through the shaving kit by the sink. O'Reilly had left out on the dressing table a bottle of Tom Ford cologne. The kit held nothing but ordinary toiletries, a razor, and a travel-size bottle of aspirin. "No prescription medications, no alcohol stash," said Booth.

"The barman at the pub said he had nothing but coffee with his dinner."

Kincaid frowned. "Would he have taken aspirin if he had a heart condition?"

"I'll ask the pathologist. But if he took some form of digoxin, it's not here."

There was something about the paucity of possessions and the worn clothing that struck Kincaid as a little sad, and certainly did not fit his idea of a successful chef.

When they went downstairs, the receptionist had printed out O'Reilly's address for them. "Chelsea," Booth said, scanning it. "Viv Holland said he used to live in Chelsea."

Jane had gone back to scrolling down her computer screen. "Our register shows Mr. O'Reilly as a returning guest. I didn't realize he'd stayed here before. Ah." Her frown cleared. "That explains it. I work Wednesday through Sunday. It was a Monday night, almost three weeks ago."

"What the bleeding hell," Booth said as he and Kincaid walked back towards the pub. "No one I spoke to said anything about O'Reilly being here three weeks ago."

Kincaid was thinking it out. "So, are Viv Holland and her staff lying, or did they not see him?"

"Well, I intend to ask them. But one person at a time, and not until I know more."

The sun had set, leaving a lingering rose stain on the underside of the clouds. The lights in the pub shone like beacons in the gloom. When they reached the roundabout and Booth turned towards the pub, Kincaid said, "I thought Nell's cottage was to the left."

"Yes, but I know that road and I don't fancy walking that lane in the dark. I'll drop you at the Talbots' after." Booth had glanced at him as he said it and Kincaid suspected that the detective, like Melody, was coddling him. But if he was honest, he had to admit that the doctor's pain pill had worn off some time ago. He wasn't, however, going to pass up his chance to learn more about Nell Greene. And he was glad enough to settle into the leather seat of Booth's Volvo.

"Nice car."

"What will you do about yours?" Booth asked.

Kincaid shrugged. "No idea. It will have to be something that will hold kids and dogs."

"That's called *the wife's.*"

Kincaid thought he saw Booth smile in the dark.

Booth drove through the center of the village, then took the road that branched off by the mill. Hedges flashed by in the glare of the headlamps, and once he had to brake sharply when a rabbit darted across the road. When he slowed for Nell's cottage, Kincaid saw why he had missed it when he and Ivan had driven by that morning.

A long, low building in the ubiquitous Cotswold stone with a neatly thatched roof, it was set back from the road and faced north, towards the village, so that the front entrance was hidden from the lane. The dark bulk of the rising hill loomed behind it, and only one faint light shone from a window by the front door. Booth stopped the car in the drive and they got out without speaking. The air felt still and heavy and the only sound was the distant call of a bird.

"Storm coming," Booth said softly as he fished out the key.

As soon as they stepped inside and switched on the lights, Kincaid could see that no expense had been spared on the place. The floors were bleached wide plank, the walls a pale mint, and the upholstered furniture looked comfortable.

The cottage was feminine, and above all, tidy. Tidier, God knew, than his own house ever looked, between the kids and the cats and the dogs. Here there were no stacks of newspapers, no empty tea mugs, not even any dog toys littering the kilim. A few issues of *Country Life* were stacked neatly on the ottoman that served as a coffee table, the television remote aligned perfectly in the center. In a basket at the end of the sofa, he found a current issue of the *Radio Times* and some knitting.

Bookcases had been built in on either side of the hearth. Examining the volumes, Kincaid found popular novels, some classics, as well as some books on gardening and knitting.

There were two framed photos on the bottom shelf. Kincaid recognized Nell instantly, even though he'd only seen her in the dark and in pain. Both showed Nell with a black-and-white border collie—Bella, he presumed. In one, Nell was smiling at the camera. In the other, she was facing the dog, which was placed in a perfect sit. Kincaid wondered if Mark Cain had taken the photos.

Although Kincaid had another look among the books and objets d'art, there were no other photos, and nothing to suggest that she had kept in touch with work colleagues or extended family.

Kincaid picked up the first photo and held it in the lamplight. Nell Greene had been a trim woman with an ordinary, pleasant face and short light-colored hair that might have been described as blond. The photo did not highlight what he remembered the most. She had had beautiful eyes.

"The woman alphabetized her spices," Booth called from the kitchen. Photo in hand, Kincaid joined him. Booth was peering into a drawer beside the cream-colored Aga. The only spots of color in the room were provided by a turquoise teakettle on the Aga and a bowl of green apples on the kitchen table. Kincaid spotted a few cookery books grouped on an open shelf, but when he looked more closely he saw that they were well-thumbed copies of Nigella and Nigel Slater, homey rather than challenging.

Looking about, Kincaid saw a couple of unopened bottles of wine in a rack and a bottle of sherry beside the salt and pepper mills. "No other alcohol?"

"No. And no sign she'd been drinking in her initial blood test last night, which corroborates what the bartender told me. He said she only had coffee and a glass of tap water."

Kincaid held up the photo for Booth's inspection. "Would you say she was blond?"

"You mean could she have matched our receptionist's description?" Booth squinted at the image. "Maybe. At night, in the right light."

"Questionable, I agree."

Neither of them said that no one could mistake Viv Holland for anything *other* than blond.

The dog's bowls, Kincaid discovered, were by the back door, and the basket with her toys and chew bones was under the kitchen table. There were only a few stray tufts of black-and-white hair on the bare floors. Having grown up with collies, he thought Nell must have vacuumed every day to have kept the house in such a pristine state.

He had always found searching the property and the possessions of the recently dead a complicated business—fascinating, because how people lived and what they lived with told so much about them, disturbing, because it seemed such an elemental invasion of privacy.

"I don't think we'll find anything in here," he said, abruptly. "I'll just check the rest of the house."

The only bathroom was off the hall and, unlike the kitchen and living areas, did not seem to have had much updating. It was clean, however, and the toiletries were organized in pretty baskets. Checking the medicine cabinet, he found toothpaste and various over-the-counter medications. Behind these were two prescription bottles.

He wasn't carrying gloves, so using a tissue as a precaution, he turned the bottles until he could read the labels. One was an antianxiety drug, the other a common antidepressant. Both were nearly full, and both were dated nearly a year ago.

The bedroom held a neatly made double bed, nightstands, a dresser, and an old-fashioned freestanding wardrobe. He tried that first, running his hands gently over the hanging things. The business suits were of good quality but had a layer of dust on the shoulders. The other things in the wardrobe were the sort of simple, practical things one wore for life in the country, much of which was spent outdoors.

Carelessly, he'd used his right hand to move the hangers in the wardrobe and now it was throbbing badly. With a grunt of pain, he sat down on the edge of the bed and opened the nightstand drawer with his left hand. Bookmarks, hand cream, a small torch. And beneath the detritus, a framed photograph, facedown. He held it to the light.

It was Nell's wedding picture. The clothes were dated, the dress the overly ruffled fashion made popular by Princess Diana. The young Nell looked hopefully out at him, perhaps a little too seriously for a wedding day. The groom had been a good-looking man with dark hair and heavy eyebrows, but Kincaid thought that even then his expression showed the beginnings of a certain pomposity.

What had become of this young couple? And why had Nell kept the photo if she couldn't bear to look at it?

CHAPTER THIRTEEN

"Fire two duck, two steaks, medium well," Viv called out.

"Two duck, two freaking wasted steaks," Ibby muttered. "Medium well, this beef, might as well throw it in the bin." The steaks were rib eyes, heritage beef, with mushrooms and red wine sauce, and they were the most expensive thing on the menu.

Viv agreed with him, but his grousing was the last thing she needed right now. She took a second of her attention from the plates at the pass to glare at him. "Make that, 'Yes, Chef,' and keep your opinions to yourself."

"Yes, ma'am." From the sauté station, Ibby gave her an exaggerated bow.

"Shut the hell up, Ibby. Tonight, of all nights." She could strangle him. But that would be after she strangled Fergus, who *had walked out in the middle of service and left her to expedite, tonight of all nights.*

"Back in a tic," Fergus had said, and that had been half an hour ago. It meant they were one down on the hot line. They were beginning to lose it, and the tension had seeped into front of house. Not that front of house wasn't tense enough as it was.

The buzz had started at lunch. A last-minute booking for one at half seven, under an innocuous name, but one that the maître d' thought he had seen before. The man had come alone a month ago, wearing a suit. He'd sampled several of the house specialties, had one glass of wine, and asked some knowledgeable questions about the menu—all the hallmarks of a Michelin inspector.

It was now a quarter to eight, so if the man had been on time, his starter order should be coming off the printer at any moment. And if they were right about him, they absolutely could not afford to screw up. Which brought her back to it—where the hell was Fergus? There had been too many nights recently when he'd slipped out and come back a little more wired than he should be, but he'd never done it when so much was at stake.

Viv tried to concentrate on the plate in front of her. A calf's sweetbread with an old-school sauce soubise, it tasted fabulous but took an artist's hand with the garnish to make it look like something anyone would want to eat. That was Fergus's strength, not hers. Give him a squeeze bottle and a pair of tweezers and he was bloody Picasso.

She'd just arranged the last bits of thyme and sorrel when Danny, the maître d', came clattering down the kitchen stairs with the ticket in hand. "I think it's him," he said. "He's ordered the breast of quail."

It was a recipe she'd tweaked, adding a hint of truffle, and it had since become one of the house specialties. That was one of the signs restaurants looked for—a Michelin inspector ordered the signature dishes, not run-of-the-mill roasted chicken.

"And, wait for it," Danny went on, his eyes wide.

"One glass of wine," they chorused, and Viv couldn't stop her grin. That was the third hint—Michelin inspectors, who visited two restaurants a day, had to watch their alcohol intake.

"Let's do this," she said. "And if it turns out it's Joe Blow from Brighton, we'll give him the best meal of his life."

Danny looked round the kitchen. "Where's—"

"Don't even start." She glanced over her shoulder. "Ibby, fire one quail."

"One quail, Chef," he answered, without a hint of truculence. Ibby wanted this as much as she did.

Viv wiped the sweat from her brow with her towel and bent again over the plates at the pass. She had to focus.

The concentration paid off. It wasn't long before they'd found their rhythm and had begun to catch up. "Nailing it, Chef," Ibby called out as he passed her a sea bass with black garlic.

She didn't even notice Fergus come in. Looking back to take a plate, she saw him working the line with Ibby, quiet and efficient. He must have sensed what was happening.

"Chef." Straightening, she set down the tweezers and wiped her hands.

Fergus shook his head. "No. You keep on."

"But—" She stopped herself. He was right. A switchover at this point would disrupt the kitchen.

Danny came down the stairs himself again, his color high. "Table six. The veal."

"Shit." It was a new recipe she and Fergus had worked on together, a slow-roasted rump of veal with a white bean ragu. What if they hadn't got it right? Too late now. "Fire one veal," she called out, swallowing her nerves. "Any trips to the loo?" she asked Danny.

"Once, so far." Michelin inspectors never took notes at the table. They were rumored to take their notebooks into the toilet for quick between-course recording—although some supposedly had photographic memories. "He asked what I recommended," Danny added.

"Good job." She managed a smile. "Fingers crossed he goes with the tart for dessert." She and John had dreamed up a lemon-rhubarb custard tart that was a showstopper. The other option was a warm chocolate pot with pistachio toffee that Viv had thrown together that morning.

He chose the tart.

The kitchen did a quick round of high fives when the plate came back clean.

It wasn't until service was over that they all had a chance to dissect the evening.

"Was it the same bloke who came before?" Viv asked Danny.

"Yeah, I think so, wearing jeans this time instead of a suit. He's so ordinary. Forties, medium height, medium build, shortish hair. Very polite. Asked a couple of questions about the food, but not too fussy."

"Did he go back to the loo?"

"Once, yeah, and was in there a few minutes."

Ibby pumped his fist. "This could be it. The big one."

"If he's looking at us, he'll come back one more time," said Fergus. He'd gone upstairs and come back with the bottle of *twenty-five-year-old Glenfarclas he kept locked under the bar. Now, he gave it a wipe with the towel in his apron, and pulled the cork. "Gather round, children," he said, and they all held out a random assortment of cups and glasses.*

Viv watched him as he poured and they all raised their drinks in a toast. He was too bright, almost feverish, and she didn't like it. She knew about the coke, of course. It went along with the after-hours drinking and the leggy society girls who were slumming it a bit with the Irish chef. But she'd never seen him use during service, and she had a nasty suspicion that was what accounted for the missing half hour tonight.

When she looked up, he was watching her. "Viv, darlin', not celebrating? It's all down to you, you know, the evening's success." His tone was teasing, but the look in his eyes said he was not. Fergus O'Reilly knew he had lost it.

Viv raised her glass. They were watching her, Fergus and Ibby and Danny, Mikey and John, Magnus the kitchen porter and Geraldo the dishwasher. "It was a good effort tonight on everyone's part. But we can't coast on this. We were good but we can be better. If he comes back, Mr. Michelin, whatever his name is, we are going to have to raise our game. To O'Reilly's." She drank, and the whisky went down like fire.

Supper had been a casual affair. Addie had brought in cold meats and salads from the Daylesford farm shop, along with a selection of cheeses and fresh-baked baguettes. They'd served their plates from platters in the kitchen, then carried them through to the long table in the dining room.

"We can seat ten," Addie had told Gemma, "so nine is quite comfortable."

"Are you sure you want children in the dining room?" Gemma had asked, worrying about Charlotte and Toby's table manners.

"They'll be fine," Addie assured her, bringing Charlotte a booster cushion from the sitting room.

Gemma hated to admit how seldom they ate anywhere but the kitchen in their own house and vowed to do a better job of civilizing her children.

But in the end there was no worse damage than scattered bread crumbs, and no worse gaffes than Toby feeding a bite of something he didn't like to Polly the terrier under the table. Still, Gemma breathed a sigh of relief when it was time to clear up.

Everyone had been quiet during dinner, subdued perhaps by the events of the day, although Addie and Ivan had kept polite conversation going. Sitting across from Kincaid, Gemma watched his eyelids droop and his face become more drawn as the meal went on. "Go and take another one of your pills," she whispered to him as she helped clear the table, and it was rather to her surprise that he nodded and disappeared up the stairs.

All three of the Talbots waved off her offers of help with the washing up. "You need to get the kids settled," Melody told her, adding, "and besides, Dougie needs to make himself useful," earning her an offended look from Doug.

But Gemma was glad of the respite. She made sure the boys had everything they needed, then took Charlotte upstairs. They found Kincaid stretched out on the bed, still in his clothes and shoes, his eyes closed. "I'm just resting," he said, blinking and starting to sit up. "Ivan wanted me to have a drink."

"Nonsense. He's just being polite. And you have no business drinking alcohol with pain pills."

"I can just have a tonic or something to be sociable."

"Stay put while I get Charlotte ready for bed. Char, give Daddy a kiss. Gently."

Kincaid gathered Charlotte into his uninjured arm, murmuring, "Love you, sweet pea," into her hair.

By the time Gemma had got Charlotte into jammies, teeth brushed, and tucked into bed with her new Alfie book, Charlotte's eyes were closing. Kissing her, Gemma pulled up her covers and went back to check on Kincaid.

He was sound asleep. Carefully, she pulled off his shoes, then covered him with a spare blanket. He didn't stir. With a sigh, she sat beside him and smoothed the hair from the unblemished side of his brow. The bruising around the cut on his forehead was ugly, the skin beneath his eye beginning to darken. The stubble on his cheeks and chin looked patchy—he'd done a lousy job of shaving left-handed that morning—making him look even more disreputable.

In the few minutes she'd had to talk to him in the hall before dinner, he'd told her what he and Booth had learned at the hotel. "Was it Viv, do you think, that O'Reilly met in the garden?" Gemma asked.

Kincaid shrugged, then winced and touched his ribs. "There's too much we don't know. We can't even be certain it was a woman—the receptionist just said that was her impression."

"What about Nell Greene's cottage, then? Did you find anything there?"

"There was nothing to indicate she had any connection with

O'Reilly." Kincaid sounded irritated, as if she'd touched a nerve with the question. "She was just an ordinary woman living an ordinary life. Divorced. Maybe lonely. Making the best of things. She loved her dog."

"Well, if O'Reilly was here three weeks ago, who did he see if it wasn't Viv? Or Nell?"

"I don't have the foggiest idea." His tone was unnecessarily sharp.

Melody had called them to dinner then, but Gemma had been replaying the conversation ever since. Kincaid was unusually touchy. She could put it down to pain, or the shock of the accident. And maybe that was the case.

But Gemma knew her husband, and she would bet her life that there was more to it than that. There was something he was not telling her.

Somewhere along the river, a barn owl hooted. On the summer nights when Joe sat out on his small dock, he would see them swooping over the field across the river, their undersides glowing ghostly pale against the velvet darkness of the sky.

Tonight, however, he was huddled under the porch overhang, as close as he could get to the warmth generated by the wood stove in the cabin without actually sitting inside. The temperature had dropped with dusk and he could smell rain in the air. Another owl called. They were busy, hunting ahead of the storm. He wondered if the voles and mice scurrying in the field could sense their impending doom, or if it came on them only with the sudden flurry of wings.

Shivering, he sipped at his coffee, but it had gone cold. He'd made a pot, trying to counteract the whisky he'd drunk after Roz had left. When he'd found himself staggering, he'd mumbled, "Enough is enough," and tossed the dregs of his glass into the river. It would help nothing if he ended up falling in after them.

Now his head was beginning to clear in the cold air. There had to be a way to get himself out of this mess. Should he confess to Addie? God, how could he, after everything she'd done for him? He'd never meant to betray Addie's trust. But he hadn't known how to tell her about his family. Addie and Ivan had accepted him from the beginning for who he was—or at least who they thought he was. Would that change if they knew more? And if he didn't confess to skimming the funds, and Roz told Addie . . .

That, he couldn't contemplate. If Addie fired him, he had nothing. Nothing for himself, nothing for his mum, nothing to help his stupid little brother.

It all came down to Roz. Was his trespass worse than hers? Either way, they both had too much to lose. And Roz was frightened. Did that tip the balance in his favor?

He was going to call it a stalemate, for now. And he would do everything in his power to make sure it stayed that way.

The owl called again, near enough this time to make him jump. Lightning flashed in the distance, raising the hair on his arms. Blinking in the aftermath, he thought he saw something in the old elm across the river. It was the owl, and its white heart-shaped face was turned towards him, watching.

"Are you sure I can't give you a lift, Jack?" asked Viv, coming into the bar from the kitchen. The dining rooms were empty, floors mopped, tables set for tomorrow's morning coffee. Jack was wiping down the bar and racking the last of the clean glasses. She peered out the front windows. "I think there's a storm coming."

"I'll be all right, Chef." Jack's words were a little slurred. When Viv turned to study him, she thought he looked a bit befuddled. Jack wasn't teetotal, but it was unlike him to drink during service. Sometimes the customers would buy him a pint, but it usually sat unfinished on the bar. It was a cardinal rule of the restaurant business she'd learned early on—never hire a bartender who drank. Jack had never disappointed her.

"Are you all right?" she asked, frowning.

"Fine. I'm fine. Don't you worry, love. You should get some rest."

That was true enough. She was so knackered she wasn't quite sure how she'd got through service. Ibby had been right beside her the whole evening, filling in the things she'd missed. But he was gone now, having caught a ride to Moreton-in-Marsh with Angelica. Although Ibby had an old banger of a Toyota, that was his usual Saturday-night routine, staying with friends, then getting a lift back in time for Sunday service at the pub.

Bea had left as well, a half hour ago, saying she'd have a quick look in on Grace before she went home.

Still, Viv hesitated, loath to leave Jack. Loath to leave the pub, if truth be told. It looked safe, and ordinary, and familiar. It let her think that this day had been like any other day, that nothing in her life had changed.

"Go." Jack flapped a tea towel at her. "Don't fuss, Viv. I'll lock up."

"If you're sure . . ."

"I mean it. Out, now."

Viv summoned a smile. "I like it when you're bossy. See you tomorrow, then."

But when Viv stepped into the courtyard, she saw that it wasn't empty. Someone was sitting on the little stone bench by the cottage door. Her heart thumped. Then, as the figure rose, she saw that it was Bea.

"What are you doing here?" Viv whispered when they met in the middle. "You scared me silly." Then her quick relief turned to panic again. "Grace—is she all right?"

"She's fine. Sound asleep." Bea seemed to hesitate. "Viv. I never had a chance today. I just wanted to tell you that I was sorry. I know this must be hard for you." She enfolded Viv in an awkward hug—awkward, because Viv was a good deal taller, and awkward, because Viv could not let herself relax into it.

"Thank you. Really." Viv gave Bea's arm a squeeze and stepped away. "I don't think I want to talk about it just yet. And not with Grace. Don't say anything more to Grace."

"No, of course not. Sleep well, then."

As soon as Bea reached the car park, Viv let herself into the cottage. The television was still on, the sound muted. She went into Grace's room first. Grace lay on her back, the duvet thrown half off. Without her glasses and the frown that was becoming habitual, she looked like the child she had been. She still was a child, for a little while longer, Viv reminded herself. Pulling up the covers, she bent down, kissed Grace's soft hair, and whispered, "Sleep tight, pumpkin." She thought she saw Grace's lips move in a smile.

She went out, closing the door only partway, and stood gazing into the jumble of the sitting room. Fergus had asked to come in and she had refused him. She'd been angry at him, but she'd also been ashamed. Her furniture was secondhand and shabby. The prints on the walls were amateurish Cotswold watercolors, inherited from the previous tenant. Her cookbooks littered the coffee table and slid off onto the floor, along with Grace's discarded socks and shoes. The place was a tip.

Viv started to tidy up, then sank onto the sofa, her head in her hands. What sort of life had she made for herself, and for Grace? She worked all the time, and she was tired when she wasn't working. Would things have turned out differently for them if she hadn't been so bloody stubborn all those years ago?

And what if Fergus had known he was ill, when he'd finally searched her out, and then she'd turned him away? What had she cost herself? And even worse, what had she cost her daughter?

She pressed a hand to her mouth. The sobs came at last, silent and racking.

Melody made herself a hot drink in the kitchen, then carried it upstairs to the guest room she was occupying in lieu of her own room. She'd left Doug ensconced in her dad's study, talking about computers. Her dad, by nature, had always been a good listener. Her mum had gone up before her, half an hour ago.

The house felt quiet and yet alive, humming with the presence of its occupants, and Melody found it odd but comforting. She hadn't known what it would be like to have her friends here, had wondered if she'd feel too exposed, or if they would feel awkward. But even the children had fit in as if they belonged here.

Slipping off her shoes, she curled up on the bed and sipped her Ovaltine. That was certainly a childhood holdover, the hot drink, and a habit she seldom indulged in London. London . . . she didn't much want to think about London at the moment, or her real life.

When her phone dinged, she was tempted to ignore it. But of course she didn't. She picked it up and checked the incoming text. Andy. Again. He'd rung just at the beginning of the luncheon, when she'd had an excuse not to pick up. And later, when she'd been unloading the van at the pub, she couldn't have talked then, either. But when the house had calmed down after dinner and she might have managed a little privacy, she hadn't rung him back. He'd texted her since then but she hadn't responded.

How was she going to admit how hurt she'd been by the stupid photo Doug had shown her? But how could she talk to him and ignore the whole thing?

They were adults, after all, and neither had ever actually committed to an exclusive relationship. But Andy had told her from the beginning that there was nothing between him and Poppy, and she'd believed him. Had she been a fool? One of the things that had drawn her to Andy Monahan in the first place was his rejection of pretense. He was who he was, and he didn't lie about things.

Had he lied to her?

Another text came in. This one said simply "Please tell me what's wrong."

But she couldn't, not tonight. Even though she knew that the longer she put it off, the harder it would be.

The rain started just as Jack left the village behind, a spattering of drops at first, then a hail that stung his head and face like bullets. Hunching his shoulders, he pulled up the hood on his anorak. He should have taken Viv up on her offer of a lift, but he knew she was exhausted. That, and he hadn't wanted her to see how tipsy he was. He was ashamed of turning to drink out of weakness. The last thing he'd ever meant to do was let Viv down, but he hadn't been able to wipe last night's images from his mind. The man, O'Reilly, nursing his coffee. Nell, doing the same. In his bar.

And then there was the other image, the fuzzy one. He hadn't wanted to be alone with Viv, hadn't wanted to give in to the temptation to tell her what he thought he'd seen, not until he was certain. He didn't want to believe it himself.

The verges had dwindled away as he left the last houses of Lower Slaughter behind, so that now he was walking in the lane itself. But he took this route every night, along Copsehill Road north towards Lower Swell. His bungalow was not much more than half a mile, just before the first junction. He knew where the muddy patches were, and the thickness of the trees and hedges crowding in from either side at least gave him some cover from the rain.

When he heard the car coming, he automatically moved as close to the left-hand hedge as he could get. It was another few yards to a layby, but the back of his anorak was reflective so that even in the dark and the rain he should be easily visible. The car came round the bend in the lane behind him, the headlamps picking out the slanting raindrops and the glisten of the wet leaves in the hedge. The car had slowed and he was just about to lift his hand in a wave of thanks when the sound of the engine changed. It was revving up, the engine squealing with sudden acceleration.

Turning, he was shouting, "Slow the fuck do—" when the searing lights cut him off, blinding him.

The impact caught him by the side, threw him hard into the hedgerow, then into the road. He lay on his back, stunned. Looking up, he thought disjointedly how odd it was to see the falling rain from beneath, silvery in the light of the headlamps. The moisture was trickling down his neck, into his jacket. The car had stopped, but it was still running, he could hear the engine ticking over. A door creaked open. There was a swish of footsteps and a moment later a familiar voice said, "Oh my God. Are you all right?"

Jack tried to raise his head, tried to answer, but no sound came. He couldn't feel his legs.

A torch glared suddenly in his face, pinning him to the tarmac. Then the beam swung wildly. He felt a crushing blow, and darkness descended.

CHAPTER FOURTEEN

The rain had stopped sometime in the early hours of the morning. Mary Thompson avoided the worst of the puddles in the farm's yard. It was her turn on the altar guild rota at St. Mary's in Lower Slaughter and that meant a very early start. There had been a cold snap with the rain, and it was her job to turn the heaters on in the church so that by the time anyone turned up for the service, the church would be warm enough that they wouldn't shiver in their coats.

Her old four-by-four was cold as well. She huddled deeper into her fleece-lined jacket as she waited for the engine to catch. But it was a beautiful morning, she reminded herself, the first rays of the sun just catching the treetops, the clear sky a pale lemon yellow. Careful of the ruts at the end of the drive, she turned into the road and headed south towards the village. Water stood on the verges, and the foliage in the hedges drooped with the weight of moisture.

Mary settled into her seat as the car began to warm, enjoying the sense of being early abroad and owning the morning. The trees seemed to have turned overnight and when there was a gap in the hedges, she could see smudges of reds and golds in the distance.

She'd just switched Radio 4 to Radio 2 to fit her upbeat mood when she saw something at the side of the road. A deer, she thought with the first stab of dread. It happened. The deer darted out, and if whoever had hit this one hadn't sustained serious damage, they were lucky. But she couldn't bear wondering if the poor beast was still alive and should be put out of its misery. Worst case, she'd ring her husband and ask him to bring his hunting rifle. She glanced at the dashboard clock as she passed the huddled shape. It was still early—she could stop.

She pulled into the next layby and left the truck. The crisp air nipped at her lungs as she took a deep breath and started back up the road, walking fast, her boots squelching in the sodden fallen leaves. Something niggled at her. The shadows were still deep at ground level, but something about the shape hadn't looked right. Her unease grew as she rounded the gentle curve. Now that she could see more clearly, the shape looked more like a bundle than a deer—perhaps she'd been mistaken and someone had thrown rubbish into the hedge. But as she drew closer, she made out what looked like legs, canted slightly towards the road. And there, almost under the hedge—was that the pale blur of a face? Her stomach lurched. Dear God. Her steps slowed, then she shamed herself for her fear and stumbled the last few yards.

"Jesus Christ," she whispered, an invocation.

She didn't need to touch the body that lay before her to know that he was dead. The man's eyes stared heavenwards, sightless. And she knew him.

Colin Booth poured beaten eggs into the frying pan, adding a dash of cream and a few grinds of salt and pepper as he began gently stirring. The eggs would be cooked slowly, just the way his mum had taught him to make them. Bacon was draining on kitchen paper, the first lot of granary bread already in the toaster, coffee made, butter and jam ready. It was his Sunday routine, making breakfast for his wife and son. He'd been for a run, picking up a Sunday paper for Jessica on his way back. Humming along with something he vaguely recognized on Radio 2, he used his free hand to pull the plates from the warming oven. The eggs were almost there. He pressed the toaster lever.

"Lucas," he called to his son, who was sprawled on the floor in front of the television in the sitting room. "Two minutes. Tell your mum. And TV off."

"But, Dad, it's *Match of the Day*—"

"I know you're recording it. You can catch up after breakfast."

"But it won't be the same."

Booth sighed. His son was football mad. The eggs had reached the perfect, silky texture. Spreading the plates on the work top, he divided the eggs and bacon among them. He was about to step into the sitting room when he heard his wife's voice and then the television went blessedly silent.

Jess padded into the kitchen and slipped her arm round his waist. "Mmm. If you ever decide to give up policing, you can be my short-order cook."

"I already am your short-order cook." Kissing the top of her head, he handed her a plate, then nodded towards the sitting room.

"He's coming. Let him sulk for a bit. It will be his own fault if his eggs are cold." She put the hot toast in the toast rack and more bread slices in the slots while Booth poured the coffee.

"He's still upset about yesterday?"

Jess shrugged. "He made two goals. Of course he was disappointed that you weren't there."

"I'll take him out for some practice today." Booth had been football mad himself, had even dreamed of a professional career before a knee injury had sidelined him at sixteen. Sitting down across from his wife, he thought how much he liked the sight of her on Sunday mornings, in tracksuit bottoms and a T-shirt, her sandy hair falling loose round her shoulders, her freckled face free of weekday makeup.

"I was hoping he might pick up a game with some of the boys," she said with a grin that let him know exactly what she was thinking they might do in that eventuality.

Before he could respond, his mobile vibrated. "Oh, bloody hell." He reached for the phone where he'd left it on the work top, frowning when he saw the name on the ID. "It's Dr. Mason," he murmured to Jess as he answered.

"Colin." The pathologist's voice was loud in his ear. "Sorry to disturb you on a Sunday morning, but there's something I think you should see."

"Is this about O'Reilly?" he asked. He'd told Jess last night about the death of the chef they had both so admired. It was Dr. Mason who'd found the digoxin in O'Reilly's system and she had intended to test Nell Greene as well. "And the Greene woman?"

"Not exactly. You know I'm on rota this weekend. I got a call this morning to look at the victim of a presumed hit-and-run. The accident was less than a mile from your village."

"You mean Lower Slaughter?"

"Yes, but to the north, unlike Friday night's accident. Still, I thought three deaths in the same vicinity was a bit much of a coincidence."

Booth had lost all interest in his breakfast. "Are you at the scene?"

"Yes. I'm ringing from my car." She gave him directions.

"You said *presumed* hit-and-run. You don't think it was an accident."

"There are injuries that are inconsistent with those caused by the vehicle," Dr. Mason said carefully. "And there's another thing, Colin. The victim was the bartender at the pub where both of the Friday-night victims had their dinner."

Sunday-morning breakfast had been a haphazard affair in the Talbot household, with cereals, fresh fruit, and bread for the toaster set out so that everyone could help themselves. Melody's mother had left for the early service at St. Paul's, the church up the hill in Upper Slaughter. Ivan was sequestered in his study with newspaper business—his usual excuse when it came time to go to church. Gemma and Duncan had taken the children for a walk in the grounds.

Melody had managed a piece of toast, but a night of tossing and turning, waking up periodically to check her mobile, had left her without much appetite. Andy hadn't texted her again. Now she was regretting not answering his calls or texts yesterday, but she couldn't quite see how to apologize gracefully. With her second cup of coffee in hand, she went looking for Doug.

She found him in the sitting room, his laptop on the ottoman, two empty coffee cups rather precariously balanced on the arm of his chair. Unread Sunday papers were stacked on the coffee table and a small fire crackled in the grate. Through the French windows, she saw the tops of Gemma's and Duncan's heads traverse the view—they must be walking across the bottom terrace.

"What *are* you doing?" she said to Doug, a bit more sharply than she'd intended, but she was feeling cross, and for the first time that weekend, a bit territorial.

"Reading about Fergus O'Reilly." Doug looked up at her, apparently oblivious to her irritation. "The celebrity chef had fallen on hard times, I'd say." He glanced back at his screen. "His Chelsea restaurant won a Michelin star in 2007, but lost it the next year. Two years later, O'Reilly's closed. There were lots of tabloid reports of a wild lifestyle—drink, drugs, rock and roll, and models. Have a look."

Melody sank down on the sofa next to his chair as he turned the laptop screen towards her. The photo Doug had pulled up showed O'Reilly, wearing his trademark fedora, with his arm wrapped round a waif-thin, high-cheek-boned, pouty-lipped young woman. Melody's immediate impression, as it had been when she'd occasionally caught O'Reilly on television, was how extraordinarily good-looking the man had been. The curls and dimples might have looked feminine on another man, but with O'Reilly's strong bone structure had just made him more striking. For the first time, Melody had a real sense of the shock of this man's death.

"Then he partnered with a London restaurateur for a couple of years," Doug went on. "And after that, another venture on his own, reopening O'Reilly's in a new location in Hammersmith.

The reviews were only so-so. Two years later, O'Reilly's 2.0 went the way of its predecessor. Somewhere along in there"—Doug scanned the screen— "that would have been in 2010—there was a marriage. That didn't last much longer than the restaurant. And, then, a year after the divorce, his ex-wife died of a heroin overdose."

Melody grimaced. "Ouch."

"Very. Fergus O'Reilly disappears from the London scene for a while after that, although there's no indication that he was involved with his ex at the time of her death. I think he did some American food programs."

"Ouch again."

"Right. I'm not coming up with anything recent. If I were Booth, I'd contact O'Reilly's former partner, the restaurateur, fellow by the name of Colm Finlay. Another Irishman."

"I'm sure DI Booth will appreciate the suggestion." Melody's slight irony was lost on Doug, as she had thought it would be. "What's Finlay doing now?"

"He has a couple of successful West End restaurants." Doug named one in Kensington where they'd both eaten.

"So he's the real deal," said Melody, impressed, then added thoughtfully, "So in all this research you've been doing, have you come up with anything about Viv Holland?"

"Only connected to the original O'Reilly's. After that, nothing. No news items, no social media, not even a listing on LinkedIn."

"The pub must have some kind of Internet presence."

"Yes. And nicely done, too." Doug pulled up a page displaying the pub's flower-decked exterior, then clicked over to a dinner menu, presented against a background photo of the bar area, complete with sparkling glassware and its welcoming fire. "But Viv's name is nowhere on it."

Melody's coffee sat forgotten on the side table. "No one disappears that thoroughly unless they mean to. So, what—or whom— was Viv hiding from? O'Reilly? And if it was O'Reilly, how did he find her here? She—" The light dawned and Melody swore. "My mother. My lovely, interfering mother. I remember her saying Viv was reluctant to do the luncheon, but Mum thought her talent was unappreciated—obviously, we know now, as she was good enough to be cooking in a Michelin-starred restaurant. The invitation list wasn't public, but what if one of the guests knew O'Reilly and just happened to mention it, or mentioned it to someone who passed it on to O'Reilly . . ."

"Duncan told me last night that the hotel receptionist said O'Reilly was here three weeks earlier, just for one night. What if he came to see for himself?"

"That it was really Viv?" Melody stared out into the bright, sun-washed garden, visualizing it as it had been yesterday, full of guests and the buzz of conversation. "In which case, why wait until the day before the luncheon to turn up again? What if— You said his career had taken a dive. What if it wasn't Viv he came back to see? What if it was someone who was coming to the luncheon? Someone important. Maybe—"

"That's all very well, but—" Doug jabbed a finger at the screen. "You've just skipped over the big question. Assuming Viv was hiding from O'Reilly—and that's a big if at this point, but if that's the case—why?"

Melody stared at him. "Oh, well. Maybe he was violent. Maybe she owed him money. Maybe—"

Doug's mobile pinged with a text. "Bugger." He sounded annoyed, but pulled the phone from his pocket and tapped the screen. His eyes widened as he read the message. "Uh-oh," he muttered. Then, with a glance at Melody, he hastily put the mobile away.

"What is it?"

"Oh, nothing. Um . . ." He pushed his glasses up on his nose. "Bloke at the rowing club broke his ankle."

"There must be a lot of that going round, then." She gave a pointed glance at the ankle he had torn so badly when he fell off the ladder in his sitting room.

What on earth was he up to? she wondered. Doug Cullen couldn't tell a decent lie to save his life.

Doug looked mulish. "It happens." He closed the laptop with a snap. "Come on, let's go outside. Do your hostess duties and give me a proper tour of the garden."

"You look much better this morning," said Gemma as she and Kincaid stood at the end of the pergola, looking down on the lawns and gardens spread below them.

"Even with the shiner?" He touched a fingertip to his cheekbone, tentatively.

"It's not too bad. You could do the dissolute rock star thing and wear sunglasses to cover it up."

"Our friend Andy might not appreciate the 'dissolute rock star' description," Kincaid said with a grin.

Gemma squeezed his arm. "I'm just glad you're all right."

A gust of breeze sent a flurry of pink rose petals swirling down upon them. "Look, Mummy," called Charlotte, who had been skipping back and forth on the gravel path, singing to herself. "It's con-fitti."

"Confetti," Gemma corrected absently, still admiring the view. The rain had given everything a new-minted brightness and the air seemed suddenly ripe with autumn. The trees across the river seemed to have been brushed with gold and russet just since yesterday.

Toby and Kit had found a football somewhere and were kicking it about on the bottom lawn, watched by the two dogs, who looked like referees on the sidelines.

Squatting, Charlotte began gathering the petals. "I'm going to make you a present, Mummy. You can take it home." It was the first time they'd taken Charlotte to stay with strangers and she'd done remarkably well. Perhaps her separation anxiety was abating.

Gemma bent down to examine the petals filling Charlotte's small hand. "That's lovely, darling. We can make a sachet. But we'll need something to put your petals in." Fishing in her jacket pocket, she found a clean tissue. "How about this? We can wrap them up."

Kincaid had moved to the edge of the terrace. He stood, his hands in his trouser pockets, his gaze abstracted.

Going to him, Gemma said softly, "It is lovely here, isn't it? I didn't think I'd like it quite so much."

"You'd better not get too accustomed to the lap of luxury," he teased.

"It's not that—although I have to admit it is nice. It's just that I didn't expect the place to be so . . . I don't know. Relaxed, maybe. I will be glad to get home, though."

They'd decided at breakfast that Kincaid would stay another day to deal with any issues that might arise with the car insurance, and that Melody would run Gemma and the children to the train after Sunday lunch. Melody and Doug would drive back later in the afternoon in Melody's car. The Talbots had planned to stay another few days and had assured Kincaid that he was welcome.

"Ivan wants to take me to look at a car in the morning," Kincaid said now. "He says he has a friend who can make me a really good deal."

"Not on anything we can afford, if he's in Ivan's league." Gemma was horrified at the idea. "And we don't know yet what the insurance will pay on the Astra—"

"Don't worry, I won't do anything rash. But it only seemed polite to accept the offer. And we are going to need a car as soon as possible."

"Well, just don't—"

"Mummy," said Charlotte, running to her with the crumpled tissue, "I have lots of petals. What's a *sashay*?"

Gemma wasn't quite ready to tackle homonyms, so said simply, "It's something you put in a drawer to make it smell nice. Shall I keep your petals for—" Gemma stopped as Ivan stepped out onto the terrace.

"Is Melody about?" he called to them. He was holding one of the house phones and looking perplexed. As he came to meet them, he added, "Doug said she was going to take him round the gardens but she seems to have disappeared."

"I haven't seen her," Gemma said. "Can we help?"

"I've just had Viv Holland on the phone, ringing for Addie. She sounded quite hysterical. Something about her bartender being killed."

"What?" said Gemma. "Not Jack?" Kincaid gave her a surprised glance. "I spent half an hour with him yesterday," she explained. "He was feeling very bad about Nell Greene. What on earth happened?

"A hit-and-run, she said. She heard it from the woman who found him, apparently."

"So the police haven't been yet?" Kincaid asked, frowning.

"Not that Viv said. Since Addie isn't back from church, I thought Melody might go down and lend a bit of support."

"I'll go," Gemma said quickly.

"There's no need for you to do that, lass. You're our guest—"

"No, I want to go." Gemma couldn't quite wrap her mind round the fact that the friendly barman who'd insisted she try his special gin was dead. She wanted to know exactly what had happened.

The boys, pink-cheeked from exertion in the crisp air, had come up from the bottom lawn. Toby was examining Charlotte's petals, but Kit had come to stand with them.

"Well, if you're certain," said Ivan, not putting up much resistance. "I'll just give you a lift down."

"To the pub?" asked Kit, who'd missed the first part of the conversation. "Can I go, too? Grace texted and asked if I could walk the dog with her."

Gemma started to refuse, then thought that it might be a good idea for Grace to be otherwise occupied for a while. She'd explain the situation to Kit on the way. "Okay," she said. "If you're ready now."

Charlotte, sensing a disturbance, came and clung to Gemma's leg. "Mummy, I don't want you to go."

Gemma picked her up and kissed her cheek. "I'll be back soon. You stay with Dad, lovey."

She glanced at Kincaid, who nodded and took Charlotte's hand as Gemma let her slide to the ground, saying, "Come on, sweet pea, we'll find your mum some more petals."

Knowing Toby would protest, too, Gemma turned away, but not before she'd seen Kincaid slide his mobile from his pocket.

CHAPTER FIFTEEN

Booth picked up on the first ring, sounding irritated.

"It's Kincaid here." He could hear road noise in the background. "Sorry to bother you, but I thought you should know there's been another death associated with the pub in Lower Slaughter."

"The hit-and-run? The pathologist rang me. She's still at the scene and I'm on my way there now. How did you know?"

"Viv Holland called for Addie. Apparently she's in quite a state. The victim was her bartender."

"Bugger," Booth muttered. "I was hoping to break the news to her myself. You're still at the Talbots'?" When Kincaid confirmed it, Booth said, "I'm just coming into the village. Why don't I swing by and pick you up? I suspect you'll want to see this for yourself."

Kincaid agreed and rang off before he remembered that Gemma

had left him in charge of the children. Bloody hell. How could he have forgotten that? He'd felt odd since the accident—things he would ordinarily remember kept slipping from his mind. Now what was he going to do? He wanted to see the accident scene but he couldn't leave the kids unattended.

Charlotte had gone back to picking up rose petals, singing to herself, but Toby had been listening. "Where are you going, Dad? Mum said you'd watch a video with us."

"That's not exactly what she said," Kincaid corrected, but it had given him an idea. "Let's find Melody, shall we? Maybe there's something on the telly." He urged both children towards the house, Charlotte clutching her rose petals. Doug came out through the sitting room French doors. "Did Melody turn up?" Kincaid asked him.

"No. She said something about finding the gardener. Um, boss, I think maybe I've done something a bit stu—"

"Look," Kincaid broke in. "Could you do me a favor? You heard about the hit-and-run?"

"Ivan told me, yeah, when he was looking for Melody."

"Ivan's run Gemma down to the village, to see what she could do for Viv, and Booth's just said he'd pick me up on the way to the scene. Could the kids hang out with you for a bit?"

"Me?" Doug sounded as if he'd been asked to practice surgery.

Kincaid couldn't help grinning. "It's not hard. You had the boys on the train."

"Yes, but, Charlotte—I don't know what to do with a girl."

"I'm sure you'll think of something. I've got to go. Booth will be here any minute." He started to clap Doug on the shoulder, thought better of it when his arm protested. Was the pain getting worse? Probably just his imagination, he told himself, shrugging it off. He didn't have time for that now. "I'll owe you a pint," he told Doug. The children had run out to the lawn with the dogs, so he took his chance to escape, just murmuring, "Back as soon as I can."

Booth was already waiting in the drive, talking to Ivan, who'd returned from taking Gemma down to the village.

Ivan didn't ask questions, just nodded and said, as Kincaid got in the car, "Keep us informed, will you?"

When Ivan dropped Gemma and Kit at the Lamb, Gemma saw that although it had gone ten o'clock, the CLOSED signboard was still out in the car park. A disgruntled-looking couple in hiking gear passed them, muttering about wanting their morning coffee. Hearing voices from the courtyard, Gemma and Kit bypassed the main entrance and walked through the courtyard archway.

On the grass near the garden play area, Grace was putting a pretty black-and-white collie through obedience exercises. When the collie saw them and started to bark, Grace firmly put her back in a sit.

Viv, who was sitting on the kitchen steps, rose and came to meet Gemma as Kit went over to Grace and the dog. Viv looked hollow-eyed, even more exhausted than yesterday. Her bright, spiky hair had gone flat, and she hugged herself as if she had a chill. "Gemma, I wasn't expecting you. Grace said she'd asked Kit to walk the dog with her. I hope you don't mind me drafting him." She gave Grace a worried glance, and Gemma guessed that she hadn't told her daughter the news about Jack.

"Mark didn't want to leave the dog—that's Bella, Nell's collie—

on her own all morning. He thinks she's pining for Nell, and he had to help out a neighbor with a ram." Turning away from the kids, she said more quietly, "Ibby and Angelica and the servers are all late. I told Grace that's why we haven't opened yet. But I don't want her to be here when I tell them about Jack—" Her voice broke and she wiped trembling hands on her apron. "And Bea—Bea's in Cheltenham. She goes to church with her father. I texted her saying I needed help with lunch service. I didn't want to tell her over the phone. She should be back soon. I don't know what I'm going to do—"

"First things first," said Gemma. "Kit is happy to go with Grace and Bella, and I can certainly help with whatever needs doing. Or saying." Putting a light hand on the other woman's shoulder, she added, "Let's start with getting you a cup of tea."

"Yes, okay. Thanks." Squaring her shoulders, Viv led the way across the courtyard to the kids. Grace, who was demonstrating the dog's heel, looked happier than Gemma had seen her yesterday. "Listen, love, Kit's mum is fine with him going with you, but don't stray too far out of the village. And be—"

"*Careful*," Grace mocked her. Her frown returned. "Although I don't see what you think could be *dangerous* on a stupid walk. And Kit's grown up. I'm sure he doesn't need his mum to tell him what he can do."

Viv's face flushed. Before she could answer, Gemma said, "Sometimes he does, actually. But as we're not leaving until after lunch, a walk is fine. You two have fun."

Grace gave her a dirty look but turned her attention back to the dog. Kit gave Gemma a raised eyebrow, a look so like his dad's that it always shocked Gemma. "You go," she mouthed. "Tell you later."

"Come on, Grace," Kit called. "You can show me round." When the children had disappeared through the courtyard arch, Gemma gently turned Viv back towards the kitchen door and led her inside.

The kitchen smelled of roasting meat and vegetables and fat, a heady, mouth-watering combination that instantly took Gemma back to long-ago Sunday dinners cooked by her mum in the flat above the bakery in north London. Stainless steel bins held neatly prepped vegetables and garnishes, and pots of stock simmered on the big commercial cooker. Several delicious-looking cakes sat under glass covers on a serving counter.

"We do Sunday lunch," said Viv, "so I start even earlier than usual. But now— How can I— The staff will be here any minute and I have to— I don't know how I'm going to tell them—" She pressed a hand against her mouth, suppressing a sob.

"Right this minute," said Gemma, "you're going to have tea."

"But I—"

"Kettle. Mug. Teabags," Gemma directed. "Then we can sit for fifteen minutes and sort things out. You've had a terrible shock."

"Oh, right. Okay. If you're sure." Viv dabbed at her eyes with the hem of her apron, but she turned to the kitchen shelves, fetching an open box of Yorkshire teabags and a couple of chipped mugs. She filled an electric kettle, then turned to Gemma as it began to heat. "I'm so sorry about Grace being so rude. I know she's upset about yesterday—she was fond of Nell—but it's more than that. Lately, she's been so hateful all the time—I don't know what to do with her. And now I have to tell her about Jack. He was so good to her, you know. He has—had a grown daughter, so he knew how to talk to her—" Viv stopped, shaking her head. "I can't think what—"

"Tea first," Gemma interrupted. The kettle boiled and she poured hot water over the teabags she'd plopped in the mugs. When the tea had steeped for a couple of minutes, she added milk and sugar without asking. "Is there somewhere we can sit, just for a bit?"

Nodding, Viv led her, not into the bar area, for which Gemma was grateful, but into the smaller dining room behind Bea's office. As they sat at the nearest table, she said, "Grace is how old? Eleven?"

Viv nodded.

"Well, it's a hard age, isn't it?" Not that Gemma felt she could offer expert advice. Kit had been eleven when he'd come to them, true, but his circumstances, like Charlotte's, had been traumatic. And, besides, weren't girls supposed to be harder to deal with than boys at that age?

"Yes, but—" Viv cradled the blisteringly hot mug in both hands, as if it could warm her from the outside in. "I know kids start needing to assert their independence, but this seems different. And the last few weeks, she's seemed almost . . . I don't know. Sly." She sipped at the tea, making a face as it scalded her mouth. "I don't know. Maybe I'm imagining it all. But I do know that she's going to be devastated about Jack, and that she won't let me comfort her. And that she's going to blame me—and maybe she should."

"What?" said Gemma, startled. "Why?"

"He wasn't himself last night. He was drinking, and Jack didn't drink, not really. I offered to drive him home but he said he was fine. He wanted to walk. It was what he always did. And I didn't press him. I went in and checked on Grace and when it started to rain I didn't even think Jack might be getting soaked, and all the while—" Viv gulped at her tea, seeming not to notice the heat now, or the tears sliding down her cheeks. "All the while he must have been lying in the road and no one— If I had insisted on driving him—" Viv set down her cup and wiped a shaking hand across her cheeks.

Gemma reached in her pocket for a tissue and handed it to Viv. "You couldn't have known what would happen. You said Jack always walked home?"

Viv nodded. "He has a car, a little Renault, but he doesn't use it often. He says the walking keeps him fit. He's ex-army, you know."

Gemma found that didn't surprise her. And she couldn't imagine that Jack, even drunk, had not got out of the way of an oncoming car.

"What about family?" she asked. "Was he married?"

"Divorced for yonks. There's a grown daughter—lives somewhere up north. I don't even have a contact number—" Viv's face crumpled again.

"Don't worry about that now. The police can take care of it." Gemma thought for a moment. "Viv, if Jack's drinking was out of the ordinary, did he do or say anything else unusual last night?"

"No. He told me not to fuss. But—" She frowned. "He seemed, I don't know. Maybe worried. He—"

Viv broke off at the sound of car doors slamming in the pub car park. Footsteps crunched on the gravel and the kitchen door banged. Viv set down her mug, her face draining of color.

Ibby came into the dining room from the kitchen, his mouth set in a scowl.

"What the hell, Viv? It's after ten. Why aren't we open? Sarah and Jack were probably held up the same as us, but you could have managed serving coffee and bloody cake, if that's not too far below your high and mightiness. The police had the whole freaking road shut down and we had to go the long way round, can you believe it? You'd think they'd realize people had to get to—" The expression on Viv's face finally seemed to penetrate his tirade.

Ibby stared at them, glancing from Viv to Gemma. "Viv? What is it? What the hell's happened?"

"Your black eye is coming along quite nicely this morning," Booth told Kincaid as they drove down Becky Hill Road towards the village.

Kincaid smiled. "Thanks. You're not the first person to encourage me this morning. But I do feel a bit better," he added, although he was not sure it was true.

"I expect you look a damn sight better than the poor bugger they found in the road," Booth said, all levity gone. "I talked to him yesterday. Nice bloke."

Kincaid wished now that he'd gone into the pub and met the man himself. "Gemma spoke to him as well."

"Yes. Your wife has a knack for talking to people. A good cop, I think." Slowing as they reached the village, he glanced at Kincaid. "Did you meet on the job? If you don't mind me asking."

"We were partners," Kincaid admitted, a little ruefully. "Very un-PC of us. But the only thing I regret about it is not working with her on the job any longer. You're right—she has good instincts. And she's definitely the person you want on your side in a crisis." They were alongside the Lamb now. The village was already busy with walkers and tourists, but the pub car park looked ominously empty. "Addie was out when Viv Holland rang. Gemma's gone in her stead."

Booth whistled. "That was quick work."

"It sounded as if Viv needed some support."

Passing the pub and the church, they quickly left the outskirts of the village behind. Copsehill Road ran north and Kincaid had not been this way before. Glimpses of open fields to either side were quickly eclipsed by trees and hedges. The arching trees began to connect overhead, shutting out the crystalline blue of the sky. The light turned a leafy green and Kincaid had a hard time visualizing the road in the dark, in the rain. Spots of color appeared ahead— red traffic cones, just beyond a layby, and then the bright blue and yellow of a patrol car, pulled sideways across the lane. The uniformed officer standing beside the car came towards them as Booth brought the Volvo to a stop and rolled down his window.

"Sir, if you could just—"

Booth held out his ID.

"Oh, sorry, sir. Dr. Mason's expecting you. If you could just pull your car up there," he added, gesturing towards the wider spot.

When Booth had parked the car, they got out, Kincaid carefully avoiding the muddy pools at the road's edge. As they threaded their way through the cones and walked round a slight curve, Kincaid saw other vehicles, a mud-splattered Jeep and a mortuary van, parked on the verge. Beyond those, he glimpsed another patrol car blocking the road from the opposite direction.

A woman wearing a disposable paper overall came towards them. Middle-aged, square-faced, with alert brown eyes, she had obviously pulled the overall over her puffy jacket. She looked a bit like the Michelin Man. "Booth," she said, shaking his hand. "Sorry to roust you on a Sunday morning. Who's your walking-casualty friend here?" she added, turning her sharp eyes on Kincaid.

"Detective Superintendent Kincaid, from the Met. He was in the other car in the Friday-night crash."

"Ah. The friend of the Talbots." Kincaid must have looked surprised because she smiled. "News travels fast in these parts. Well, I'd say you were the lucky one in that collision. I won't ask you to shake—I can see that arm is plaguing you—but I assume you want to have a look at our victim as well."

Leading them to the muddy Jeep, she opened the rear hatch and pulled out the requisite paper suits and booties. Kincaid struggled getting his injured arm into the overall, but persevered, determined not to be kept away from the scene.

"Accident-investigation team not here yet?" Booth asked, steadying himself on the Jeep as he pulled on the paper booties.

"As soon as they finish the crash scene on the motorway. I came straight from there. Drug driving on a Sunday morning, I ask you. Driver survived, too, the idiot."

When they were ready, the doctor led them past the mortuary van, and for the first time Kincaid glimpsed the victim.

The man lay on his back at an angle to the road, his head nearest the hedge and lower than his torso. The back of his head and his shoulders were partially submerged by the rainwater that had pooled in the dips at the side of the road. Kincaid had to suppress the urge to move him to a drier spot—the man was past caring about the cold or the damp.

Sturdily built, the victim wore dark trousers and a dark anorak. One of his shoes—black rubber-soled lace-ups of the sort worn by people who stood on their feet all day—had come off and lay a few feet from the body. His socks, although both dark, didn't match.

Dr. Mason squatted beside the body and stretched out a gloved finger. "See here, just above the right knee? There's not much tearing to the trouser fabric, but his leg is broken, I'd say from the initial impact. Also, I suspect his pelvis is fractured."

"He turned towards the car as it came on?" Kincaid looked back the way they'd come, trying to work out the point of impact. Had the victim been thrown five feet? Ten? Taking a step back, he studied the tarmac. "There aren't any skid marks, unless they've been washed away by the rain."

"I'm not certain even last night's downpour would have completely washed away burnt rubber," Booth commented, having followed the direction of Kincaid's gaze.

"I'm inclined to agree," the pathologist said. "And there are also injuries to the back of the head that are consistent with our fellow's initial contact with the tarmac. However"—Dr. Mason moved, squatting again by the man's head— "this one is not." She pointed to an indentation at the top of the man's forehead. "There's no blood, of course. If he bled, it will have been washed away by the rain, and I'd guess that there wasn't much to begin with. His skull was fractured and if the blow didn't kill him immediately, he probably didn't live long afterwards."

Kincaid winced. The position of the blow to the bartender's skull was almost identical to the lump on Kincaid's forehead, but much easier to see as the man had kept his thinning hair buzzed short. A dapple of sunlight moved over the face of the corpse, giving it a sudden eerie animation.

"So what you're telling us," Booth said, straightening up, "is that someone deliberately hit this bloke with their car, then got out and bashed him in the head?"

The doctor shrugged. "It's possible that the driver simply didn't see him. Although"—she touched the anorak with her gloved fingers—"this jacket has highly reflective panels. It's also possible that he rolled as he fell and hit his head on a stone. But I think either scenario is highly unlikely. I think this is where he landed after impact. And then I think someone hit him on the head, hard." She stood to face them. "I think you're looking at a murder, Detective Booth. And a particularly brutal murder at that."

CHAPTER SIXTEEN

Wanting an excuse to grab a few minutes to herself, Melody had told Doug that she wasn't the right person to show him round the garden. He'd looked a little offended, but it served him right for being so squirrelly over whatever it was he was keeping to himself. Relenting, she said, "Seriously. Let me find Joe. He's the expert here. Mum likes to putter and read gardening books, but Joe's the one who puts in the hard graft." With that, she let herself out onto the terrace and surreptitiously checked her phone. There was nothing from Andy.

Damn. Was it too late to grovel? Did she even want to grovel?

Gemma and Duncan were out under the pergola with Charlotte, watching something the boys were doing on the lower lawns. Realizing that she didn't want to speak to anyone at the moment, she slipped quickly along the terrace and took the path to the glasshouse. She stepped inside, breathing in the warm, humid, humus-scented air. It was a comforting smell, dirt, and she'd often taken refuge here as a child. Of course, before Joe came, when the garden and glasshouse had been the domain of Old Ted, the place had been much less tidy and more suited to childish imaginings.

But Old Ted, who had let Melody push his wheelbarrow and bury things in his borders with her trowel, was living out his days with a sister in Bournemouth, and the garden, under Joe's care, had gone from a place pretty but rather ordinary to a showpiece, a stunning adaptation of a Gertrude Jekyll design.

Joe, however, talented as he was as a gardener and landscaper, seemed a bit of an odd duck. Several years ago, her mother had discovered him working at a garden center in Cheltenham, and after hiring him a few times for contract work through the nursery, had offered him a full-time job. Together, they'd hatched a plan to restore the gardens to their Edwardian glory. Once Joe had begun implementing the long-term plan for the ornamental gardens, he had tackled the derelict kitchen garden. Within a year, he'd been harvesting much more produce than the household could use, and he and her mum had decided to sell the excess to local restaurants. Melody thought it was about that time that Joe had asked her parents if he could fix up the old fishing hut, and in return her mum had offered to let him live there. That, Melody couldn't imagine. No electricity, no hot water, and heaven forbid, no Internet.

Leaving the glasshouse, she wandered down through the kitchen garden and, her curiosity piqued, took the path along the river. Even though the morning was warming nicely, when she reached the hut's clearing, a faint wisp of smoke drifted from the woodstove chimney. Otherwise, there was no sign of habitation, and she felt suddenly unsure of herself, trespassing on Joe's privacy. Although she often chatted with him when she came for weekend or holiday visits, she couldn't say that they were exactly friends.

Before she could either call out or change her mind, Joe came out onto the hut's porch and looked round, as if he'd sensed her presence.

"Melody. What are you doing here?" He did not sound pleased to see her. He was dressed in a woolly jumper so ancient it might have been Old Ted's, and his thick brown hair stood out like a thatch, obviously uncombed.

"I came to ask a favor." She took a few steps forward but stopped shy of the porch. "I didn't mean to intrude, especially on your Sunday morning."

"I do have a mobile, you know," he said, but then his shoulders relaxed a little and he added, "I don't suppose you have the number."

"No. Look, it wasn't important. I'll just—"

"No. I'm sorry. Didn't mean to sound a total shit. Had a bad night." He raked a hand through his hair, subduing it a bit. "I was just making some coffee. Why don't you come in and have a cup while you tell me what I can do for you."

"Thanks." Melody wasn't about to turn down a chance to see what he'd done with the inside of the place. In her granddad's day, it had been full of cobwebs, broken fishing rods, and disintegrating lawn chairs.

Following him, she saw a single wooden garden chair on the porch, a tartan rug thrown over its arm, and beside it, a pair of muddy boots that Joe seemed to have been in the process of cleaning with a palette knife. "I used to come fishing here with my granddad, when I visited my grandparents as a kid," she said. "But I haven't been here in years—Dad never having held a fishing rod in his life."

Although it was hard to tell through the beard, her little aside brought what might have been a smile from Joe as he held the door open for her. Her father, brought up in working-class Newcastle, not only abhorred golf, but had refused to take up the expected country pursuits of hunting and fishing.

"He comes down here sometimes," said Joe, surprising her. "For a drink. Likes the quiet. I keep a bottle of single malt set aside just for him."

Stepping into the single room, Melody inhaled the scent of fresh-ground coffee. There were no more cobwebs. A kettle simmered on a gas cookstove set atop a long waist-high wooden bench on one wall. Beside the cookstove sat a cafetière and a metal contraption that looked like an oversize pepper mill. "Oh," she exclaimed, when Joe twisted it open and dumped coffee into the cafetière, "it's a grinder."

"I'm not uncivilized," Joe said tartly.

"No, of course not." This was certainly obvious from her quick glance round the room. It was as orderly as any army quarters, but considerably more colorful. Crockery, utensils, and pots and pans were neatly stacked on the workbench, alongside straw baskets filled with just-harvested fruits and veg. There were apples and pears, a bowl of blackberries, cabbage and carrots and Brussels sprouts and broccoli, and a large butternut squash. She wondered how he could possibly cook all of it with such meager equipment.

A single bed on the opposite side of the room was covered with another bright tartan rug. There was also a copper tub with some sort of shower rig suspended over it, a sturdy oak table with two chairs, and in a niche created by two half-height bookcases, a toilet. A beautifully designed camping lantern hung from a long hook in the ceiling. "I'd say you have everything you need here. How does the toilet work?" she added, curious.

"Composting. That was my biggest expense, but it beats a chamber pot." Joe sounded as though her interest had thawed him a bit.

While he made the coffee, Melody perused his eclectic selection of books. There were at least half a dozen on Edwardian garden design, including one faceup on the top of the bookcase about the restoration of the Jekyll garden at Upton Grey in Hampshire. There were books on philosophy and history, and a good selection of classic novels. Most of the volumes looked secondhand. A small table at the head of the bed held a battery-powered lantern.

Joe, who she assumed was about her own age, had never said anything about his education. "Did you do a university course?" Melody asked, tracing the title on a quite nice volume of T. S. Eliot's collected poems.

Pushing down the plunger in the cafetière, Joe shook his head. "No time, no money. But my father taught history and philosophy in Czechoslovakia—as it was then. So books were always treasured in our house. And without electricity there's not much else to do here in the evenings," he added with another faint smile.

"It sounds quite idyllic. Waldenesque."

Joe poured the coffee into two stoneware mugs. "Not so much in the winter, when it's dark early and you have to sleep in your long johns. Milk?" he asked, holding up her mug.

"You have milk? Oh, sorry." Melody colored as Joe frowned. She'd offended him again.

"Of course I have milk." He reached under his work top and lifted the lid on an insulated cool box, pulling out a glass bottle of milk, organic, with cream on top, which, at her nod, he poured into her coffee.

"I keep the ice blocks in the freezer at the house," he said with a shrug. "So I'm not really all that self-sufficient. I charge my mobile there, and do most of my washing."

Melody took the offered mug. "Self-sufficient enough, I'd say." Melody cringed at the thought of her life, filled with ready meals and takeaway. She really must make more of an effort. But it was hard on her own—although apparently not all that hard for Joe— and the "on her own" brought her round again to Andy.

"Thanks," she said quickly, cradling the mug in her hands and inhaling the steam rising from it. Searching for a change of subject, she said, "I didn't see you when I was here the last time, in August. Mum said you were on holiday. Where was it—Prague?"

This only earned her another frown. "Yeah. Near there. My mum insisted we visit some long-lost relatives, when I should have been here. Too much to do in the gardens that time of year."

Leaving his drink on the workbench, Joe picked up one of the chairs and nodded towards the porch. "Let's sit outside. It's too fine to be in, and these days won't last." There was an elegiac note in his tone. Melody picked up his cup and followed him, intrigued.

She supposed she could understand, she thought as she sat beside him and gazed at the sun sparkling on the river, how the loss of these golden autumn days could seem like a personal depri-vation.

When Melody had tasted her coffee, which was delicious, Joe said, "So what can I do for you?"

"Well, you've given me a respite, for starters," she said with a smile. "And I really don't want to intrude on your time, but my friend was wanting a tour of the garden, and I thought you were certainly better qualified than me."

"Harry Potter?"

Melody grinned. "Doug. Yes. I'm the one got him started on the gardening thing, so I feel responsible."

"I thought you didn't garden?"

"I don't. I live in a mansion block. But Doug, he'd bought a little house in Putney with a derelict back garden. And things were sort of rough for him last spring, so I thought . . . you know, it would be therapy. But it's turned into a bit of a monster."

"That happens." A glance at Joe's face told Melody it had been said in all seriousness. "But there are worse things," he added. "Your friend—he seems all right for a— Oh, shit, sorry. I didn't mean—"

"For a nerd, you mean?" Melody felt comfortable enough now to tease him. When Joe's mouth relaxed, she wondered what he would look like without the beard. Better, in her opinion. But she supposed shaving and the rustic life didn't go all that well together. "For a cop, yeah, Doug's a good guy. Even though he's a pain in the arse sometimes."

"Your other friends—they're cops, too?"

"Yes. Gemma's my boss."

Joe sipped his coffee and Melody waited, wondering where he was going with this.

"Did you know who this bloke was, the one in the car crash? Did Viv really work for him?"

"A long time ago, apparently."

"I didn't want to put my foot in it, when I talked to her."

"You're friends, you and Viv?"

"Well, yeah. We work together all the time, with the produce for the pub. But I had no idea she'd ever worked in that sort of a restaurant, or with somebody famous."

"I got the impression that no one else knew, either, if that helps."

"Yeah. Thanks. Did Viv say what the guy was doing here?" Joe rotated his mug with his long fingers.

"Not that I've heard."

Joe nodded, as if she'd given him a positive answer rather than a negative one. Finishing his coffee, he stood. "If you'll tell your friend I'll be up in a few minutes, I just need to clean up a bit."

Realizing she'd been dismissed, Melody finished her coffee and stood, too. "If you're certain—"

"Yeah. No problem."

"Well, okay, thanks. See you, then." Feeling awkward, Melody stepped off the deck, then raised her hand in a little wave as she turned away.

"Melody?"

She turned back.

"You won't say that I asked about him? O'Reilly? It's just that I wouldn't want Viv to think I was . . . putting my nose where it didn't belong."

"No. Of course not," Melody said, but all the way back to the house, she wondered why Joe didn't want to ask Viv himself.

"Where are we going?" Kit asked, shortening his stride to keep pace with Grace as they walked back through the village.

"I don't know—you'll see," Grace mumbled, keeping her eyes on the dog. Rather than staying on the road towards Beck House, she turned left at the little roundabout across from the mill.

Kit was beginning to regret agreeing to this. He glanced at the girl beside him, her frizzy hair pulled up in a lopsided ponytail, her shoulders hunched, her eyes still on the ground. Her face looked puffy from the crying she'd done yesterday. Maybe she'd been upset enough over the lady dying in the car crash to excuse her being so rude to her mum, but he'd certainly never get away with that.

Grace had released the dog from her heel, and now she ranged out in front of them, sniffing back and forth at the hedgerows and threatening to tangle them in her lead. The lane was barely wide enough for two people to walk abreast. The sun was warm and Kit began to wish he hadn't worn his hoodie. Bees buzzed in and out of the blackberry brambles and the air smelled ripe and green.

"So, how much obedience training has Bella done?" Kit asked, breaking a silence that felt increasingly awkward. "I did trials with my terrier, Tess. She's a rescue."

"It wasn't official training, like classes or anything," said Grace. "Just basic stuff. Mark was helping Nell teach her to herd."

"Mark? Who's he?"

"Bella was one of Mark's puppies," said Grace, as if Kit were dumb for not knowing. "Mark breeds herding collies, really good ones. They win sheep trials and everything. Nell bought Bella from Mark when she moved here. It's Mark who's keeping Bella now, until . . ." Grace's voice quavered. "Until someone decides who she belongs to."

"Nell didn't have any family?"

"Some niece who lives in Australia or something."

Bella was forging ahead, pulling Grace along on the lead now. When Grace gave her the heel command, the dog only pulled harder. Grace started jogging to keep up.

"Do you want me to take her?" said Kit, worried the dog was going to pull Grace down. He was running now, too.

"No, she just—" was all Grace managed as the collie pulled her off the road and through an open gate. Kit saw a thatched cottage, set back from the road.

"Bella, stop!" Grace shouted. With both hands wrapped in the lead, she managed to bring the dog to a stop. The collie panted and whined even as Grace reached down and unclipped her. Bella shot towards the cottage and began barking at the door. "She just wanted to go home," finished Grace, panting as well, hands on the knees of her ripped jeans.

"This is Nell's cottage?" Kit wasn't at all sure this was a good idea. Bella seemed frantic now, running back and forth along the front of the cottage, then bolting round towards the back. Running after her, they found her pawing at the kitchen door.

"She needed to see there was no one here for her. She's got me now."

"I thought Mark was taking care of her."

"That's just because she belonged to him once. He won't want to keep her for good." Grace sounded mulish again.

"Well, right now, Bella's really upset." Taking the lead from Grace, Kit walked slowly towards the dog, saying, "Hi, Bella, you're a good girl," in a singsong voice. He took a few more steps. "Shh, that's it, you're a really good girl, everything is going to be okay."

Bella stopped pawing at the door and looked at him, but she was still panting and wild-eyed.

"Shh, that's it, that's a good girl." When Kit was almost within touching distance, he said, "Bella, sit," in his dog-training voice, and she did. Another step and he slipped his fingers round her collar and clipped on her lead. Dropping to his knees, he stroked her head and murmured to her until he felt her relax. "Okay, then," he said, standing and patting his leg. Bella moved into place by his knee. "Let's go," he said to Grace.

"She'd have been okay," Grace muttered as they walked back towards the lane. "She'd have given up and she wouldn't have wanted to come back here anymore."

"Maybe," Kit said, not wanting to argue with her. "But right now I think we should take her back to the pub."

"Can we go just a bit farther? I don't want to go back. And there's something cool I was going to show you."

Kit considered as they reached the lane. The dog seemed calmer, and Grace hadn't asked him for the lead back. "Okay, but let's not go too far. We're supposed to be going back to London after lunch."

"Okay." Grace gave a little skip, curiously childlike for some-one who was trying to be so grown up. As they walked on, the lane began to climb and the sun grew warmer. Kit was ready to say it was time to turn back when Grace stopped and pointed at a barred gate on the right. "That's Mark's farm, through there. It's really big."

Beyond the gate, a drive crossed a deep rill carpeted with fallen leaves. Trees arched overhead, forming a tunnel that after a few yards opened up to a green field and farm buildings of golden

Cotswold stone. Bella's ears had pricked up again and he hoped they weren't going to have a repeat of the scene at Nell's cottage. He tightened his grip on the lead. "I really think we should—"

"No, wait. Just a little bit farther." Grace walked on up the lane and stopped after a few yards. There, an impenetrable hedge gave way to another barred gate, and beyond it Kit could see a field. "Look, here," said Grace, pointing to a hollow under the gate. "We can go over and Bella can go under."

"But that's somebody's field."

"It's Mark's, actually. And he doesn't mind. The sheep are all in the other pastures just now. We can cut across and pick up the public footpath."

"And that goes back to the village?"

"Well, yeah, obviously. Along the river."

"Okay, then," agreed Kit, happy not to take Bella back past the cottage. Grace climbed over the gate and he followed, holding tight to Bella's lead, then urging her through the muddy dip under the gate.

They crossed the field at an angle, managing another gate on the far side the same way they'd done the first. "See, the footpath," Grace said, leaving him to manage Bella as she slid down a steep bank. "And there's the river."

Kit and Bella scrambled after her. He would have called it a stream, he thought as he looked round, but she was right. It crossed under the path, then ran bubbling along on their left. The water was shallow and so clear it reflected the trees overhead like glass.

"It's the River Eye. It used to be spelled E-Y, not E-Y-E. It runs into the Windrush and the Windrush runs into the Thames, so this water ends up in London. I like to think about that." She glanced at him as they walked along. "What's it like, living in London?"

Surprised, Kit said, "It's okay, I guess. But I used to live in a village a lot like this and I liked it, too."

"Why did you move?"

Kit really didn't want to answer this, but after a few minutes, he said, "My mum died. I went to live with my dad."

"Did you know your dad before?"

"No. I didn't."

"Were they divorced or something, your mum and dad?"

"Well, yeah, they were, but it was . . . complicated." There was no way Kit was explaining any further.

"So Gemma's your stepmother?"

The question always took Kit aback. He didn't think of Gemma that way—what did "step" mean, anyway? It somehow made their relationship seem like second best, and he didn't think Gemma loved him any less than she loved Toby. Or Charlotte, and Charlotte wasn't related to Gemma or his dad. "Yeah, she is," he answered at last.

Picking her way ahead of him along the track now, Grace said over her shoulder, "You're lucky, then. Gemma seems nice."

"She is," Kit said, puzzled. He'd thought that conversation was finished. "Why would you think she wasn't?"

"Because." Stopping on the narrow track, Grace bent down and picked up a flat stone. "My mum isn't." She threw the stone at the water so hard that the splash sprayed them both.

When the accident-investigation team arrived, Kincaid, Booth, and Dr. Mason left them to their measuring and photographing and walked back to Mason's Jeep.

"So, what are we looking for in terms of a vehicle?" Booth asked the doctor as they started peeling off their paper suits.

"Well, obviously I'll have to do some measuring as well. But from initial observation, I'd say something with a fairly high clearance—an SUV or a four-by-four, or possibly even a van. I'll know more when I've got him on the table, so don't quote me on that."

"That's three-quarters of the county right there," Booth muttered.

"And the blow to the head?" Kincaid asked, making an effort not to touch his bandaged forehead.

"There, you've got your classic blunt object, I'm afraid." Dr. Mason took their paper overalls and booties and wadded them up in a ball, which she stuffed in a rubbish bag in the back of the Jeep. "Again, I'll know more when I get some measurements from the impact site on his skull. I do have something for you, though, Colin. Your female victim in Friday night's accident, Nell Greene, did not have any digitalis in her system. Or anything else toxic that I can find."

"Then what—"

"She had a ruptured aorta from the collision. Nothing could have saved her. Until she ran into your car, Mr. Kincaid, she was a remarkably healthy woman."

Nell Greene's imploring face, in those moments as her life slipped away, was imprinted in Kincaid's memory. She'd had a new home, a dog, friends, and an expectation of a long and productive life. He realized that he had to know if all that had been taken from her by anything other than the purest chance.

"I'll ring you, Colin," Dr. Mason continued, "just as soon as I can get to this one. Nice to meet you, Mr. Kincaid. If I were you,

I'd have those injuries looked at." She nodded briskly at them and climbed into her Jeep.

Booth and Kincaid watched as she backed skillfully up, made a U-turn in the narrow road, and drove off towards Lower Slaughter.

Gemma poured boiling water into an ancient Brown Betty teapot that Angelica had rooted out of a cupboard for her. This was the second—or was it the third?—pot she'd filled in the last hour. The capacity of people in a crisis for hot tea never failed to amaze her, but she was happy to oblige. She'd been the one to break the news to Ibby and Angelica. Viv hadn't managed to get out more than Jack's name before she'd pressed her hands to her mouth again, shaking her head.

Ibby, after a shocked "You're shitting me," had sunk down in the chair next to Viv. It had been Angelica who'd rallied and organized more tea, even though she was red-eyed and sniffing.

Putting the kettle back on the cooker, Gemma touched Angelica on the shoulder. "Are you all right? I can manage here if you want to go have a sit-down."

"No. No, I'm fine. Well, I'm not fine, but it's not often I have a chance to see Ibby speechless." Her laugh turned into a half-choked sob. "Jack would have thought that was bloody hysterical." She pulled a sheet off the kitchen roll and blew her nose before refilling the milk jug. "I just can't believe he could be so stubborn or so stupid." Turning a red-rimmed gaze to Gemma, she said, "If there was one thing Jack wasn't, it was careless."

"Do you have any idea what was bothering him yesterday? Viv said he seemed distracted."

Angelica shook her head again. "No. He liked Nell. Of course he was upset, wasn't he? We all were."

"When I spoke to him yesterday, he said something about a row."

"Oh, that." Angelica picked up the steeping pot. "Fergus bloody O'Reilly. I cannot believe I've worked here for going on three years, and Viv never said a word about working with him. I mean, I knew she and Ibby had worked together in London, but anything more you asked either of them, they just clammed up."

She set the pot down again and looked at Gemma, her face pink with emotion. "Honestly, sometimes I wondered if it had been a really crap restaurant, something they were ashamed of. Except that they're both too good. In which case, why the hell are they working here?"

That, thought Gemma, was a very good question. But before she could say so, her phone rang. Excusing herself when she saw it was Kincaid, she stepped out into the yard to answer.

"We're on our way to the pub," he said without preamble. "Or we will be, as soon as Booth finishes organizing uniform. The pathologist says the hit-and-run was deliberate. And that someone then bashed the victim over the head to make doubly sure he died. I thought you would want to be forewarned—but probably better not to steal Booth's thunder."

"Right." Although she couldn't have said why, Gemma found that she was not all that surprised. And she agreed—she couldn't break that news to the group assembled in the dining room. Then she thought of Kit, and Grace. "Got to go," she told Kincaid. "I'll explain later."

Ringing off, she punched in Kit's number and held her breath until he answered. "Listen, love," she said hurriedly, "I can't explain right now, but can you keep Grace out with you for a while longer? Maybe take her up to the house?"

"Um, I'm not sure . . ."

"Please try. Your dad's coming with DI Booth, and she doesn't need to be here."

"Oh, yeah, sure, that'll be fun," Kit said with studied casualness, and she knew he'd understood. No one knew better than Kit that bad news should be broken gently to a fragile eleven-year-old.

CHAPTER SEVENTEEN

Ignoring the CLOSED sign, Kincaid and Booth let themselves into the pub by the main door. In a small dining room off the lounge they found Gemma, Viv Holland, and two people Kincaid hadn't met, a thin man with a forbidding expression, and a slightly stocky, pink-cheeked woman. Kincaid put both in their midthirties, and from what he'd heard from Gemma and Melody, he guessed they were the other cooks, although they were still in street clothes. From the expressions of all three he could tell that they were shocked and upset, but Gemma's slight shake of the head indicated that she had not told them the worst news.

Gemma stood to greet them. "Inspector Booth. Duncan, you've met Viv. This is Ibby, and Angelica. They work in the kitchen." She touched Kincaid's arm. "This is my husband, Duncan Kincaid." Angelica stood to shake his hand, while Ibby gave him only the barest of nods.

Taking a chair, Booth said, "Miss Holland. I think you've all heard that Jack Doyle died last night, struck by a vehicle as he walked home."

Nodding, Viv pressed her lips together tightly in an obvious effort to contain their trembling. "I can't believe—"

"Some bastard," broke in Ibby. "Some bastard just knocked him down and drove on? How could anyone do that? How could—" He stopped, blinking.

"Miss Holland," said Booth, "is the rest of your staff not in yet?"

"No," she whispered, then cleared her throat and said more strongly, "No. Most of them come from Moreton or Stow by the back road. I suspect they're held up by—by—" She couldn't finish.

Kincaid had not sat when Booth did, but had instead stepped back a pace. He stood where he could see them all, cradling his injured hand with the good one. Although the day had been warming nicely, it was cold inside the pub, and he suspected Viv had forgotten to switch on the central heating. From his vantage point, he could glimpse the hearth in the lounge bar's great fireplace, cold, and still clogged with yesterday's ash. He could see, though, that under other circumstances the pub would be a cheerful and welcoming place.

"And Bea," Viv went on, "Bea goes to church in Cheltenham. I haven't told her yet . . ."

"Yes, I can understand that," Booth told her, with a gentleness Kincaid hadn't seen before. "But I'm afraid that when she does arrive, you're going to have even worse news for her. We believe that Mr. Doyle was run down deliberately."

"What?" Viv just stared at him, her face blank.

Ibby sat forward in his chair, his fists clenched. "What do you mean, 'Run down deliberately'? That's bollocks."

"I mean that the scene of the accident and Mr. Doyle's injuries are consistent with a deliberate assault by a vehicle." Booth left out, Kincaid noted, the blow to the head.

"But you must be mistaken," whispered Angelica. "No one would want to hurt Jack."

"It's highly unlikely that a deliberate hit-and-run was random, I'm afraid, Miss Lockhart. Do any of you know why someone would have reason to harm Jack Doyle?"

All three chefs shook their heads, but Kincaid thought he saw a slight hesitation in Viv's face.

"He was working here at the pub last night?" Booth asked.

Viv found her voice. "Yes. Yes, it must have been close to midnight when he finished up in the bar. I told Gemma, I offered to drive him home but he insisted on walking even though it was coming on to rain. He always walked."

"Did he say or do anything unusual before that?"

Glancing at Gemma again, Viv said, "He was—he was drinking, which wasn't like him. But he didn't say anything. I just assumed he was upset about Nell Greene."

"Were they friends?" Kincaid asked, wondering if they had missed something here. The bartender and Nell Greene would have been about the same age, both single, both apparently divorced.

Frowning, Viv said, "Well, not outside the bar, I don't think. But he always made a special effort to chat with her when she came in. Maybe he would have liked . . ." She trailed off, as if processing the idea that Jack's attention to Nell might have been more than professional. "Bea would know better than me, since she's front of house."

"Who would have known that Jack walked home after closing?" Booth asked.

"Everyone who came in regularly," Viv answered. "He liked to tell people that it stretched out the kinks from standing all day."

"Were you the last to see him, Miss Holland?"

Viv nodded, tearing up again. "We closed up together." Gemma, who was sitting beside her, gave her arm a comforting squeeze.

Booth took a notebook out of his jacket pocket and Kincaid sensed the atmosphere in the room change. Everyone sat up a little straighter, their eyes fixed on Booth.

"I'm going to have to ask you all where you were last night," Booth said, pen now poised over an open page.

Viv answered first. "I was here. After Jack left, I checked on Grace—that's my daughter—then I went to bed."

"You live on the premises?"

"In the cottage across the courtyard."

Booth made a note, then looked up at the other two.

Angelica spoke first. "Ibby and me went to Moreton. Usually on Saturday nights, Ibby stays with my partner and me in town. We go out, have a few drinks. We must have left right before Jack—he was just finishing up in the bar. If we'd given him a lift—"

"What kind of car do you drive, Miss Lockhart?" Booth asked.

"A VW Golf."

Booth looked at Ibby. "Do you confirm this, Mr. Azoulay?"

"Yeah. I don't drink-drive. That's really messed up. Me and Angie had a few beers with one of the chefs there in Moreton, then I kipped on Angie's sofa."

Spots of color had appeared in Viv Holland's cheeks. "You can't think that Angie or Ibby had anything to do with what happened to Jack. That's ridiculous—"

"We just have to eliminate them—and you—from our inquiries, Miss Holland," said Booth. "I take it the van in the courtyard belongs to you?"

"Yes."

"Do you own another vehicle?"

"No," Viv said, her voice still clipped with anger.

Booth made a notation, then slipped his notebook back into his pocket. "Thank you. I will need to speak to all of your staff when they come in. You must realize this is a very serious mat—"

A car door slammed loudly and a moment later the pub door flew open and Bea Abbott came in. "Viv! What is going on? We should be serving morning coffee—" She stopped, taking in the group huddled in the otherwise empty dining room. Then, as she fixed her gaze on Booth, she paled. "Oh my God. What's happened now?"

Booth persuaded Bea to sit down while he told her what had happened. She simply stared at him and shook her head. Dressed in a dark skirt and a floral blouse, her hair loose, she looked softer, more vulnerable. Finally, she said, her voice raspy, "You must be mistaken. Everyone loved Jack. I can't believe someone wanted to hurt him." When her eyes filled with tears, Gemma went to the kitchen to make yet another pot of tea.

When she returned with the pot and more cups, Booth had his notebook out again.

"A Fiat," Bea was saying. "I drive a little Fiat runabout."

"And where were you last night?" Booth asked.

"Home. Jack was still finishing up in the bar, so I left Viv to lock up. If only I'd—"

Whatever she'd meant to say was cut off by loud voices and the excited yipping of a dog coming from the car park.

Grace burst through the door, hair disheveled, glasses askew. Right behind her was Kit, with the collie, Bella, beside him.

"Why are you trying to keep me away?" Grace shouted at her mother. "What have you done now?"

Viv rocked back in her chair as if she'd been slapped, then stood and went towards her daughter with her hands outstretched. "Grace, love, I didn't want you to be upset. There's been an accident."

Grace stepped backwards, away from Viv, almost treading on Kit, who was trying to quiet the panting dog. Catching Gemma's eye, Kit mouthed, "Sorry."

"What do you mean, an accident?" Grace seemed to take in the presence of the others, and of Booth, in his official-looking dark suit, and she suddenly looked more frightened than angry.

"It's Jack, love," said Viv. "He was hit by a car last night. I'm so sorry. I didn't want to tell you."

"You mean he's . . . dead?" Grace must have seen the answer in all their expressions. Her face crumpled and she began to cry, little hiccupping sobs. "It's your fault," she managed to gasp at Viv, then the sobs grew to a keening wail.

Gemma was on her feet, but Bea was quicker. She reached the girl in two strides, wrapping her arms round her and turning her towards the door. "Let's get you home," she murmured to Grace. "You'll be all right, love." Kit, who'd managed to calm the dog, stepped out of their way as they went out.

Viv sank back into her chair, looking utterly defeated.

July 2007

"Irish?" Fergus had said when she'd put it to him. "You have got to be taking the mickey. No decent chef does Irish. It's all pubs with Guinness and bloody leprechauns."

"So, we can do Irish fine dining. Call it British-Irish if that helps. You can't tell me there's not cooking being done in Ireland at that level," Viv insisted. They were sitting in Fergus's tiny office, having been the last to finish scrubbing down the kitchen after that night's service. She'd been doing her homework the last few weeks, studying recipes, checking sourcing, wanting to have all her ducks in a row before she suggested this.

"Well, no, but . . ." He stretched his long legs out under the two-top from the dining room that passed for his desk, seemingly unaware that his feet were touching hers.

Sensing him wavering, she'd gone on, trying to keep her excitement in check. "We can get wild Irish venison. I've checked. We can get Irish beef, Irish fish and scallops. And we could source the very best veg locally, but add an Irish twist to the recipe. Why couldn't we make the most divine potato and leek soup that anyone's ever tasted? Why not make soda bread the house bread? We could make lamb sausages, smoke Irish trout. All with gorgeous presentation."

"Mmm." Fergus still hadn't been convinced. "But why should we do this? The kitchen is clicking. We've got a reputation to maintain now. Why should we take that sort of risk?"

He was right about the kitchen, Viv knew. They'd found their rhythm over the last couple of months. They were turning out better food, and doing it consistently. But all that made her more determined. Sweating a little because she was still in her whites and it was stifling in the little room, she said, "So how many restaurants in London are doing a menu like ours and doing it well?" When Fergus frowned, she went on, encouraged. "A dozen, at least. If we want to stand out, we've got to be just that bit different."

The frown was still there—it still surprised her that frowning made his dimples deeper. "Not sure I want to be reminded of Ireland every day of my life," he said. "It wasn't exactly fun and games, you know, in those days." He seldom talked about his boyhood in Belfast.

"You must have some good memories of food, though, growing up," Viv ventured, hoping to bring him back from whatever he was seeing.

"Baked beans on toast for tea every night?" Fergus countered, focusing on her, but there was a hint of laughter in his voice now.

"What about Belfast? There must have been something good in the restaurant there. It held a Michelin star for years." She knew he'd started as a kitchen boy in the best restaurant in Belfast, before he moved to London.

"Family meal," Fergus said, grinning now. "I didn't care what it was as long as there was plenty of it. Growing boy." He studied her. "You're not going to give this up, are you, darlin'?"

Viv shrugged, pressing her lips down on a smile and suspecting that just made her look prissy.

"I can see it now. You'll give me no peace, woman. We'll start with one thing, and we'll see where that takes us. Deal?"

"Deal." Viv did her best to sound casual, then ran into the staff toilet and did a fist pump. It was going to be brilliant. She knew it.

The weeks flew by. They tested recipes at night, after service, staggering into work hollow-eyed in the mornings. They worked

*all day in the kitchen on Sundays, when the restaurant was
closed.*

*They made Caesar salad with Cashel Blue cheese. They made
Irish lobster confit in Kerrygold butter. They made black pudding
the way Fergus remembered it from his childhood, and lamb sausages so delicate they almost melted in your mouth. Everything
they put on the menu got raves.*

*The leggy models grew few and far between, as Fergus had
no time to accommodate them. Viv would never have admitted
to jealousy, although she did allow herself to think that in
spite of the workload, Fergus seemed healthier. There'd been
no more episodes like the night he'd walked out in the middle
of service, although she suspected he was still doing coke on
the nights he managed to go out with the boys.*

*When they'd refined a new recipe enough to put it on the
menu, they'd repair to the little flat Fergus was renting off
Old Church Street, not far from the restaurant. There, they pored
over cookery books and scribbled endless notes on scraps of
paper.*

*It was a Sunday night, and after working all day in the
kitchen, trying to perfect a foie gras and apple stuffed chicken,
they'd walked up to the King's Road in the warm summer evening and bought fish and chips to carry back to the flat. Fergus
filled her kitchen tumbler with a second glass of expensive white
Burgundy and raised his own glass in a toast.*

*"Have I told you lately that you're brilliant?" he said, plop-
ping down on the tattered sofa beside her as he crumpled his empty
chips paper. Fergus might like his designer clothes and handmade
shoes, but he cared nothing about decor and the flat looked as if
it had been furnished from a charity shop. Which it had. The*

thought made Viv giggle. "That's funny?" Fergus asked, giving her a look of mock offense.

"No," Viv said hastily, eating a last chip. "I was just thinking we should do pork belly. Maybe with parsnips."

"Peasant food. Poor Irish peasant food," Fergus said, but without heat.

"Uh-huh," she agreed. "Good peasant food, though. And cheap is good for the balance sheet."

They sat, tired feet propped on the onion-crate coffee table, sipping their wine in companionable silence, both in the Sunday jeans and T-shirts they'd worn under their whites. Viv felt her breathing take on the rhythm of his. They'd worked side by side for months, touching, bumping, synchronized in the intimate dance of the kitchen. He had never flirted with her, other than his occasional lapse into broad Irish teasing when something was going particularly well. Although there were times she'd caught him looking at her intently, his brow furrowed, as if something about her puzzled him.

Her eyes drifted closed. "Citrus-smoked salmon," she murmured. "With avocado crème fraîche."

"They don't have avocados in Ireland, darlin'."

"I never meant we should put ourselves in a box," Viv said, trying to blink herself awake. "No need to be rigid about the Irish thing."

"No?" Fergus took the tilting wineglass from her hand and set it on the crate. "Woman, do you never think about anything but food?"

"Sometimes." She was suddenly aware of the warmth of his thigh against hers, but she felt as if she were mired in treacle, powerless to move.

"Good." Fergus reached over and touched her chin, tilting her face up so that he could meet her eyes. "Come to bed," he said, and there was no hint of Irish brogue, and no laughter now in his voice.

She went, as if her life had never held any other possibility, and when she kissed his scarred fingers, they tasted of vinegar and salt.

CHAPTER EIGHTEEN

As soon as Bea and Grace had left the room, Gemma went to Kit. "What happened?" she asked quietly, moving him away from the others.

"I don't know. She seemed okay with what you said—I told her you'd invited her to lunch and that the kids would like to meet Bella. But we had to walk back through the center of the village and she saw something. Maybe it was the closed sign still out in front of the pub. Then she started yelling at me and ran straight across the road. I couldn't stop her."

"I know, love. Thank you for trying." Gemma gave his shoulders a squeeze, then bent to stroke the dog's silky head. "I'm sure Grace will calm down. But in the meantime, what are we going to do with this lovely girl?"

"I don't want to give her back to Grace."

Gemma looked up, surprised. "Why ever not?"

"Grace isn't responsible. She's a baby. She doesn't understand that what's good for the dog comes first, not what *she* wants."

What exactly had Grace done? Gemma wondered. But before she could ask, her mobile vibrated in her pocket. When she saw that it was Melody, she realized she hadn't even had a chance to ask Kincaid what on earth he'd done with the children. "Just hang on to Bella for a bit," she told Kit. "We'll work something out. I've got to get this."

She stepped into the lounge bar and answered the call. "Melody, are the kids okay?"

"That depends on whether you call playing croquet with Doug 'okay,'" said Melody. "But other than that, they're fine."

"I'm so sorry." Gemma puffed out a breath of relief. "I didn't mean for you to be landed as a babysitter. I left them with Duncan. He's here at the pub now with DI Booth, but I haven't had a chance to ask him what happened."

"Doug says Booth got a heads-up from the pathologist and picked Duncan up on the way to the scene. I came back to find Doug and both kids glued to *Frozen* and made them go outside."

"Where were you, anyway?" Gemma asked.

"Having an interesting visit with Joe."

"The gardener?"

"One and the same. I'll tell you about it later. Listen, boss, Dougie did actually make himself useful this morning, other than child minding—which was probably good for his constitution. He did some research on Fergus O'Reilly."

As Melody started telling her what Doug had learned, Gemma said, "Hang on," and looked round for something to write on.

Yesterday's newspapers were still on the reading shelf by the bar, but there was no pen. Ducking behind the bar, she seized on an order pad and a pencil and began making notes. "Colm Finlay?" she repeated, and double-checked the spelling. She took down the name of the deceased ex-wife, and the approximate dates of Fergus's different restaurant ventures. "So Fergus was in bad shape financially?" she said, tapping the pencil on the pad.

"Certainly looks that way. What's going on with the bartender?"

Gemma stepped into the empty dining room on the other side of the lounge. "All I know is that Booth and the pathologist don't think the hit-and-run was an accident." Frowning, she added, "Melody, can you and Doug manage the kids just a bit longer? And please apologize to your mum and dad if we don't make lunch? I'll ring you back in just a few."

Ringing off, she crossed the lounge again and stood in the doorway of the smaller dining room. Kit, the dog at his side, had joined the chefs, who seemed to be arguing. Viv was shaking her head as Ibby spoke to her urgently. Kincaid was huddled with Booth, discussing something Booth had pulled up on his phone. Watching her husband, she noticed how drawn his face had become over the last two days. There were hollows under his eyes and the lines between his nose and mouth seemed etched more deeply. He was still cradling his right hand and wincing when he moved. Could she be certain that he'd see the doctor again tomorrow if she left this afternoon?

She was worried about Viv Holland, but it was concern for Kincaid that tipped the balance. Crossing the room, she touched him gently on the arm and whispered, "Need a word." When he'd excused himself to Booth, she led him back into the empty lounge and urged him to sit down with her at the table by the cold hearth.

"I don't think we can just leave this," she said quietly. "Not that I don't think DI Booth can do a good job, but there's a lot going on here that he may not have access to. And I think Viv Holland needs some serious support. I want to stay on at least another day. We can all go back to London together, tomorrow or the next day."

Kincaid frowned. "What about the kids? They have to be back in school tomorrow. And work? I've let my team know I'll be held up, dealing with the car, but you're due back at Brixton in the morning."

"I'll ring the kids' schools first thing and get them excused. I don't think the boys have anything they can't make up. And you know I've got leave due—I worked straight through the last two weekends because other people were out."

Kincaid nodded, and she thought he looked relieved not to be left on his own. "Won't we be making a nuisance of ourselves with Ivan and Addie?"

"I'll speak to Addie as soon as I get back up to the house. She said they were here until midweek and we were welcome to stay as long as we needed." Leaning closer, Gemma said, "So tell me about the hit-and-run."

"No visible skid marks. Which doesn't rule out an accident, but the pathologist thinks someone hit him over the head once he was down."

"Oh, bugger," whispered Gemma. She considered this for a moment. "I don't think it can possibly be coincidence, the deaths of Nell Greene and Fergus O'Reilly, then this. And it all starts with O'Reilly. What was he really doing here? Why was he here three weeks ago? If Viv spent years hiding from him, which is certainly what it looks like, why? Was he violent?" She relayed what Melody had told her about O'Reilly's restaurants. "I'd start with the London address you and Booth got from the hotel here. And the name Doug found of his former partner in London."

"Someone will have to follow up on those leads," Kincaid agreed. "But Booth will have to liaise with the Met and that may take some time."

"I have an idea," Gemma said, and smiled for the first time since Viv had called Beck House.

Seeing that Doug and the kids were still occupied with their croquet game, which looked as though it was becoming a bit Alice-esque, Melody went back into the house.

She found Addie in the kitchen, arranging sliced ham and tomatoes on a platter. "I just spoke to Gemma," Melody told her. "She and Duncan are still at the Lamb. She said to apologize if they didn't make it back for lunch."

"I'm not surprised," Addie said. "I'm just putting out some ham for sandwiches. There will be plenty left for them whenever they get back. Your dad told me about the bartender." She shook her head. "What a shame. Poor Viv."

"It's worse than that. Gemma says they don't think it was an accident."

Addie stopped, hands arrested over the ham. "Oh, no. That's dreadful. Surely, they're wrong."

"I don't get the impression that DI Booth makes a habit of being wrong." Melody helped herself to a slice of tomato—delicious, and undoubtedly from their garden.

"No." Addie went back to her task, adding farmhouse bread to the platter. "I'd agree with you on that. But I can't imagine that anyone would want to hurt poor Jack Doyle. Such a nice man. This will be horrible for Viv and Bea. I must see what I can do for them."

"It sounds like a zoo at the moment, with Gemma and Duncan at the pub as well as DI Booth. I'd go down myself except I promised Gemma I'd look after Toby and Charlotte." Melody leaned back against the work top. "Mum, what do you know about Joe?"

Addie looked up, surprised. "Joe? Why do you want to know?"

"We were just chatting a bit ago. I was curious why a good-looking young guy would want to live like a monk."

"I wouldn't exactly say that." The corner of Addie's mouth turned up. "He does go down to the pub as well as into town, regularly, and there have been quite a few times when I've seen him coming back early in the morning. Where he chooses to spend the night is certainly none of my business—although I do like having him here on the property when we're in London."

"He wanted to know what I knew about Viv and Fergus O'Reilly, but then he didn't want me to tell Viv he'd asked. I just thought it was odd."

"Oh." Addie considered this. "Well, as far as I know, they're just friends. Of course he would be concerned. Roz," she called out, "has Joe spoken to you about Viv?"

"I didn't realize Roz was here," said Melody.

"She was just finishing up some correspondence that needed to be done by tomorrow. We got a bit behind, with the luncheon."

A moment later, Roz Dunning came in from the hall. "Did you call me, Addie? I was just on my way out." She added, "Oh, hi, Melody. I thought you were out in the garden with your friend. He seems to be getting on famously with the little ones."

"It's not important," said Addie. "Don't let us keep you. I'll see you tomorrow."

"Okay, if you're sure. Bye now." Roz gave them a little wave and a moment later they heard the front door open and close.

"I do hope my luncheon idea wasn't responsible for bringing O'Reilly here," said Addie, looking down at her finished platter with an unexpected expression of regret. "If he hadn't come, neither he nor Nell might have died. And now this, with Jack Doyle . . ."

"Mum." Melody put her arm round her mother's slender shoulders. The silk of Addie's blouse felt cool under her fingers. "Whatever happened to Nell and Fergus O'Reilly, it was not your fault. Now, what about these sandwiches?"

"Right." Addie smiled, but Melody wasn't entirely convinced. "If you'll fetch Doug and the children," Addie said, "I'll just tell your father. He's been on the phone all morning trying to find a good car for Duncan." She looked at Melody. "If Duncan had been hurt very badly—or died—I don't know how I would—"

"Mum!" Melody cut her off, shocked. "Don't be silly. That's not like you at all. I might as well hold myself responsible because I invited them."

"I suppose you're right, darling." Addie sighed. "I just feel a bit like the thing that started the dominoes falling."

"You have certainly never been described by anyone as a *thing*," Melody said, laughing, and earned a rueful smile in return. "Come on, then—"

The doorbell rang, startling them both.

"Who the hell?" grumbled Melody. Neither Gemma nor Duncan had keys, but the front door had been purposely left off the latch for them. Perhaps Roz had forgotten. "I'll get it," she said, starting for the hall, but Addie followed her nevertheless.

"I'm so sorry," Melody said as she opened the door. "Did you get locked—"

The words dried up. Neither Gemma nor Duncan stood on the porch. Gaping, she looked into Andy Monahan's very blue eyes.

As Gemma and Kincaid walked back into the small dining room, she could tell that the discussion among the chefs was getting more heated. Kincaid went to speak to Booth, while Gemma saw that Kit had apparently fetched a bowl of water for Bella from the kitchen, and now knelt beside the dog as she drank, listening intently to the conversation.

"We can't," Viv was saying. "We just can't. It's disrespectful. What would people think?"

"What are people going to think when they start turning up at noon for the Sunday lunches they've booked, and they haven't even had a phone call telling them their reservation is canceled?" argued Ibby.

"That doesn't matter." Viv sounded near to tears again.

"It does, actually," Angelica put in, quietly. "The locals will have to be told about Jack, whether it's today or tomorrow. But we have tourists and people from outside that are only going to know that their day is ruined. And what are we going to do, otherwise? Sit in the kitchen while the food spoils? I don't know about you, but I'd rather be working."

Gemma jumped as Bea spoke from behind her shoulder. "Angelica's right. We've got people already pulling into the car park. We can't just turn them away," Bea continued as she joined the group. "Sarah and the rest of the servers are here. Sarah is manning the car park until we can get ourselves sorted out in here. Viv?"

"But we can't just—" Viv shook her head. "What about Grace?"

242 OF DEBORAH CROMBIE

"I've got her settled on the sofa with a duvet and a video. I'll check on her in a few minutes."

Bea, Gemma decided, was the sort of person who met a crisis with action.

"But what about the bar?" said Viv. "We can't pull anyone out of the dining rooms—"

"I can mind the bar," put in Ibby. "Angie's right. We can't just sit here all day. We'd go spare. But you'll be shorthanded in the kitchen."

Kit had stood up. "I can help."

"Would you?" Viv gave him a grateful look, then glanced at Gemma. "If it's all right with your mum, we might be able to manage with an extra hand."

"Of course, that's fine, if Kit wants to help. And I'm glad to do whatever I can, as well."

"But you'll have to take Bella if I help out," he said. "I can't have her in the kitchen. You will watch out for her, won't you?" he added, with a return of the worried frown he'd worn earlier.

"Of course I will," Gemma assured him, but before she could ask what was bothering him, the chefs, having made a decision, whisked him off to the kitchen, and Gemma was left, quite literally, holding the dog.

When Bella whined after Kit, Gemma reassured her, then took her over to Kincaid and Booth. "They're going to open," she told them. "And we need to find a place to talk."

Roz escaped into the forecourt at Beck House and walked fast up the drive until she reached the road. There, she stopped and drew a shaky breath.

She'd been about to walk into the kitchen when she'd heard

Melody mention Joe's name. Hardly daring to breathe, she'd listened until Addie had called out for her, then waited a moment to enter, a smile pasted on her face. Dear God, she'd never dreamed that Joe would be stupid enough to ask questions about Fergus of Melody, of all people. What else had he told her? She considered going back to confront him now, but someone might see her and she didn't want to chat.

Hunching her shoulders, she started up the road towards her cottage. The sound of a car coming up the lane made her look back, but all she saw was the flash of tail lamps as a car turned into the Beck House drive. Roz shrugged and continued up the hill. Not her problem, whomever it was.

As she reached the high point of the village, a flock of black birds rose from the churchyard, wheeled in the air above her, then settled on the power wires, their voices raucous and mocking. They might have been laughing at her.

As well they might. She meant to go home and erase any trace that Fergus O'Reilly had ever entered her life.

And then she was going to deal with Joe.

"Andy, what are you doing here?" Melody managed to gasp when her tongue had unlocked itself.

"Surprised to see me, then?" He didn't smile.

"How did you—"

"Know where to find you? I rang Doug. I was worried about you. Apparently, I needn't have been."

"Doug? But why did he—" A movement made Melody realize that her mother was still standing right behind her. Stepping back, she said, "Oh, Mum. This is Andy. Andy, this is my mother, Addie Talbot."

Andy held out a hand to Addie. "Andy Monahan. Melody's *friend*." There was a definite emphasis on the *friend*. "Pleased to meet you, ma'am."

Addie shook his hand warmly, then studied him with a slightly puzzled expression. "Don't I know you from somewhere? Oh." Her face cleared. "I've seen you on the television—was it *Breakfast*? You and your partner, the adorable girl who sings and plays the bass. Poppy."

"Yes. Poppy Jones."

"You're the guitarist. I think the two of you are so talented."

Melody glanced at her mother in shock. What was she doing, gushing like a smitten teenager? Not that Andy looked the rock star today. His usually tousled blond hair was neatly combed. He wore a quite smart navy blazer over a blue button-down shirt, and jeans with his bespoke brown leather boots—those, one of his few concessions to his recent celebrity.

"Remember, darling?" Addie turned to Melody. "I told you how much I liked that song?" She hummed a bit of Andy and Poppy's hit from last summer—perfectly in key. Melody could have sunk through the earth. "Why didn't you say you two were friends?"

"I— It just never came up—"

"Well, in any case, do come in," Addie said before Melody could dig herself in any deeper. "We were just about to have lunch. You must join us, Andy."

"I'm very sorry, Lady Adelaide, but I can't stay. I've just come to have a word with Melody. It won't take long."

CHAPTER NINETEEN

Gemma, Bella, Kincaid, and Booth repaired to the farthest table in the garden. It had grown so warm that it felt more like balmy summer than late September. Bees zoomed among the splash of red roses still blooming on the nearby stone wall and visited the small pot of lavender on their table, coming perilously close to Gemma's egg mayo and watercress sandwich.

The pub car park was now full, and most of the other tables in the garden were occupied with Sunday lunch diners making the most of the weather. Viv had insisted that they take something to eat from the kitchen, and Gemma had had to admit that her bite of breakfast had long since worn off. She'd promised Viv that she'd help out in the pub wherever needed—the least she could do was bus tables—but not until she'd had a chance to make certain that she, Kincaid, and Booth were all up to speed. And not until they'd finished their lunches. Booth had ordered the ploughman's, Kincaid the roast chicken sandwich, but she noticed he didn't manage to eat more than a few bites.

When she and Booth, at least, were mopping up crumbs, she said, "I've been thinking, trying to work out what might have happened here on Friday night. Fergus O'Reilly apparently walked out of the bar without his coat or mobile. We assume he'd just stepped out and meant to come back, right? But why did he go outside? He didn't smoke, did he?"

"Nothing indicates that he did," agreed Booth. "Maybe it was too warm in the bar and he just needed some air."

"Or maybe he needed to cool off for another reason—the argument in the kitchen," said Gemma. "Jack Doyle told me that O'Reilly was slagging off Viv's food the entire evening. Then he barged into the kitchen and he and Viv had a shouting match. Did anyone you interviewed say exactly what it was about?"

Booth gazed into the distance, then said, "The two cooks said that she told him to get out of her kitchen, that he had no right to be there. Viv Holland just agreed with them."

"So." Shooing a wasp away from her glass, Gemma took a cautious sip of her lemonade before going on. "If O'Reilly was sniping at her food and sending it back, I'd guess he was already angry with her. Why? Because she turned down the job he offered her? That seems a pretty extreme reaction."

"Famous chef, offering her a plum job, and she doesn't want it," mused Booth. "Maybe his ego was wounded. He was never exactly a self-effacing bloke."

"*Formerly* famous chef," put in Kincaid. "According to what Doug Cullen found this morning." He repeated what they had learned from Doug's research.

"Well, if he wasn't doing well, it must have really smarted to be turned down." Booth ate his last potato crisp and eyed Kincaid's plate.

"Maybe." Gemma mulled this over. "But you know what bothers me about this? The mobile. Who leaves their phone behind these days when they step outside for a breath of air?"

"Who leaves their mobile in their coat pocket to begin with?" countered Booth. "Instead of keeping it in hand or on the table?"

"True. Although the reception is iffy here. But, I've been thinking. What if Fergus left his coat and his mobile not because he was angry, but because he wasn't feeling well? We know he must have died very shortly after he left the pub." She took out her own mobile, checked the bars, and pulled up a Wikipedia page. Scanning the page, she said, "Listen to this. Symptoms of digitalis poisoning include vomiting, loss of appetite—that could be why Fergus kept sending Viv's food back—blurred vision, and confusion. We've never come up with any explanation for what Fergus O'Reilly was doing in Nell Greene's car, or any connection between them.

"But what if he simply felt very ill and was trying to get back to his hotel? When Nell leaves the pub, say, half an hour later, she finds him wandering in the village, obviously ill. Nell was a hospital administrator. She certainly had enough experience to know he needed medical attention urgently."

Slowly, Booth nodded. "That intersection, where she crashed into you, Duncan, would have been the quickest route to the hospital in Cheltenham."

"Oh my God." Gemma felt suddenly queasy as the idea came to her. "Everyone says how sensible Nell was. We see car crashes caused by distracted driving every day—people fussing with their Happy Meals or sending texts—but Nell was responsible, and careful. But—what if she looked over at her ill passenger and real-ized that O'Reilly had died?"

"Christ," Kincaid said, his voice strangled. "She said— She tried to tell me something, but it didn't make any sense to me then. She seemed so distressed, and not for herself. She said, 'Tell them he—' and that was all she managed."

Looking at Kincaid, Gemma saw to her dismay that his eyes had filled with tears. "You didn't tell me you spoke to her."

"I— It was only a few seconds. Waiting for help. And then she was—gone." Kincaid stood up, almost tipping over his wooden chair. "Excuse me, would you?" Without waiting for an answer, he left them, walking quickly across the courtyard and disappear-ing through the arch into the car park.

"He's a bit upset, I think," Booth said to Gemma.

She took in his lack of surprise. "You knew, didn't you? That he spoke to Nell."

"Sometimes it's easier to tell strangers when something really gets to you." Booth leaned forward, keeping eye contact with her. "You know. You know how it is on the job."

After a moment, Gemma made an effort to relax her shoulders and let her breath out in a sigh. "Yes. You're right. But still—"

"Head injuries can do funny things as well. Emotionally, I mean. I got seriously smacked once, playing rugby for the police team. I cried for weeks over anything, even telly adverts. You can imagine how well that went over on the job. I'd recommend that you make sure Duncan gets that head injury checked out."

Gemma realized then what had been nagging at the edge of her awareness—how odd it had seemed that Kincaid hadn't tried to run Booth's investigation, whether it was officially his case or not.

So accustomed was he to being in charge that it came as naturally to him as breathing, and ordinarily he'd have been organizing and suggesting, politely, of course. But he wasn't. She said, "I've decided I'm not going back to London tomorrow. And I'll make certain he sees someone first thing in the morning." Looking towards the car park, she added, "Should I go after him?"

Booth shook his head. "No. I'd give him a few minutes to sort himself out."

Gemma shooed a few more wasps while she tried again to order her thoughts. From the kitchen, she heard the rattle of dishes and the hum of voices, but she couldn't distinguish the speakers. "Have you ruled out the possibility that O'Reilly might have overdosed on his own medication?" she asked Booth.

"Not entirely, until we can check out his home address. But I think if he'd been taking prescribed tablets, we'd have found them in his hotel room or on his person. Dr. Mason—the pathologist—says the toxic dose is five to ten times the therapeutic dose, but we're still talking small tablets. The lethal amount would depend on the person's health and sensitivity."

Gemma scanned her phone screen again. "This says onset of symptoms from a lethal dose is thirty minutes to two hours. But it might not have been heart tablets. Apparently, all parts of the plant are highly poisonous, even dried seeds and leaves."

Booth met her gaze. "Because of Jack Doyle's death, we have to seriously consider the possibility that Fergus O'Reilly was deliberately poisoned. And, given the time frame, that it happened in or near the pub."

"And that it's highly likely the digitalis had to have been administered in his food or drink," added Gemma, not liking this at all. "Which puts the pub staff squarely in the picture." Looking towards the kitchen again, she shook her head. "I just can't believe that any of them would have done that."

"Well, we don't know where O'Reilly was before he came to the pub Friday evening, so we can't rule out the possibility that he ingested it somewhere else. And the plant grows bloody everywhere."

Including the garden at Beck House, thought Gemma. She remembered seeing the distinctive leaves in what Addie had told them was the White Border, modeled on Gertrude Jekyll's white borders. Hybrids of the foxglove seeds Jekyll had developed were available even now from catalogues, Addie had added.

"Nor do we know where he stayed those nights he didn't use his hotel room," Booth went on, still focused on O'Reilly. "Or who he met. Damn the man."

"We need to get into his mobile," said Gemma, then realized that with the plural, she'd just included herself in an official investigation, but Booth merely nodded in agreement.

"I've got forensics working on getting a fingerprint or facial recognition scan from the body, but that will take some time. I also need to liaise with the Met on checking O'Reilly's London address. But it's Sunday, and I doubt I can get anyone to return a call before tomorrow morning. And I'm seriously understaffed this weekend on all fronts."

"I might be able to help with the London end," said Gemma, hoping her idea would float. "I have a friend, a DCI at Kensington nick. I could give her a ring, see if she could check the place out. And maybe she'd be willing to track down Fergus O'Reilly's former partner as well."

✖

"Can we talk somewhere away from the house?" Andy said, when Addie had gone in.

Nodding, Melody walked across the drive and Andy followed her. "How on earth did you get here?" she said, turning to face him.

"Taxi. From your little town where the train stops. Moreton-under-Puddle, or whatever it's called."

"I'd have fetched you from the sta—"

"Oh, right, when you got round to answering your texts or your phone calls? I'd have had a long bloody wait."

"I was going to ring you. I just—"

"Doug told me he showed you the stupid paper. I can't believe you fell for that crap," Andy said, his voice tight.

"Did *you* see it?" Melody shot back, beginning to feel angry, too. "The pair of you looked like 'love's young dream.'"

Andy shook his head in disgust. "And how many hundreds of shots do you think it took that photographer to find one that looked like more than it was? You can't be so naive. I told you from the very beginning that there was nothing between Poppy and me, and I've never given you any reason to doubt it. But you—you just flat-out lied to me, Melody."

Her legs suddenly felt boneless. "What? What are you talking about?"

Andy leaned so close she could feel his breath on her face and punched a finger at her chest. "You said your dad was in the newspaper business." He gave a bitter laugh. "Although I suppose you could say that, couldn't you?" he added, dripping sarcasm. "So I look up this house when Doug gives me the directions, and I see it belongs to Sir Ivan and Lady Adelaide freaking Talbot. *The*

Ivan Talbot." He shook his head. "I'd feel really stupid for not seeing the connection, except why would it have occurred to me that it was more than coincidence, you sharing a last name with the owner of the bloody *Chronicle*?"

"He's not the owner. The paper is legally my mother's. Passed down from her parents. Dad's just the managing editor." Melody knew as soon as she said it that she'd sounded horribly prim and condescending, but she couldn't take it back.

"*Just* the managing editor. Okay. Like this place is *just* a little weekend cottage." Andy waved a dismissive hand at the house.

"The house isn't that bi—"

"Oh, spare me," Andy snapped, rolling his eyes. "You're a freaking heiress, Melody, and you didn't bloody tell me. Were you ashamed of me? Your working-class bit of fluff?"

"Oh, no. God, no! How can you think that?"

"Well, I do think. I think we've been going out, what, almost a year, and you said nothing. Were you ever going to tell me?"

"You don't understand." She reached out to touch him, but his look stopped her. Pulling her hand back, she crossed her arms in front of her chest and began to shiver. "I didn't tell you at first because I thought it would frighten you off. Once they know, no one ever looks at me the same way—you've just given me proof enough of that. But the longer I put it off, the harder it got. And, then, I thought if it ever got out about us in the tabloids, then everyone on the job would know who I was—"

"Oh, right," Andy broke in. "You can invite three cops home for your mum's charity do, and not me?"

"It wasn't like that." She was pleading now. "They're the only ones who know. I had to tell Gemma, and Doug found out. And I'd never invited anyone at all here, before this weekend." She could tell from his face that she wasn't moving him and she felt helpless, unable to stop this argument spinning out of control. "Look, I'm sorry I was upset over the photo, and I'm sorry I didn't tell you about my parents. Can't you come in? We can talk about this—"

Andy shook his head. "No. I'm getting the next train back to London. I had the taxi wait in the village." He gave an exaggerated shrug. "And, besides, I don't have anything else to say. We're finished, Melody Talbot."

She stared at him, her stomach dropping. "You can't mean that."

"Give my regards to your mother. It's been nice knowing you." With that, he turned and started up the drive, his head down, his hands shoved in his blazer pockets.

"Andy, please," she called after him, but he didn't pause, and he didn't look back.

Kerry Boatman put down her phone and pushed her chair back from her desk, still smiling after her conversation. The first thing Gemma had said was "Caught you working on a Sunday, didn't I? I can hear the sirens in the background."

"Just finishing up," Kerry had told her. "The girls went to church with their grandparents, so I thought I'd get a head start on Monday. What's up with you? I thought you were out of town this weekend, hobnobbing with the country set."

She and Gemma had first met on a case a couple of years earlier, when Kerry had been a DI at Lucan Place Station in Chelsea. Now, sadly, the station had been sold off by the Met. Kerry had been promoted to DCI and moved to Kensington Station on Earl's

Court Road. Then, last spring, she and Gemma had worked together to solve the murder of a young nanny in Notting Hill. Since then, they'd become good friends.

Kerry had come to respect Gemma's professionalism and instincts on the job, and often wished she had her on her own team. So when Gemma had given her a brief rundown of the events in Lower Slaughter, Kerry said, "Trust you to run smack into one, if not two, possible murders. So what can I do for you?" She'd jotted down Gemma's requests and said she'd get back to her as soon as she could.

Now, she studied her notes and did a quick Internet search. Colm Finlay, the restaurateur, would have to wait until the morning, as she could find only a corporate contact number. But she might be able to work in taking a look at the flat in Chelsea that afternoon while she was shopping for her daughter's birthday.

CHAPTER TWENTY

SEPTEMBER 2007

On a night in the first week in September, Viv checked her mobile at the end of service and found she'd missed half a dozen calls from her dad. That was unnerving, but worse, there were no messages. She ran up the back stairs and out into Margretta Terrace in her whites, her heart pounding. Alone in the street, she pressed her dad's number. When he answered, his usually hearty voice was almost unrecognizable.

"Dad? What's wrong? What's happened?"

"It's your—" He broke off, and she thought she heard him choke back a sob before he said, "Darling, it's your mum. She went into hospital yesterday. A cut on her knee had got infected. By the time I got her to agree to see the GP, they said it had gone septic and that she needed an emergency operation—"

"What? Why didn't you call me?"

"It all happened so fast, love. They said she just needed to stay in hospital for a couple of days, for the antibiotics, and we didn't see any reason to worry you." Her father made that small choking sound again. "But she's got worse. They say the first drugs aren't working. They can't get the infection under control."

It was a moment before Viv could gather enough breath to say, "What hospital, Dad? Where is she?"

"Redditch. The Alexandra."

"Is she—" Viv swallowed hard. "How bad is it, Dad?"

"They're trying a new round of antibiotics. But—they say it could be touch and go. She—she's asking for you. Can you come, Viv?"

"Of course. Of course I'll come." Viv tried to work out the logistics. It was already almost eleven—she'd have to manage with what she had in her locker. "I can get the train to Birmingham and from there to Redditch, but it'll be a god-awful hour of the morning before I get in."

"That's fine. Not going anywhere," her dad said, and she could hear the effort he put into that bit of humor.

"What about Adam?" Her younger brother was still at university in Bristol.

"He's borrowing a car from a friend. He should be here by breakfast."

"Okay, I'll ring you from the station." Pausing, she tried to steady her voice. "Dad, I love you. Tell Mum, too, okay? And tell her she's going to be fine." She rang off before she completely lost it. Scrubbing at her wet cheeks with her apron, she checked the train times before she went back down to the kitchen. If she hurried, she could just make the 22:57, which, with a change in Birmingham, would get her into Redditch at 6:41 in the morning.

The crew was almost through with the scrub down. Fergus, who was bent over cleaning the gas rings, frowned as he looked up at her. "Where have you been? We're almost done here." Nothing was more reviled in the kitchen than slacking off on your part of the cleanup.

As Viv saw the expectant faces turn towards her, no doubt looking forward to watching a bollocking, she realized she couldn't get through this in front of the whole crew. "Fergus. Can I have a word? In your office?"

"Can't it wait until we've finished here?"

"No."

For the first time, he seemed to realize something was wrong. "Okay." Handing his scrub rag to John, he said, "Finish this for me, will you, mate?" and followed Viv into the tiny office cubicle. "What is it?" he asked when he'd closed the door.

"My mum. She's really ill. I have to go."

"What do you mean, go?" He seemed perplexed. "We were going to work on the duck liver parfait after service."

"No. I mean I have to go to Redditch. Tonight. She's in hospital there."

Fergus still looked blank. "But you can't. We're rolling out the crispy duck leg on the menu tomorrow. I need you here."

"Fergus, it's my mum." She wanted to shake him. "Don't you understand? She might—" Viv couldn't say it. She shook her head. "Ibby can take over my station. He'll be fine. My mum needs me."

"I need you," Fergus said, but his face had lost its impatient

tightness. He reached out, cupping her cheek with a moth-light
touch, something he only did when they were alone.

    "Ring me when you get there, all right?" he said, but she had
seen the distance in his eyes.

Melody sank down on the front step. She was too shocked even
to cry. What had just happened? Had Andy really broken up with
her? Her little blue car was parked to the side of the garage, and
for a moment she thought about going after him. She could catch
him before he reached the village. But what could she say that
she hadn't already said? And she couldn't face his rejection again.

    She had no idea how much time had passed since she'd walked
so unsuspectingly to the front door. Petals from the St. Swithun's
roses on either side of the porch fluttered past her, shaken loose by
the breeze, and the sun danced in the treetops of the Woodland.

    After a bit, she realized she could hear the sound of voices
coming faintly from the dining room. Lunch. Her mother. What
was she going to tell her mother? And then she thought of Doug,
and that was enough to get her to her feet.

    She was going to kill him.

    Stepping quietly into the hall, she stood in the pocket of shadow
just outside the kitchen, where she could see into the room without
being noticed. Her mum was loading plates into the kitchen dishwasher. Toby was bouncing a dog ball into the scullery for Polly.
Mac was stretched out on his side, taking up as much of the kitchen
floor as possible. Ivan still sat at the table, Charlotte leaning against
his knee. He was telling Charlotte the *Three Little Pigs* in broad
Geordie, just the way he used to tell it to her, and every time he

said, "And then he blew the house doon," Charlotte shrieked with laughter and told him to do it again.

Then, her mother seemed to sense her presence, and turned. "Melody?" When she didn't move, her mother wiped her hands on a tea towel and came to her. "Melody, what are you doing out here, darling? Where's your friend? Is he not staying for lunch?"

"No," Melody managed to croak. "No, he's not. He had to go."

"Oh, what a shame," said Addie, but it was obvious from her keen look that she knew something was wrong.

"Where's Doug?" Melody managed to ask before Addie could say anything else. "I need a word with him."

"In the sitting room, I think. He said he had some email to answer."

"Thanks." Melody turned away, her fists already clenched, but she could feel her mother's eyes on her back as she walked out of the room.

When she reached the sitting room, Doug's laptop was open on the table, but he was scrolling through something on his mobile. He started when he heard her and closed the phone screen. Looking up, he said, too casually, "Oh, it's you. Um, where's Andy?"

"You mean he hasn't told you already?"

"What? Why would he—"

She cut him off. "You bastard, Doug. You absolute bastard." Fury coursed through her. "How could you bring him here when I hadn't—I didn't—" She gulped back a sob.

"I was only trying to help—"

"You had no right. No right!" Melody realized she was shaking. "You are an interfering shit. Now he knows about Mum and Dad—"

Doug stood up so that they were face-to-face, separated only by the coffee table. "Melody, for God's sake, be sensible. How could you *not* tell him? He was bound to find out, and better sooner than later—"

"That wasn't for you to decide. It was none of your—"

"Melody, calm down." Doug looked, she noted with some small, cold compartment of her mind, frightened. But he said, "What did you think would happen if you kept that from him? I'm your friend, for heaven's sake," he added, in a voice so reasonable that it made her want to strike him. "I only wanted—"

"*Were. Were* my friend. Did you know Andy broke up with me? Did you? This is your doing, Doug Cullen. This is all your fault."

She expected him to argue, but he just looked at her. After a long moment, he shook his head and said, so softly that she could barely hear him, "No. No, really, Melody, it's not."

Somehow Kincaid ended up with the dog.

He'd walked out of the pub car park and crossed the road, standing for a while on the bridge over the Eye, waiting for his breathing to return to normal. He couldn't stop thinking about Nell. What if Gemma was right about what had happened? And why hadn't he worked it out himself? He could see it all too clearly, now, Nell stopping to help, getting O'Reilly into the car but not managing to fasten his seat belt, talking to him, perhaps, as she drove, trying to figure out what exactly was wrong so that she could phone ahead to the hospital. Realizing her passenger wasn't responding, looking over just as she was coming up to the T-junction and finding him slumped in his seat . . .

Kincaid had driven that road with Ivan, had seen how little

warning there was of the upcoming intersection. And in the dark, in a panic . . . His head swam and he held on to the wooden bridge railing. What was wrong with him?

Was it the accident that was making him feel so strange? When he closed his eyes, he had moments of frightening disorientation in which he replayed over and over how he'd felt when he'd come to, upside down in the car.

He had to pull himself together.

The sound of a car coming from the direction of the mill had made him look up and move off the bridge. It was a local taxi. Glancing at the car's back window as it passed, he could have sworn he recognized the passenger's profile. He'd watched the taxi turn right at the roundabout and vanish from sight beyond the manor. Could that really have been Andy Monahan? Here? Melody hadn't said anything about Andy coming this weekend. Shaking his head, he decided he must have been mistaken.

As he'd turned to walk back to the pub, the churchyard caught his eye and his thoughts had gone back to Nell. Would she be buried? And, if so, here? Who was looking after her arrangements? Perhaps Mark Cain would know something.

Reaching the pub, he'd seen Gemma coming towards him across the car park, the pretty black-and-white collie at her heels.

"Are you okay?" asked Gemma when she reached him. "I was getting worried about you."

"Fine. Just needed some air." Across the car park, he saw Booth, now in rolled-up shirtsleeves, standing by his Volvo with his mobile to his ear. "What's going on?"

"Booth is organizing a house to house along Jack Doyle's route and calling in help to take official statements from the pub staff.

I've rung Kerry Boatman and she's agreed to check some things in London. And I've rung Melody to say we're staying over, but I had to leave a voice mail. She must be busy with the kids."

Kincaid started to tell her he thought he'd seen Andy, but Gemma went on, "Viv says Mark Cain texted her that he's home now but he can't fetch the dog. I've promised Kit I'd help out in the kitchen but I can't do it with the dog in tow," she added, sounding exasperated.

The dog in question sat patiently at Gemma's side, her head tilted as if wondering what these two unfamiliar humans were going to do with her next. She was a beauty, Kincaid thought. His mother had always favored the classic black-and-white coats in her border collies, and these were the dogs he'd grown up with.

"You are a love, aren't you?" he said to the dog, holding out his uninjured hand for her to sniff, then stroking her head.

"I was just going to take her up to Cain's myself," said Gemma.

"I'll take her," Kincaid offered. "I wanted a word with him about Nell, anyway."

Gemma frowned at him. "You sure you're up to it?"

"I'm fine. I'm perfectly capable of walking a dog."

Her eyes widened at his tone. "I know, love. It's just—take it easy, will you?" She handed him Bella's lead. "You know where it is, right? You've been to Nell's cottage. Viv says Mark's farm is the first place on the right after that."

"I can find it," he said, and knew he'd sounded cross again. He didn't understand why he felt so irritable. Reaching for the dog's lead, he leaned in and kissed Gemma's cheek. "Sorry, love, I didn't mean to be snappy. Don't worry, okay?" He gave her his best effort at a cheeky grin and walked away, the dog trotting at his side.

It was a good thing, he thought a few minutes later, that Bella had been trained to heel properly on the left, and to walk calmly. He couldn't have managed with his right hand. Once he had made the turn across from the mill and was well into the lane, the sun felt warm on his head and shoulders, and the scents from the hedgerows were heady. There were still blackberries among the brambles and he stopped to pick one. It was tart on his tongue, a tangible memory from his childhood.

When they neared Nell's cottage, Bella began to pull a little, but he tightened her lead and talked to her soothingly. There was no sign of activity at the place. Bella relaxed when they had passed the drive. The lane began to climb more steeply and trees filled in the hedgerows, shading Kincaid from the sun. When Bella's ears pricked up and her pace quickened, he began looking for the entrance to Cain's farm, although a drive seemed unlikely among the thick growth. But Bella whined and bumped his knee as she tried to cross in front of him, and then he saw it, a break in the trees. A barred gate was set just off the road, and beyond that a raised causeway crossed a deep, leaf-filled rill. On the far side of the rill, the belt of trees gave way to an open pasture, and on either side of a curving drive sat a substantial stone farmhouse with a wooden barn and outbuildings.

The gate, Kincaid saw, was only loop latched, so he opened it and led the excited dog through, then made certain it was fastened behind him. There was a tractor in the farmyard, and an older-model Land Rover with a light trailer attached.

Kincaid had nearly reached the yard when Bella yipped and two other black-and-white collies came streaking out of the barn, barking madly. He stood still as they circled round him, greeting Bella and sniffing him enthusiastically as well.

"Wally! Sprig! What the hell are you doing?" Mark Cain came

out of the barn, wiping his hands on a rag. "Oh, it's you," he added when he saw Kincaid. He nodded at Bella, who was quivering, her swishing tail beating against Kincaid's leg. "You can let her loose. She's fine in the yard. I just like to keep an eye on her in case she decides to scarper back to Nell's."

Kincaid managed to unhook the lead with his left hand and Bella joined the other dogs in a race round the farmyard.

"She's still a pup, really," said Cain as he watched the dogs. "Thanks for returning her. I told Viv I had to get the hay unloaded from the trailer before I could fetch her." He gestured at the trailer, which still held a few bales of hay.

"I didn't mind. She's a lovely dog. And I wanted a word with you anyway."

Studying him, Cain said, "Well, I could use a break. You'd better come in." He led Kincaid round to the back door of the farmhouse and exchanged his boots for slippers before inviting Kincaid inside. The dogs came with them, heading straight for their water bowl and lapping noisily.

It was a big, stone-flagged kitchen, with a center island and sleek fittings. After washing his hands, Cain opened the fridge and pulled out two unlabeled brown bottles with stopper-sealed tops. He held out one to Kincaid. "Have a cider. It's a gift from my friend with an orchard up Stow way. Presses and bottles it himself every year." When Kincaid accepted, Cain clicked his bottle against Kincaid's. "Cheers." Taking a long swig, he wiped his mouth with the back of his hand and leaned against the work top.

Kincaid drank. The tart, fresh, green-apple taste seemed to explode in his mouth and made his eyes water. "Bugger, that's stout stuff," he said when he'd managed to swallow and blink back the tears.

Cain grinned. "No alcohol percentage regulations on home-made cider. More than two of these will make you sorry the next day." The smile faded. "What did you want to talk to me about, then?"

Kincaid sipped more gingerly before answering. "I was wondering about Nell, whether there was anyone to make funeral arrangements."

"Ah. Good question. I had a word with the vicar last night. She was trying to get in touch with Nell's ex. There is a niece somewhere but I don't think they were close. I know her sister died a few years ago. If no one steps in, the vicar's going to organize a service in the church here and a little reception in the village hall. Viv said she'd provide the tea and cakes."

Kincaid nodded, feeling relieved. "I'm glad she'll be looked after. Did Nell attend the church?"

"Yes, pretty regularly. I don't think she was all that religious but she wanted to fit into the community." Cain shook his head. "It's a bloody shame. She was a nice woman. And now this business with Jack Doyle. I still can't believe it."

"Did Viv tell you?"

"Yes. She rang me not long after I'd dropped Bella here off this morning. But the news will have gone all round the farms by now." Frowning, he drank some more of his cider. "I don't understand it. Jack was not a careless fellow. And Viv is punishing herself for not having insisted on driving him home. She told me last night that he was a bit tiddly, but I didn't think anything of it."

"You spoke to Viv last night?"

"I went round after she'd locked up."

"To the cottage?"

"God, no. We had a drink in the bar after she'd made certain Grace was asleep. I don't know why Viv's so convinced that Grace would be traumatized if she knew there was anything going on between us." Cain drank some more cider. "We've been sneaking about for months. I mean, Grace and I get on fine. Why should she be horrified for her mum to have a relationship?"

"Maybe Viv thinks it would be hard for Grace if things didn't work out between you," Kincaid offered, hoping that sounded sensible. His head was beginning to swim a bit. Setting his half-finished cider down on the work top, he tried to concentrate on the important bit in what Cain had told him. "Mark, how long after Jack left did you arrive at the pub?"

"Hell, I don't know. Five or ten minutes? Viv said she'd seen him off, then gone in and checked on Grace and changed out of her whites."

"And Viv hadn't been anywhere else?"

Cain frowned at him. "No. I just told you. Where the hell would she go? Why are you asking?"

"Did you drive down to the pub?"

"Of course I drove," said Cain. "It was pouring buckets. Why are you asking me all these questions?" Cain sounded much less friendly now. "I thought you wanted to talk about Nell."

"Viv didn't tell you, when you spoke to her about Bella earlier?"

"I didn't talk to her, I texted her. She was in the middle of service. Tell me what?"

Cain would hear it soon enough, if not from Viv, then from Booth.

"We"—Kincaid corrected himself— "that is, the police, think Jack Doyle was run down deliberately."

Kerry Boatman had done herself a favor and parked in the Marks & Spencer parking garage on the King's Road. She quickly finished her shopping. Then, swinging her colorful paper bag, she'd walked west along the King's Road until she reached Old Church Street. She found the address Gemma had given her halfway down the street, across from the Pig's Ear, a pub well known as a hangout for coppers.

The buzzer for the second-floor flat was labeled BUSBY. Kerry took out her mobile and checked Gemma's instructions again. She had the right address. She pushed the buzzer and the front door clicked open before she could identify herself over the intercom.

As she climbed the stairs, a female voice came from above. "Oi, did you forget the blinking wine?" Looking up, Kerry saw a young woman with crayon-red short hair peering down at her. "Ow, sorry," the young woman said in deepest Estuary. "I thought you was my mate. Who're you?"

"Police," answered Kerry, a bit puffed as she reached the top landing. "I'm looking for Fergus O'Reilly's flat."

"You'd better come in, then," said the young woman. She stood back, allowing Kerry to step into a large sitting room, brightly lit by the west-facing bay window. The place seemed to be furnished entirely in Ikea and bean bags, with pride of place given to the monster flat-screen TV on one wall.

Introducing herself, Kerry showed her warrant card even though she hadn't been asked. People really should be more careful.

The girl, who was wearing leggings and an oversized jumper

that would have made Kerry's daughter swoon, put out a chubby, be-ringed hand. "Valerie Busby. Yeah, he used to live here, that chef bloke. But he moved out about a year ago—some TV gig in la-la land, according to my landlady, who was right pissed off, I can tell you."

"Why was that?"

"He didn't pay his last month's rent, did he? And he didn't leave no forwarding address."

CHAPTER TWENTY-ONE

SEPTEMBER 2007

To Viv's enormous relief, the second cocktail of antibiotics checked her mother's infection. But it was forty-eight hours before the doctors cautiously said she might be out of the woods. The doctors warned, however, that the severity of the infection might have damaged her heart, and that her recovery would be slow.

Viv's brother had gone back to university on the third day, but it was a full week before Viv could bring herself to leave her dad to manage her mum's convalescence on his own.

Having stopped to drop off a few things at her flat in Selwood Place, she walked across the King's Road and into the restaurant kitchen just as evening service began.

Fergus, whom she'd texted that she was on her way back, barely looked up from the starter he was plating. "Nice of you to put in an appearance," he said, making it sound like she'd been off sunning herself somewhere other than the chicken coop on her parents' smallholding.

It was Ibby who stopped what he was doing long enough to give her a hug and ask after her mum. She changed and slotted herself into her usual place on the line, but she could tell from the very first that the atmosphere in the kitchen had changed. It was so tenuous and indefinable, the synergy of a kitchen. When everything worked, it was an almost liquid thing—one station flowed smoothly into another and the communication on the line was seamless. But now their timing was off, tempers were frayed, orders were got wrong. Fergus was irritable and edgy, and she had a horrible feeling that he was back on the coke.

At the end of a night that had seemed interminable, he walked out halfway through the scrub down after an argument with John, and didn't come back.

Exhausted and disappointed, she was fighting tears as she changed into her street clothes. Ibby tapped on the office door. "Viv, how about I see you home."

She hadn't realized how much she'd been dreading that walk until he offered. "Yeah, sure," she said. "Let me get my jacket." The nights had turned chilly just in the short time she'd been gone—autumn was upon them.

They made desultory chat about her stay in Evesham and that night's near disasters in the kitchen until Viv swallowed and said, "What's up with Fergus, then?"

She could feel Ibby shrug as he walked in step with her. "Nerves, I think. First of October is coming up." That was the date for the release of the next year's Michelin guide.

"I think it's more than that."

"Yeah, well. You were his buffer. He's been an absolute shit the whole time you've been gone. But there was no way he was going to admit that he missed you. To be honest, I think it scared the crap out of him."

The day after the first time she'd slept with Fergus, Viv had gone into work feeling like she must have a big red S for SHAGGED stamped on her forehead. It was only when no one seemed to notice that she realized they'd all assumed she and Fergus were having it off all along—and then it was too late to protest.

"He's been using again, hasn't he?"

"Yeah, well, he's been out with the boys a few times."

"And the girls?"

There was a long pause. She knew Ibby was trying to figure out how to answer. "Yeah, a couple of times," he finally said.

"Works fast, doesn't he, our Fergus."

"I wouldn't take it too seriously, Viv. They were just fluff."

Fluff. Entertainment. While she'd been afraid her mother was dying.

Christ. What had she expected?

They'd reached her flat. "Look, Ibby, thanks for—"

"Can I come in for a drink, Viv?" He shuffled, hands in his pockets. "I won't stay long."

Viv frowned at him. There was nothing flirtatious in his manner, but she couldn't figure out what it was that he wanted. "Sure. Okay. Just a quick one." And to be honest, she was glad of the company.

In the summer, she'd moved from the flat she'd leased for years in Hammersmith, near the restaurant on the river where she'd first trained. Although the rent was steep because of the location, *she loved the new flat, loved being able to walk to work. Or to Fergus's—or so she'd thought.*

She unlocked the door and Ibby followed her in.

"Nice," he said as she switched on the lights. The sitting room was small, but she'd painted the walls a soft white, then centered her meager furniture on an Indian carpet in deep greens and blues. She'd hung some original artwork, pride of place over the mantel taken by a large watercolor of the rolling Cotswold Hills near Evesham.

It was the kitchen that had sold her on the place. It was big enough to actually cook in, with a German gas range and a center table that could be used for prep. French doors led out to a small back garden.

"What can I get you?" she asked, when she'd stashed her bag in the pokey bedroom.

"Gin and ice, if you have any."

Viv fetched two tumblers from the kitchen and filled them with ice from a bag she kept in the freezer, then cut up a rather shriveled lime and added wedges to both glasses. Going to the restaurant dessert trolley that served as her drinks cart, she poured them both a generous slug of Bombay Sapphire and handed Ibby his glass. "Cheers."

Ibby sat on the sofa, but she switched on the gas fire, then stood with her back against the mantel.

"I'm glad your mum is better," he said. "Fergus said it was an infection."

"I'm surprised he remembered. But thanks." Shivering as the first swallow of cold gin hit her stomach, she moved directly in front of the fire.

Ibby swirled the ice in his glass, avoiding her gaze. He seemed hunched into the jacket he hadn't removed, and Viv realized that she'd been so caught up in herself that she hadn't realized how unhappy he looked. In spite of his grousing in the kitchen, Ibby was, she'd learned, a pretty decent guy as well as a good cook. Better than good, but she doubted he'd ever make head chef. He hadn't the people skills needed to manage a kitchen.

"The kitchen totally sucked without you," he said. "We were in the weeds every night. I'd forgot how it was before you came. And you were right about the blow. Fergus and Danny have been out every night. Danny had a nosebleed during dinner service yesterday." Danny, their maître d', was Ibby's closest friend. They'd come to O'Reilly's together.

"Christ." Viv took another swallow of gin, hoping the alcohol would generate some warmth from the inside. "How bad was it? Tell me Michelin didn't come again."

"I don't think so. But there's this." Ibby pulled a folded newspaper clipping from the inside pocket of his leather jacket and stood to hand it to her. "I thought you should see it."

It was from the Times. Viv unfolded it with trepidation. It was not, however, a bad review, but an interview. The restaurant critic had quizzed Fergus about the success of O'Reilly's new menu, asking him what had inspired his foray into Irish-influenced fine dining. Fergus had waffled on about the glory of Irish products, missing his homeland, even adding some nonsense about his poor dead mam's cooking. But not once had he mentioned Viv.

Melody slammed out the front door of the house. She knew she'd promised to drive Doug to the station, but he could bloody well get a taxi.

Following in Andy's footsteps, she walked up the drive, then stood, irresolute, at its end. She didn't want to go down to Lower Slaughter. It would be too difficult to avoid Gemma and Duncan, and what if they had seen Andy, and then she'd have to explain? So she turned right and walked uphill, towards Upper Slaughter.

The smaller of the two Slaughters, the village boasted only a church and a rather lovely country-house hotel, along with its few streets of cottages and the occasional B and B. Most of the village was hidden from the road—you could pass it without ever knowing you'd missed it.

She turned on Rose Row, which ran downhill and into the village proper. But it also led to the church, and it seemed to Melody that the churchyard in the middle of a Sunday afternoon was one place where no one was likely to bother her. She'd played hide-and-seek round the giant yew hedges as a child, and as a teenager had sneaked into the churchyard for the occasional illicit drink and a snog with one of the boys from the village. She had no idea what had happened to him—he was probably married with three kids. It was she who'd rebelled against all those expectations, and look where that had got her.

So involved was she in that morose train of thought that she was almost past the woman washing her Mercedes SUV in front of one of the cottages before she recognized her. She'd completely forgotten that Roz Dunning lived in the village.

Looking up, Roz seemed just as startled to see her. "Melody, what are you doing here?" she said, sounding unexpectedly hostile. Roz, who was always so well turned out, looked cross and thoroughly untidy in cropped yoga bottoms and a baggy jumper, her hair escaping from its ponytail in damp straggles.

"Just taking a walk," Melody answered, making an effort to be pleasant. "Good day to do something outside, isn't it?"

"Oh, yes." Roz pushed back a strand of hair, leaving a soapy streak on her forehead. "Must make the most of it, this time of year, mustn't we? I'm glad the weather held for yesterday's party."

Roz seemed friendlier, now that she knew Melody hadn't come to interrupt her, but Melody could have kicked herself for having introduced that staple of polite and awkward English conversation—the weather. "You'll be going back to London today?" Roz asked, and it was only then Melody realized that with Gemma and the kids staying over, she hadn't worked out what to do herself. As little as she'd wanted company, the thought of driving back alone today, and of the empty flat that awaited her, seemed more than she could face.

What if she stayed as well? At the moment she didn't much care whether it would piss off her super if she didn't come in to work in the morning.

"Um, I'm not sure. My friends are staying over another day, so I may, too." Roz had left the door of her cottage standing open and Melody glanced in, curious in spite of herself. She knew from her mum that Roz had been widowed quite young. She and her husband had owned an accountancy firm before her husband died of a heart attack, and Roz had sold the business. She hadn't done too badly for herself out of it, Melody thought, considering the cottage and the car.

"Well, I'd better get on, while the sun lasts." Roz gestured at her bucket and the dripping sponge she'd set down on the car's perfect silver paintwork.

"Oh, right." Melody felt surprisingly rebuffed. "Well, good

luck with it, then." She nodded and walked on to the church, with no more disturbance than the caws of the churchyard's resident crows.

Sunday lunch had wound down to a last few guests lingering over coffees and the dregs of their wine. Gemma had done whatever she'd been told by Bea or Ibby or the serving staff, and her feet were beginning to complain.

Viv and Bea had decided that they would close the pub after Sunday lunch service. Bea had been able to cancel the few evening bookings, and had already put the CLOSED sign out front again. She'd then taken over the bar and sent Ibby back to the kitchen so that Viv could go and check on Grace.

"Well, we got through that, at least," Bea said to Gemma as she racked the clean glasses Gemma had just brought her from the kitchen. She looked shattered, her pale skin almost translucent and the hollows under her eyes almost as dark as bruises.

Gemma chided herself for having been so concerned over Viv's welfare that she hadn't thought about Bea's, especially as she'd overheard some of Bea's low-voiced conversations with the locals who'd asked after Jack. "This must have been so tough for you today," she said.

Bea sighed. "Better not to have turned people away. And the locals who'd already heard the news wanted to talk about it. And to offer condolences." She smiled at Gemma. "But you have been a star today. I don't know how we'd have managed any of this without you."

"But, I only—"

"Viv finds you a comfort. I'm sorry you'll be leaving us. Today, is it?"

"I think the kids and I are going to stay over until tomorrow, at least. Duncan has to sort out things with the car, and, to be honest, I want to make sure he gets those injuries looked at again. I hope he didn't overdo it, taking the dog up to Mark Cain's. He should have been back by now." She'd meant to ask Melody if she'd mind giving him a lift up to Beck House, but Melody hadn't answered her calls. "If you can spare me for a few minutes, I need to make a phone call."

"You go right ahead." Bea summoned a smile. "You've done more than enough today already."

Thanking her, Gemma walked out into the car park. It was almost empty now, and Booth's Volvo was gone. First, she tried Kincaid, but the call went to voice mail. Then, instead of trying Melody again, she rang Doug's number. He picked up on the first ring.

"Doug? Melody's not answering her phone. Is everything okay there?"

"If you mean are the kids okay, they're fine. They're having a proper tea party on the terrace with Ivan and Addie." Doug's voice sounded strained and starchy.

"Where's Melody?"

"I don't know. She left."

"What? In the car?"

"No, on foot, I guess. I heard her go out. Her car's still here."

Frowning, Gemma said, "Doug, what the hell is going on? Why would Melody leave the kids when she said she'd look after them?"

"It's my fault. I did something really stupid."

As he explained the whole sorry business, Gemma started tapping her foot in exasperation. "Doug, how could you be such an idiot?"

"Good question. And now I've stranded myself. She was going to take me to the station. I'll feel like a prat asking Ivan or Addie. And wasn't she supposed to drive you and the kids back to London?"

"We're staying over. She knows that. I talked to her earlier. But you—I don't blame her for being furious with you. You'd better stay until you can sort things out with her. If you leave, it's going to fester, and you may never be able to put it right."

"But she won't talk to me."

"Then keep trying until she does. Look, let me see if I can collect Kit, and find Duncan. Apologize to Addie and Ivan for me. I'll be there as soon as I can."

She rang off, shaking her head. How could someone as smart as Doug Cullen be such a pillock? He did care about Melody, in his own prickly way, and he probably had thought he was doing the right thing. That didn't make his interference any less wrong—or damaging. Poor Melody. Poor Andy, for that matter. But there was nothing she could do for either of them at the moment.

She turned and went through the arch into the courtyard, intending to fetch Kit from the kitchen. Viv and Bea were sitting on the bench outside the cottage. Bea had her arm round Viv's shoulders and Viv looked as if she was crying.

"What's wrong?" Gemma asked as she reached them.

Viv raised a tear-stained face. "She won't even speak to me. I don't know what to do."

"Grace?"

"You just have to give her time, love," Bea said, giving Viv's shoulders a squeeze. "I'll have another talk with her, shall I? See if

I can convince her she's being unreasonable." Getting up, she went into the cottage. Gemma sat down in her place on the bench.

"I'm so sorry." Viv sniffed and fished a tissue out of the pocket of her apron. She blew her nose, then gave Gemma a watery smile. "I promise I'm not usually such a mess. First, Fergus, and poor Nell Greene. And now, Jack. But I think I could cope with all of that if it weren't for Grace being so angry with me. Thank God she'll talk to Bea."

"They're close, aren't they? You're lucky to have that." Gemma thought of all the support her friend Hazel had been to her and her kids.

"Bea and I both lost our mums. That's how we met, you know. I came back to Evesham when my mum was ill—she had a heart condition—and got a job in a pub there. Bea was the front of house manager. After my mum died, Bea and I invested in this place. We've been like family ever since."

The kitchen door opened and Kit and Ibby came out, carrying bags of rubbish to the big bin. Ibby seemed to be telling Kit a story. Kit was listening, rapt, and laughing as they went back in. He hadn't even noticed Gemma and Viv.

"Ibby's all right, too," said Viv. "In spite of the attitude. He's known Grace since she was a baby. If anything were to happen to him—" Viv balled her tissue in her fist and met Gemma's gaze. "Gemma, who could have done such a terrible thing to Jack?"

"I'm sure that Detective Inspector Booth will find out. But these things take time. Try not to—"

But Viv was shaking her head. "I don't feel safe here anymore. I thought I made the right choice, raising Grace on my own. Coming here. Now I wonder if any of my choices were the right ones." Her voice rising, she went on, "I should never have agreed to the luncheon. I got greedy, thinking I could have more than this, thinking I could push my cooking up a notch, thinking maybe I could actually have a relationship with Mark. Sometimes I wonder if it was just my wanting those things that brought Fergus here."

Before Gemma could ask what she meant, Kincaid and Colin Booth came through the archway from the car park. One look at Kincaid's face told Gemma that the most important thing she had to do right this instant was to get him to rest. Anything else would have to wait.

LATE SEPTEMBER 2007

The next few weeks went by in a blur of long shifts and short tempers. One of the line cooks quit after Fergus had given him a royal bollocking in the middle of service, leaving Viv and Ibby to take up the slack until Fergus could hire somebody new, which he didn't seem bothered to do. Even before that, Viv had struggled to get the kitchen running with any kind of precision again. The food was good, Fergus's plates were exquisite, but the kitchen had lost its chemistry.

Like a cancer, the disruption spread. There was discontent in front of house. Plates were sent back by dissatisfied customers. Fights broke out among the waitstaff. Front of house got in a brawl after service one night with the crew from a neighboring restaurant, and one of their best waiters ended up in the A and E getting stitches in his head. Viv had been furious, not least because one of the waiters involved had been Ibby's friend Danny, and for days afterwards Ibby had been impossible to work with.

She'd carried the newspaper clipping tucked into her work bag, intending to confront Fergus over it, but she was afraid if she let her anger boil over, the situation in the kitchen would become untenable. She had too much invested in this job and this place to risk losing it all. So she avoided being alone with Fergus as much as possible. She cooked, she smoothed ruffled feathers. And then she went home after service to her flat. Alone.

The days crept by towards the first week in October, and the closer it came to the release date for the Guide, *the higher the tension grew in the kitchen. There was constant gossip in both front and back of house—someone knew someone who'd heard a leak—but there was no mention of O'Reilly's.*

On the morning of publication, they all gathered early in the kitchen. Fergus looked as though he might be ill, and Ibby was chewing his nails and sniping at everyone. When Viv volunteered to go to the nearest newsagent's, no one objected.

She felt a little queasy herself as she watched the newsagent unpack the newly arrived box, then pull out and ring up her copy of the red book. Taking her package outside, she stood, watching the traffic whiz past on Edith Grove, trying to still her shaking hands. Well, it was not going to get any easier, she thought, and slid the book from its plastic bag.

She thumbed through the pages, breathing hard, despair mounting.

Then she saw it.

O'Reilly's, Chelsea. With the distinctive red rosette. "For an innovative and beautifully presented take on traditional Irish cuisine."

They had done it.

Her mobile rang, then rang again, but she didn't answer. This news had to be delivered in person.

She jogged back to Phene Street, and when she reached the restaurant, she almost tumbled down the kitchen stairs. She stood in the doorway, her hands behind her back, trying to keep her poker face. They all turned to stare at her, looking stricken. Before Ibby could start to swear, she thrust the book up overhead and whooped, "We did it! We got the bloody star!"

"Jesus fecking Christ," mumbled Fergus, looking like he might faint. Then he crossed the kitchen, grabbed her round the waist and whirled her round before kissing her soundly in front of everyone. Then he snatched the book from her hand. "Woman, did you mean to give me a heart attack?"

They all gathered round. Fergus read the entry aloud, then the book was passed reverently from hand to hand.

Lunch and dinner service passed by in a blur. Everything went exactly the way it should and Viv thought they'd never turned out more sublime food. A good thing, too, as the word had spread quickly and the house was packed, with barely a letup in midafternoon.

When dinner service was finally over and the last work top had been washed down, they were still buzzing. Fergus called for a celebration and opened bottles of champagne for front of house and for the kitchen. A few glasses in, Ibby wrapped one arm round Viv and one round Fergus. "Tattoos," he mumbled, already a little owlish. "Just the three of us. All the same. With the star."

Viv looked at him askance. At heart, she was still a Cotswolds girl, and while lots of cooks sported art, she'd never got up the nerve. "At this time of night?"

"I know a good place. They'll open for us, tonight," Ibby assured them.

Fergus waved his glass. "I think it's a grand idea. The Three Musketeers of the fecking rose, that'll be us." And so they piled into a taxi to Soho.

When they emerged from the tattoo parlor a few hours later, all three bore matching crossed chef's knives and honing rods below the small red rosettes on their left forearms. Fergus hailed a taxi for Ibby and sent him on his way. Then, he looked down at Viv, who'd begun to shiver. It was cold and her arm was smarting. "Come to mine," he said.

"No."

"I'll come to yours, then." Looping his arm round her shoulders, he scanned Frith Street for another taxi. Viv tried to stop herself leaning into his warmth.

"Fergus, it's not a good idea—"

"And why is that? Don't be stubborn, darlin'. You know I've missed you."

She pulled away. "Fergus, why didn't you mention me in that interview, the one in the Times?"

He looked down at her, surprised. "Is that what's eating at you, then? Of course I mentioned you. But I had no say over what he decided to print, did I?"

A taxi was coming, its yellow light glowing like a beacon. Fergus pulled her to him again as he flagged down the cab. "This is our night, yours and mine, Viv. I told you, I need you." In the light from the streetlamp, his expression was suddenly naked. "On my life, I've never said a truer thing."

And Viv knew then that she was lost.

❧

Somehow, Melody had got through the rest of the afternoon. She'd come back to the house to find Doug still there, playing croquet with her parents, Gemma, and all the children, while Kincaid sat in a lawn chair someone had carried down to the croquet lawn for him. "I feel like the invalid uncle," he said with a smile as she sat on the grass beside him, but she could tell he didn't feel well. The bruising round his eye had deepened since she'd seen him that morning, and she thought he looked flushed.

"No, Char, you can't hit it back through the hoop!" Toby shouted, picking up Charlotte's ball, and it took Gemma's intervention to get the game back on track.

"You're not playing?" asked Kincaid.

"I don't think I'm up to my father's killer croquet," she said. "It makes you think it's a good thing he never took up golf." Although at the moment, he was patiently coaching Kit in the nuances of a shot.

"I'm glad we came. In spite of everything that's happened." Kincaid's expression was rueful. "I haven't really had a chance to thank you for inviting us. Your parents have been great. They're officially promoted to auntie and uncle status."

"They'll love that," Melody said, while wondering if Doug had talked to him about Andy. And if Gemma knew as well.

Doug kept shooting loaded glances at her, but she was determined not to let him get her alone. She didn't want his apologies—assuming he even meant to apologize.

When the light began to fade and the croquet set was put away—her father having very obviously allowed Toby to win—Melody helped Gemma get the younger kids up to the house for dinner. As they walked, she said quietly, "I'm sorry about this afternoon."

"Not to worry. They had a great time with your mum and dad. Melody"—Gemma stopped her with a touch— "I know you're upset. But Doug meant well." So that answered one question, Melody thought. Doug must have told her. "He does care about you, you know," Gemma added gently.

"Funny way of showing it." Melody was horrified to find the tears threatening again.

"You should give him a chance to make amends."

Melody was saved from answering that by the children scuffling over who got to wash their hands first.

Her mother had, of course, managed to gracefully feed the unexpected masses, pulling a huge fillet of salmon from the freezer, poaching it, and serving it with dill sauce and a cucumber salad. Her father had opened several bottles of his best Grüner Veltliner wine, of which Melody drank considerably more than her share while pushing the salmon round on her plate.

When everyone had finished, she busied herself with clearing the table and rinsing plates, topping up her wineglass in the process. But when Gemma and Duncan excused themselves to get the little ones ready for bed and Melody saw Doug coming towards her with a tea towel, she simply stopped what she was doing and walked straight out the scullery door.

The temperature had dropped rapidly since dusk and she was still in only jeans and a T-shirt. It was dark, too, and the light thrown through the French doors served only to cast the rest of the terrace into deeper shadow. Bumping against a chair, she stumbled, then picked her way across the terrace with her arms held out in front of her, like a blind person.

It was even darker once she left the terrace. The glasshouse loomed in front of her, and for a moment she thought of taking refuge in it. But it was too close to the house. She went on, down through the kitchen garden, falling once and skinning her knee on the edge of one of the boxed herb beds. When she reached the river path, she stepped right into a puddle left from last night's rain, soaking both feet.

Reaching the clearing, she realized she'd known all along where she was going. As before, Joe seemed to sense her presence and came out before she reached the porch.

"Melody? What on earth are you doing here?"

"I don't know," she said honestly. She couldn't seem to stop her teeth chattering and her feet felt like blocks of ice. "Can I come in?"

"Of course."

She stumbled again on the porch step and he hurried forward to help her, putting his arm firmly round her shoulders and propelling her through the door. "What happened to you?"

"Fell. Stupid," she managed, trying to push the hair back from her face, realizing too late that she must look an awful mess. "Needed to get out of the house."

The hanging lantern cast a soft light, and a fire crackled in the woodstove. Joe had obviously been sitting at the table, using a little battery-powered work light to tie fishing flies.

"You're freezing." Fetching the tartan rug from his bed, he draped it over her shoulders and urged her into the other chair, then studied her. "And you look a bit pissed, if you don't mind me saying so."

"Not a'tall," Melody said, not sure if she meant she wasn't pissed or that she didn't mind him saying so. "Can I have some of that good whisky you keep for my dad?"

He raised an eyebrow at that, but fetched the bottle and tumblers and poured them both a generous measure.

"Ta." Melody accepted the proffered glass, took a swig, and coughed. Joe thumped her on the back.

"You sure you're all right?" he said, sitting down beside her when she'd got her breath back.

Melody sipped more gingerly. "I'm fine. Really. It's just . . . things."

"I heard about Jack Doyle." Joe studied her, his dark eyes serious. "Is it true? That someone ran him down on purpose?"

"I don't know. I mean, I know the police think it's possible. But I haven't really been in the loop today." Her head was swimming. She tried to blink the room into focus. "Did you know him?"

"Well enough. Nice bloke." Joe drank half his whisky in one swallow. "Can't imagine why anyone would want to do that to him." It sounded like a question. "You're still shivering," he added, frowning at her.

"Feet. Stepped in a puddle."

"Why didn't you say?" Joe knelt beside her and slipped one shoe off. "You're sopping. The bottoms of your jeans are soaked, too." He pulled off her other shoe, then fetched a towel from the bookcase by his bed and rubbed her feet briskly. Blotting her shoes, he said, "I'll put these by the stove, okay? Take your jeans off and we'll dry them, too."

"But—"

"I won't look. You can wrap up in the rug." He turned his back.

Standing unsteadily, Melody slid her jeans down round her ankles, then wrapped the rug haphazardly round herself before plopping back down in the chair. The tartan wool was scratchy against her bare skin. "All clear," she said, and giggled.

Turning, Joe knelt and pulled her jeans free, then rubbed her feet again, this time with his hands. "Christ, you are cold. I always thought you were an ice princess, Melody Talbot."

"Not." She drank some more of the whisky. "I'm not, really. I promise."

Joe sat back, looking up at her, and she wanted to tell him to keep doing whatever he'd been doing to her feet. "I have an idea." Standing, he turned the gas on under the kettle on his little cook-stove.

On the table beside Melody, his mobile buzzed. He ignored it. "Don't you want to get that?" she asked.

With a quick step, he swiped the mobile from the table before she could read the caller ID, then switched the power off. "No. There's no one I want to talk to more than you."

Melody felt a clutch of panic as she realized she'd left her mobile in the house. But then she sat back, trying to tuck her feet under the rug and sip her drink at the same time. No one would be calling her, she didn't want to talk to anyone, and she didn't even want to think about Andy Monahan. "Are you making me a hot toddy, then?"

"No. A foot bath." Joe carried the now-steaming kettle over to his copper tub and poured the boiling water in. Then he moved his own chair to the edge of the tub and said, "Come on, shuffle over, sit here. The tub is cold, so the water will cool fast."

Setting her almost empty drink on the table, Melody did as she was told, edging carefully onto the chair and lifting her feet. Joe dipped a finger in the water, then splashed in a bit more from the big jug that stood beside the tub. Swirling the water, he said, "Okay, try it now."

Melody eased her feet in, gasping at the tingle. "Ow."

"Too hot?"

"No, no, it's lovely. It's just that I can feel my feet now."

Joe left her, refilling the kettle and putting it back on the gas. "I'll keep topping it up for you." When the water boiled again, he knelt beside the tub and carefully tipped a little more in. "Good?"

"Heaven." Melody could feel her damp hair curling into her flushed face. She had a sudden vision of Joe naked in the tub, and that made her turn even pinker.

Joe grinned up at her. "Melody Talbot, you are an enigma. Not so prim and proper, after all. Tell me," he added, suddenly serious, "is there a boyfriend?"

Swallowing hard, Melody said, "No. No, not anymore. But I, um, I think I need to get out now. I should go." She stood, clutching the rug at her waist, then wobbled as she attempted to step out of the tub. "I'm not sure I can do this gracefully."

"That's fixed easy enough." Standing, Joe simply wrapped both arms round her and lifted her over the lip of the bath. When Melody let go of the rug to put her arms round his neck, neither of them noticed it fall away.

CHAPTER TWENTY-TWO

On Monday morning, Kincaid's right hand was so stiff and swollen that he couldn't move his fingers. What he didn't tell Gemma was that the redness and swelling was also moving from his hand into his arm—she'd been worried enough as it was.

Gemma had meant to borrow Melody's car to take him to the A and E in Cheltenham, but Melody didn't come down to breakfast. It was Ivan who'd rung his GP for an appointment for Kincaid, and Ivan who'd insisted on driving him to Cheltenham. Addie, not to be outdone, had planned an outing for Gemma and the kids to the bird park in Bourton-on-the-Water while the fine weather held.

"I can't keep you from work," Kincaid protested to Ivan. "You've put up with enough trouble from us as it is."

"I've been working since five this morning," Ivan said with a chuckle. Having seen the array of computer screens in Ivan's home office, Kincaid hadn't doubted him. "I could use a break," Ivan added. "And I have an ulterior motive. A friend of mine has found a car you might want to look at."

Kincaid had checked in with his team at Holborn Station, then left Doug, who was ensconced once again with his laptop in the sitting room, to manage the bulk of the case management with their Holborn DI, Jasmine Sidana.

It wasn't until he was on the way to Cheltenham with Ivan that Kincaid suddenly realized his head felt clearer. While that was encouraging, it made him wonder just how muddled he'd been yesterday.

When they reached Dr. Saunders's surgery, however, she gave him a very critical eye. "Do you mind if Ivan comes in with you?" she asked, before ushering him into her consulting room.

"So I need a responsible adult?" Kincaid joked, but the sharp look she gave him said that was exactly what she meant.

"I feel much better," he protested as he sat on the exam table. "Really. It's just my hand that's playing up."

"Well, let's have a look at you," Dr. Saunders said briskly. She shone her pencil light in his eyes, checking his pupils. "Still equal and reactive, so that's a good sign. Headaches?"

"Not since yesterday."

"Taking it easy?"

"Um, more or less." Ivan's presence in the room made it impossible for Kincaid to tell an outright lie.

"Ribs?"

Kincaid grimaced. "Still pretty sore."

The doctor took the small pillow from the exam table and

positioned it against his right side. "Press this to you, bend over it, and cough."

"Ouch. That hurts like hell."

"I want you to do that two or three times every couple of hours. It's to keep you from getting pneumonia, so no slacking. Now, let's have a look at that hand." It was all Kincaid could do not to grit his teeth as she gently removed the dressing.

Shaking her head, Dr. Saunders clucked disapprovingly as she examined the spreading redness. "Cellulitis." When Kincaid looked blank, she added, "Bacterial skin infection. I'm going to clean and dress your hand again, but you'll need to start on antibiotic tablets straightaway. No missing a dose, mind. This can be dangerous if not treated, besides being bloody uncomfortable."

Dr. Saunders glanced at Ivan as she worked. "I heard about the poor fellow hit by the car Saturday night."

"That news traveled fast," Ivan said, quirking an eyebrow.

"Pathologist is a friend. We had drinks last night."

He grinned. "Is there anyone you don't know, Carol?"

"Small world, the medical community. As is your village, apparently. What a shame for Bea Abbott, all this. That young woman has had more than her fair share of tragedy."

"I seem to remember hearing something about her family," said Ivan, frowning. "When she and Viv Holland first bought the pub. Didn't her mother commit suicide? But that must have happened years ago."

"Bea was a teenager. A year or two above my daughter in school." She shook her head, her expression grim. "How someone can leave a child to live with that, I'll never understand."

A mobile phone rang. It was a moment before Kincaid realized it was his, still in the pocket of the jacket he'd left draped over a chair. "Sorry," he said, but he was held captive by Dr. Saunders's ministrations to his hand. Ivan obligingly handed him the mobile.

Kincaid had meant to decline the call, but when he saw it was Colin Booth, he murmured, "I'd better get this."

"Kincaid here," he answered, then listened, frowning. "Let me call you back," he said, and rang off.

"That was Booth," he told Ivan, adding for the doctor's benefit, "the DI investigating the Lower Slaughter deaths. He's going to interview Nell Greene's ex-husband and wants to know if we can meet him."

"Bruce Greene?" said Dr. Saunders, finishing Kincaid's new dressing.

"You know him, too?" asked Ivan.

"Yes, of course. I send my patients to him if they need a more thorough internal medicine workup than I can provide. He's not a bad sort, Bruce, aside from the fooling-around business."

Kincaid frowned as he rolled his shirtsleeve down. "You mean when he was married to Nell?"

Dr. Saunders sighed. "With one of his nurses, yes. But, as she's the second Mrs. Greene now, and we see them socially, I suppose I can't be too critical."

Taking a packet of tablets from the cupboard near the exam table, she handed them to Kincaid. "I want you to start these now. Take one three times a day, and I'll write you a prescription for more." As she fetched him a paper cup of water from a standing dispenser, she added thoughtfully, "You did know that Bruce Greene used to be partners with George Abbott, Bea's father?"

Kincaid stopped in the midst of buttoning his shirt cuff, an act he'd learned was quite difficult single-handed. "What? When was this?"

"Oh, it was years ago. Bruce dissolved the partnership after George's wife's suicide."

"Do you know why?" Kincaid asked.

"I have an idea, but it's not for me to tell you. You'll have to ask Bruce Greene."

"Oh, God." Melody managed to peel one eye open, then shut it again. Why was it so bloody bright? She rolled away from the light and the room swayed alarmingly. With the rush of nausea came a flash of memory, and that made her feel even more ill.

What on earth had she done? And just how big a fool had she made of herself?

"Oh, God," she said again, this time a moan, but she managed to open both eyes. Familiar ceiling. Familiar window. The guest room at Beck House. That at least was some comfort. She recalled now, in a jumble of images, waking in Joe's narrow bed before dawn, leaving him sleeping as she stumbled back to the house, quaking with cold.

Joe. She sat up, head pounding, and fumbled for her mobile, left last night on her bedside table. A glance at the time readout brought another unpleasant jolt—it was after ten. There were no texts from Andy. And there had only been one missed call, at half past eight, from Gemma, wanting to know if she could borrow her car.

Shit. What must Gemma be thinking? What must everyone be thinking?

Swinging her legs off the bed, she listened. The house was completely silent. Had they all packed up and gone back to London without her? Surely not. But that meant she was going to have to face everyone, and she was going to have to make up some excuse for lying in this morning. And she was going to have to apologize to Gemma.

But there was something she had to do first.

A shower and clean clothes having made her feel marginally better, she crept through the house, determined to avoid speaking to anyone, especially Doug, until she'd set things straight with Joe about last night.

She slipped out the front door and walked round the garage towards the kitchen gardens, hoping to find Joe somewhere out of sight of the house. She'd reached the glasshouse when she saw him coming towards her up the path from the kitchen garden.

"Melody," he called, hurrying to her. "Are you okay? I was worried sick about you. I couldn't ring you because I don't have your number, and I didn't want to come up to the house—I just wanted to say I was sorry about—"

"Yes, me, too," Melody broke in with a rush of relief. When he looked a bit hurt, she added, "Oh, I don't mean— Oh, this is awkward." Parts of the night came back vividly now and she flushed. "But we shouldn't have—"

"No, *I* shouldn't," Joe broke in with touching earnestness. "I shouldn't have taken advantage of your, um, of the situation—of you—"

"I was royally pissed, if that's what you're trying to say. And I put you in a terrible position. I wouldn't want anything we did to affect your job, or to embarrass you—"

The look he gave her was searching. "I thought maybe *you* were embarrassed about being with me—the gardener."

Melody shook her head. "Oh, Joe. Don't be daft. Of course I'm not embarrassed about you. But we can't— I mean I have—" She swallowed. "I guess you could call it unfinished business."

"The ex-boyfriend?" Joe said, and she could see the disappointment, quickly masked.

"Yes. That's why I was— Anyway, I need to try, at least, to sort things out. Things ended rather badly." An understatement, she thought, if ever there was one.

Joe nodded, his shoulders slumping. "I understand, but if things change . . ." He hesitated, his rueful smile vanishing. "Look, Melody, there's something else. Can we talk?"

"We are talking," she said, perplexed.

But Joe gave an anxious glance round, as if someone might be lurking in the shrubbery. "No, I mean—" He gestured toward the glasshouse. "Can we talk in there? It's sort of personal. There's something I need to tell you."

In her experience, those words never presaged good news. With a little cold lump of dread in her stomach, Melody followed him into the glasshouse. What, she wondered, could be more personal than apologizing for drunken shagging?

For once, the warm, earthy atmosphere in the glasshouse did not feel comforting. In its close confines, she could smell the wood smoke on Joe's clothes, and the scent of his soap.

Turning away from her, Joe gazed down at the neat rows of vegetables in the kitchen garden. "I'm not sure where to start."

Melody began making a mental list of dread diseases. "Look, Joe, if this is about—you know—what we did last night, you'd better tell me and get it ov—"

He swung round to face her again, looking shocked. "No, it's not about that at all. It's about that chef. The one who died in the car crash with Nell Greene."

"What?" Melody was completely blindsided. "You mean Fergus O'Reilly? What does he have to do with—"

"He was here. In the house."

It was a moment before Melody could do anything but stare. "You mean in *my* house?"

"Well, yeah, your parents' house, anyway."

"But surely not," Melody protested, frowning. "My parents didn't even know him. You must be mistaken."

Joe gave her a half smile. "Not likely. His wasn't a face you'd forget. Not that his face was the first part of him I saw."

Taking a step back, Melody connected with a pile of bagged mulch and inadvertently sat. "You'd better explain."

"It was maybe three weeks ago—"

"Then my parents wouldn't have been here. They only came down the beginning of last week."

"No, they weren't here," Joe agreed. "Roz was."

"Roz Dunning?" Now Melody was really baffled. "But she never said she knew O'Reilly."

"Well, I can tell you that she did know him—at least in the biblical sense." Joe sounded surprisingly snappish. "I came up to do my washing. I didn't know Roz was here that day. So when I walked into the house and heard thumping noises coming from upstairs, I thought the house was being burgled. I grabbed the emergency torch and crept upstairs as quietly as I could. By the time I'd reached the top I was pretty certain it wasn't burglars, but I kept going to your parents' bedroom." Joe winced. "That was a sight I wish I could un-see. But, then, they weren't best pleased to see me, either."

"Roz was with Fergus O'Reilly? They were . . . having sex? In my parents' room?"

"They certainly weren't playing charades."

"But——" Melody tried to wrap her mind round this. She wished her head would stop pounding. "This was three weeks ago?"

"Yeah. I usually do my washing on a Monday, so it was three weeks today."

According to what Melody had heard from the others, Fergus O'Reilly had checked into the manor house in Lower Slaughter three weeks ago, but hadn't spent the night in his hotel room. Had he been with Roz Dunning? "But if she knew Fergus, why see him here? She lives alone, right?"

"Roz says she didn't know him. He came to see your mother. He was hoping for an in with Viv, and a ticket to the luncheon. But of course your mother wasn't here, and Roz just——fancied him, I take it. I gather he was willing."

"But she——but he was a complete stranger? How could she——" Melody was appalled. But she couldn't pass judgment.

"Okay," she said. "So Roz was shagging Fergus O'Reilly, at least once that we know of. But after Fergus died, why on earth didn't she say she knew him? She was here when the police came to notify Viv."

"Maybe she didn't want your mum to think badly of her. Then, when there were rumors about his death, she didn't want to admit she hadn't been honest in the first place."

Melody frowned, thinking things through. Something didn't add up. "Joe, what I don't understand is why *you* didn't say anything before now."

He shoved his hands in his pockets and prodded a bag of mulch with the toe of his boot. "Because I've been an idiot. At first, I thought that Roz lying didn't matter, that the car crash was just an unfortunate accident. But then yesterday, when I heard Jack Doyle had been killed, I started to wonder. And I couldn't figure out why Roz was so determined no one find out about her and O'Reilly."

Melody remembered how hostile Roz had been yesterday when she'd happened on her washing her car. *Washing* her car. Christ. "Oh, God, Joe. You don't think Roz could have run down Jack Doyle? But—"

"Melody. Listen. There's more." He took a deep breath and she saw that he'd clenched his hands into fists. "I didn't say anything because Roz was blackmailing me," Joe blurted out. "You know she trained as an accountant, right? And that she keeps the business books as well as your mum's personal accounts?" He looked away. "Well, she found . . . discrepancies . . . in the business account. She threatened to tell your mother if I said anything about her and O'Reilly."

"But—" Melody could only stare at him. "Joe, are you telling me that *you* took money from the account?"

"I was going to pay it back." His gaze was pleading.

Melody had never known anyone who lived a more frugal life—not even Andy in his pre-fame days. "I can't believe that. Why would you do such a thing? Why not just tell my mother if you needed money for something?"

"Because I was ashamed. It's my stupid youngest brother. He's got himself in trouble for serious drugs, and my parents needed the money for the lawyer's fees. I didn't want your mum and dad to think badly of my family."

"Oh, Joe." Melody shook her head in exasperation. "You've been a bloody idiot. Listen to me. You are not responsible for your brother's actions. Neither are your parents. But this— You are going to have to deal with this."

"I know. And I know I have to tell Addie, but I had to tell you first. After last night, I didn't want you thinking I'd . . . Oh, God— that there were any false pretenses in what we . . . that I'd used you in any way. Christ, I've made a balls-up of things."

Melody remembered something. "Was that Roz who called you last night, when I was there?"

Joe nodded. "She was getting more and more . . . um, aggressive . . . in her threats."

"Have you spoken to her since?"

"No. I've blocked her number. She'll be livid."

"Don't speak to her, Joe. Not under any circumstances. You know I have to inform the police straightaway?"

He nodded. "I know."

Melody made an effort to pull herself together. "Okay. I don't think anyone's at home right now. But as soon as my mum comes back, you'll have to speak to her. You don't want her to hear about this from someone else." Melody hesitated, then added, "And, Joe, after what happened to Jack Doyle, just be careful, okay?"

Kerry Boatman reached Colm Finlay through his restaurant group's corporate offices first thing on Monday morning. To her surprise, he'd been eager to talk to her. He'd set up an appointment to meet with her at eleven o'clock at his Kensington restaurant, Pomme. The place was on Abingdon Road, just off Kensington High Street, a few minutes' walk from the police station.

When she reached the address, she found an unassuming shop

front occupying the ground floor of a bland postwar, three-story building. She knocked as Finlay had directed.

A moment later he opened the door, introduced himself, and ushered her in. "I had to meet with some suppliers here this morning," he said, "and I thought it would be easier for you than coming into the West End."

Finlay's corporation, Kerry had learned, owned several successful London restaurants, including one in a renowned Mayfair hotel. Finlay himself was short and sturdily built, with wavy dark hair going gray, a close-trimmed gray beard, and alert blue eyes. "If you'll just follow me back, we can chat in the chef's office." Even after years in London, Finlay's Belfast accent was still pronounced.

The interior of the restaurant surprised Kerry. She wasn't sure what she'd expected of a Michelin-starred venue, but the dining room was casual, wood floored, with square wooden tables, simple black-and-white chairs, and glossy white subway-tiled walls. A sleek black-framed gas fireplace anchored the dining room's far end.

As he led her past the gleaming bar, she had only a quick glimpse into the kitchen, where chefs were already at work, prepping for that night's service. Something already smelled fabulous.

Finlay led her into a small office behind the bar and seated her in front of a paper-strewn desk. "Can I get you anything? A coffee? Some tea?"

When she demurred, he got right down to business. "I only heard about Fergus yesterday. Jesus, I still can't believe it. I'd been trying to reach him for days, but I never imagined something like this . . ."

No one, Kerry thought, ever did.

"The newspaper said he was killed in a car accident in the Cotswolds," Finlay went on, "and I thought it must be a mistake. Fergus didn't drive, you know. Is it true, then?"

"I'm afraid it is," said Kerry. "I'm very sorry. I understand you were friends. Can you tell me why you were trying to reach Mr. O'Reilly?"

"Because I'd made him a job offer. But there were conditions, and there was a time limit on his acceptance." Finlay leaned back in his chair with a sigh. "I hope I'm not in some way responsible for what happened to Fergus, because I was the one who sent him haring off to the bloody Cotswolds. The restaurant group had recently acquired a new property in the West End, but the chef who was to take on the place had to renege at the last minute. Fergus had been in touch with me, looking for a job. We started in the same hotel in Belfast, you know, and we had a brief partnership after O'Reilly's went under. Before he came to me a couple of months ago, I'd never have considered working with him again."

"Why was that?" she asked.

Rocking forward again, Finlay picked up a pencil and tapped it on the nearest stack of papers. Kerry got an impression, not of nerves, but of the suppressed energy in the man. "Because Fergus snorted our profits up his nose. I'd heard rumors, of course, about O'Reilly's, but I thought he was good enough to compensate for the bad habits. Turned out I was wrong.

"But then Fergus turned up on my doorstep last summer, swearing he was clean, had been for more than a year. I even let him stay in my flat, because I wanted to see for myself. I'd been toying with the idea of giving Irish fine dining another try." He flashed a sud-

denly mischievous grin. "Not that I'd attempt to give Dickie Cor-
rigan a run for his money, mind you. There's only a limited market
for three-star dining, while restaurants like this one"—he waved
an expansive hand— "have a very good chance of succeeding with
the right formula. And Fergus—a sober Fergus—seemed like a
godsend."

"Then why send him to the Cotswolds?" Kerry asked, not quite
following the logic.

"Because of Viv Holland. *She* was the condition. I'd heard
about this luncheon she was catering from my reviewer friend at
the *Chronicle*, and I wanted her on board. The thing is, Fergus is—
Fergus was—brilliant. But Viv was pure bloody genius." Finlay's
tone was reverent. "She was the secret ingredient in the sauce, if
you'll forgive me the cliché. Together, they were dynamite."

"So Fergus went to the Cotswolds to make Viv an offer?"

"One she surely couldn't refuse. Viv Holland, cooking in a
bloody pub kitchen." Finlay grimaced. "Sweet Jesus, what a waste."

"Did she accept?"

"The thing is, I don't know." Finlay tapped his pencil again.
"Fergus kept putting me off, said they were still ironing things out
and he needed to go down there again. That was last week. That
was why I'd been ringing him. His time was up as of today. I had
to make a decision."

Kerry made a few quick notes, then looked back at Finlay with a
frown. "You mentioned rumors about O'Reilly's. What were you
referring to?"

"Ah, well, that's ancient history. I probably shouldn't have
mentioned it. One of the staff died suddenly. The story was that it
was a cocaine overdose."

DECEMBER 2007

Viv had already thrown up three times that night when they got the news, halfway through service.

Danny, their maître d', hadn't shown up for work and hadn't answered his mobile. One of the servers had gone to his flat to check on him, but that had been hours ago. When the girl finally stumbled down the stairs into the kitchen, her face chalky, Viv felt the sickness rise again. "What's happened?" she said.

The girl stifled a sob. "He's dead. Danny's dead. I got his neighbor to let me in. He was slumped on his sofa. He'd been ill— Oh, God, it was awful."

They had all stopped in midtask. Ibby came up to her, his face drawn in shock. "No, that's bullshit. Danny can't be dead."

"I swear it's true. I called an ambulance. The paramedics said he'd been gone for, like, hours. Maybe a stroke or a heart attack. And he had"—she touched her nose—"you know, all down his front and on the coffee table—"

Fergus was shaking his head. "No, he was okay when I left him last night. He was fine."

Ibby rounded on him, crossing the kitchen in two strides. "You! You bastard, Fergus. You were with him. You must have seen he was doing too much—"

"Bloody shut up, Ibby," Fergus spat back at him. "We had a couple of drinks, that's all, then he went home. He was fine." They were almost nose to nose, with Ibby standing on his toes to get right in Fergus's face.

Ibby shook his finger at him, poking Fergus in the chest. "Don't give me that bullshit. If he's dead, it's your fucking fault, Fergus."

"Fuck off, Ibby." Fergus knocked his hand away. "It's too bad about Danny, but we've got a service to finish." He turned away, reaching for a squeeze bottle.

But Ibby lunged, grabbing him by the throat. Fergus had the advantage of height, but Ibby's hands were strong and Fergus struggled to loosen his grip.

Viv was nearest. She bolted towards them, grasping Ibby round the waist with one arm while she tried to break his grip on Fergus's throat with the other. The rest of the cooks piled on and after a few seconds of straining and a flurry of blows and swearing, they managed to drag the two apart.

Fergus, panting with fury, shook off their restraining hands and faced Ibby. "Get. Out. Of. My. Kitchen," he bit out. "I'll see you never work in this city again, you little shite."

Viv still had a hand twisted in the back of Ibby's white jacket. She could feel him breathing, short and sharp, until he jerked out of her hold. But he didn't go for Fergus again.

Very slowly and deliberately, he pulled the ties on his apron and let it drop to the floor. Then he unbuttoned his white jacket and shrugged out of it, all the while never taking his eyes from Fergus. When the jacket had joined the apron, he spoke with deadly calm. "You can keep your bloody kitchen, Fergus O'Reilly. But I'm going to make you pay for this, you wait and see if I don't."

CHAPTER TWENTY-THREE

Ivan dropped Kincaid at the elegant detached house in St. George's Road near the hospital, where Dr. Greene had his practice. Booth was already waiting for him in the parking area, leaning on his Volvo while checking his mobile.

"Going to live?" Booth called as Kincaid got out.

"Hopefully." Kincaid lifted a hand to Ivan as he drove away. "Nice place," he said, indicating the surgery. He'd seen other surgeries in similar properties along the road, as well as a day nursery and a care home. A few of the houses still seemed to be family homes, but Kincaid imagined the soaring cost of real estate had driven these large places above most family budgets.

"The practice has a good reputation," said Booth, pocketing his phone. "My wife has a friend who sees one of the doctors here. This interview is really just ticking the boxes, making sure that Nell Greene didn't have some connection with O'Reilly that hasn't yet come to light. Dr. Greene's agreed to see us between appointments."

As Kincaid followed Booth into the building, he wondered if Dr. Abbott had practiced from this house as well. A plump, middle-aged receptionist greeted them and took them immediately into Dr. Greene's office.

Even if he'd passed him in the street, Kincaid would have recognized Dr. Bruce Greene from the wedding photo Nell kept in her bedside table. The man was still trim and youthful looking, and would, Kincaid thought, have been handsome if his face had not been lined with shock.

When they'd introduced themselves and taken the visitors' seats, Dr. Greene sank heavily into the leather chair behind his desk. "I still can't believe it," he said. "I was away at the weekend—a cottage in the Lake District with no mobile reception. It wasn't until we started home yesterday afternoon that I got the messages. Everyone at the hospital knew before me. I feel as though I should have been here, that Nell had no one—" He broke off, blinking. "I don't understand what Nell was doing with that man in her car."

"We were hoping you might tell us," said Booth. "Do you know of any previous connection your wife might have had with Mr. O'Reilly?"

"That chef? Why would Nell have known a London chef?" Greene seemed affronted by the very idea. Kincaid wondered if he'd have been just as incensed at the idea of any man with his ex-wife.

"Was your wife not interested in cooking, then?" asked Booth.

"Nell was always very career oriented. That was one of the

reasons I—" Greene seemed to think better of what he'd been about to say. "Nell's idea of dinner was a ready meal, I'm afraid. And the occasional Sunday roast. I couldn't imagine what she meant to do with herself when she took early retirement." There was definite disapproval in his tone now, and Kincaid felt a bit less favorably disposed towards him. The man had thought his wife should be more of a homemaker, but hadn't liked her leaving her job when she was no longer married to him.

"I take it you two were still . . . cordial?" Kincaid asked.

The bristle seemed to go out of Dr. Greene. "Well, we weren't in each other's pockets, but I'd say we were on friendly enough terms." He hesitated, then added, "I've just had a call from Nell's solicitor. This is very awkward. It seems I was still the designated beneficiary of Nell's estate. And her executor. I never thought—" Closing his eyes, he steepled his fingers beneath his nose for a moment.

"Does that estate include Nell's cottage?"

"Yes. And her savings and investments, which were not in-considerable. I don't want— Well, I shall have to see what's to be done."

"And the dog?"

"It will have to go back to the breeder. I'm allergic, I'm afraid." Greene brushed his hands together, as if disposing of a problem. "I've spoken to the vicar," he went on. "I'm to meet with her in the morning about arrangements, and then I suppose I'll have a look at the cottage."

"Dr. Greene," put in Booth, glancing at his notebook, "is there anyone who can confirm that you were away the entire weekend?"

Greene frowned. "Well, my wife, of course. And I suppose the owner of the cottage where we stayed in the Lakes. What sort of a question is that?"

"Just part of our inquiries. There were some irregularities in the death of your ex-wife's passenger."

"Irregularities? What are you talking about? And what can that possibly have to do with our weekend away?"

"Nothing, I'm sure. It's just that it appears Mr. O'Reilly died prior to the accident."

"What?" Greene stared at him. Kincaid thought his skin looked suddenly papery against his dark hair—and that the hair was perhaps a bit too evenly brown to be natural for a man in his fifties.

"His heart, apparently," Booth said. "The Mercedes coupe parked out front, the E-Class? Is that yours?"

"Well, yes." Pride replaced some of Greene's irritation, although he still looked at them suspiciously. "It's quite new. That's one of the reasons we took the weekend in the Lakes. I wanted to try it on a long drive."

Booth closed his notebook with a snap and slipped it back in his pocket. "Thank you, Dr. Greene. We won't take up any more of your time. I'm sorry for your loss."

As Booth started to stand, Kincaid said, "One more thing, Doctor. I understand that at one time you shared your practice with a Dr. Abbott."

Greene seemed suddenly wary. "What of it? That was years ago."

"Would you mind telling me why you dissolved the partnership?"

"I don't see—" Greene gave an impatient glance at his watch, then sighed. "Well, if you must know, there had been issues . . . I'd long worried that George was a bit too free with his prescriptions. On top of that, Nell and I disliked the way he treated his wife. Frankly, he was a bully. Then, when Laura died—" His gaze grew distant with the recollection. "It was a terrible time. She—" Greene cleared his throat before going on. "She cut her wrists in the shower. And if that wasn't bad enough, they found medications in her system, things George had prescribed. Rumors were flying. It was all just too . . . awkward. I felt I couldn't continue to associate with him."

"Is George Abbott still practicing?" Kincaid asked.

"No. He retired a few years ago. Rather reduced circumstances, I believe."

"Did you know that George Abbott's daughter lived in the same village as your ex-wife?"

Booth gave Kincaid a sharp glance as Greene's eyes widened. "No," said Greene. "I had no idea."

Kincaid shrugged. "Well, small world, I'm sure." He knew he was going to have to answer to Booth for throwing the Abbott thing out without filling him in first, and he wanted time to think about it. "My condolences, Dr. Gre—"

"Did you say you were a superintendent?" Greene broke in, rising from his chair, the bristles back in full force. "What is a superintendent doing asking questions about my wife, and my practice? You'd better tell me what's going on here."

"I'm not with the local force, Dr. Greene. My interest is personal. I was in the other car."

Melody saw that both garage spaces were empty, but her little Clio still sat pulled to one side, so Gemma hadn't taken it. When she went inside, she found the house silent, the kitchen post-breakfast tidy. It still smelled faintly of coffee and bacon.

Both Gemma's and her mother's handbags were missing from the hall bench, and her father's Barbour was gone from its hook. Melody stood in the hall, listening. From the sitting room came the faint click of a keyboard.

Well, there was nothing for it. She walked quietly across the hall and stopped at the sitting room door. He was sitting on the sofa, turned away from her. Light from the end-table lamp glinted on his fair hair.

"Doug."

He gasped and stood, just catching the laptop before it crashed to the floor. His eyes looked enormous behind the round lenses of his glasses. "Melody! What the— You scared the crap—" He stopped, and she saw his Adam's apple move as he swallowed hard. Clutching the laptop to his chest, he said, "Listen, Melody, I want to talk to you—"

"Not now, Doug." She took a step farther in. "Something's happened. I've got to ring Duncan, and then I need your help."

The bird park in Bourton-on-the-Water turned out to be much more enjoyable than Gemma had anticipated. It was well-planned and in a lovely setting, along the River Windrush and within walking distance of the village center. All three children enjoyed the exhibits, especially the penguins and the dinosaur trail, although Charlotte had got a bit whiny by the end. To keep the peace, Gemma bought her a stuffed flamingo in the gift shop, as well as books and puzzles for the boys.

Afterwards, they walked back along the Windrush to the town

center, where Addie chose a café on the river called the Rose Tree for their lunch. After Addie had a friendly word with the hostess, they were given a table in the front window, with a view of the riverside.

"Go on, have a glass of wine, Gemma," Addie encouraged when they placed their orders. "You're not driving, and you've had quite the weekend."

"You've been too generous, looking after us all," Gemma responded, but she took Addie's advice and ordered a glass of white wine to go with the grilled aubergine salad Addie had recommended. The menu had a special gin section, and reading through it had made Gemma think of Jack Doyle with a pang, remembering the Cotswolds Dry Gin he'd insisted she try.

"Have you heard from Duncan?" Addie asked. The children were occupied, Toby reading aloud to Charlotte from the book on penguins Gemma had bought him, Kit engrossed in something on his mobile even though electronics at the table were against their usual family rules.

Gemma had repeatedly checked for messages while they'd been at the bird park, and again just as they'd walked in. "No, nothing," she said.

"I'm sure he's fine. I have every confidence in Dr. Saunders."

"Yes, and Duncan did seem a bit brighter this morning. But—" Gemma struggled to put her worries into words. "I think he somehow feels responsible for what happened—not at fault, just responsible. A sort of debt, because he lived and they didn't, Nell and Fergus O'Reilly. I hate for him to go home with that weighing on him."

"Are the police no further forward? With either matter," Addie added circumspectly, with a glance at the children.

"I've not heard anything, but then I'm not exactly in the loop."

When their food arrived, it was as good as Addie had promised, and Gemma was soon busy with making sure the younger two children minded their manners.

"Can we look at the ducks, Mummy?" Charlotte asked when the children had finished.

"If Kit goes with you," Gemma said, lingering over her last sip of wine while Addie signaled for the check—which she refused to let Gemma pay. "Addie, really," Gemma protested, "that's too much, after everything you've done."

"I've enjoyed every bit of it," Addie told her firmly. "It's been too long since we've had children in the house—or a houseful at all—and I'm glad we've had a chance to get to know you and your family." With a sigh, she slipped her bank card back into her purse. "Melody never brings anyone home, you know. She thinks we disapprove of her job, but that's not true at all. We were afraid she was putting herself in an untenable position, because of her connection with the paper. What we didn't expect"—Addie stopped, a frown barely crinkling the corners of her blue eyes—"was the young man who turned up at the house yesterday. I recognized him, you know. He was there at St. Pancras, when the bomb went off. We've watched the videos from that day, over and over. But I had no idea he and Melody were—whatever they are. Why didn't she tell us?" The slightest catch in Addie's voice betrayed, for once, her polished exterior.

"Oh, you know Melody," Gemma said, perhaps too breezily. "She's very good at compartmentalizing things. It's only the past few months that she's even had any of us round to her flat. I think that was a big step for her—she's been so determined to separate work from her personal life."

Addie was not to be deflected. "Is she serious about him?"

"I'd have thought so, yes. He's a nice bloke, Andy. I hope she hasn't—" Gemma realized her tongue was running away with her. She gave Addie an apologetic smile and reached for her handbag. A glance out the window told her that Toby was leaning too far over the water. "Well, anyway, we should probably be going before Toby falls in with the ducks."

As they left the restaurant, Addie took a phone call while Gemma went to join the children. The wind had risen, lifting Charlotte's hair into a dandelion puff, and the sky had gone milkily opaque. Gemma shivered.

Having shooed the little ones back from the river's edge, Kit came over to stand beside her. "Weather's changing," Gemma said. "I'm glad we had a nice morning." When Kit didn't respond, she looked at him more closely. "What is it, love? If you're worried about your dad, I'm su—"

"No. I mean, yes, of course, I hope he's okay, but that's not what— I was wondering what was going to happen to Bella."

"The collie?"

Kit nodded. "Grace was texting me. I gave her my mobile number. I mean, she's nice, but she keeps asking me all these weird questions."

"What sort of weird questions?"

Scuffing his shoe against the verdant green of the riverside grass, Kit looked into the middle distance. "Like, what it's like, living in London."

"I don't think that's so weird."

"Yeah, but she wanted to know if I knew Dad before my mom—before I came to live with him. And she kept trying to prove something with the dog. It was like she had to make Bella love her more than she loved the lady who died, Nell, and that's just"—he shrugged his thin shoulders—"well, wrong. It's not fair to Bella."

Gemma considered this. "But that's understandable, don't you think? Grace is still a child after all." An oddly self-centered child, Gemma had to admit.

"Yes, but—" Kit turned to her, serious and intent. "I like Viv," he went on. "I think she's really cool. And nice, you know, a nice person. But Grace keeps saying her mother is mean to her, like deliberately. That her mum hates her and doesn't want her to be happy."

"But all kids go throu—"

Kit was shaking his head. "This isn't like griping 'cause you're grounded or you've lost your mobile privileges. This is like she really believes this stuff and it's just . . . weird. She seems to think her mum deliberately kept her from seeing her dad."

Gemma slipped her arm round his shoulders in a quick hug. "I'll have a word with Viv, okay? See if I can sort out what's going on." She gave him what she meant to be a reassuring smile. Kit might be overly sensitive, but she'd learned to trust his instincts. Something was not right between Viv Holland and her daughter.

Back in the surgery car park, Kincaid had just begun to explain to Booth about his conversation with Dr. Saunders when Melody rang. He listened, alarm growing, as Melody filled him in on what she'd learned from Joe about Roz Dunning. "Wait, wait, slow down," he told her. "He's sure this was three weeks ago? Why didn't he tell us this before now?"

"I don't believe anyone asked him, for starters," Melody responded with a hint of sarcasm. "And . . . he, well, she was holding something over him, but I don't think it has any bearing on this."

Kincaid decided to pursue this point later. "Is Doug with you?" When she said he was, he said, "Can you keep an eye on Dunning until we get there? Assuming she's at home. But don't approach her, understood?"

"Yes, sir."

He and Booth had stopped, by chance, beside Dr. Greene's white Mercedes. Booth ran a hand over its bonnet rather covetously as he listened to Kincaid's side of the conversation. "How long will it take us to get to Upper Slaughter?" Kincaid asked him.

"Not long." With a wicked grin, Booth popped the door locks on his Volvo. "You can tell me what this is all about on the way."

Kincaid should have known from Booth's smile that he'd be gripping the Volvo's door handle the entire way. He recognized nothing as the rolling blue-tinted hills sped by, punctuated only by the occasional glimpse of a few houses clustered in a hamlet, and a few sheep. "Where the hell are we?"

"Back roads," Booth answered, gearing up again as the car zoomed out of a hollow, climbing steadily. Kincaid's stomach lurched. "Almost there," Booth added, with another grin.

A signpost for Upper Slaughter appeared and was gone in a blink. Then Booth slowed and made a sharp downhill left turn into what appeared to be a driveway, but was, Kincaid realized, a lane. Tucked into the side of the hill, the village had been invisible from the road. Slowing to a sedate ten miles per hour, Booth checked the sat nav for the address Melody had given Kincaid. "It should be just to the left here, near the church."

A few cars were parked on one side of the tiny triangle of a green. Among them was Melody's blue Clio, but Booth carried on a bit farther until they spotted the name of the cottage. The silver Mercedes SUV Melody had described was parked in front.

As Booth pulled up, Melody and Doug emerged from behind a parked van. "Is she still inside?" Kincaid asked quietly as he climbed from the car.

"As far as we can tell without announcing ourselves." Melody still sounded out of sorts.

Booth was examining the gleaming paintwork on the SUV. "You could eat off this thing." He bent over to scrutinize the front bumper. "No visible damage here."

"What the hell do you think you're doing?" Roz Dunning stood in the open door to her cottage. In jeans and a flax-colored baggy jumper that fell off one shoulder, she looked nothing like the polished and efficient personal assistant Kincaid remembered from Saturday. Her hair was loose and unbrushed and her mouth was tight with anger.

Kincaid sensed Melody take a breath, but before she could speak, Booth stepped in front of her and held out his warrant card. "Mrs. Dunning, we'd like a word."

Roz had admitted them with ill grace and an uneasy glance at Melody.

The cottage, which had been gutted and renovated as open plan, was a study in expensive neutrals unbroken by color—rather, Kincaid thought, like its owner. She didn't invite them to sit, but stood with her back to the kitchen island, so that she seemed to be presiding from in front of the bench.

"Yes, I knew Fergus," she said in response to Booth's question. "I met him when he came to the house trying to cadge a ticket for the luncheon. But I didn't see that it was anyone else's business. There was no official inquiry."

"He came to the house and you slept with him in my parents' bed," Melody blurted out, as if she couldn't restrain herself.

"And what little bird told you that?" Roz gave her a sly glance. If she was surprised, she didn't show it. "Joe? He was jealous, you know, so I wouldn't put too much stock in what he says. And even if it was true, it's not a crime."

Melody gaped at her, turning pink, and Kincaid stepped in. "This was three weeks ago, that O'Reilly first came to the house?"

"Something like that," Roz admitted with a nonchalant shrug.

"Did he see anyone else on that visit?"

Roz appeared to give the question consideration. "I think he meant to talk to Viv. But he must have changed his mind, because he asked me not to tell anyone that he'd been here."

"Not that you would have mentioned it, under the circumstances," said Melody, and Kincaid shot her a quelling look.

"I'd merely have told Addie that the quite delicious chef turned up, hoping his celebrity would get him a ticket to the sold-out luncheon. Anything else that passed between us was, as I said, no one else's business. We were both single and certainly consenting adults."

Kincaid was trying to fill in a time line. "That Monday, O'Reilly checked into the manor house and then came to Beck House."

"And what if he did?" Roz said in the same dismissive tone.

"And the next day?"

"He said he had to see to some things. Late in the afternoon, he came here and I ran him to the station in Moreton."

"He didn't tell you what he'd been doing?"

"No. But he was, I don't know, preoccupied. Less charming." She shrugged again, but she might, Kincaid thought, have been a little offended. "I didn't think I'd see him again until he rang me the night before he died. I said I'd meet him in the hotel bar for a drink, but he was still being secretive."

"So he met you in the manor gardens instead?" Kincaid hadn't thought of her as a blonde when he'd seen her on Saturday, but now, with her hair loose, he could see how she might give that impression if caught in a certain light.

Roz looked surprised, but nodded. "I gave him a lift up here. But he was a bit disappointing, if you must know," she added, with a look that intimated she was assessing the three men in the room as potential replacements.

This was a woman to be avoided like the plague, but there was a certain rawness to the unfettered side of her that appealed to baser instincts. "And then?" Kincaid asked.

Roz shifted restlessly and the loose top slid a little farther down her shoulder. "Then, nothing. He left after a coffee the next morning. I never saw him again. I was as shocked as anyone when the police came on Saturday and said he was dead."

"He didn't tell you what else he meant to do that day?"

"No." Absently, Roz pulled her hair back into a knot. "But . . . he got a text, early. And I'd say that after that, he had an . . . agenda."

Booth asked if she could account for her movements on Friday.

"I was with Addie all day at Beck House. I only came home just before the Talbots' guests arrived."

"And you didn't see O'Reilly after that?"

"No. I told you, I didn't see him again after that morning."

"Did he ever say anything to you about Nell Greene?" Kincaid put in.

"No. As I said, he only mentioned knowing Viv, because they'd worked together. That was his whole thing, supposedly, with the luncheon ticket, to surprise his old friend." Roz straightened. "Now, really, are we quite fin —"

Booth interrupted her. "What about Saturday night, Mrs. Dunning? Can you account for your movements then?"

She frowned at him. "Why should I?"

"Because we're looking into the circumstances of Jack Doyle's death."

"What?" Roz gaped at him in what appeared to be genuine astonishment. "What has that to do with me? I didn't even know the man."

"You must have had drinks at the pub."

"Well, yes, but that doesn't mean I knew him. And he certainly wasn't my type."

"Then you won't mind telling us what you were doing on Saturday night."

"I do mind, actually," she snapped, folding her arms. "I will tell you that it had nothing whatsoever to do with that bartender, and that's all I'm going to say."

It was almost a challenge. If Booth had been prepared to take it, he was interrupted by a phone call. He excused himself, and when he returned a few moments later, he thanked Roz for her time.

"Don't worry, Detective Inspector," she said, with a tight little smile. "I'm not planning to abscond to South America.

Although"—she directed this at Melody—"I was planning to resign from your lady mother's employ, so you needn't worry your little head about my corrupt morals."

Before Melody could respond, Booth motioned them all outside.

"That was forensics," Booth said. "They've managed to unlock O'Reilly's mobile."

DECEMBER 2007

Viv had managed to hold her tongue through the remainder of service, but as soon as the door closed behind the last of the staff, she turned on Fergus. "How could you? How could you do that to Ibby? Danny was his friend."

Fergus didn't raise his eyes from the griddle he was scrubbing. "How could I do what?"

"For God's sake, Fergus. How could you be so bloody callous?" Viv found she was shaking with exhaustion and outrage. Not only had she had to cover Ibby's station, the tension in the kitchen and in front of house had made the rest of the evening a nightmare. She was surprised they'd made it all the way through service without a disaster—although she couldn't imagine worse than what had already happened.

"What did you expect me to do?" asked Fergus, finally glancing up at her, his expression cold. "Close down the kitchen and hold a prayer service? Danny was a fecking bomb waiting to go off and Ibby was the only one who couldn't see it."

"If you knew he was using last night, why didn't you do something?" Viv had given up any pretense of working and stood with her fists clenched as tightly as Ibby's had been.

For a few weeks after the Michelin star, she'd thought things might go back to the way they'd been in the summer between her and Fergus. But the attention and the notoriety had been siren songs to him, and soon there were more nights spent partying and fewer and fewer with her. The last few weeks she had barely seen him outside the kitchen.

"What is it you think I should have done? Sent him home to his mam?"

His mockery made her even more furious. "You are such a shit, Fergus. You should have done what any friend would do—looked after him. We're more than friends here, we're family. You know that. You have a responsibility." She took a gulping breath and tried to bring her voice down from a shriek. "And not only were you cruel to Ibby, you've left us a cook short and I can't manage—" The nausea hit her suddenly, twisting her gut without warning. Clamping a hand to her mouth, she ran for the staff toilet and vomited nothing but bile. The sickness had been so persistent the last few days that she hadn't been able to keep anything down. She'd managed to wipe her mouth, flush, and take a shaky seat on the toilet lid when Fergus appeared in the doorway, looming over her.

"What the hell is wrong with you, Viv? You've been heaving your guts up for days, so you can't blame that on me."

She started to laugh. She couldn't help it. "I can blame it on you, Fergus. At least partly. I'm pregnant."

If Viv had ever wanted to see him gobsmacked, she had her wish. He gaped at her. "But . . . you . . . you can't be."

"What we've been doing, Fergus, is generally how babies are made." Even though she knew it wasn't the least bit funny, she

was still stifling giggles, so light-headed she might have been drunk.

"You were on the pill," he protested.

"Yeah, well, when I went to Evesham, I didn't take any of my things, remember? And after that, I didn't see much point continuing."

He backed up a step, as if it might be catching. "Of all the bloody stupid things to do, Viv—"

"I thought my mum was dying." She stood, all the urge to laugh gone. "And I wasn't exactly planning to sleep with you again, or have you conveniently forgotten that?"

His face had gone the color of clotted cream, the dimples marking his cheeks like tiny craters. "Well, you can't have it," he said. "You'll have to get rid of it."

"What?" She stared at him. "What are you talking about? This is your child, too, Fergus!"

"It's my fecking restaurant! I can't have a pregnant cook in my kitchen. And you—how exactly do you plan to be a chef with a bloody baby to take care of?" He'd made baby *sound like a dirty word. "Don't be daft. You get this taken care of and then we'll—"*

"No." It wasn't until the word left Viv's lips that she realized she had made a decision. "I won't do it, Fergus. I can't." She tried to shove her way past him but he caught her arm.

"Let me go."

"Viv, you can't mean it." His fingers were pinching her. "I can't manage— You can't leave this. You can't leave me."

She saw it then, the fear in his eyes, and for just an instant she felt sorry for him.

It didn't last. "Let me go, Fergus," she said again, and this time there was something in her tone that made him release her as if he'd been burned. "Find yourself another chef."

Forgoing Ibby's grand gestures, she carefully hung up her apron, put her jacket on over her whites, and walked out.

After her talk with Kit, Gemma had wanted to have a chat with Viv, but the phone call a few minutes later from Kerry Boatman made a visit to Viv seem even more urgent.

As much as she hated to ask another favor of Addie, she couldn't discuss things with Viv with the children in tow. She had Addie drop her at the Lamb in Lower Slaughter. It was well after lunch by this time and the car park was nearly empty. A small Volkswagen pulling out beeped its horn at her and, seeing that it was Angelica, Gemma waved back.

There was a mud-spattered Land Rover parked near the archway that Gemma didn't recognize. Hoping for a private word with Viv, Gemma slipped into the hallway. She was about to enter the kitchen when she heard a man's voice. Mark Cain.

Taking a step forward, she peered into the kitchen. Viv stood at the central hob, stirring something, with Mark beside her. "I've got to finish unloading the hay," he was saying. "But I'll be back. Try not to worry, love." Gently, he pulled her to him and kissed the top of her head.

Gemma had seen him comfort Viv before, but there was a tenderness in this gesture that made her heart contract. And when Viv looked up at him, Gemma felt the intensity all the way to her toes. This was more than a dalliance.

She was trying to back up gracefully when a voice in her ear said, "Gemma, whatever are you doing here?" Startled, she stepped back and trod on Bea Abbott's toes.

"Oh, Bea, I'm so sorry. I was just going to have a word with Viv, but I didn't want to intrude—" she began, but when she looked back into the kitchen, Mark was gone and Viv was stirring her pot with great concentration.

"Well, don't mind me," said Bea briskly. "Viv, I'm just off to the bank with the cash receipts from the weekend."

"Okay, see you later," Viv replied, then smiled at Gemma. "Come in, Gemma, do. I've sent Ibby and Angelica for a break. Tonight will be slow and we all needed a bit of a breather."

"I was hoping we might have a chat."

Viv's eyes widened. "Has something happened?"

"No, no, I just wanted to talk."

"Let me finish seasoning this soup, then, and I'll make us a cuppa."

"What is it? It smells divine."

"Cream of mushroom. Come and taste." When Gemma came to stand beside her, Viv dipped some soup into a tasting spoon and handed it to her. "We've a local farmer growing mushrooms for the markets, so I buy whatever he has on hand. This has brown mushrooms, shiitake, and some dried porcini, for depth of flavor."

Gemma took a little sip from the spoon. "Oh, I see what you mean," she said in surprise. "It's delicious, but it's somehow more—mushroomy."

"It's not balanced yet. It needs more salt." Viv added a generous palmful from a dish by the hob and stirred the pot thoroughly. Grabbing two more spoons, she tasted it herself, then handed a spoonful to Gemma. "Now try."

Obediently, Gemma tasted. This time the flavors seemed to pop on her tongue. "Oh, my goodness. It's not salty—it just tastes . . . I don't know . . . brighter?"

"That's what salt does. It's a flavor enhancer. You have a good palate." Viv turned the flame down to a low simmer and fetched cups from the crockery shelf. Plopping a few Yorkshire teabags into the old Brown Betty pot that Gemma had used so diligently yesterday, she filled the pot from the already steaming kettle. "Maybe Kit has inherited that from you."

"I'm afraid not," Gemma said a little ruefully. "I'm his step-mother, you see."

"Oh." Viv looked startled. "I'm so sorry. He never said. I just assumed . . ."

"No need to be sorry. I couldn't love him more or be more proud of him." Gemma decided to take advantage of the open-ing. "Speaking of Kit, he's a little concerned about Grace. She was asking him all sorts of questions about going to live in London with his dad. She wanted to know if he knew his dad before that."

Viv, filling Gemma's cup, sloshed scalding tea on her hand. "Shit!" Setting the cup down, she stuck her hand under the cold tap, her back to Gemma.

"Viv, are you all right?"

"It's nothing." Viv turned off the water and patted her hand with a towel, her expression tense. "What else did she say to Kit?"

Gemma wasn't sure how to put it delicately. "This is like she really believes this stuff and it's just . . . weird. She seems to think you deliberately kept her from seeing her dad."

The color drained from Viv's face. "Oh, Christ. The bastard. The absolute bastard."

Her reaction took Gemma by surprise. "Who, Viv? What are you talking about?"

"Fergus, of course. Bloody Fergus. He swore not to tell her. I should have known he wouldn't keep a promise."

"Dear God," said Gemma as realization dawned. "Fergus was Grace's father?" She'd only seen the mortuary photo of the man, and she hadn't caught a resemblance. "I knew you used to work for him, but—"

"That's why I left O'Reilly's. He never wanted her, you know. And, then, to show up here, demanding to see her, after all this time—" Viv wiped at tears.

Giving Viv a moment, Gemma finished pouring the tea while she thought it through. "Viv, a friend in the London police talked to Colm Finlay this morning. You said that Fergus had offered you a job working for him in a new restaurant in London. Colm Finlay said that *Fergus's* job was dependent on *you* taking that offer."

Viv stared at her. "Oh, the idiot," she breathed. "I should have known. Did he think I wouldn't find out? That Colm wouldn't eventually tell me? That's why he was so determined I should do it." With shaking hands, Viv reached for the cup of tea Gemma brought her.

"Here, your fingers are like ice," said Gemma. "Wrap your hands around that and tell me exactly what happened."

"I told the truth. Just not all of it," Viv admitted after a moment, with a sigh. "Fergus showed up here on Friday morning, out of the blue, telling me he had this great opportunity, that Colm was setting him up in a place and he wanted me in on it. I hadn't seen him in nearly twelve years. It was . . . a bit of a shock, I can tell you. And he still— I was still— Fergus could be so bloody charming, even after everything that happened between us." Viv sipped at the tea, wincing. "But I said no, I'd made a life for myself here. Then, he said it was our chance to be a family, the three of us. He'd seen Grace, I don't know how. He seemed obsessed with her, with wanting to be a father. Or so I thought," she added with a grimace. "How could I have been so stupid? He needed me to get the job. And he needed Grace to get me."

"What happened when you told him no?"

"I thought it might be okay, that he might leave it. But he came back in the afternoon, and this time he told me that if I didn't agree, he would sue me for partial custody. He said he could have the court order a paternity test, that I couldn't deprive him of his rights as a father. I told him to get stuffed.

"But he wouldn't let it go—I'd forgot how persistent Fergus could be when he set his mind to something—he kept pushing me. Hanging about in the courtyard, talking to Grace. And then later, coming in the dining room, ordering food, then sending it back, with the *chef's compliments*."

A horrible thought occurred to Gemma. She'd never seriously considered the possibility that Viv had poisoned Fergus. What chef in her right mind would poison someone in her own restaurant? But it sounded more and more as if Viv had good reason to want rid of Fergus—and quickly, before he made further inroads with Grace.

Viv had known exactly which plates were going out to Fergus. But, still, even if she'd had the intent, would she have had digitalis on hand? Or foxglove itself? The plant was common enough, but certainly no part of it would be kept in a kitchen, and Gemma hadn't seen it growing in the pub garden.

Unaware of Gemma's ruminations, Viv continued, "When he came into the kitchen during service that night, I just lost it. I shouted at him to get out and not to bloody come back. I never thought . . ." She looked stricken. "I never thought he would die!"

Viv Holland had still loved Fergus O'Reilly, Gemma realized, in spite of his faults.

She didn't believe Viv could have harmed him, and certainly not through the very thing that was the touchstone of her life— her food. "Viv," she said slowly, "who else knew about Fergus and Grace? Or Fergus's offer, for that matter?"

"Well, Bea knew about the offer. It was only fair to tell her, even though I didn't mean to take it. And of course Ibby knew about Fergus and Grace. Ibby was—" Viv's expression softened. "Ibby was the only one who was there for me when Grace was born. He's known Grace her whole life."

Once they'd left Roz Dunning's house, Booth told them that he'd asked a uniformed officer to meet him with O'Reilly's mobile. "I'm all for the glories of fingerprint recognition," Booth said. "But I don't want some anorak in forensics texting me what *he* thinks is important. And"—he nodded at the cottage they'd just left—"I want to keep an eye on this nice lady for a bit, see if she rabbits. She's a right piece of work, that one. Your mother," he added to Melody, "had better hope she hasn't hijacked the family silver."

"They're bringing the mobile here?" Doug looked as eager as a puppy promised a treat.

"To the green. I'd better move my car, though, someplace a bit less conspicuous, so Ms. Dunning won't see us. We can sit in yours."

"Mine, actually." Melody sounded thoroughly irritated. "The Clio."

Booth's raised eyebrows conveyed his opinion of her automotive judgment. "Well, you all pile in, then. I'm going to move my car to the hotel down the road."

"You know this village?" Kincaid asked.

"Michelin-rosette restaurant in the hotel. Anniversary date last year."

When the panda car arrived a few minutes later, there'd been no sign of activity in Roz Dunning's cottage. Doug had rather grudgingly ceded the Clio's front-passenger seat to Booth, which left him and Kincaid crammed into the back. Now Doug leaned forward, breathing down Booth's neck as Booth scrolled through the phone.

"He didn't use it much," said Booth. "Limited data plan?"

"Or it's new and he didn't transfer anything," Doug suggested. "Or maybe he was just a Luddite. Sad tosser."

Booth flicked his finger down the screen. "There's a Colm in the contacts. That would be the restaurateur, I think. Along with some missed calls from the same number." He went to the texts, holding the mobile up so that they could all see the screen. "Somebody named Abby wants to buy him a drink. But that was a month ago. Not much social life, poor bugger. Colm wants to know why he's not returning his calls; O'Reilly says he'll be in touch soon." Booth frowned. "Wait. Here's a text thread from an untagged number, just a couple of messages. He—or she—says, 'When are you coming back? Please please come soon.' He says, 'Don't worry, everything will work out and we'll be together, I promise.'"

Booth swiped again. "Then, he says, 'PS remember DONT tell your mum!'"

"The guy was a pedophile," Doug said, with disgust. "Christ. But how does—"

"No," Kincaid broke in. "I don't think so." He was remembering the child who'd played with his own children at the luncheon, with the same pinched and angry look she'd worn when she'd come tearing into the pub yesterday to shout at her mother. "I don't think that's what this is about at all. We need to talk to Viv Holland."

CHAPTER TWENTY-FOUR

There had been a moment, on Saturday, when Kincaid had caught a glimpse of the girl laughing as she played with the dogs. It had transformed her, and it was that image that he recalled now. He'd skimmed Doug's research on Fergus O'Reilly, with the accompanying photographs, and he could see it now—the ghost of a resemblance.

"When was that text sent?" he asked Booth.

Booth scanned the messages again. "Last Wednesday."

Leaning up from the backseat, Doug said, "Check the call log."

Booth tapped the phone icon. "O'Reilly made calls to that number on Thursday afternoon, and again on Friday morning. Hang on a moment." Frowning, he scrolled further back. "The first call to that number was just shy of three weeks ago. The Wednesday—"

"After the Monday O'Reilly first came to the village," Kincaid finished. "He intended to see Viv—he told Roz Dunning as much—but then he changed his mind. I think it was because he met Grace Holland."

They took both cars down the hill to the pub, Booth having now agreed that speaking to Viv took priority over keeping an eye on Roz Dunning. Melody had been oddly quiet and seemed to be avoiding speaking to Doug.

The four of them walked into the pub courtyard together, the crunching of their feet on the pea gravel sounding like the arrival of the cavalry. The noise brought Viv to the kitchen door, wiping her hands on her apron. Gemma appeared behind her, carrying a mug of tea. "Where have you been?" she said, hurrying down the steps towards him. "I was worried about you."

"I'm fine. We got caught up with something." He gave her a reassuring smile before turning to Viv. "Viv, does your daughter have a mobile phone?"

She looked puzzled, but said, "Yes, but it's just calls and texts. I wouldn't buy her a smartphone, even though she says everyone in her year has them."

"Is this the number?" Booth read it out to her from O'Reilly's mobile.

Viv blanched. "Yes, that's it. What's happened? Is Grace all right?"

At a nod from Booth, Kincaid said, trying to break it gently, "We think Fergus O'Reilly was in contact with your daughter in the weeks before he died."

"What? But how—" She glanced at Gemma. "That's why she

said those things to Kit. Oh, my God. When you said he'd been here before, staying at the manor house, it never occurred to me that he'd— He had to have met her then, hadn't he, to get her number?"

"That would be my guess, yes," said Gemma. "Viv, shall I tell them?"

"I can guess," Kincaid told her. "Fergus was Grace's father, wasn't he?"

"There's more." Gemma put a supportive hand on Viv's back. "I heard from Kerry Boatman. Viv didn't know this, but Fergus getting the job in Colm Finlay's restaurant depended on Viv accepting the offer as well. When she refused, Fergus threatened her with a paternity suit.

"Finlay also told Kerry that he was certain Fergus was not taking heart medication. Fergus was living in his flat and Finlay kept a close eye on him. He wanted to be sure Fergus was clean before he finalized a job offer."

Booth fixed a hawkish gaze on Viv. "If we can rule out self-administered, we have to look at where the digitalis came from. And when he might have ingested it."

Looking more startled than frightened, Viv said, "You can't think—surely you don't think *I* gave it to him."

"It seems to me that you had very good reason to want Mr. O'Reilly out of the way, Ms. Holland. It's highly unlikely that any court would have granted him complete custody, but a suit on his part would certainly have disrupted your and your daughter's lives—and caused your daughter untold emotional distress."

"But"—Viv threw Gemma a helpless look—"but I would never— I wouldn't even have any idea how to go about something like that!"

"Nevertheless, Ms. Holland, I'll need to ask you some ques—"

Booth broke off as tires squealed on the car park tarmac, then a vehicle flashed by, visible for only an instant through the courtyard archway. A car door slammed, and Ibby came charging through the arch. Without the cheerful bandanna tied over his hair, he looked older, and far more menacing. Kincaid tensed, but Ibby came to a stop a few feet from them, his hands on his hips.

"Who the hell has been messing with my truck?" he said, glaring at them.

"What are you talking about?" Booth asked. "What truck?"

"My four-by-four. I was going to run into town to buy some"— Ibby broke off, shooting a guilty glance at Viv— "I mean I had an errand to do. But my seat and my mirrors are off. I hate anyone—"

"You never said you had a four-by-four," broke in Booth.

"You never asked. I said I didn't drink-drive, not that I didn't drive."

That much was true, Kincaid remembered. And he knew Booth had checked Ibby's and Angelica's alibis for Saturday night—they were both confirmed to have been at a pub lock-in from eleven o'clock until two in Moreton-on-Marsh. "When did you last drive?" he asked.

"I don't know. Last week. I rode with Angie on the Saturday and yesterday morning—as you bloody well know. And I hadn't needed to go anywhere until just now."

With a scowl, Booth strode across the courtyard and through the arch, the rest of them following. A battered and muddy red Toyota RAV4 stood alone and slightly askew in the car park. "This is it?"

"I didn't come in a bloody pumpkin."

Booth walked round it and, squatting, examined the front

fender. The others followed and peered over his shoulder. "It's about the right height. And it's pretty dinged up, but I can't tell if the damage is old or new."

"What do you mean, dinged up?" Sounding even more incensed, Ibby pushed through the group to stand beside him.

"Look, here, just left of center. There's a crack in the grill."

"That wasn't there. I'm sure that wasn't there. What the hell is going—"

Booth stood. "Who else has access to your car?"

"What?" Ibby stared at him. "Well, Bea, of course, but I thought—"

"What do you mean, of course?"

Ibby seemed just as baffled. "Because I lodge in her house. Just at the top of the village. You took our details. You must know—"

"Wait. Just wait a minute." Viv slipped past Ibby to stand in front of Booth. "Are you saying that it might have been Ibby's car that hit Jack? Is that what you're talking about? Ibby wasn't even here when Jack was run down!"

"We know that, Miss Holland." Booth sounded as if his patience was strained. "But Mr. Azoulay here seems to think that someone else has driven his car. And his car fits the profile of the vehicle involved in Jack Doyle's death."

"But that's ridiculous. That means Bea— You can't think Bea had anything to do with— Someone must have stolen Ibby's keys—"

"They were right where I normally keep them," protested Ibby. "But someone drove my car. I'm not imagining it. Everything is just a bit off-kilter. Not to mention, the seat lever is jammed, and when I went to take a look at it, my bloody torch was missing."

Kincaid heard a quick indrawn breath from Gemma. The blow

to Jack Doyle's head was knowledge the detectives had kept to themselves. A torch would have made a handy and effective blunt instrument.

"You kept it in your car?" asked Booth.

"Well, yeah, in the glove compartment. Where else would I keep it? Look, this is bonkers. Bea's never driven my car—why would she do that?"

"Because," Kincaid said slowly, thinking it through, "if you had the idea to run someone down, it would be wise not to do it in your own vehicle. Especially in a smaller car that might be less effective and sustain more damage. And just say it was a last-minute decision, and there was another vehicle, readily available, but not likely to be associated with you."

They all stared at him. "But why?" whispered Viv. "I don't believe it. Why would Bea do such a thing?"

"Because Jack Doyle knew something about what happened to Fergus O'Reilly—something that would have proved dangerous for him to share," Gemma said with sudden certainty. "Jack was not himself that night—you told me that, Viv. He was upset. He was drinking, which was unusual. You thought it was because he was grieving for Nell. But what if it was more than that? What if he'd seen something, something that only had significance when he learned that Fergus might have been poisoned? Who besides Jack would have served Fergus in the bar that night?"

Frowning, Gemma fished in her jacket pocket, pulling out a crumpled note and smoothing it with her fingers. "I needed to write something down yesterday. I grabbed an order pad from the bar, but first I tore off the top page." She held it up. Scrawled across the sheet was the word *COFFEE* followed by a question mark.

338   DEBORAH CROMBIE

"That's Jack's writing," said Viv, with obvious reluctance.

"Wasn't Fergus drinking coffee?"

"Yes, but—" Viv bit at her fingernail, then said, "Okay. Bea was helping Jack in the bar. You think Jack saw her put something in Fergus's coffee?"

Glancing at Booth, Kincaid guessed they were thinking the same thing. Bea Abbott's father was a doctor with a reputation for being a bit free with his prescription pad. What might Bea have had access to?

"But even if she did," Viv went on, "why? Why would she do something like that?"

"You told her about the job offer. Who had the most to lose if you changed your mind and accepted Fergus's offer?" asked Gemma.

"But I wouldn't have. And she didn't know he was Grace's—"

"Viv," broke in Ibby, her name a plea. "*I* told her about Fergus and Grace. I'm sorry. I know I shouldn't have, but I was so pissed off when he showed up that afternoon. He was chatting Grace up in the courtyard, making her laugh, wearing that stupid hat like he was freaking Gandalf or something. Bea saw them together, too."

A sudden gust of wind swirled round the car park, raising little eddies of fallen leaves. Just as Kincaid looked up and realized that heavy clouds were massing in the western sky, Gemma said, alarm in her voice, "Where *is* Bea? She said she was going to the bank ages ago."

"Oh my God." Viv gripped Gemma's arm. "Grace. Grace should be home from school by now. Where the hell is she?"

"Right here is fine, Mrs. Johnson." Grace bared her teeth in a big fake smile as she got out of the car in front of St. Mary's Church.

"I can walk across the road," she said, adding under her breath as Mrs. Johnson waved and drove off, "I'm not two, you know." She could even walk home from school if her mum would let her, along the river path. It was only a couple of miles. She knew the way, but of course her mum said she was too young and what if it was muddy or something stupid like that.

Usually Bea alternated picking her and Alesha up from school with Mrs. Johnson, because her mum, of course, was always too busy. Grace wished it had been Bea today, but then Bea had been short with her that morning, so maybe it was just as well.

Just thinking about going home gave Grace a sick feeling in the pit of her stomach. Everybody was whispering round her, like she didn't know there was something weird about Jack being hit by the car. She couldn't bear to go in the bar because it made her think about him.

And she really couldn't bear to think about Fergus. She didn't want to believe he was dead. Maybe he'd just gone away and her mum was only telling her that because she didn't want them to be together. He'd been fine on Friday—he'd whispered to her that he was going to make her mum see sense and that they would all go to London to live.

Maybe her mum had made him go away. Maybe Fergus would come back and take her to London and it would be just the two of them.

But that thought made her feel funny, too. As much as she hated her mum, she didn't want to think that something bad might happen to her, like what had happened to Kit's mum. Or to Nell.

She shivered. Alesha said that meant someone was walking over your grave, but that was stupid. She was just cold, that was all. The sky had gone a weird sort of muddy purple and the rising wind tugged at her hair and rustled in the leaves of the trees in the churchyard. A storm was coming.

She wondered if Mark had left Bella out in the farmyard. Bella didn't like storms. Would she be scared if it thundered? Coming to a sudden decision, Grace slipped her backpack over the churchyard wall. Nobody would steal it from out of the churchyard, and she wouldn't be gone long. And it wasn't like her mum would notice if she didn't come home right on time.

It occurred to her too late that Mark might tell her mum that she'd come without permission. They were always talking and sometimes she thought that Mark actually liked her mum in *that* way, which was gross. But Bea said not to be silly, that her mum couldn't manage things as it was and she certainly had no business having a *relationship*. Besides, her mum had to have loved Fergus, hadn't she, if Fergus was her dad?

Well, she would just check on the dogs, in case Mark wasn't at home. The farmhouse door was always left off the latch, and she could just put the dogs inside. Carefully, she opened and closed the gate, aware of the too-loud sound of her trainers crunching on the leaves that lay like a gold blanket over the drive. But there was no sound from the dogs.

She walked on. When she came out into the open field, she saw that the sky to the west was almost black and it had grown twilight dark. There was still no sign of the dogs. But there was Mark's Land Rover, in the yard, so he must be inside with them. The back was down on the trailer and all the hay was gone.

Grace was about to turn back to the gate when she saw there was another car pulled behind Mark's, invisible until she'd turned the curve in the drive. It was Bea's little Fiat. What was she doing here? Bea didn't even like Mark.

Curious, Grace crept closer, afraid that the dogs would sense her, even from inside the house. When the wind dropped, she heard voices coming from the barn. Tiptoeing now, she crossed the farmyard, keeping out of sight of the door. She knew there was a crack where the frame of the door didn't quite fit the old wall of the barn, and she thought she could peek through it.

One voice grew louder. Mark's. "I'm sick and tired of you interfering in Viv's business, Bea."

Grace edged closer until she could put her eye to the gap. Mark and Bea were facing each other. Mark had been stacking hay bales and his face was red.

"I'm only saying what's best for Viv and for the child," Bea said, sounding bossy and just as cross. "I saw you today with Viv, carrying on. What do you think that would do to—"

"For Christ's sake. We were not carrying on. And the *child* is nearly twelve and needs to grow up."

Grace felt a little flush of pleasure at the *nearly twelve*. But then Mark said, "And it's about time she had a man in her life. You're warping that child, Bea. Viv is the only one who can't see it. Even Jack thought so, and he had a soft spot for you."

"Jack? What did Jack tell you?" There was something in Bea's voice that Grace didn't like. She almost bolted, but she was afraid if she moved they would hear her and then Bea would be really, really cross.

Mark shoved the hay fork into a bale and left it sticking there. "He saw you with Grace's mobile on Friday afternoon. She'd left her backpack in the bar. You were spying on the kid."

"So what if I was?" Bea said, and Grace frowned in surprise, wondering if she'd heard wrong. "It was for her own good," Bea went on. "She should learn not to put in her pass code where people can see it. She was texting O'Reilly— Did you know that? He told her he was her father."

Mark's face went blank. "What?"

"Oh, Viv didn't tell you that either, did she?" Bea said, in a nasty, baiting voice.

But Mark shook his head. "Don't try that shit on with me, Bea. You're not turning me against Viv. She did tell me. But she didn't know that Grace knew."

"O'Reilly told Grace her mum was going to take the job in London and they would all play happy families together." Bea snorted. "And Grace believed him, the little ninny. He needed Viv for his restaurant, and Grace was a way of getting to her."

Grace clapped a hand over her mouth to stop herself crying out. It couldn't be true. Fergus had wanted to be her dad, she knew he had. Now she just wanted to go home, but the stunned look on Mark's face kept her rooted to the spot.

"You believed it, didn't you?" he told Bea. "You thought Viv would really take the job. And where would that have left you? Out in the cold?" Mark took a step towards Bea and Grace shrank back.

Bea laughed but there was nothing funny about the sound. "Don't be stupid."

"You were there, in the bar that night," Mark said slowly. "You must have been panicked after you saw those texts on Grace's mobile. Maybe you decided to take matters into your own hands. Did you give him something, Bea?" He must have seen an answer in Bea's face because his eyes went wide. "You did, didn't you?" He sounded surprised, as if he hadn't quite believed it until then. "What about Jack? Did he see you do it?"

"Nobody will believe you, you know." Bea's quiet voice was somehow scarier than her shouty one.

But Mark just shrugged, and Grace suddenly wanted to call out to him, but she didn't. "I'm going to tell the police what I think, regardless. And I'm going to tell Viv. You can deal with the consequences." Turning his back, he reached for his hay fork.

Quick as lightning, Bea grabbed the manure shovel that was propped against one of the sheep pens. She swung it high with both hands, like a cartoon warrior, cracking it against the back of Mark's head with a sound like a ripe melon hitting the tarmac.

Grace doubled over, stifling a moan of terror.

When she could bring herself to look again, Mark was in a heap on the ground, and Bea was stooping over the emergency lantern Mark used when there was a power outage. Bea tipped it over, spilling the white petrol into the loose straw on the floor of the barn. Her back was to Grace now, but when Grace heard the flicking sound she knew instantly what it was—the little butane lighter Bea used to light the table candles in the pub. A wisp of smoke rose from the floor.

Grace could just make out Mark's body slumped against the hay bale. He wasn't moving.

She had to get help.

Hardly daring to breathe, she backed up a step, then another one. Dark clouds now blotted out the sky, leaving the farmyard in a weird gray-green twilight. Grace turned, but she'd misjudged her step and she bumped against the empty trailer, making the tow bar clank. Inside the house, the dogs began to bark.

"Who's there?" called Bea.

Grace froze, praying that Bea wouldn't come to see. But a moment later, Bea appeared in the barn door, peering out.

"Who's there?" she said again, a little uncertainly. Then she caught sight of Grace on the far side of the trailer. Taking a step farther into the yard, she called, "Grace! What are you doing here?"

Grace turned and ran.

Gemma and the others followed Viv as she looked in the cottage, then in the restaurant. As they were searching, Angelica arrived with the two evening servers, and then a couple of early customers came into the bar. Ibby quickly began making drinks while the rest of them crowded into the kitchen after Viv, who grabbed the mobile she'd left on the work top.

"I think she's overreacting," Gemma heard Doug mutter to Melody as Viv dialed Grace's mobile number. But Gemma knew that if it were any of her children, she'd be panicked, too.

"She's not answering," said Viv, turning a stricken face to them. "She keeps her phone switched off at school, but she's supposed to turn it on again as soon as school's out."

"Have you tried the friend who was giving her a lift home?" asked Gemma. "Maybe she was delayed."

Scrolling through her contacts, Viv rang another number, while Angelica, filling orders, tried to maneuver round all the bodies taking up the kitchen work space. After a moment's murmured conversation, Viv rang off, shaking her head. "She dropped her off an hour ago," she said, her voice rising.

Gemma glanced out the kitchen door. Dusk had come early with the heavy clouds, and out in the courtyard she'd felt the prickle that presaged a thunderstorm.

"Where exactly did your friend drop her off?" asked Booth. "There are enough of us to organize a search. Where else do you think she might go?"

"Lizzy Johnson says she dropped her right in front of the pub, on the churchyard side of the road. I don't know where she might go. She doesn't have any friends in the village. Before, she might have gone to Nell's, but now . . ."

"We'll start at the last-seen point and work outwards, then. Ms. Holland, you had better stay here in case she comes back. Keep trying to ring her."

"But what about Bea? What if she comes back?"

"I'll stay here with Viv," Kincaid said.

Gemma didn't like that idea at all. "I don't think you ought—" she'd begun, when Viv's mobile rang.

"It's Grace!"

"Put her on speaker," Gemma said hurriedly as Viv swiped the screen.

Then Grace's terrified whisper filled the kitchen. "Mummy, she hurt Mark. You have to do something. She set the barn on fire!"

"Grace, where are you? Who hurt Mark?"

"Mummy, I'm scared. She saw me. I have to—" There was a gasp, then a thud, then silence.

"Grace!" Viv shouted, but the call had failed. When she tried to ring back, the mobile went unanswered. Turning to them, Viv said, "She has to be at Mark's farm. I'm going—"

Booth interrupted her. "You and Gemma take the van. Duncan and I will come in my car." He turned to Doug and Melody. "You two, call it in, all services. Then stay here. Deal with Bea Abbott if she shows up."

Booth got his Volvo out of the pub car park before Viv could back her van round in the courtyard. This time, Kincaid didn't mind Booth's driving. They tore up King's Well Lane, a bloody storm-tossed sunset filling the sky ahead. Lowering the window as they reached Nell Greene's cottage, he could smell smoke. "Just ahead," he directed as Booth drove on. "The farm entrance is where the trees are thickest. I'll get the gate."

But there was no need—the gate stood open. Booth drove over the rill and down the farm drive. As the yard came into view, Kincaid could just make out Mark's Land Rover and the unattached trailer in the gathering gloom. There was no sign of Bea, or of Grace, but smoke was snaking from under the bottom of the barn door. Booth slammed the Volvo to a stop and they scrambled out just as Viv's van rolled up behind them. Inside the house, the dogs barked frantically.

"Christ," Booth shouted as they reached the barn. "The door's been blocked." A piece of timber had been pulled across the bottom of the barn door, but the two men managed to shift it quickly enough.

"Stand back," Booth directed as Gemma and Viv came up behind them. He moved to one side as he pulled open the door, but still the cloud of smoke set them all coughing.

Blinking, Kincaid peered inside. Flames flickered, fanned by the inrush of air, but as the smoke cleared he could see a huddled shape against the hay bales on the barn's far side. He recognized the denim jacket Mark had worn when he'd visited yesterday. "It's Mark. We've got to get him out."

"You can't lift him," Gemma said. "Stay back. Viv and I can help."

As much as he hated it, Kincaid knew she was right. He'd only been able to grip the timber blocking the door with one hand. "Be careful."

As the three of them ran crouching into the barn, Mark began to cough and try to push himself up. Kincaid breathed a prayer of relief. "Wait, wait, we've got you," said Viv as they reached him and lifted him up. With Booth on one side and Viv on the other, they supported him across the barn and out the door. Gemma trailed behind, looking round, then ran after them as she began to cough, too.

"I don't think Grace is in there," she gasped as she reached Kincaid and the open air. Booth pushed the door to behind her, stopping the wind from feeding the flames.

"My head," moaned Mark. "I don't remember—she must have bloody hit me." He put a hand to the back of his head, wincing, and when he pulled it away his fingers were dark with blood.

Kincaid grasped his shoulder. "Mark, take it easy. Who hit you?"

"Bea. It must have been Bea. She was saying crazy things about O'Reilly—" Realization seemed to hit him. "My barn! Christ! Get some water!"

"I know where the hosepipe is," said Viv. "But, Mark, where's Grace?"

"Grace? What are you talking about?"

"She saw Bea hit you."

Mark shook his head, then grimaced. "Bloody hell. No, she can't have—Viv, get the damned hose."

But Booth loomed out of the dimness, dragging a coil. "Viv, go turn the tap." The sound of sirens came faintly on the wind as Booth eased the barn door open and shouted, "Now!" The jet of water hit the smoldering straw with a hiss and a billow of dark smoke.

Viv reappeared beside Kincaid and Gemma, her face smudged

with soot. "I've got the torch from the van," she said. "We've got to find Grace."

Gemma and Kincaid followed Viv down the lane toward Nell Greene's cottage. Their eyes had grown accustomed to the twilight and they made their way without using the torch, which Viv gripped more like a weapon than an implement. Looking back, Gemma saw the strobe of blue lights coming from the opposite direction.

"We know Grace was here," Viv had insisted back in the farmyard. "And that she was on foot. She's terrified, and she could be hurt. I don't think she will have gone far. We should try Nell's—she'd feel safe there."

"Viv's right," Gemma had said, although she knew the thud they'd heard over Grace's mobile might have been a blow, and that Bea might have bundled the injured girl into her car and taken her God knew where. But Booth had already put out an alert for the Fiat, and they had to cover every other possibility. "We should go on foot. If Bea is searching for Grace as well, we don't want to warn her that we're coming."

Reluctantly, Booth had agreed, but he'd stayed behind to direct the emergency operations and to make sure the farm was searched thoroughly. "Be careful in the lane," he told them. "Don't forget what happened to Jack Doyle."

Not having seen the accident scene, Gemma could only imagine, but she was doing that all too well as they crept along the very edge of the narrow lane, listening for the sound of an oncoming car, a crackle of movement in the hedgerows—or the cry of a distressed child.

The thunderstorm seemed to have collapsed with the dusk, thank God, with only a brief spatter of droplets on their cheeks as they set off. The air had gone dead still. She could hear Kincaid breathing right behind her. A heavy, green scent rose from the grass on the verge as their feet crushed it.

With a clap, a bird exploded from the hedge right in front of Viv, who swore and almost dropped the torch. When their hearts had stopped thudding, they moved even more carefully, until Viv brushed Gemma's arm with her fingers and tilted her head to the left. They must have reached the drive to Nell's cottage, and so far had seen no sign of either Grace or Bea.

But when Gemma looked, she realized that they would have to move out into the open to reach the cottage itself. She tapped Viv, who was still wearing her kitchen whites, and mimed taking off the jacket. Viv slid out of it and tucked it into the bottom of the hedge.

They kept to the grass, avoiding the crunch of the gravel in the drive. As they drew closer, there was no sign of light or movement in the cottage. Kincaid had just whispered that they should split up when Gemma saw it, a crouched shape moving around the corner of the cottage, then rising to try the door—a shape too large to be a child, the movement too furtive to be Grace. She clutched at her companions, but they'd seen it, too.

Viv wrenched herself out of Gemma's grasp and took off at a dead run, her trainer-shod feet only whispering on the springy grass. Too late, the shape rose and turned, and Gemma saw the pale moon of Bea Abbott's face beneath her dark hair.

Then Viv was on her in a rugby tackle. The impact took them both to the ground, then Viv was on top of Bea, punching and pummeling, while Bea twisted and kicked at her, grunting with the effort.

Gemma reached them first, and between them she and Viv managed to get Bea facedown. Gemma slipped off her light anorak and, with Viv's help, managed to tie Bea's wrists together while Kincaid pinned her feet.

Once secured, Bea twisted away from them until her back was against the cottage wall. "What is wrong with you?" she shouted at Viv. "Have you lost your mind?"

"Where is she?" spat Viv, shining the torch in her face. "Where's Grace?"

Bea flinched away from the light. "I have no idea. Viv, listen to me—"

"You killed them. You poisoned Fergus, didn't you? I *loved* him," Viv cried. "You knew I loved him and you—"

"Don't be stupid, Viv. Of course I didn't—"

"We found Mark Cain," put in Kincaid, still panting. "He's okay, no thanks to you, and he remembers what you did."

Bea went still. Her expression turned calculating. "So? It's his word against mine."

"Grace saw you." Dropping the torch, Viv grabbed her by the shoulders and started to shake her. "What have you done with Grace?"

"Let me go!" Bea tried to scoot away from her grasp. "I'm telling you, I haven't hurt Grace! Everything I did was for Grace! O'Reilly was going to ruin everything, don't you know that? I only meant to make him sick."

"What did you give him, Bea?" Gemma asked quietly. "Did you put something in his coffee?"

For a moment, Gemma thought Bea wasn't going to answer. But then she shrugged and said, "Diet pills. It was just a few of my mum's old diet pills. I took too many once and they made me ill—that's all I thought they would do to him. And then he'd go away—"

Headlamps suddenly illuminated them as a car bumped down the drive, then another one behind it. Booth's Volvo, Gemma realized, as he climbed out, and a panda car. Booth left the lights trained on them as he and two uniformed officers walked over. "Well, well, what have we here?" he said. "Miss Abbott. Where's the child?"

Bea glanced right and left, then blinked up at him, looking cornered. "I don't know."

With a nod to the uniformed officers, Booth sent them to search round the cottage, but they came back shaking their heads. "No sign of the girl, sir," said the female officer. "And both the cottage doors are locked. But we did find a Fiat pulled round behind the garage. The keys were in it. We checked the boot. Nothing there."

Gemma felt a wash of relief. That had been her worst fear, that they would find Grace stuffed in the boot of Bea's car. But Bea had been searching, too, which meant that she might be telling the truth about not knowing where Grace was.

But they still had a missing child.

Kit had been uneasy ever since he'd told Gemma about the things Grace had said. He felt like he'd betrayed a confidence and he wasn't sure he'd done the right thing, or what the consequences of it might be for Grace. To make matters worse, Gemma and his dad had now been gone for hours. Melody and Doug hadn't come back, either.

When he and Addie and the kids got back to the house after dropping Gemma at the pub, Joe had been waiting for Addie. They were closeted in her study for a long time. From Addie's tight-lipped expression when Joe left, Kit gathered the meeting had not been a pleasant one.

When dusk came on early and still no one had returned, he found Addie in the kitchen making the little ones their tea. "Is it okay if I walk down to the village?" he asked. "I need to talk to Gemma about something."

"I'll run you down," said Ivan, who had come in behind him. "I want to see what's going on."

"Oh, cool," Kit breathed as he climbed into the restored Land Rover, and he and Ivan talked cars on the short drive down the lane to Lower Slaughter. When they reached the pub, Kit saw immediately that Viv's van was gone, which seemed odd. Why would she go somewhere during dinner service? Melody's little blue Clio was in the car park, however, so he hoped that someone was there.

Glancing in the kitchen as they went in, Kit saw Angelica, but not Viv. Ibby, however, was behind the bar, and Melody and Doug were huddled on the other side, all three of their heads together in what looked like a heated discussion. When they looked up, he saw a flare of hope in their expressions, then disappointment.

"I've got to give Angie a hand," Ibby said, and went into the kitchen.

"What's going on?" Kit asked, the feeling of dread growing. "Where is everyone?"

"It's Grace," said Melody. Although there were punters in the dining rooms, there was no one else in the bar at the moment. Still, Melody lowered her voice. "Bea Abbott attacked Mark Cain and set his barn on fire. Apparently, Grace was there. She rang her mum but the call was cut off. They've caught Bea, but they still can't find Grace."

"My mum and dad—are they okay?"

Melody gave him a surprised look but said, "Yes, Gemma and your dad are fine. They're with DI Booth and the police. So is Viv. I didn't mean to frighten you."

"There's rain coming," put in Ivan. "Storms are building up again. What can we do to help?"

"Did they check Nell's cottage?" Kit asked before Melody could reply. "Grace might have gone there, if she was scared."

"That's where they are now. And they've searched the farm. There's no sign of her."

"The village?" Ivan asked.

"We've looked," said Doug. "Booth is organizing a search party. The girl just seems to have vanished into bloody thin air."

Kit's mind raced. "Do they know exactly where she was when she rang Viv?"

"No. She just said that Bea had hurt Mark, and that the barn was on fire. Then the call dropped. She—"

"Wait," broke in Melody. "There were dogs barking. I could hear them in the background. But they weren't too close. So—"

"I think I know." Kit realized he was butting in, but he couldn't help it. He was remembering the lane, and the bolt-hole under the gate into the pasture. And then the footpath that ran, dark and slippery, along the river. "Let me look."

"Can't you just tell us?" asked Doug. "We can let the search party know—"

"No. I need to do it," Kit said, his urgency mounting.

"We should check with your parents first," said Melody. She and Doug exchanged a look Kit recognized. It didn't mean that they thought he couldn't find Grace—it meant they were afraid he'd find something bad if he did.

Kit swallowed and used his most reasonable voice. "She could be hurt. And Ivan says there's more rain coming."

"The lad's right," said Ivan. "I'll go with him. I've got an emergency torch and supplies in the Land Rover. Tell me where we're going, lad."

"Behind the inn. The footpath."

"Ah." Ivan nodded. "That'll be nasty enough in the dark, never mind the rain. Let's get on with it, then."

"I'm coming with you," said Doug, but Kit could tell he wasn't thrilled.

Melody nodded, however. "I'll hold the fort here. Check in with me right away if you find her. Or any sign of her," she added quietly to her dad.

They went single file, Kit leading the way, Ivan bringing up the rear. They each had a torch, and Ivan carried an emergency pack. "Always good to be prepared when you live in the country, lad," Ivan had said. He'd talked steadily to Kit as he prepared. Kit thought it was Ivan's way of trying to keep him from worrying.

The lights had been blazing in the manor house across the road as they entered the footpath, but after the first twist of the path they were plunged into a darkness that seemed absolute. The torches were necessary but disorienting. Kit found that if he didn't hold his steady he felt woozy. The surface under their feet was slick with a coating of mud. And worse than mud.

"Horse shit," Doug muttered, and he wasn't swearing. The pungent smell caught in Kit's throat.

"It's a bridle path along this bit." Ivan seemed unperturbed. "Grace!" he called out. His voice seemed to boom back and forth between the trees pressing in on either side. They all stopped, listening, but there was no answer.

"The river goes under just here," Kit said when they reached the little crossing. He was beginning to think he'd been wrong. But they had to go the whole way, in case Grace was somewhere between here and the pasture.

Then, as they neared the spot where he and Grace had scrambled under the last fence and slid down the steep bank onto the path, he thought he saw something. "Grace!" He ran ahead, barely managing to keep his footing. "It's her!"

She might have been a bundle of rags, caught in the glare of the torch, and for a moment Kit's heart nearly stopped. "Please," he whispered. "Please be okay."

Then the bundle moved, resolving itself into Grace's white T-shirt and dark jeans, with a flicker of safety yellow from the reflective bits on one of her trainers. The other shoe lay to the side of the path. She was huddled into the bank, but her sock-clad foot stuck out at a funny angle.

"Mum?" she said groggily, squinting into the light.

"No, it's Kit, Grace." He sank to his knees beside her. "We came to find you." He swallowed hard, afraid he was going to cry like a bloody baby.

Ivan knelt beside him. "Looks like you've hurt your ankle, love," he said gently. "Can you stand?"

Grace shook her head. "No. I slipped. My ankle—I was running. After I dropped my mobile in the pasture, Bea—she was looking for me—" She pushed herself back into the bank, the whites of her eyes glinting in the torchlight.

"Bea can't hurt you, Grace. The police have her."

"But—" Grace seemed to have trouble taking it in. "But Mark—"

"He's fine, too. Don't you worry. I reckon that you ringing your mum saved his life."

"Oh. I was so scared— I thought he was— I'm so cold . . ." Grace sighed, her eyelids drooping closed. Kit was afraid she'd fainted, but then he saw the tears on her cheeks. Kit's face was damp, too, he realized, but not with tears this time. The rain had begun.

"Let's get you out of here, lass," said Ivan, scooping her up in his arms as if she weighed no more than Charlotte.

"I want to go home," whispered Grace. "I want my mum."

CHAPTER TWENTY-FIVE

DECEMBER 2007

Blindly, she left the restaurant and turned towards the river. The Albert Bridge beckoned, its lights bright as a web of tiny stars against the hard winter sky. Her feet seemed to take her past the old gingerbread guardhouse and up the incline of the bridge of their own volition. She stopped at the apex, gripping the railing, looking down at the dark mass of the Thames swirling below.

What was she going to do? Pregnant, jobless, her mother ill, her rent due on the first of the month. Terror made her heart pound painfully against the wall of her chest. Her head swimming, she gripped the railing tighter and tried to breathe, tried to look away from the water.

"Excuse me, miss," said a voice in her ear. Startled, Viv looked up. A man in a bulky overcoat stood beside her, his face

creased with concern. "Are you all right?" he asked. "It's just that you looked a bit . . . lost."

"No, I'm fine," she said, when she could find her voice, and as she spoke she realized that she meant it.

She was fine. She would be fine. She would manage somehow. She would make it all work.

And she would be a good mum in the bargain.

Letting go of her grip on the railing, she rubbed her hands together to warm them. "But thank you for asking."

She summoned a smile and turned away, walking with quick, firm steps, back the way she had come.

The rain must have stopped in the very early hours of the morning, because when Gemma woke and went to the window, the sky was a pure bright blue, unmarred by any cloud. Mist hung over the treetops, muting the beginnings of autumn color, and the hills climbed green into the distance. Gemma sighed.

"What is it, love?"

Turning, she saw that Kincaid was awake and had pushed himself up in the bed. She went to sit beside him. "I was just wishing I could keep that picture in my head on days when London is full of traffic and shouting and petrol fumes."

"You're homesick, aren't you?" he said with a grin.

"Desperately," she agreed, laughing. "But I've liked it here much better than I thought I would. Aside from the complications."

Which, thank God, had turned out much better than they might have, in part due to Kit's initiative in finding Grace. Last night, Doug had rung Melody from the walking path, and by the time Ivan had carried Grace back to the pub, the ambulance—and Viv—had been on their way to meet them.

Viv had gone with Grace to hospital in Cheltenham, Booth had taken Bea Abbott into custody, and the rest of them—including a bandaged Mark Cain—had gathered in the pub bar to wait for news of Grace. Ibby and Angelica had made them sandwiches and chips. Then, when the last customer had left, Ibby locked the doors, stoked the fire, and poured them all a generous measure of the bar's best whisky. All except Kit, that is.

"Ginger beer for you, kiddo," Ibby told him regretfully.

"Give him a sip," said Kincaid. "He deserves it. And he should learn to recognize good whisky so he won't be tempted to drink the bad stuff."

Kit had taken one little taste, blinked watering eyes, and made a face. "I think I'll pass on that, thanks," he said, coughing, but he'd looked pleased to be the hero of the hour.

When Viv rang at last, she said the scans showed Grace's ankle to be badly sprained, not broken. As Grace had also been dehydrated and slightly hypothermic, they expected to keep her under observation for a few more hours. Mark had wanted to go to hospital to wait with Viv but had been cautioned against driving, considering the blow to his head.

It was Ibby who insisted on going to Cheltenham, taking Viv's van as Booth had warned him that his truck would be impounded by forensics. "We need to have a word, me and Viv," Ibby had said. "She's going to be gutted. But this was not her fault, not any of it."

With Ibby's departure, they had all gone their separate ways, but Gemma had sensed a reluctance, as if no one wanted to face the reality of the things Bea Abbott had done.

"Kids not up?" Kincaid asked, yawning, bringing Gemma back to the present with a start.

"I thought I heard the thump of little feet. I'd better check."

Addie had put Charlotte to bed with Toby before they'd returned from the pub the night before, so heaven knew what the kids were getting up to this morning. She suspected it was only strict orders from Addie and Ivan that had kept them from coming in and jumping on the bed. "How's the hand?"

Kincaid flexed his fingers. "Better. Look. The redness is already fading. Ribs hurt like hell this morning, though."

"I'm not surprised." Gemma rubbed Kincaid's stubbly cheek, then brushed the hair from his forehead. "You have a bit of a lie-in, love. I'll bring you a cuppa."

But when she returned from the kitchen, he was up and dressed and ready to accompany her down to the village after breakfast. They'd promised Kit that he could say goodbye to Grace before they left for London, but first Gemma wanted a chance to talk to Viv on her own. Kincaid had something he wanted to do as well, so after tea and toast, they walked down the hill together in the bright fresh morning, matching steps, her hand tucked into the crook of his left arm. Gemma was painfully aware of how close she had come to losing him on Friday night.

They parted at the Old Mill, Gemma cautioning him to wait for her before walking back up to the house. "Just in case you need a push," she'd added.

She found Viv sitting in the sun on the bench against the cottage wall, head back, eyes closed. At the sound of Gemma's footsteps on the gravel, Viv started, then sat back with a sigh of relief. "Oh, it's you, Gemma."

Sitting beside her, Gemma patted her knee. "It's okay, you know. Bea is going to be thoroughly tied up for the near future. And hopefully a good deal longer."

"Have you spoken to Booth?"

"No, but Duncan did. He's charged Bea with aggravated assault and the attempted murder of Mark Cain. Whether or not he can bring charges on Fergus's poisoning and Jack's murder will depend, at least in part, on the forensics."

"Ibby told me they've cordoned off her house. He's gone to Angelica's for a kip. He can stay with her while he looks for someplace else to live."

Gemma had seen that Ibby's Toyota had already been collected from the pub car park. Booth was moving quickly.

"I don't want *her* coming here," Viv said with sudden force. "Or coming anywhere near Grace. I've packed up her things from the office and left them with the police officer at her house."

"What will you do, Viv? Was it an equal partnership?"

"Yes. Mark's going to help with the day-to-day business in the short term. Beyond that, I don't know. I'm not at all sure I can raise the funds to buy Bea out. But this is my home, and Grace's home. I meant it when I told Fergus that. How ironic if it's Fergus who causes us to lose it."

"Hopefully it won't come to that. How's Grace?"

Viv's expression softened. "Asleep on the sofa. They put her in a cast boot, which at the moment she thinks is pretty cool. I've promised her mac cheese and a Harry Potter marathon when she wakes up."

"What about the dog, Bella?" Gemma asked, remembering Kit's concerns.

"Mark means to offer to buy her back from Nell Greene's ex. Grace would love to take her, but I think it's going to be a while before she's ready for that responsibility—and according to the doctors she's going to be in the cast boot for some time." Viv rubbed her face with both hands. "I still can't believe it, you know. Bea. If I hadn't heard her myself . . . And if Grace hadn't heard her, and hadn't seen her attack Mark, she might never have believed we were telling the truth about the things Bea did." She looked up at Gemma, her blue eyes shadowed. "Why? Why did she want to turn my daughter against me? And to turn me against Mark?"

Gazing out at the tidy pub garden, Gemma thought about it. If Bea had been jealous of Mark, what must she have felt about the threat presented by Fergus? "It seems to me that she couldn't bear not to be first. In Grace's affections, and in yours. Maybe, in a twisted way, it was because she loved you."

Kincaid met Mark Cain walking up Nell Greene's drive. A Mercedes he recognized as Dr. Bruce Greene's was parked in front of the cottage, and the cottage door stood open. Cain had texted Kincaid first thing that morning to say that he was meeting Greene to turn over Nell's keys.

"I thought you might come," Cain said, shaking Kincaid's hand.

"How did it go?"

Cain looked back at the cottage. "He seems a nice enough bloke—quite cut up about Nell, I think. I offered to pay him for Bella, but he wouldn't hear of it. Said Nell would have wanted her to go with me. He's meeting with the vicar shortly to organize a memorial service."

"I'd better get on, then, if I want to speak to him," Kincaid said.

"Yes, well, have a safe journey. How are you getting back to London?"

"The train, after lunch. Addie and Ivan are taking us to the station in Moreton. We'll need two cars," Kincaid added ruefully. "As neither of them drive a people carrier."

"Yes, well," Cain said again, then blurted out, "I just wanted to thank you. You and your wife, and Viv, and Detective Booth, you saved my life last night."

"You can thank Grace, not us. Maybe some regular dog-training sessions are in order," Kincaid added with a grin. Seeing that Dr. Greene had come out and appeared to be locking the cottage door, he said, "I'd better go," and they shook again. As Cain turned away, Kincaid saw the neat bandage on the back of his head and thought how lucky the man had been.

They had all been lucky. Except for Jack Doyle. And Fergus O'Reilly. And Nell Greene. He walked the rest of the way down the drive.

"Dr. Greene," he said as the man turned towards him.

"Mr. Kincaid. Or is it Detective Superintendent Kincaid today?" Greene asked, but he sounded bemused rather than irritated. In chinos and a slightly rumpled cotton shirt, he looked considerably more human than he had in his consultant's three-piece suit. He also looked as if he hadn't slept much since yesterday, and had missed a few spots shaving.

"Merely mister," Kincaid replied. "Mark Cain told me he was meeting you here this morning."

"I'd never seen the place, if you can believe it. Nell visited her aunt occasionally, but in more than twenty years of marriage, I was always too busy to come with her. I wish—" Greene sighed and shook his head. "Well, never mind. Cain told me about Bea Abbott. To think that she was in some way responsible for Nell's death, even if not deliberately . . . I would say it beggars belief, but somehow I find I'm not all that terribly surprised." He met Kincaid's eyes. "I didn't tell you yesterday—perhaps I should have. Bea Abbott was fifteen years old when she came home from school and found her mother in the shower. Laura was naked. She'd slit her wrists and left the water running." When Kincaid grimaced, Greene said, "Yes, well, that would have been bad enough. But the worst thing was that Laura had known Bea would be the one to find her. I don't think Bea Abbott was ever quite right after that. I wonder if I could have somehow intervened. Instead, I walked away from the whole sorry mess. And now Nell is dead."

"Dr. Greene, I don't think you can hold yourself responsible for Bea's actions. Or for your ex-wife's death. But there is something I wanted to tell you." Kincaid gazed out at the rolling hills, fighting the blurring of his vision and the sudden constriction in his throat. After a moment he managed to go on. "Nell was trapped in her car, but she was conscious. I—I waited with her. But by the time help arrived, she had . . ." He took a breath. "It was too late. But I thought you would want to know that she wasn't in pain. And that she wasn't alone when she died."

He and Gemma walked back up Becky Hill Road together. "All right?" she'd asked when they'd met again at the little round-about across the river from the mill, and he'd nodded.

"Yes. I'm only sorry we can't stay for Nell's service."

"We can send flowers," Gemma suggested, and with that he had to be content.

As they climbed, he thought that even with yesterday's exertions, his ribs were finally improving. When they reached the last tunnel of overarching green before Beck House, he stopped Gemma, turned her towards him, and kissed her very gently.

"What was that for?" she asked, when he'd reluctantly pulled away.

"For the weekend that might have been." Then, as he put his good arm round her and they walked on, he added, "And to remind me not to take anything for granted."

When they reached the house, there was an unfamiliar car in the drive. "Guests?" Kincaid wondered aloud.

But Ivan and Kit came bursting out the front door as if they'd been lying in wait.

"What do you think, Dad?" asked Kit, nearly hopping with excitement. "Isn't she gorgeous?"

"She?"

"The car, Dad. It's a Land Rover. A Discovery."

"I can see that." Indeed, he was nearly blinded by the sun winking from gleaming paint the color of a new penny—and of Gemma's hair. "But—"

"It takes seven people. That's five of us and the dogs and luggage—and even the cats in their carriers. Or camping gear."

"Camping gear?" said Gemma with a horrified squeak.

"Kit, it's very nice, but I don't see—" Kincaid had begun, when Ivan, who had been standing aside with a Father Christmas smirk, broke in.

"This is the car I wanted you to see. It belongs to friends who are moving to France and don't want to take a right-hand-drive car. It's a year old but the mileage is low, as they've been in France a good bit of the time. I thought it would be just the thing for you and the family."

"Ivan, you're too kind, but you know there won't be much insurance settlement on the Astra and I'm not sure we could—"

"They're asking a very reasonable price, as they've left selling the car to the last minute." Ivan quoted him a number that made Kincaid gulp. But he'd been doing some research, and he knew that it was indeed a fair price for the sort of car they needed as a family. When he didn't immediately object, Ivan moved in for the kill. "Go home, talk to your insurance people and to your bank. You can do the paperwork long distance. Then I'll drive the car up to town for you."

Kincaid looked at Gemma, who had edged closer to the car and was peering in the windows. "I admit it sounds a good deal, but any decision on a family car would have to rest with Gemma."

Gemma, who had been begging him to get rid of the Astra for ages. Gemma, who'd been putting money aside every month for a sizable deposit on a new car.

Running a hand over the shiny copper bonnet, Gemma shot him a grin. "How could I *not* like it? Can we take it for a test drive?"

Kit's whoop of delight split the air.

Melody woke late—again—and unaccountably exhausted. As she lay there, watching the sunlight play on the guest room ceiling, she thought how little she was looking forward to driving back to London on her own. Gemma and Charlotte would be going on the train with the rest of the family—as would Doug.

She was not, in fact, looking forward to going back to London at all. It felt as if all the progress she'd made the past few months had been for nothing, and she didn't know how to start again. A tear leaked and ran down her cheekbone to dampen the pillow.

"Oh, get over yourself," she said in disgust, sniffing and pushing herself out of bed with a groan.

Once downstairs, she found the house again felt strangely deserted. She made a coffee and then wandered through the rooms, looking for signs of human habitation. Doug's laptop lay closed on the coffee table in the sitting room, beside a pile of newspapers, and the children had left an unfinished puzzle on the window table. She had an odd sense of life suspended.

At last, she found her mother, sitting at the desk in her study.

"Where is everyone?" Melody asked, hating the little prickle of anxiety she felt at being left behind.

"Let's see." Addie pushed back her chair and stretched. "Gemma and Duncan have walked down to the village. Your father and Kit are off on some car scheme. And Doug and the children are playing a last game of croquet." Her expression softening, she added, "I'm going to miss the children, you know. Although I will admit that Toby can be a bit challenging. And that I am looking forward to getting in an hour or two in the garden on my own this afternoon, before we go back to town on Wednesday."

Melody almost hated to ask. "Mum, what about Joe?" She'd thought about confronting Joe over the things he *hadn't* mentioned about Roz, but decided it would only make things more awkward between them.

"Ah." Addie looked out at the garden. "He's been a bit of an idiot, but I think we'll manage to get through it. His intentions were in the right place, after all—although I don't understand why he just didn't tell us he needed help."

"And Roz?"

"Roz put her keys through the letter box this morning." Her lips pinched, Addie gestured at the account books and the piles of what looked like credit card statements spread out on her desk. "I think Joe borrowing from the business was a drop in the bucket compared to what Roz had been charging for herself on the household accounts. It seems I've been a bit of an idiot as well."

"Oh, Mum, don't be silly. You had no reason to think she was dishonest."

"Well, the last few days have been full of surprises, haven't they?" Addie fixed her with the sapphire-blue gaze that always made Melody feel like a butterfly pinned to a corkboard. "Darling, why didn't you tell us about your boyfriend? Surely you can't have thought we'd disapprove."

"No, it wasn't that," Melody protested. "It was just—I don't really know what I thought. Maybe that he would never quite see me the same way, once he knew I was part of all . . . this." She waved a hand in a gesture that took in much more than the house.

Addie shook her head and sighed. "Darling, I think your friends—Gemma and Duncan and especially Doug—have already proved you wrong on that count. You underestimate yourself. We are so proud of you, of *everything* you are. And you should be, too. You were so brave, that day at St. Pancras, and I don't think we ever told you."

If Melody had felt fragile enough before, now she thought she might come completely undone. "Mum—"

"One more thing." Addie came round the desk and gripped her shoulders, gently, saying, "We love you. You're going to be just fine, I promise."

And Melody let her mother hold her as she hadn't since she was a child.

She found Doug sitting on the steps at the edge of the top lawn, under the end of the pergola. Mac lay beside him, looking down as well, his bony haunches protruding. They might have been sentinels, human and canine, watching over their charges.

Sure enough, Melody heard the high-pitched voices of the children, and Polly's excited bark. When she reached the edge of the lawn, she could see them below, on the croquet lawn.

"They're having a last game," Doug said as she sat down beside him. "Very non-reg. They got tired of me trying to make them play by the rules."

"I can't say I blame them. You can be bloody annoying, Doug Cullen."

He glanced at her, his mouth turning up in a rueful quirk. "So I've heard."

"And who'd have thought you'd turn out to be the favorite uncle." She nodded at the kids.

"Maybe it's my childlike charm."

"There is that," she said.

He looked at her again, as if to see if she was being sarcastic, then frowned as he studied her. "Are you all right? You look a bit peaky."

Melody started to shrug the question off, then realized that if she was going to turn over a new leaf, this was the time to start. "Not really, to be honest. I've just had a mum/daughter heart-to-heart. She likes you, you know."

Doug's eyebrows shot up above the gold rims of his glasses. "And that's a bad thing?"

She laughed in spite of herself. "No, of course not. It's just that—well, anyway, I came to say that I think I owe you an apology."

He looked even more surprised, but then he fidgeted, brushing at an errant rose petal that had drifted onto his knee. "Yes, but—I probably shouldn't have told—"

Melody cut him off. "Just don't go there, okay? It's done, and probably for the best."

"Okay." They sat in silence for a long moment, then Doug said, tentatively, "What *are* you going to do about Andy? If you don't mind me asking."

"I don't know. See if he'll talk to me, for starters. But—" She hesitated, crushing another rose petal between her fingers, then she swallowed and went on. "But, in the meantime, do you fancy a lift back to London? I could use the company."

Three weeks to the day after Fergus O'Reilly had cast his long shadow across the courtyard of the Lamb, Viv once again sat on the kitchen steps after early-morning prep. But on this morning it was cold and crisp, and she huddled into a fleece jacket, the stone step chilling her bum through her kitchen trousers. When she blew out a breath, a cloud formed in the air, but she'd needed the break to collect herself for the day.

The crunch of tires on the car park gravel jolted her out of her reverie. It was an hour too early for morning coffee. She stood, ready to send overeager tourists politely on their way, but the man who came through the courtyard arch a moment later looked nothing like a tourist.

His tailored overcoat screamed *city*, as did the polished sheen on his shoes. The face, however, she recognized instantly, although the dark, waving hair was cut short and shot with gray.

"Colm Finlay. Whatever are you doing here?"

"Hello, Viv. How about a cup of coffee for an old friend?"

"Don't tell me you were just passing," she said a few minutes later, when she'd made them both espressos and sat down across from him in the small dining room.

"Never would I try on such a thing with you, Viv," he said with a twinkle, then sobered. "I came to offer my condolences. I was truly sorry to hear about Fergus." Before she could answer, he went on. "And I came to make you a proposition."

"I'm not going to London, Colm. Whatever happens here." She looked round the pub with the anxiety that dogged her daily these days.

"You've got a nice place here, Viv. I was hoping you might cook me lunch, and we could talk business."

"But—"

"Hear me out before you go running away with your *buts*. My mate at the *Chronicle* told me the whole story about what happened, and I've done a little investigating on my own. It seems your business partner is going to be in need of some serious cash for solicitors' fees."

Ivan Talbot had been down at Beck House the previous week, Viv thought. Did he have a hand in this?

"I had a meeting in Cheltenham this morning with Bea Abbott's father, who is managing her affairs," Colm went on. "He would be open to an offer on her share of the Lamb."

"But I can't raise— I've been to the bank—"

"No. But *I* can." Colm's comfortable face was as serious as she'd ever seen it. "I'd like to come in as your partner in this place, Viv. Expand my horizons outside of London, if you will."

She stared at him, coffee forgotten. "But you don't even know what I'm doing—"

"I know you're a talented cook. I've always known that, if you remember."

She did remember. He'd offered her a job not long after she'd left O'Reilly's, but she'd known by then that she couldn't take a full-time chef's position, not with the baby coming. Frowning at him, she said, "I'm not doing foams or molecular gastronomy. Or Irish food."

"Heaven forbid I should ask." The twinkle was back. "But you *can* do spectacular *local* food, with your own touch. And I think you could stretch yourself a bit—if you gave yourself permission to remember how much you loved to create cuisine."

She did remember that, too, those heady early days with Fergus, keeping herself awake nights with the rush of ideas for new recipes to try. She'd felt a bit of that again, with Addie's luncheon, and it had been glorious.

Colm emptied his cup and set it back in the saucer with a decisive clink. "What do you say, Viv? It would be your show. Will you think about it?"

"I—" She swallowed. "Yes. But—" She thought about Grace, and Mark, and Ibby and Angelica. This was not her decision alone. "There are other people who should have a say as well."

"Then I think you had better introduce me."